the Return of
Santa Paws

MW01088877

Don't miss the first book starring the lovable
dog hero, *SANTA PAWS*

the Return of
Santa Paws

by
Nicholas Edwards

AN
APPLE
PAPERBACK

SCHOLASTIC INC.
New York Toronto London Auckland Sydney

ISBN 0-590-94471-1

24 23 22 21 20 19 18 17 16 15 14   23/0

Printed in the U.S.A.   40

First Scholastic printing, November 1996

the Return of
Santa Paws

1

The dog was happy every day. Eating food was his very favorite thing to do, but sleeping was a lot of fun, too. More than anything else, of course, he loved his owners, the Callahans. After living on the streets for a long, lonely time, he had finally found a family who wanted to adopt him. Now he had a warm bed to sleep on every night, fresh water in a red plastic dish that was just for him, and Milk-Bones *all day long*!

The Callahans were the nicest people in the world. Mr. Callahan was a writer, and so the dog spent most of the day following him around the house. Mrs. Callahan taught physics at Oceanport High School, and the dog liked her because she was almost always the one who fed him and brushed him. Sometimes she would also take him to the vet, but he didn't really mind. The vet was a nice person, too.

But the dog *especially* loved Gregory and

Patricia, the Callahans' children. Gregory was eleven years old and in the sixth grade, while Patricia had just started junior high this year. They took him for lots of walks, taught him tricks, and fed him snacks under the dinner table. The dog *really* liked snacks.

While Gregory and Patricia were at school, the dog usually slept under Mr. Callahan's desk. Sometimes Mr. Callahan would sit down at the desk, mutter to himself, and then pound wildly on his keyboard for awhile. On other days, he would lie on the couch and watch television, or spend hours blaring music and pacing back and forth. No matter what Mr. Callahan was doing, though, he liked to talk to himself. The dog wasn't always sure what he was saying, but he would listen, anyway, and wag his tail a lot.

When Mr. Callahan was working hard and the dog got bored, he would play with Evelyn, the family's tiger cat. If she didn't feel like playing, he would chase her until she whacked him on the nose with her paw. When that happened, the dog would always yelp and whimper a little. Mr. Callahan would come out to see what was wrong and then give them each a treat. After eating his treat, the dog would be happy again. Then he and Evelyn would lie down and sleep some more.

Everyone in the family called him by a different name. His real name was Nicholas, but they almost never used that. The dog thought it was fun to have lots of nicknames, and he answered to all of them. Mr. Callahan always called him "Pumpkin," and Evelyn was "the little Pumpkin."

Mrs. Callahan referred to him as "Smart-Guy." When he tipped over the trash, she would look stern and ask, "Are you the one who did this, Smart-Guy?" If Patricia was around, she would say, "No way, Mom — it was Greg." The dog would just stand there, and wag his tail, and lift his right paw in the most charming way he could. The family always liked it when he did tricks.

Patricia had taught him to answer to "Princess" and "Sweetpea," because it made Gregory mad. Gregory usually called him "Nick" or "Nicky" or "Bud." Evelyn, the cat, didn't really talk to him much, but the dog was pretty sure she thought of him as "Hey, you!"

But the truth was, that the Callahans — along with everyone else in town — called him "Santa Paws" more than anything else. He had shown up in town the Christmas before, and somehow, the name stuck. The dog wasn't sure why he liked that name so much, but he would wag his tail extra hard whenever anyone said "Santa Paws." There was something really *friendly* about that name.

The only thing he didn't like people to say to him was "bad dog." It didn't happen very often, but whenever he heard "bad dog," he would slump down with his tail between his legs. Usually, the person who said it, would come and pat him right away and he would feel better. He tried to be good all of the time, and not chew shoes or break anything. That way, they would just say, "What a good dog!" Whenever he heard those magic words, he would jump around and bark a lot.

Sometimes, when he and the Callahans were riding in the car, people in other cars would wave and shout, "Hi, Santa Paws!" out the window. If they were taking him for a walk, people they passed would always yell, "Look, there's Santa Paws!" Then they would smile, and sometimes even clap.

Gregory thought it was really cool that everyone in Oceanport loved their dog so much, but Patricia was always embarrassed. As far as she was concerned, all of that attention wasn't dignified. Patricia *liked* to be dignified, no matter what. Gregory didn't care, one way or the other.

Every day, the dog slept until he heard Gregory and Patricia coming up the back steps. Then he would scramble to his feet and dash out of Mr. Callahan's office. By the time they opened the door, he would be standing in the kitchen to greet them. Right after they got home, they always liked to sit down at the table and have a snack. One of them would also give him a Milk-Bone, so he could keep them company.

It was almost Christmas, and Gregory and Patricia couldn't wait for their vacation to start. There were only two days of school left before they had a whole week off. The family was going to spend the holidays up at their grandparents' lake cabin in Vermont, and they were all really looking forward to the trip.

It had snowed twice in the last week, and the backyard was still covered with about five inches of soft slush. Gregory and Patricia were just coming home from school, and they had been bickering for several blocks. Their fights were never very serious, but they liked to have *lots* of them, just to keep in practice. At least, that's what Patricia always told their parents.

"It's *really* cold," Gregory said, for at least the tenth time. He was all bundled-up in three layers of clothes — a down jacket, a Red Sox cap, and thick ragg-wool mittens, but he was still freezing.

"It is not," Patricia said — *also* for the tenth time. Her New England Patriots jacket wasn't even zipped, and her black beret was *purely* a fashion statement. She was wearing an oversized pair of red mirrored sunglasses, too. "You're just a big baby."

"*You're* a big faker," Gregory responded. "If you were, like, by yourself, I bet you'd be all shivering, and running really fast so you'd get home quicker."

Patricia shook her head. "No way. I'm too cool to be cold."

Gregory thought about that. As far as he was concerned, *nobody* was that cool — not even Patricia. "You know what would be cool?" he asked reflectively. "If I put a whole bunch of snow down your back."

Patricia stopped walking long enough to scowl at him. "If you do, I'll put a whole bunch in your *bed*. Under the blankets, inside your pillow, and everything."

Gregory grinned at her. "Oh, yeah? Then I'll put snow in all your shoes. Especially your cowboy boots."

"Then *I'll* cover your computer with snow," Patricia said, grinning now, too. "Inside your disc drive, smash it onto your keyboard, send it through the printer — you name it."

This was the kind of fight that really upset their parents, who never seemed to understand that they were mostly just kidding. *Mostly*, anyway.

The two of them looked so much alike, with

dark brown hair and very blue eyes, that people were always asking if they were twins. He *wishes* he could be so lucky, Patricia would say. She's *way* uglier, Gregory would say.

They turned the corner, and the icy wind coming up from the ocean whipped toward them. Their house was at the end of the block, and they both walked more quickly.

"I bet the windchill's about thirty-five below," Gregory guessed.

"Give me a break, Greg. It's probably twenty *above*," Patricia said.

Gregory looked over at her dubiously. "Are you really not cold?"

"Well, maybe a little," Patricia admitted, and she zipped her jacket halfway.

Gregory laughed. "I knew you were faking."

Patricia shrugged self-consciously. "So I'm faking, so what?"

Gregory just laughed.

The weekend before, the whole family had put up their Christmas decorations, and the house looked really pretty. There were wreaths on the front and back doors, and Mr. Callahan had hung lights on the pine tree in the side yard. Their Christmas tree was in the living room, right in front of the bay windows. That way, at night, everyone who drove by the house could look inside and see it.

"Did you spend all your Christmas money?" Gregory asked.

Patricia nodded. "Most of it. Why?"

"I spent all mine, and I didn't get a present for the baby yet," Gregory said.

The baby was Miranda, their cousin. She was almost exactly a year old now, and had just started talking. Miranda's parents were their Uncle Steve, and Aunt Emily. Uncle Steve was their father's little brother, and he was a police officer in the Oceanport department. Their Aunt Emily was an advertising executive at a big firm in Boston. After the baby was born, she had arranged it so that she could work at home two days a week, and commute into the city on the other three days.

"I've only got about eight-fifty left," Patricia said, "but you can borrow it, if you want."

Patricia might tease him a lot, but she was actually really, really nice, when no one was looking. "Thanks. What did you get her?" Gregory asked.

Patricia shrugged. "Sunglasses. What else?"

As they started down the shoveled walk to the back door, they could hear delighted barking from inside the house.

"It's the Princess!" Patricia said cheerfully. "She's waiting for us!"

Gregory was not amused. "Don't call him that — it's dumb."

Patricia laughed. "Oh, what, and *Santa Paws* isn't? Come on, Greg. Get serious."

"Call him Nick," Gregory said. "He likes Nick."

"He likes *everything*, Greg," Patricia pointed out.

That was actually true, so Gregory just opened the back door instead of arguing. Whenever he was at school, he spent a lot of time thinking about his dog and wondering how he was. It was always a relief to get home and be able to play with him. Lots of people had nice dogs — but their dog was *special*.

Gregory poked his head around the edge of the door without going inside. "Where's my pal?" he asked.

The dog barked and pawed eagerly at the door.

"He waits here the whole time for me to come home, just like Lassie," Gregory told Patricia.

Patricia shook her head. "No way, he just gets up when he hears us coming. I think he takes naps all day."

"No, he waits," Gregory insisted. "Kind of like a sentry."

"Yeah," Patricia said. "Sure."

As they came inside, the dog kept barking. He wagged his tail back and forth, and jumped up on his hind legs to greet them. He had finally stopped growing, but at eighty-five pounds, he was a *big* dog. Patricia was small for her age and weighed about the same, so sometimes he knocked her down by accident.

Gregory, on the other hand, was pretty tall, and outweighed both of them. He only had an advantage of about seven pounds, but he figured that it still counted. His parents had given him some light barbells for his birthday, and he did thirty repetitions every morning when he got up, and then again before he went to bed. He and his best friend Oscar did lots of endurance exercises, too, so that when they got to high school, they would be able to make the football team.

Naturally, Patricia's reaction to this was, "Yeah. You *wish*." Sometimes, she and *her* best friend Rachel did a few abdominal crunches, but that was about it. The rest of the time, they just ate Doritos and drank Cokes.

The dog had lifted his front paws up onto Gregory's shoulders, so Gregory danced him around the kitchen a little.

"What a good dog," he said proudly. "You're the *best* dog, Nicky."

The dog barked and wagged his tail.

"Are you going to have a Milk-Bone?" Gregory asked.

The dog barked more loudly.

"Okay." Gregory stopped dancing with him, and then took off his jacket. "Let's get you a Milk-Bone."

The dog wagged his tail so hard that his whole body shook. He loved Gregory! He loved Patricia! He loved his life! He loved *Milk-Bones*!

What a great day!

2

Gregory and Patricia hung up their coats on the hooks behind the door, and dropped their knapsacks on the kitchen table. In the meantime, the dog ran around in circles, barking every so often. Since he was a German shepherd and collie mix, he had a very deep and commanding bark.

"Are you hungry, Greg?" Patricia asked.

"I'm *starved*," Gregory said.

Patricia nodded. "Me, too," she said, and opened the refrigerator.

Gregory picked up the plastic dish on the floor and carried it over to the sink. He dumped out the old water and filled it with fresh water.

The dog wagged his tail cooperatively and drank some right away. It tasted *really* good. Nice and cold.

While Gregory took out the box of Milk-Bones, Patricia studied the food inside the refrigerator.

"There's a whole lot of carrot sticks, and yogurt, and stuff," she said without much enthusiasm.

"Well, you know, you're a girl, so you like, need lots of calcium," Gregory said. He'd read in magazines that women were supposed to get more calcium than men. "So your bones don't get weird."

Patricia shook her head. "No, what I need right now, is *candy*. Or — fudge, maybe. Fudge would be good."

She opened a plastic container and looked inside. Beef stew. She closed the container, and checked another. This one had leftover macaroni and cheese, and she set it out on the counter, along with some butterscotch pudding their mother had fixed the night before.

"We could make popcorn?" Gregory suggested.

"Yeah, that'd be all right," Patricia agreed. "And maybe some hot chocolate."

They could hear music playing loudly in the den, and they both stopped to listen for a minute.

"Frank," Patricia said grimly.

Gregory nodded. As usual, their father was listening to Frank Sinatra. Sometimes, he would put on Billie Holiday or Ella Fitzgerald, but mostly it was Frank, Frank, *Frank*. Endless hours of *Frank*. "Is he singing?" he asked.

They listened again. If their father was singing along, that generally meant that he wasn't getting any work done.

"No," Patricia decided. "Just listening."

"Good," Gregory said, relieved. When their father's writing was going well, they could do whatever they wanted and never get in trouble. When he had writer's block, he was much more strict.

Patricia started fixing dishes of macaroni and cheese to put in the microwave, and then stopped. "Hey, I know!" she said. "Let's go see what he's wearing!"

Gregory's eyes lit up. "Yeah!" he agreed.

When they left for school in the morning, their father would usually be wearing pajama bottoms and an old college T-shirt. Then sometimes, during the day, he would change into outfits that he thought might help him get in the mood to write better.

"Be really quiet," Patricia said softly, as they crept through the living room. "So he doesn't hear us coming."

The music was so loud there was no *way* he would hear them, but Gregory nodded anyway. If their father knew they were sneaking up on him, he would have time to whip off any goofy hats or other silly things he might be wearing.

The dog barked and galloped ahead of them. He ran so fast that he slipped on a small braided rug and skidded into a nearby wall.

"Santa Paws, shhh!" Patricia said, and then

frowned. "Did I just forget and call him Santa Paws?"

Gregory nodded.

"Hit me next time," Patricia said.

He wasn't about to pass *that* up. "Absolutely!" Gregory promised.

When they got to the den door, they could see their father sitting at his word processor with his back to them. Computers were too mod for him. His posture was very straight and he was holding his hands motionless above the keyboard, as though he *might* start writing at any second.

Gregory and Patricia tried not to laugh when they saw that he had on a top hat and a black bow tie. Once they had caught him wearing a bright green sombrero, because he was writing a scene set in Mexico. Right now, he also had on gray sweatpants and a T-shirt with a picture of the Grinch on it.

"Bunny slippers?" Patricia whispered.

Gregory peered underneath the desk. "No, *Snoopy* slippers," he whispered back, and they both snickered. Lots of times, Mr. Callahan forgot and went out in public with his slippers on. People in Oceanport seemed to think that this was — quaint.

They waited to see if he was going to type anything, and when he didn't, they started singing, "You Make Me Feel So Young" along with Frank. Over the years, completely by accident, they had learned all of the words to an astonishing number of old songs. Their mother mostly played musicals, so they were pretty strong on those, too. When Patricia's science teacher had asked her recently to explain the concept of "osmosis," she had used their uncanny knowledge of song lyrics as an example. Her teacher had found this to be a very clever comparison, and gave her an *A* for the day.

The dog started barking again, because he *liked* singing. Singing was funny.

Mr. Callahan turned around to look at them. "You two are home early," he said, sounding surprised.

Actually, they were *late*, because Patricia had forgotten her global studies book and they had to go back to get it.

"You want to hear 'Moonlight in Vermont?' " Gregory asked. "We're good at that one, too."

Mr. Callahan smiled, saved whatever he was writing on a disk, and then stood up. Their cat, Evelyn, who had been sleeping soundly on his lap, was quite annoyed by this. She flounced over to the couch, and curled up again.

"How was school?" Mr. Callahan asked. "Are you kids hungry?"

"Fine," Patricia said, just as Gregory said, "*Yes.*"

Realizing that he was still wearing his top hat,

Mr. Callahan frowned and took it off. "Ballroom scene," he explained.

Patricia and Gregory shrugged politely, doing their best not to laugh again. However, they failed miserably.

"Dad, does Nicholas wait all day for me by the door?" Gregory asked as they walked to the kitchen. "Because he misses me so much?"

"Hmmm?" Mr. Callahan said vaguely. "Oh." He paused, and then didn't quite make eye contact. "Well, sure. I mean, yes. No question about it. Sits there nonstop. Never moves."

"That means no," Patricia said to Gregory.

Mr. Callahan examined the plastic containers on the kitchen counter. He was over six feet tall, with greying hair that was almost always rumpled. He wore thick brown glasses, and usually slouched when he walked.

"This looks good," he said, taking down a plate for himself and spooning out some cold macaroni and cheese. "But try not to spoil your appetites, okay? We're meeting your aunt and uncle for dinner at six-thirty."

"Italian?" Gregory asked. Italian food was his favorite.

"How about Mexican?" Patricia suggested. "We haven't had Mexican for a while."

"Rumor has it, it's going to be Chinese," their father answered.

17

It was a safe bet that that rumor had come straight from their *mother*.

They had finished the macaroni and cheese, and were halfway through the beef stew, when Mrs. Callahan got home. She was carrying an oversized canvas briefcase and several bulging shopping bags.

"Hi, Mom. Are those Christmas presents?" Gregory asked.

Quickly, Mrs. Callahan held the bags behind her back. "No," she said, and grinned at them. "Whatever gave you that idea?"

The dog had been sitting alertly next to Gregory, in case a piece of beef from the stew fell on the floor by accident. Smelling something familiar, he got up and went over to sniff the bags. A rawhide chew bone! He was almost *sure* that he smelled a rawhide chew bone.

"No, it's a surprise, Santa Paws," Mrs. Callahan said, and lifted the bag up out of his reach. "Go lie down."

Lie down. He knew what "lie down" meant, but right now, he wanted to sit. If he went over to lie down on his special rug, he might forget about the beef stew and fall asleep. So he sat down next to Gregory's chair and lifted his paw, instead.

"That's good," Mrs. Callahan told him. "You're a very good dog."

She thought he was good. Yay! The dog

wagged his tail, and then returned his attention to the beef stew. So far, he had managed to catch a piece of potato Mr. Callahan dropped, and he had snapped up two chunks of meat Gregory had slipped under the table.

Mrs. Callahan glanced up at the kitchen clock, and then at her husband. "We're supposed to meet Steve and Emily and the baby in about an hour and a half," she reminded him. "Maybe you all should save some room for supper."

"It's just a snack, Mom," Patricia said.

Mr. Callahan looked a little sheepish. "A *hearty* snack," he admitted.

"Whatever you say." Mrs. Callahan started out of the room with her bags, then paused. "Did anyone feed the dog?"

The dog leaped enthusiastically to his feet again. "Feed the dog" was another one of the magic phrases, right up there with "ride in the car."

"We were about to," Gregory said.

Evelyn came ambling out from the direction of the living room. She jumped up on the side counter where her small green dish was kept and meowed loudly — and sadly.

"I'll bet you were about to feed her, too," Mrs. Callahan said. "And maybe even clean up these dishes, while you're at it."

Gregory nodded. "Yep."

"Right away," Patricia promised.

Mr. Callahan was already on his feet and heading for the sink. "Count on it."

"I thought so," Mrs. Callahan said, and then she disappeared up the stairs with her many mysterious shopping bags.

When it was time to leave for dinner, the dog watched with worried eyes as the Callahans put on their hats, coats, and gloves. Where were they going? Was he going to be left alone? Would they be back soon? This was *horrible*. He slumped down on the floor and rested his muzzle miserably on his front paws.

"Can Nicholas come?" Gregory asked. He really hated to go *anywhere* without his dog.

Hearing his name — *one* of his names, anyway — the dog's ears pricked forward.

"I don't know, Greg," his mother answered. "It's pretty cold out there, and it might not be a good idea for him to wait in the car."

"But he always comes," Patricia reminded her.

Mrs. Callahan nodded. "Okay. Bring one of the beach towels, though, so he has someplace to curl up."

When the dog saw Gregory open the cupboard and take out a thick blue towel, he stood up tentatively. Was the towel for him? Was he going to have a bath, maybe?

"Want to come for a ride in the car?" Gregory asked.

A ride in the car! His favorite! The dog barked, and then chased his tail for a minute to show how happy he was.

Next to eating — and sleeping — riding in the car was the best thing in the whole world!

3

The best part of being in the car was when one of the Callahans would roll down the window, and he could smell lots of exciting scents. But he also liked just sitting and watching objects flash by. Usually they drove to interesting places, like the beach or the city, and there was always something new to see.

When they were at stores and the dog was waiting for them to come back, he liked to sneak up into the front seat. It was fun to sit in the driver's seat and gaze out through the windshield. Then, when he saw them coming back, he would quickly jump into the back again. Most of the time, he got caught, but no one ever really got mad at him, so he figured it was okay.

Oceanport always looked very pretty during Christmas. It was a small town, and the streets twinkled with bright strings of lights. All of the stores and restaurants and office buildings would put up festive decorations, and every year, there was a contest to decide who had done the most beautiful job.

During the holiday season, the municipal park had lots of special exhibits, which were called "The Festival of Many Lands." The exhibits were devoted to all kinds of different cultures, religions, and other traditions. Oceanport was proud of being a very democratic and multicultural town.

When the dog had been a lonely stray the year before, he had slept in Santa's sleigh in the park. Some of the local townspeople had noticed him there, and they had given him the name "Santa Paws." That was before he had an owner, and he was always cold and sad and hungry. He ran into a lot of people who were in trouble, and he did his best to help them, so the name "Santa Paws" seemed perfect for him. The dog was just glad when he met Gregory and Patricia, and got to go live with them. He was *still* always hungry, though!

The Chinese restaurant was right on Main Street, and Mr. Callahan found a parking place a few doors away.

"Can we walk down to the park for a minute?" Gregory asked, as they got out of the car.

"*May* you," Mrs. Callahan corrected him automatically. "Why don't we go after supper and look at the decorations?"

Gregory nodded, and carefully unrolled one of

the back windows a couple of inches so that Santa Paws would have plenty of fresh air. Then he patted him, and started to close the door.

Suddenly sensing that something was wrong, the dog stood up on the seat to look outside. The fur rose on his back and he sniffed the air uneasily, trying to figure out what was happening. He knew that there was trouble brewing somewhere — he just wasn't sure what it was.

"What is it, boy?" Gregory asked.

Across the street, Mrs. Lowell had just come out of Mabel's Five-and-Dime, carrying lots of bundles. Her four-year-old daughter Bethany was skipping along next to her, bouncing a miniature Shaquille O'Neal basketball.

The sidewalk was a little bit icy, and Mrs. Lowell slipped. She dropped most of her packages and had to bend over to pick them up. As she did, Bethany's ball bounced off a chunk of snow and rolled right into the busy street!

Bethany gasped and ran after her beloved basketball, without looking both ways first.

Seeing this, the dog leaped out of the car. Barking loudly, he raced across the street, dodging traffic. Horns beeped, and cars skidded on the ice, as people tried to steer out of the way.

"Hey!" Gregory yelled. "Look out!" He started

to chase after his dog, but there were too many cars.

The man driving the car closest to Bethany jammed on his brakes, but the car spun out of control, and headed directly toward her! Everyone on the sidewalks was frozen with shock.

The dog grabbed Bethany's hood with his teeth, and dragged her out of the way at the last second. He pulled her safely between two parked cars and then gently released her hood and nudged her to her feet.

With that accomplished, he bolted back into the street to fetch the basketball. The ball was too big to fit in his mouth, so he used his nose to roll it in front of him. He deposited the ball at Bethany's feet, and then stood there, wagging his tail.

All around them, people were running across the street and jumping out of their cars to see what had happened. Everyone was very upset, and expecting the worst.

Mrs. Lowell and Gregory reached the pair first.

"Oh, thank God," Mrs. Lowell breathed, and she hugged her little daughter tightly.

Bethany smiled up at her, not even bruised by her narrow escape. "Santa Paws saved me!" she said happily. "He's Santa's best helper!"

Mrs. Lowell hugged her closer, so relieved that she couldn't even speak.

"You all right, boy?" Gregory asked the dog. Then he swiftly checked him over, running his hands over the dog's back and legs to make sure he hadn't been injured.

The dog barked once, and wagged his tail. He really liked being patted.

Patricia and their parents rushed over to join them.

"Are they okay?" Patricia asked.

Gregory nodded. "Everybody's fine."

Hearing that, most of the people who had gathered nearby began to applaud.

"Hooray for Santa Paws!" Mabel from the Five-and-Dime store hollered, and a few people cheered.

"I don't know how to thank all of you," Mrs. Lowell said to the Callahans. "If it weren't for your wonderful dog — " She stopped, overcome again.

Gregory always carried extra biscuits in his pockets, and he took one out.

The dog barked and joyfully accepted it. He crunched up the biscuit right away, his tail thumping against one of the parked cars. No matter how many Milk-Bones he ate, he was still always surprised by how delicious they were!

"You know," Mr. Callahan said thoughtfully to his wife, "he really *is* a good dog."

It was hard to disagree with that, so Mrs. Callahan just nodded.

Mr. Callahan's brother Steve had come out of the Chinese restaurant to see what all of the excitement was about. As far as he was concerned, a police officer was *never* really off-duty, and so he liked to keep an eye on things.

"What's going on?" he asked, sounding both curious and authoritative. "Everyone all right?" Uncle Steve wasn't quite as tall as Mr. Callahan, but he was a lot more muscular. He was only thirty-two and unlike Mr. Callahan, his hair hadn't started turning grey yet. Even so, it was easy to see that they were related.

"Thanks to Santa Paws!" someone shouted.

"Oh." Uncle Steve looked around and saw that everything seemed to be fine. "Okay. Good."

Patricia moved to stand next to him, folding her arms decisively across her chest. She was pretty sure that she wanted to be a police officer, too, when she grew up — that is, unless she could be a member of the Supreme Court. "Should we tell them to move along, and go about their business, Uncle Steve?" she asked.

Uncle Steve laughed, and reached out to give her ponytail a little flip. "No, it's okay, Patty. I think they'll figure out that one for themselves."

27

The family who owned the Chinese restaurant had come outside, too. Their last name was Lee, and their son Tom was also a member of the Oceanport Police Department. Because of that, most of the police officers in town ate at their restaurant regularly. Of course, it didn't hurt that the food was *really* good.

"Was it Santa Paws again?" Mr. Lee asked the crowd in general.

Most of the bystanders nodded, and some of them started clapping again.

Mrs. Lee smiled at the Callahans. "We would be delighted to have the hero dine in our restaurant tonight."

Gregory looked surprised. "Wait, you mean, inside? *With* us?"

Mrs. Lee nodded, and held the door open with a flourish. "Please. We would be very honored."

"Whoa," Patricia said, impressed. "That is like, *so* European."

"We will prepare our finest meat dish for him," Mr. Lee proclaimed grandly. "Please, follow me."

As they walked inside, Mr. Callahan leaned over to his wife again. "If it's their very finest dish, think a certain dog will be willing to *share* it with us?" he asked in a low voice.

Mrs. Callahan laughed. "Well, maybe if you ask nicely. . . ."

The dog couldn't believe that he was being allowed to go inside the restaurant, instead of

28

waiting in the car like always. How fun! He trotted happily next to Gregory, waving his tail back and forth.

Mr. Lee led them over to the best table in the restaurant. Gregory and Patricia's aunt Emily was already sitting there with her baby, Miranda. Miranda was wearing a red velvet holiday dress, with black patent leather shoes, and she looked even more adorable than usual.

The Lees' teenage daughter, Nancy, brought out a special rug from the back room, which Santa Paws immediately sat on. He knew that small rugs were almost always meant just for him. This one was very soft and comfortable, with nice fancy patterns, and he woofed once before settling down.

Mr. Lee distributed menus, while Mrs. Lee filled their water glasses.

"Tonight, everything is on the house!" Mr. Lee announced. "Out of respect for the heroic Santa Paws!"

"Oh, no," Mrs. Callahan protested. "We couldn't — "

"We *insist*," Mrs. Lee said. "Consider it our holiday gesture."

Gregory nudged Patricia's arm. "So, should we order lobster, and shrimp, and all?" he whispered, since those were the most expensive items on the menu.

"Don't be a jerk," she whispered back. "Besides, Mom and Dad'll leave a *really* big tip, so it'll work out pretty much the same."

Gregory nodded and looked down at his menu. His favorites were Hunan flower steak and General Tso's chicken, anyway. Patricia almost always ordered broccoli with garlic sauce, because, she would explain, of the considerable health benefits. Mr. and Mrs. Callahan always laughed when she said things like that. Gregory and Patricia were never exactly sure what was so funny, and they would write it off to parental foolishness.

"So," Aunt Emily said, once they had all been served tea, and soda, and other drinks. "What should we toast to?"

"Santa Paws," Gregory said. "Who else?"

They all raised their cups and glasses. Miranda giggled and imitated them by holding up her bottle.

"Okay, Mr. Writer," Uncle Steve said to Mr. Callahan. "Let's see how profound you are."

Mr. Callahan frowned. Sometimes, under pressure, he lapsed into writer's block. "To Santa Paws," he said finally. "The best dog in Oceanport!"

"The best dog on the Eastern seaboard," Patricia corrected him.

"The best dog in the *world*," Gregory said.

They all drank to that, and then started in on their scallion pancakes and other appetizers.

The dog wagged his tail when Patricia gave him some pork strips on a small white plate. He had no idea why they were celebrating tonight, but he was certainly having a very nice time!

4

Over dinner, they all talked about their Christmas plans. Patricia and Gregory's grandparents lived in Montpelier, Vermont, but they also had a lake cabin in the Northeast Kingdom of Vermont, up near the Canadian border. It was winterized, and so this year, they were going to spend the holidays there. The drive from Boston was pretty long, but the cabin was right on a beautiful lake. There was skiing nearby, and plenty of other winter sports available.

"When are you all heading up?" Mrs. Callahan asked Uncle Steve and Aunt Emily.

Steve shook his head. "Emily's going to drive up with the baby, and take the week up there, but I have to work on Christmas, so I'm going to fly."

Hearing that, Gregory and Patricia perked up. They loved flying in their uncle's plane. He was a private pilot, and he shared a little Cessna Skyhawk with an old friend of his from the Army. Uncle Steve really loved baseball, and during the summer, he would fly all over New England and upstate New York to go to minor league games in tiny little towns. Lots of times, Gregory and Patricia would get to go along. As a result, they had seen all sorts of obscure teams play and had a large collection of souvenir caps.

"Why are they making you work on Christmas?" Mr. Callahan was asking him. "You worked on Thanksgiving."

"Well, they're giving me the twenty-third and Christmas Eve off, so at least I'll be able to spend a little time with all of you before I fly back," Uncle Steve said. "As long as I fly out early Christmas morning, I can make my shift."

"Can we go with you?" Gregory asked. "Please?" The last time they had gotten to fly in the plane had been way back in *October*.

"Yeah," Patricia agreed. "We could keep you company."

Mrs. Callahan looked up from her wonton soup. "You don't want to ride up with us?"

"Well — sure," Gregory said lamely, "but — " He stopped, and looked at Patricia.

"Planes are more fun than station wagons," she said.

Mr. and Mrs. Callahan exchanged glances.

"It seems to me that nice, loving children *like*

to ride with their parents," Mrs. Callahan said.

"While singing holiday tunes," Mr. Callahan added.

Patricia winced at the thought of that, and ate some of her broccoli instead of answering.

"Well, we'd be driving *home* with you," Gregory pointed out. "That counts, right?"

"Hey, if it's okay with all of you, it's fine with me," Uncle Steve said with a shrug.

"All right," Mrs. Callahan decided. "As long as I don't hear either of you arguing between now and Friday."

Gregory and Patricia looked at each other. "I would *never* fight with my best sister in the world," Gregory said.

"Your *only* sister," Patricia reminded him.

Gregory grinned at her. "Okay, but even if I had lots of others, *you'd* be the very best one."

"If I had nine brothers, you'd be in the top ten," Patricia retorted.

Gregory frowned, pretty sure that there was an insult in there somewhere. But his father was serving him some more rice and pork with garlic sauce, so he decided to pretend he hadn't heard her.

Then Patricia remembered something. "Oh," she said, and turned to Uncle Steve. "Is it okay if Santa Paws comes, too?"

Gregory promptly punched her in the arm. Patricia flinched and then socked him right back.

"Hey!" Mr. Callahan said sharply. "What did your mother just tell you two about fighting?"

"Patricia asked me to hit her the next time she said, 'Santa Paws,' " Gregory explained.

"Right, I forgot." Patricia tapped his shoulder where she had slugged him. "I withdraw my punch."

"Withdrawal accepted," Gregory said graciously, even though he was pretty sure he had a bruise.

"That wasn't a fight, he was just doing me a favor," Patricia told their parents. She was pretty sure *she* had a bruise, too.

Mr. and Mrs. Callahan looked suspicious, but they let it pass.

"Anyway," Uncle Steve said, "Santa Paws can come, as long as you bring his seat belt."

Gregory nodded. His mother had bought a special dog seat belt at the pet store. Santa Paws never wore it in the car, but he always wore it in Uncle Steve's plane. That way, there was no chance that he would jump around in the middle of the flight.

Then, just to make Patricia mad, Gregory reached over with his chopsticks and stole the last piece of sweet and sour pineapple from her plate.

"Greg!" she protested. "I was *saving* that."

Gregory ate the pineapple before she could steal it back. Then he plucked away a piece of her chicken, which he flipped to Santa Paws.

The dog caught the food with one quick lunge to his right, wagged his tail, and then sat politely on his rug again.

"Check your room *very carefully* before you go to sleep tonight," Patricia said in her most threatening voice.

Gregory shrugged. "Hey, no problem. When we get home, I'm going to spread all kinds of rumors about you on the Internet."

Patricia put her chopsticks down. "Oh, yeah? Well, *I'm* going to — "

Their mother frowned at them. "That sounds almost *exactly* like bickering to me."

Remembering that their plane trip hung in the balance, Gregory and Patricia instantly put on very sweet and innocent smiles.

"Never happen," Gregory assured her.

Patricia nodded. "Not us."

"*No way,*" Gregory said.

Two whole days of not arguing was going to be a challenge!

On Friday, school was only in session for a half-day and everyone was dismissed at eleven-thirty. Mrs. Callahan came to pick up Gregory and Patricia, and they went home to eat a quick lunch. Uncle Steve wanted to take off in the early afternoon, so that they would land before it got dark.

He kept his plane at a small airfield just over the New Hampshire border, and Mrs. Callahan drove them up there to meet him. Gregory and Patricia had each packed a small knapsack, and Gregory was also holding a picnic basket on his lap. Their parents would bring the rest of their stuff up to Vermont in the car. The plane was too small to carry bulky things like skis and heavy suitcases.

"I can't *wait* to go skiing," Gregory said, as they zipped along Route 95. "When're we going to go, Mom?"

Mrs. Callahan shrugged, and glanced in her rearview mirror. "I don't know. Monday or Tuesday, maybe?"

"Cool," Gregory said. He had asked for a new pair of ski goggles for Christmas, and he really hoped that he would get them. Either way, skiing was one of his favorite things to do.

"Can we go skating, too, Mom?" Patricia asked from the back. It had been so cold that the lake by the cabin was probably frozen by now.

"Sure," Mrs. Callahan promised. "If we're lucky, maybe we'll even be able to blast your father out of the house."

Gregory and Patricia laughed.

"Not likely," Patricia said.

"Never happen," Gregory agreed.

Feeling the holiday excitement in the air, the dog had trouble sitting still in the backseat. Gregory had given him a bath the night before, so his fur was nice and fluffy. Then Patricia had braided two red and green ribbons together and tied them around his neck in a big bow.

When they got to the airfield, Uncle Steve was busy filing his flight plan and running through a preflight checklist. It was really cold outside, so Gregory and Patricia waited in the car with their mother. Right before takeoff, they would give Santa Paws one last walk.

The runway had been plowed, of course, since the last snowstorm, and there was a huge pile of snow at the end of the tarmac. The small air-traffic control building had been shoveled out, but a lot of the small parked planes still had several inches of snow on their wing covers.

"Are you sure you two are dressed warmly enough?" Mrs. Callahan asked, looking worried. "You know how cold it gets up there."

"I have on like, *five* layers, Mom," Gregory said. With long underwear, a fleece turtleneck, and a hooded sweatshirt, plus a down vest under his ski jacket, he figured he was pretty well covered. He was also wearing a blue hat, a plaid wool scarf, his ski mittens, and a pair of heavy Gore-Tex lined hiking boots.

Mrs. Callahan turned around in her seat to

check on Patricia. "What about you? Are you going to be warm enough?"

Patricia was listening to her Walkman, and she lifted one of the headphones to one side. "What?"

"She wants to know if you're going to show off, and not zip your jacket and all," Gregory said.

Since they *were* going to Vermont, Patricia was wearing her Sorel winter boots, along with her Patriots jacket and ski gloves. She had also selected a pair of neon-yellow sunglasses to complete her ensemble. Other than that, she just had on a turtleneck and ragg wool sweater with her jeans.

"Where's your hat?" her mother asked.

Patricia looked down at herself. "I'm fine, Mom," she said. "I'm not cold."

Mrs. Callahan took off her own scarf. "Here, put this on. Where's your hat?"

Patricia checked the backseat, and then shrugged. "I don't know. I think I forgot it."

Mrs. Callahan sighed, and held out her own homemade knitted hat next.

"It's, um, nice and all," Patricia said politely. "But, um, well — it has a *pom-pom* on it."

Mrs. Callahan sighed again. "Humor me, Patricia. Okay? It's Christmas."

Reluctantly, Patricia tugged the hat on over her headphones. Pom-poms were *completely* not cool. Just in case they passed someone she knew, she slouched down in her seat so that her head was below the window.

Thinking that it might be the beginning of a game, the dog pawed her arm playfully.

"No, Santa Paws," Patricia said, and brushed his paw off. *"Sit."*

The dog sat.

"Good boy," she said, and then turned up the volume on her Walkman.

"Think you'll have enough to eat?" Mrs. Callahan asked.

Gregory grinned, and patted the heavy picnic basket. It was full of sandwiches, carrot sticks, homemade brownies, sodas, and juice boxes. There was also, of course, a small plastic bag full of Milk-Bones. "This'll hold us for *at least* an hour," he said.

Mrs. Callahan smiled, too. "All right, all right. I just can't help worrying." Then she pointed out through the windshield. "Okay, let's get ready. Here comes your uncle."

Before getting out of the car, Gregory reached for Santa Paws' harness. It snapped on around his chest and front legs, and then Gregory would adjust it to fit him just right. Once they were in the plane, he could thread the seat belt through the loop on the back of the harness. When that was done, Santa Paws would be safe in his seat for the rest of the flight.

"Extra large," Gregory said to him as he put on his leash. "Because you are a good, *big* dog."

The dog wagged his tail. Gregory thought he was good! He really didn't like the way the harness felt, but if Gregory wanted him to wear it, he would.

"Okay if I take him for a quick walk before we go?" Gregory asked his uncle.

Uncle Steve nodded, and checked his watch automatically. "Sure thing," he answered. He was wearing old army jungle fatigue pants, black work boots, an Oceanport PD cap, and a heavy-weight flight jacket. For warmth, he had added leather gloves, and a long striped scarf.

"Aren't you supposed to have on a bomber jacket and a white silk scarf?" Patricia asked.

Uncle Steve winked at her. "Fashion, I leave to *you*, my friend," he said. Then he lifted the picnic basket out of the front seat. "Weather looks great all the way up," he said to Mrs. Callahan.

Mrs. Callahan nodded. "That's good. We should get there by about nine tonight."

After walking along a stretch of bushes, Gregory brought Santa Paws back.

"Okay," he said cheerfully. "We're ready."

Mrs. Callahan hugged Patricia first, then Gregory, and finally, Santa Paws. "Okay, now be good," she said to all three of them. "Make sure you do everything your uncle tells you to do."

41

"Drop and give me twenty!" Uncle Steve said without missing a beat.

Gregory and Patricia both laughed, but didn't move.

Recognizing the *sound* of a command, if not the actual words, the dog sat down obediently and lifted his front paws in the air.

Uncle Steve bent down to pat him. "Good boy. At least someone's paying attention."

The dog barked. Uncle Steve thought he was good, too!

After saying one more good-bye to their mother, Gregory and Patricia crossed the airfield to the waiting plane. The Cessna was very snug, with just four seats inside. The outside of the plane was painted white, with red markings. There was a single propeller on the front, and the wings were attached to the top of the plane, instead of coming out from the sides. The landing gear was two fat rubber wheels at the bottom of the plane.

"Whose turn to sit up front?" Uncle Steve asked.

"Me!" Patricia said eagerly. Whoever sat up front would get the extra benefit of a little flying lesson. Uncle Steve always showed them how to use the rudder pedals to control the plane and let them steer for a minute. When they were old enough, he had promised that he would give them *real* lessons, and maybe they would be able to get pilot's licenses of their own.

Uncle Steve loaded their knapsacks and the picnic basket aboard and tied them down with rope. Then Gregory let Santa Paws into the back, and climbed in after him.

"Here you go, boy," he said, patting the seat on the right.

The dog woofed once, and bounced up onto the chair. Being in a plane was like riding in the car, but lots bumpier. He had flown with Gregory and Patricia before, and he knew what he was supposed to do. So he sat quietly, until Gregory attached his harness to the seat belt.

"Okay, good dog," he said. "Stay."

The dog wagged his tail, and then lounged back against the seat. Since they were still on the ground, he couldn't see much out through the window, but he could pretend.

Gregory reached into his jacket pocket. "Want a Milk-Bone?"

The dog tried to get up, but the seat belt kept him where he was. So he settled down and let Gregory hand the biscuit to him, instead.

Up front, Patricia was belting herself into the copilot's seat. In the meantime, Uncle Steve had put on his headset and was going through his final preflight check.

Gregory's favorite part of flying was when the

engine first started. The small cockpit would be filled with noise, and he could feel the whole plane seem to shake with excitement. It was usually too loud to talk when they were flying, but he enjoyed looking out the window so much that it didn't really matter.

Flying up to the lake cabin was always especially great, because the view of the mountains was *amazing* from the air. On a clear winter day like today, they would be able to take some really pretty pictures.

"Got plenty of gas?" Patricia asked.

Uncle Steve smiled and indicated the gas gauge. Then he twisted in his seat to check on Gregory and Santa Paws. "Everyone all set?" he asked.

Gregory and Patricia nodded, and the dog panted.

"Okay," Uncle Steve said. He gave them all a thumbs-up, and started the engine.

At first, the thundering noise always seemed deafening. But after a while, Gregory and Patricia would get used to it. The rumbling of the engine was so loud that they could feel it echoing inside their own chests. The propeller started off by spinning very slowly, but soon, it was whipping around so fast they almost couldn't see it anymore.

Once they were cleared for takeoff, Uncle

Steve taxied into position. They had to wait for a Piper Cub to take off, first.

When it was their turn to go, Uncle Steve gave them one final thumbs-up. Gregory and Patricia returned the signal enthusiastically.

Then they roared down the runway, picking up speed, until suddenly, they lifted off!

They were flying!

5

Gregory and Patricia peered out the windows as the plane banked to the right and climbed high into the sky. They watched all of the cars and buildings gradually get smaller and smaller, until even the broad stripes of interstate highways looked tiny.

After climbing up to their cruising altitude of about five thousand feet, Uncle Steve leveled the plane off.

"Do *not* feel free to move about the cabin!" he yelled over the noise of the engine.

Gregory and Patricia knew he was kidding, so they just grinned. Even if they had *wanted* to move around, there wasn't exactly much room.

Gregory reached over to pat Santa Paws and make sure he was all right. The dog licked his hand once, and then went back to gazing out the window at the clouds and bright blue sky.

"Do you think he likes it?" Gregory shouted to Patricia. "I can never tell!"

"He seems to, yeah!" she shouted back.

The dog looked alertly out the window, even though there wasn't much to see out there. But he wanted to be ready, just in case.

The flight was very smooth now, and Gregory opened the picnic basket to get them some snacks. There was a thermos of hot coffee, and he carefully poured out a cup and handed it up front to his uncle.

Uncle Steve nodded his thanks, but didn't say anything because he was busy talking into his headset.

Gregory passed Patricia a juice box and a tuna fish sandwich. Then he took a meat loaf sandwich and another juice box for himself.

Smelling the meat, the dog perked up. Gregory broke off part of his sandwich and fed it to him.

Soon, each of them — including Santa Paws — was eating a butterscotch brownie for dessert.

"These are *great*!" Uncle Steve yelled. "Remind me to tell your mother that!"

Gregory and Patricia nodded. They both really liked chocolate chip cookies, but these brownies were their favorite. On the other hand, even the *worst* cookies they had ever eaten had still been pretty good.

They were flying over the mountains now, and the wind had picked up. The turbulence made the plane jounce a little in the air, and Patricia grabbed the arm of her seat for a second before remembering that it wasn't cool to do things like that. She glanced back to see if Gregory had noticed. He was laughing, so she knew that he had.

For a while, they could see lots of small cities like Concord and Laconia, as well as wide, smooth highways. The mountains were covered with snow, and there were pine trees everywhere. If they had been on the ground, they would have been able to see other kinds of trees, but from the air, the mountains looked like one big Christmas tree farm.

As they flew further north, the landscape below them grew more beautiful and deserted. There were a few little towns in the White Mountain National Forest, but there were also miles and miles of wilderness.

The previous summer, they had hiked up Mount Monadnock in southern New Hampshire with their parents. It had been fun, but they got pretty tired. Other than that, the only time they ever made it to the tops of mountains was when they rode up on ski lifts. The Blue Hills in Massachusetts probably didn't count.

The White Mountains were really something, though. Tall, and craggy, and rugged. There were more clouds than there had been before, and they made the snow-covered mountains seem dark and mysterious.

"This is great!" Patricia yelled to Gregory.

"Yeah, I wish I remembered my camera!" he yelled back to her.

Then, all of a sudden, Uncle Steve tensed in his seat.

Patricia was the first one to notice. "Is anything wrong?" she asked.

He didn't answer, which *was* an answer.

The engine was beginning to cough and sputter, which got Gregory's attention. Before he could ask what was happening, the plane abruptly lost altitude and Uncle Steve had to fight the sluggish controls to keep them aloft.

They dropped again, and Gregory felt his stomach swooping down, too. There was a strong smell of burning electricity, and wisps of smoke floated out through the instrument panel.

Sensing the anxiety around him, the dog whined softly next to him. He wanted to stand up, but the seat belt held him in place.

Just as Uncle Steve started to call the emergency in, the engine died. In the sudden, shocking silence, they all stared at each other for a second.

"Okay, okay," Uncle Steve said. His face was pale, but he sounded very calm. "Okay." He stared at the instrument panel, and then made a few adjustments. "Okay." He tried to get the radio to work, but they were below the level of the mountains now, so it was mostly just static.

Seeing Patricia tighten her seat belt, Gregory quickly did the same. He also leaned over to make sure that Santa Paws was securely hooked up.

Uncle Steve did his best to smile at them. "I think we've got a little problem here, guys."

Gregory and Patricia looked at him with wide eyes. Santa Paws whined again, and Gregory put his hand out instinctively to pat him.

The plane sailed soundlessly through the air, but they were losing altitude very fast. Below them, there was nothing but mountains and endless forests.

"Are we crashing?" Gregory asked.

Patricia glared at him.

"I'm sorry," he said defensively. "I just wanted to know."

"Take the positions I taught you, okay?" Uncle Steve ordered, as he struggled to keep the plane in the air. "Keep your eyes closed, and don't look up until we come to a stop!"

There didn't seem to be any place to land, as the trees rushed closer and closer. One of the mountains had a small bald spot near the top, and Uncle Steve guided the unresponsive plane toward it.

They were falling, more than dropping, now.

Gregory and Patricia both bent forward in their seats, and covered their heads with their arms, trying not to scream in terror.

"Lie down, Santa Paws!" Gregory yelled without lifting his head. *"Lie down,* boy!"

They smashed down into the snowy clearing, but there wasn't enough room to stop. The landing gear collapsed on one side, and sent them sliding wildly out of control. The right wing slammed into a tree, and the force of the collision tore it right off the plane! They flipped over, and then spun backward across the snow. They spun around and around, crashing through bushes and snapping through small trees.

Finally, the plane came to a stop, and it was very, very still.

The dog was the first one to react. Hanging upside down made him feel panicky, and he yelped as he struggled frantically to get out of his harness.

Gregory opened his eyes, completely confused. Freezing cold air was rushing toward him from somewhere and a flailing paw scratched his face.

"Hey!" he protested, not sure where he was or why sharp claws had just raked across his cheek.

He couldn't understand why everything looked so strange, but then he realized that he was suspended upside down, that the plane had crashed, and — Patricia!

"Patty!" he shouted. "Uncle Steve! Are you okay?"

Neither of them were moving, and he could see that the windshield and instrument panel had been crushed. Were they all right? They *had* to be all right! Gregory gulped, feeling frantic tears fill his eyes.

"Patricia!" he shouted more loudly. "Uncle Steve! Wake up!"

Swinging helplessly next to him, the dog barked and yelped in a total frenzy of fear. What was happening? Why had they fallen out of the sky like that? He had mashed his side against the window, and it hurt a lot, so he yelped even more loudly.

"Santa Paws, no!" Gregory said. The terror was contagious, and he tried to fight it off. "*Shhh!* No! Good dog! *No!*"

Up in the front, Patricia groaned quietly.

"Patty, are you all right?" Gregory asked, trying not to cry. He could see that there was blood on her face, so she must be hurt. "Patty, wake up!"

He tore at his seat belt until he finally managed to unsnap the clasp. He landed hard on what would once have been the ceiling, and the plane lurched precariously to one side. Gregory was disoriented, but he made himself roll over until he was sitting upright.

Patricia's eyes opened partway, and she blinked a few times. Then she frowned at him.

"Why are you upside down?" she asked.

"*You're* upside down," Gregory said.

"Oh." She blinked again, her voice sounding strange and sluggish. "Why?"

Gregory started crying for real now, and it was hard to think. He rubbed his jacket sleeve across his eyes, and then forced himself to take a couple of deep breaths.

The skin of the plane had been torn open when the wing sheared off, and it was bitterly cold. Most of the fuselage — which was the metal body of the plane — on the right side was gone and the passenger's door was crumpled in.

"I-I don't — " Patricia was still blinking. "I'm not — " Suddenly, she figured out what was going on and her eyes flew open. "Greg! Are you okay?"

"I'm fine," he said shakily. Okay, she sounded like herself now. This wasn't as scary when she sounded like herself. "I'm coming up there to help you."

Patricia looked around, her expression much more alert now. "Wait. Calm the dog down first, he seems really upset."

The dog yelped and dug at the back of her seat with his paws. His side hurt! It hurt a whole lot! He was still caught in the seat belt and he desperately squirmed around, trying to get free.

"Come on, take it easy, boy," Gregory said, doing his best to stop him from struggling.

Patricia turned to check on Uncle Steve, who was unconscious. It was hard to tell exactly where he was injured, but blood was spreading down the front of his flight jacket. "Uncle Steve?" She put a trembling hand out to touch his shoulder. Then she gave it a gentle shake. "Are you okay? Uncle Steve?"

"Is he breathing?" Gregory asked.

"I don't know! I mean — " Patricia stopped for a second, so that she could calm down. "Yeah. I see his chest moving. I think he's really hurt, though."

Gregory got scratched on the face again, but then he wrapped his arms around Santa Paws to hold him still.

"It's okay, I've got you," he said soothingly. "Take it easy." He held his dog tightly, feeling both of their hearts pounding. Then he unhooked the seat belt and pulled it free of the harness.

Santa Paws fell on the roof of the plane with a loud thud and the plane lurched again. Landing that way made his shoulder hurt, too. He whimpered once, but then scrambled to his feet, and the plane swayed in response.

"Why's the plane moving?" Patricia asked uneasily.

Gregory shrugged. "I don't know. Maybe we're on some ice. Can you open your door?"

Patricia tried to pull the handle, and then made a tiny sound somewhere between a gasp and a moan.

"What?" Gregory asked, alarmed.

"I, uh, I must have banged my arm a little," she said, but her voice was so weak that Gregory knew she wasn't telling the whole truth.

"You're hurt," he said, "right?"

"I'm fine." Patricia gritted her teeth against the pain, and then bent to check the badly dented door. "I don't think it'll open, anyway. It's all smashed in."

The only thing Gregory knew for sure was that Patricia needed his help. "Good dog, stay," he said to Santa Paws. "I'm going to come up front now, Patty, okay?"

As he crawled toward her, the plane unexpectedly slid a few feet. He stopped, not sure why the plane was tilted on its side now, instead of being upside down. Then he lifted one hand to start forward again.

Patricia caught on first.

"Greg, don't move!" she shouted. "We're going to fall!"

He froze right where he was. "What?"

"I don't know where we landed," she said, "but — it's not good."

Well, no *kidding*. Their plane had crashed; of *course* it wasn't *good*. *None* of this was good.

"Don't anybody move!" Patricia said, her voice extremely crisp with authority. "Don't let Santa Paws move, either. I have to figure out what's going on here."

Outside, there was a distinct creaking sound, and the plane pitched forward again.

"What was that?" Gregory asked nervously.

"I don't know," Patricia said. "Just don't move."

She turned her head cautiously, looking in every direction. The plane seemed to be bobbing up and down, and she couldn't figure out why. When she squinted through what was left of the shattered windshield, she could see swaying tree branches and then — nothing at all. Empty air. Looking out through the cracked window in her door, she could see broken pine branches, snow — and more empty air.

"I think we're on top of a tree," she said slowly.

Gregory shook his head. "No, we're on the ground. We hit *way* too hard for it just to be a tree."

"Well, only the back part of it is on the ground then, because — " Then she sucked in her breath. "Oh, no."

They could hear more creaking, and what sounded like wood splintering. The plane bobbed

56

more, as though either the tail or the remaining wing was caught on something.

"What is it?" Gregory asked, his heart thumping in his ears.

Patricia took a deep breath, trying not to panic. "I think we're right on the edge of a mountain," she said.

6

Peering outside from his angle, Gregory saw that she was right, and that the front of the plane was suspended in midair. The only thing keeping them from falling over the cliff was a small fir tree. The tree was bent over from the weight of the plane, and he realized that the creaking sound was the trunk gradually breaking in half.

"It's okay, I can get you out," he said quickly. "I'm just going to reach over and — " As he leaned toward her, the plane lurched down another foot over the side of the mountain.

"Don't!" Patricia said.

Gregory edged back to where he had been, but the plane kept teetering.

"Just stay really still," Patricia said, her voice trembling. "If any weight shifts, we might — "

The dog stood up to see what was going on, and the plane teetered even more precariously.

"Don't!" Patricia said. "Make him sit!"

"*Sit*, Santa Paws," Gregory ordered, and then pressed down on his hindquarters.

Hearing the tension in his voice, Santa Paws quickly sat down. What was happening here? Gregory *never* got angry at him.

For the next minute, the only sounds were the wind whipping through what was left of the plane and the tree trunk creaking. Gregory and Patricia were both holding their breaths, too scared to budge.

"How high up are we?" he whispered.

Patricia was afraid to look again, so she didn't answer right away. "I don't know," she said finally. "Um, *high*, I think."

The plane swayed. The tree trunk creaked.

"Look," Gregory started. "If I — "

"Is the hole in the side big enough to crawl through?" Patricia asked.

The shell of the plane had been torn apart, so there was plenty of room. Most of the fuselage along the right side had been ripped away.

Gregory glanced over his shoulder. "Yeah. No problem. We can all fit."

There was more splintering, and the plane abruptly plunged down another foot. Patricia and Gregory gasped, and held their breaths again, as Santa Paws whimpered anxiously.

"Okay," Patricia said finally. "You and the dog get out."

Gregory stared at her. "What?!"

"Get out," she said, sounding very sure of herself. "Move as fast as you can."

"But — " Gregory stopped, and thought about it. Was that a good plan? Something didn't sound right to him. "No. That's a really bad idea."

The plane bobbed up and down. The tree trunk creaked. They might have minutes of safety left — or they might only have *seconds*.

"Just do it," Patricia said, so quietly that he could barely hear her. "Okay?"

Gregory shook his head. "*No*. If we do, there'll be way too much weight up front, and you'll fall."

"If you *don't*, *all* of us are going to fall," Patricia said through her teeth. "Just go, already!"

They stared at each other, Patricia still hanging awkwardly from her seat belt.

"You got a better idea?" she asked.

Suddenly, Gregory *did*.

"Yeah," he said, nodding. "How much does Uncle Steve weigh? Like, two hundred maybe?"

Patricia considered that. "Probably, yeah."

"And you weigh the least of any of us. So if we could get *him* out of the front, there'd be a whole lot more weight in the *back*, and we might be okay," Gregory said. "At least long enough to get us all out."

They stared at each other again.

"Well, I guess we can tell *your* mother's a physics teacher," Patricia said finally.

It was silent for a second, and then they both

laughed. *Feeble* laughs, but at least they were laughing.

"See if you can get your seat belt off, while I do his," Gregory suggested.

Patricia nodded, and fumbled awkwardly with the cold metal clasp. "He's going to be really heavy. Are you strong enough to pull him out?"

"*Santa Paws* is," Gregory said.

Hearing his name, the dog's ears pricked up.

Patricia nodded again. "You're right. Get some of the rope he used to tie our stuff down."

"Yeah." Then Gregory frowned. "Is it okay to move him? Maybe we're not supposed to. What if he hurt his back, or neck, or something? We could make it worse."

"It's okay," Patricia said. "I kind of think this counts as an emergency."

Well, that was true. If this wasn't an emergency, what *would* be? Gregory was having trouble unfastening their uncle's seat belt, and he finally realized that the metal part had been badly bent in the crash.

"What do I do? I can't open it, Patty," he said, hearing his voice shake. "We're going to fall, I *know* we are."

The plane kept bobbing up and down, and the tree kept creaking. Still too anxious to bark, the dog whined softly. First, he would sit, then he would get up, then he would sit down again. He knew that there were bad things happening here, and he wasn't sure how to help. So he just moved around skittishly in the back of the plane.

Patricia thought fast. "Go through his jacket pockets. Doesn't he have a Swiss Army knife?"

Gregory's hands were trembling so much that it was hard to make them work right. But he found the knife in the right side pocket and tugged it out. He chose the biggest blade and began hacking away at the thick seat belt.

He worked for a minute, but didn't make much progress. So he switched to one of the saw blades, yanking it back and forth as quickly as he could. He had expected Patricia to crawl over and help him once she got her seat belt off, but for some reason, she hadn't.

"You all right?" he asked over his shoulder.

"Unh-hunh," Patricia said without much expression in her voice. "Hurry up."

Was there something else wrong? She sounded like something else had gone wrong. *Everything* had gone wrong so far. But Gregory nodded and sawed even harder. When he had cut almost all the way through the seat belt, he paused.

"When I break through this, the weight's going to shift a bunch," he said tentatively.

"Unh-hunh," Patricia answered.

They both knew what might happen next, but there wasn't much they could do about it.

Gregory ripped through the last frayed

strands of the seat belt and Uncle Steve's body sagged limply into his arms. The unexpected weight was too much for him, and they both fell heavily onto what had been the ceiling.

In response, the plane swung violently to one side and then slipped forward another foot. More branches snapped off, and plummeted over the side of the cliff.

"Whatever we're going to do, we have to do *fast!*" Patricia yelled.

With his uncle's full weight crushing him, Gregory wasn't even sure if he could get up. Plus, he was so scared that —

"Don't think about it, Greg!" Patricia shouted from the front. *"Move!"*

A cold nose pressed against his cheek, and Gregory looked up at Santa Paws. The dog wagged his tail encouragingly, and then licked his face.

Okay, they all needed him to be brave right now — even Santa Paws. Gregory stretched his arm up toward what had been the floor of the plane and yanked on the first rope he saw.

The cargo underneath came tumbling down and the plane pitched forward again. There was the sound of more wood splintering, and then, a distinct *snap*. The plane sagged lower.

"Hurry!" Patricia said.

Gregory kicked the stuff out through the

shredded fuselage and shifted around until he could sit up. "Once I get him back here, you start climbing over, too, okay?" he said.

"Unh-hunh." Patricia gulped. "I mean, I'll try."

Gregory wrapped one end of the rope around Uncle Steve's chest and tied it tightly in a square knot, which was the only kind of knot he knew how to make.

"He's bleeding a lot, Patty," he said unsteadily.

"Go on!" she ordered.

Gregory nodded and pulled the rest of the rope through his hands until he got to the other end.

"Santa Paws?" he asked, looking around. "Come here, boy."

The dog wagged his tail gratefully and tried to climb onto his lap. He wasn't really sure what was going on, but they had never acted like this before. It was scaring him.

Gregory threaded the rope through the harness and tied another knot.

"Okay, Santa Paws," he said. "Go!"

The dog cocked his head to one side.

Gregory pushed him toward the hole in the fuselage. "Go on!"

The dog cocked his head the other way, perplexed.

Gregory yanked the rope, pretending that they were going to play tug-of-war. "Pull!"

Now, the dog understood. He knew the word

"pull." He grabbed the rope in his teeth and tugged as hard as he could. His legs were rigid, and he strained backward with all of his strength. His ribs were throbbing, but he just tugged harder.

"Good boy!" Gregory praised him. "Keep pulling!"

With the two of them working together, they were able to drag Uncle Steve over to the torn fuselage. Uncle Steve still wasn't conscious, but he was mumbling something Gregory couldn't quite hear. He thought he caught the words "call backup," but he wasn't sure.

"Pull, boy!" Gregory said again. "Good dog!"

The plane was still swaying back and forth, and more branches were snapping off.

When Uncle Steve was halfway outside to safety, Gregory turned to help his sister.

"Come on," he said, holding out his hand. "I'll pull you over."

She looked up at him, and he was shocked to see that she was crying. Patricia *never* cried.

"What?" he asked, afraid to hear the answer.

"I'm sorry," she said, crying harder. "My leg's stuck. I can't get it loose."

They were never going to get out. Never, never, never. Pretty much out of both courage and ideas, Gregory just stared back at her. Then he saw that from the knee down, her right leg was trapped underneath the smashed instrument panel. She was struggling to get free, but her leg was jammed there.

"Is it broken?" he asked.

Patricia shook her head, and rubbed some of the tears away with the side of her glove. "I don't think so. I'm just stuck."

Not sure what else to do, Gregory put his arms around her and pulled with all of his might.

Suddenly, the load in the back of the plane lightened and they pitched forward again. From his position, Gregory could see that there was a huge rocky ravine down below them. It went down at least two hundred feet, and — there was *no way* that they would survive, if they fell. And any second now, they might — he closed his eyes tightly and kept tugging.

"I'm sorry," Patricia kept saying, mainly to herself. "I'm really sorry."

"What if I get another rope?" Gregory asked. "Okay? I'll tie it around the back of the plane, and — "

There was a loud crack, and the plane plunged forward another couple of feet. Without looking, Gregory could tell that *most* of the plane was now hanging precariously over the edge of the cliff.

There was no time to lose!

"Santa Paws!" he bellowed.

Hearing his name, the dog sprang obediently

back inside the plane. Did they need his help? Whatever they wanted him to do, he was ready! Having his weight there made the nose of the plane rise a few inches.

"Okay, good dog. Stay," Gregory said, and crawled forward far enough to yank at the bottom of the instrument panel with his hands. "Maybe I can pry it up, and — "

Patricia shook her head. "I tried, it won't work. I don't think we can — " Then she stopped, her eyes brightening. "Oil! Get me some oil."

Gregory nodded and dug underneath the pilot's seat until he found a small plastic bottle of motor oil. He twisted the cap off, and handed it up to her.

Patricia shook the oil onto her jeans leg, forcing as much of the slippery liquid as she could below the instrument panel. Then she twisted back and forth, trying to get loose.

A few more branches broke, and they slid down another foot.

"It's not working," she said weakly. "I can't — "

No more time to fool around here — it was now, or never. "Close your eyes!" Gregory yelled. He snatched up the fire extinguisher that was also underneath the pilot's seat and sprayed the full contents at her leg. Then he threw the canister down and wrapped one arm around her. "Santa Paws! Come here!"

Instantly, the dog bounded over and Gregory grabbed onto his harness with his free hand.

"Pull, boy!" he shouted. "Go!"

The dog strained toward the torn fuselage, whimpering in frustration.

"Harder!" Gregory shouted, using his own legs to try and get them started. "Pull!"

Patricia gasped in pain, but then suddenly, her leg popped free and they all sprawled down in a heap.

"Come on!" Gregory said.

All three of them dove for the hole in the fuselage, scrambling out just as the fir tree finally gave way. The plane whipped past them, gathering speed until suddenly, it disappeared over the side of the mountain.

They had barely made it!

7

Gregory and Patricia lay in the snow, too exhausted to speak. After a minute, Patricia lifted herself up enough to look over the edge of the cliff, and then she sank back down. It was a *very* long drop.

"Is Uncle Steve okay?" she mumbled.

Gregory turned his head and saw their uncle's chest rising and falling as he breathed. He still seemed to be unconscious, though. "I think so," he answered. "He's breathing and everything."

They lay there for a few more seconds, in total silence, trying to catch their breaths. The snow was about a foot deep, and if they'd had enough energy, they would have been shivering. As it was, breathing in and out took all of their attention. Patricia didn't even have enough strength to worry about how badly her right arm hurt.

"We should have just driven up with Mom and Dad," Gregory said finally.

Patricia nodded. "Too bad we're not nice, loving children."

That broke the tension, and they snickered a little. Then they slumped back into the snow to rest some more.

Worried, the dog came over to check on them. They had never acted like this before! Why wouldn't they get up? Were they sick? This was scary! He sniffed Patricia's face, and then nudged Gregory's shoulder with his paw.

Gregory opened his eyes and lifted his hand to pat him. "It's okay," he said. "You're a good boy, Santa Paws."

That was more like it! Feeling better, the dog promptly turned in two circles and curled up between them in the snow. He rested his muzzle on Gregory's chest, and Gregory kept patting him. Patting his dog made it seem as though everything was going to be okay.

"If Santa Paws hadn't helped me pull, we wouldn't have gotten out in time," he said aloud.

"Yeah," Patricia agreed, and then paused. "You should give him a Milk-Bone."

The dog's ears flew up, and he looked at them hopefully.

It wasn't much of a reward, but Gregory fished around inside his jacket pocket until he found one. He gave it to Santa Paws, who wagged his tail and began crunching. Then Gregory stood up and looked around to see where they were.

There were craggy, tree-covered mountains in every direction. Mountains, mountains, and *more* mountains.

"Can you see any houses or anything?" Patricia asked.

Gregory shook his head. There were no signs of civilization at all. "I don't even see *roads*. We're in the like, *total* forest."

There had to be a town *someplace* nearby. It wasn't as though they'd crashed in the Yukon, right? "How about streetlights?" Patricia asked. "Or — I don't know — telephone poles, maybe."

Gregory looked and looked, but all he could see were mountains and trees. Hundreds and thousands and millions of *trees*. Dark, overcast sky. What might be a frozen lake off in the distance. Wherever they were, it looked as though they were on their own.

As though they were in *very* serious trouble.

Behind them, Uncle Steve started moving restlessly and saying something that sounded like "eltee." It didn't make any sense, but he seemed to be regaining consciousness.

Gregory hurried over to see if he was okay. Patricia followed him, wincing from the pain in her arm. The rope was still tied around their uncle's chest, and Gregory pulled it off.

Uncle Steve shifted his position, and then mumbled again.

"What's he saying?" Gregory asked. "L-T?"

Patricia shrugged as she took off her scarf and pressed it against the blood on his chest. Her right arm wouldn't work at all, so she had to do it one-handed. "I don't know," she said, trying to stop the bleeding. "Maybe he thinks this happened at work, and his lieutenant is here."

Gregory used *his* scarf to pick up a small handful of snow. Then he used the damp scarf to wipe the blood away from Uncle Steve's face. Most of it came right off, and he saw that it had all come from a cut on his forehead. The gash didn't seem to be very deep, but he would definitely need stitches. There was a huge, dark bruise there, too.

Washing his face with the cold snow must have helped, because Uncle Steve's eyes opened partway, and he squinted at them. He tried to sit up, then groaned and fell back down.

"Call backup," he whispered. Then his hand went down to where his holster would have been, if he was on duty. "Where's my service revolver?"

Gregory and Patricia looked at each other uneasily. Did he have amnesia, maybe? That would be really bad. He might even think they were perpetrators! If he suddenly started giving them their Miranda rights, it would just be too weird.

"Well — I think it's in Massachusetts," Gregory answered.

Uncle Steve looked confused. He tried to get up again, but then collapsed.

"I don't think you should try to move," Patricia said. "You might be really hurt."

Uncle Steve stared up at her in sudden recognition. "Patricia?" he asked in a dazed voice. "What happened? Are you all right?" He managed to lift himself onto one elbow, and then looked around anxiously. "Hey! Where's the plane?"

Gregory and Patricia shrugged and pointed over the edge of the mountain.

Uncle Steve's mouth dropped open. "What?! How did we get out?"

Patricia pointed at Gregory, and Gregory pointed at Santa Paws.

Uncle Steve's mouth stayed open, as he tried to take all of this in. Then he started shaking his head. "I can't believe I got you kids into this," he said softly. "I am *so* sorry."

"You should just lie down," Patricia advised. "I don't think it's good for you to be, you know, agitated."

Uncle Steve narrowed his eyes, trying to piece together what was going on. He might not have amnesia, but he still seemed pretty out of it.

"Because you're *hurt*," she elaborated.

Uncle Steve nodded, looking — even though he was an adult — a little overwhelmed for a second. Then he gave his head a shake and put on a more confident expression.

"Okay," he said, sounding very sure of himself. "Don't worry, everything's going to be okay." He tried to sit up all the way, and winced. Noticing the makeshift scarf-bandage, he raised one edge to look underneath.

"I think you maybe have a sucking chest wound," Patricia said uneasily. "Or — a pneumothorax."

Uncle Steve stared at her, and then, unexpectedly, he grinned. "Oh. You think so, Doc?"

Patricia looked a little offended, but then she grinned, too. She turned to Gregory. "Get a CBC, Chem seven, type and cross for two units, chest films, and hang a dopamine drip, *stat*," she said crisply.

Gregory looked at her suspiciously.

"Now!" she barked. "He's in v-tach!"

Instead of just grinning, Uncle Steve laughed outright when he heard that. "You know what? I think your sister watches too much television," he said to Gregory.

Gregory nodded. Sometimes Patricia even referred to herself as "Queen of the Remote Control." "Yeah," he agreed. "And she's like, in *love* with George Clooney."

Uncle Steve's face was tight with pain, but he laughed again. "Well, what would old George do in this situation?" he asked.

"Well — call nine one one, probably," Patricia said logically. "I mean, he's an *actor*." She paused. "That is, after he kissed me hello."

All three of them laughed this time.

The dog wagged his tail, because everyone seemed happy now. Things must be okay. Maybe they would go ride in the car soon. That's what they *usually* did after they got out of the plane. He didn't really know where the car *was* right now — but they would know. They *always* knew. So he sat down in the snow to wait, watching them alertly.

"Don't worry," Uncle Steve said to Patricia. "I think it's just my collarbone. Looks like a compound fracture, that's all." He took a deep breath and started to sit up all the way, but then his face paled.

Patricia looked scared. "What?"

"And maybe my hip," he said in a faint voice. He tried to move again, and then sucked in his breath. "Oh, boy." He smiled feebly at them. "I, uh, might've wrenched my back a little, too."

Patricia and Gregory exchanged nervous glances.

"What do we do?" Gregory asked.

"Let me think for a minute, okay?" Uncle Steve said, speaking with an effort.

Gregory and Patricia waited nervously for him to open his eyes again. The dog moved into a worried crouch, since they all seemed to be upset again. He whimpered once, and Gregory automatically patted him.

"Okay," Uncle Steve said finally. His voice sounded a *little* stronger, but not much. "First things, first. Are either of you hurt?"

Gregory shook his head, but Patricia didn't answer.

"Patricia?" Uncle Steve asked more firmly.

"I kind of banged my arm," she muttered.

Since her right arm was just hanging uselessly at her side, it was pretty obvious that she had broken something.

"Okay," Uncle Steve said gently. "We're going to get a splint on you as soon as we can, and — it'll be okay. How bad's the pain?"

Patricia shrugged, avoiding his eyes.

"Okay," Uncle Steve said. "I hear you." He let out his breath. "Did either of you turn on the ELT?"

The ELT was the Emergency Locator Transmitter, which looked sort of like a walkie-talkie. ELTs sent out emergency signals, so that rescue planes would be able to find downed aircraft easily. And — they hadn't turned it on. In fact, neither of them had even *thought* of it. They had just assumed he meant "lieutenant." Patricia and Gregory both ducked their heads and looked guilty.

"Okay, no problem. Don't worry about it," Uncle Steve said calmly. He pulled in a deep breath.

"Where's the survival pack? I've got a handheld one in there."

Patricia and Gregory looked even more guilty. Then Gregory pointed miserably over the side of the mountain. After all of the times they had flown in the plane, the one time there was a *real* emergency, they hadn't remembered what to do. And now, it might cost them their lives.

Uncle Steve closed his eyes briefly, but then gave them a reassuring smile. "Okay. No problem," he said again. "I had to go a little off-course to get us down, but I filed a flight plan, so they'll know where to start looking. It just might take a little while."

"Will they be here today?" Gregory asked.

Uncle Steve glanced up at the sky. Ominous grey clouds had rolled in, and it was starting to get dark. "Probably in the morning," he answered.

So they were going to have to spend the night out here, alone, in the middle of the wilderness, in *December*.

"We're going to die," Gregory said grimly, "right?"

That was the *last* thing Patricia felt like hearing, and she couldn't help giving him a little shove.

Uncle Steve shook his head. "We are *not* going to die. We're going to stay really calm, set up some kind of shelter, and get a fire going. Okay?"

Thinking about sitting in front of a warm fire, Gregory and Patricia suddenly realized that their teeth were chattering. It was very windy on the mountain, and even Santa Paws seemed to be shivering.

"We'll all feel a lot better once we get warm," Uncle Steve promised.

At the moment, neither Gregory nor Patricia could imagine how they could feel much *worse*.

"I'm really sorry about the survival stuff," Gregory said. "I — I just forgot, I — "

Patricia interrupted him. "*I* should have remembered. I'm older than he is."

"And *I* should have figured out a way to land in the middle of some nice little town common somewhere," Uncle Steve said. "Look, we all got out of the plane in one piece, right? *That's* what's important."

"Yeah, but — " Patricia started.

"It's going to be dark soon," Uncle Steve said, cutting her off. "We need to move quickly here. Greg, take the dog, and go see how much firewood you can find." He looked around the mountain face, and then pointed to a spot surrounded by a thicket of pine trees. "See where those rocks are? And that fallen tree? That's where we'll settle in. We should be protected from the wind up there."

Gregory nodded, and climbed stiffly to his feet.

"Come on, Santa Paws," he said, giving him a short whistle.

The dog jumped up, relieved to be *doing* something. Maybe *now* they would go to the car. Sitting here in the wind was just too cold.

Patricia and Uncle Steve watched as Gregory and Santa Paws went trudging off through the foot-deep snow.

"So," Uncle Steve said wryly. "We having fun yet?"

Patricia tried to smile.

So far, her Christmas vacation had been anything but *fun*.

8

Patricia knew she should be doing something constructive, but she was too tired to think. It was easier just to rest for another minute. Uncle Steve looked even worse than she felt, but he motioned her over.

"Come here, honey, and let me look at you for a minute," he said.

Patricia got up, and moved to him. Uncle Steve held her chin gently so he could examine her face. Then he picked up the scarf Gregory had dropped, and used the end to blot away the blood below her nose and on her chin.

"Did you bite your lip?" he asked.

Patricia thought back, and then nodded. "When we crashed, I think."

"Okay," he said, and dabbed lightly at the cut. "You went right through. It looks like you had a little nosebleed, too. Do your teeth feel okay?"

Patricia ran her tongue around the inside of

her mouth to be sure, and then nodded. None of them seemed to be loose or anything.

"How about your head?" Uncle Steve asked, looking concerned. "Do you think you hit it?"

"Well — it doesn't hurt," Patricia said uncertainly.

"Good." Uncle Steve rolled some snow into the scarf, and then handed it to her. "Hold that against your lip, and let's see if we can get some of the swelling down."

Patricia nodded, and pressed the snow on the spot that hurt the most. "Do you think *you* have a concussion?" she asked, her voice muffled by the scarf.

"Who, me?" he asked cheerfully. "This is nothing. I used to play *football*, remember?" Then he indicated a couple of objects half-buried in the snow. "What're those?"

Patricia went over to see, surprised to find herself limping. Apparently, she had twisted her knee while trying to get free from the instrument panel. It hurt, but not nearly as much as her arm did. She bent down on her uninjured leg to examine the things that must have been knocked out of the plane during all of the confusion.

"My knapsack," she said. "And — I think this might be a life jacket."

Uncle Steve's eyes lit up. "*Good.* I've got some

MREs, and I forget what else, wrapped up in there."

MREs were Meals-Ready-to-Eat, which were Army rations. Patricia had never had one before, but *anything* would taste good right now. She was starting to get really hungry. Just in case, she kept poking through the snow with the toe of her oil-and-foam-stained boot to see what else she might find. Her knee felt swollen and clumsy, but she could still bend it a little.

"I see some stuff from the picnic basket, too," she said. "There's a Coke, and — I see the brownies!"

Uncle Steve nodded. *"Outstanding.* See if you can get all of it piled together, and then when Gregory gets back, he can carry everything."

While she was doing that, Uncle Steve dragged himself over to the edge of the cliff. It must have hurt a lot, because he groaned a few times, but he would just grit his teeth and keep going.

He studied the broken fir tree, and shook his head. "Was the plane caught on this?"

Patricia nodded.

Uncle Steve nodded, too, before shaking his head again. Then he peered down into the deep gorge. There was a sheer rock face on both sides, and the whole thing was coated with ice and snow. He stared at the wreckage down on the rocks, and then let out his breath.

"How close did we come to going over?" he asked.

Really close. "Um, about a second and a half," Patricia said.

Uncle Steve let out a low whistle.

Patricia glanced behind her to make sure that Gregory hadn't come back yet. "I, um, I pretty much panicked," she confessed. "I thought I was maybe even going to throw up or something. But Greg was *really* brave."

"I'm guessing you did fine," Uncle Steve said, and stared at the battered wreckage some more. "In fact, you kids are really something."

Patricia shrugged self-consciously. The only thing she could remember was how terrified she had been, every single second. Just being *scared* — which was how she felt right now — was definitely an improvement. "Do you think we can climb down there, and maybe get the ELT and all?" she asked.

Uncle Steve looked at her incredulously. "I don't think a team of fully-equipped *paratroopers* could climb down there," he answered.

Patricia nodded, and then couldn't help shivering. A couple of seconds either way, and she would have fallen onto those rocks. It made her dizzy to look down there, so she concentrated on gathering up the stray cargo, instead.

Across the clearing, Gregory was stomping around near the fallen tree with a huge armload of wood. He saw them watching, waved, and hiked back over. Santa Paws galloped playfully next to him, barking every so often.

Gregory's face was red from all of the exercise, but he was smiling. "There's a whole *bunch* of wood over there," he said. "Dead trees, and all. We found most of the wing, too. Can we maybe use it like a sled for you, Uncle Steve?"

"Let me see if I can get over there by myself, first," Uncle Steve suggested. "Then we'll use it to help build a shelter."

"Okay," Gregory said, sounding remarkably chipper. "We'll go get it. Come on, boy!" he called to Santa Paws, and they headed off again.

"Why don't you carry what you can," Uncle Steve said to Patricia, "and I'll catch up."

Patricia nodded and unzipped her knapsack. There was just enough room inside to pack in the few things she had found from the picnic basket. When she came across the plastic bag of carrot sticks her mother had cut up for them, she had to stop for a second so she wouldn't cry.

Did their parents know what had happened yet? Were they upset? What if she never saw them again? She squeezed her eyes shut and tried to remember the last thing she had said to both of them.

Her mother had been worried that she hadn't dressed warmly enough for the trip. And — her mother was *right*. Her father had stayed back at the house, because he was waiting for some overnight mail to come from New York. But he had given each of them a big hug before they left, the best kind where he lifted them right off the ground and spun around a couple of times.

"You all right?" Uncle Steve asked.

Patricia nodded and swung the knapsack over her good arm. That way, she could also carry the rolled-up life jacket in her hand and only have to make one trip. Then she started limping toward the rocks.

Watching Uncle Steve drag himself inch by inch through the snow made her want to cry all over again. His jaw was very tight, and he kept his eyes closed most of the time. He was breathing really hard, and every few feet, he would groan softly and suck in his breath.

"Um, maybe we *should* make a sled," she said hesitantly.

For a second, she thought he was going to yell at her. But then, he just shook his head.

"I'm fine," he panted. "Okay? It's just going to be slow."

Patricia nodded. Her father was always talking about how incredibly stubborn his little brother Steve was — and so, she wasn't about to argue. And, hey, *she* had been accused of being pretty stubborn, too.

About fifty feet away, she could see that Gregory had managed to tie the rope to the sheared-off wing. Now he and Santa Paws were pulling it toward them like an ungainly pair of Santa's reindeer.

A large branch was poking up out of the snow, and Uncle Steve paused long enough to tear off a thick twig. He stuck it between his teeth, and bit down *hard*. Then he resumed crawling. He had only made it about ten more feet, when Gregory and Santa Paws got to them.

"Taxi!" Gregory announced brightly.

Uncle Steve hesitated, but then gave up. Slowly, he eased himself up onto the metal wing. Once he was aboard, Gregory tugged on the rope, but the improvised sled didn't move.

"We pulled him before," he said to Santa Paws, "remember? We can do it again."

The dog cocked his head.

"*Pull*, boy," Gregory said. Then he yanked on the rope, using all of his weight.

Santa Paws joined in, ignoring the pain in his side, but it still didn't budge.

Uncle Steve swung his uninjured leg over the side and pushed powerfully against the snow. With that extra effort, the wing-sled squirted forward. Using the momentum, Gregory and Santa Paws started pulling the wing-sled across the drifts.

It seemed to take forever, but finally they all made it over to the fallen tree. Patricia and

Gregory sat heavily on top of a rock, while Uncle Steve stayed right where he was, trying to catch his breath. Even Santa Paws looked tired. It was dusk now, and they had to squint through the shadows to see each other.

Uncle Steve broke the silence. "Thanks, guys. Sorry to be so much trouble." He slid himself off the wing, his face grey from exhaustion and pain. "Greg, if you can lift the wide end up on the tree, and the other side onto that rock, we'll be in business."

"I can help," Patricia offered.

Uncle Steve shook his head. "No, why don't you get some more wood, while it's still light enough to see. But *don't go out of sight.*" Then he felt around inside his right jacket pocket and frowned.

"Oh," Gregory said, and reached into his own pocket for the Swiss Army knife. "Are you looking for this?"

Uncle Steve nodded. "Thanks."

While Patricia gathered wood, and Gregory worked on the shelter, Uncle Steve began to cut pine boughs from some of the nearby trees with his good arm. Normally, of course, he would never have damaged trees that way — but, this wasn't exactly a normal situation. When survival was at stake, the rules changed.

For lack of a better idea, the dog followed Patricia around. He liked to carry things in his mouth, so when Patricia gave him a stick, he happily took it. She kept going back and forth with single armloads of kindling and thicker sticks. Each time, he would dance along next to her.

"Are you a good boy?" she asked him.

The dog barked, which made the stick fall out of his mouth. He grabbed it back up and shook his head playfully from side to side. If he was lucky, maybe she would throw it for him! Just because his ribs hurt, didn't mean that he couldn't still have fun!

"No, not now," Patricia said. Her hands and feet were so cold, and her arm was throbbing so much that the *last* thing she felt like doing was playing fetch. Besides that, her knee was beginning to ache more than ever. "Leave me alone, Santa Paws!"

The dog lowered his ears and stopped wagging his tail. Then he dropped the stick into the snow. Did she think he was a bad dog? She *must*.

Patricia sighed, ashamed of herself for having shouted at him. After all, only about an hour ago, he had helped save her *life*. "I'm sorry, you're very good, Santa Paws," she apologized. "It's just — right now, we have to work."

The dog still kept his head down, with his tail between his legs. He must have done *something* wrong, but he didn't know what it was. Now his side hurt even more than it had before.

Seeing him upset was more than she could take, and Patricia felt tears start down her cheeks. She let the sticks she was clutching fall, and then she sat down in the snow. It was cold, but she didn't care. She was *already* so cold that she couldn't think straight, anyway.

Her arm hurt so much that it felt like it was on fire. She hunched over it, rocking slightly. Gregory and Uncle Steve — and Santa Paws — were so brave, and she just wasn't making it, here. She buried her face in her sleeve and cried as quietly as she could. If they heard her, or came to look for her, she would feel even worse.

The dog *couldn't stand it* when he saw anyone cry. He hated it when people were sad. Especially *his* people. He sat down and nuzzled up next to her, trying to get as close as he could.

Patricia put her arm around him and hugged him tightly. His fur felt warm, and comforting. She had never been outside in the forest like this before, and she couldn't believe how *dark* it was. How frightening it seemed. The clouds were so thick that there weren't even any stars out.

Then she heard Gregory calling her name, his voice sharp with fear.

"Patricia!" he yelled. "Patricia, where are you?"

Santa Paws was already on his feet. Patricia hung onto his collar to help herself stand up faster. Then she stumbled through the snow in the direction of her brother's voice.

"What's wrong? I'm over here!" she yelled back.

"Come quick!" he said, sounding frantic. "I need help!"

9

It was hard to see in the dark, but Santa Paws was galloping ahead of her. Patricia just kept watching for a moving shape, and then she would race after it.

Then she ran into Gregory — *literally* — at the edge of the clearing.

"What's wrong?" she asked, out of breath. "Are you hurt?"

"Uncle Steve fainted or something," Gregory said, sounding very close to tears. "He was helping me make a fire pit, and then he just passed out. I didn't know what to do!"

Patricia put her hand on his shoulder to calm him down. "Just show me where he is, okay?"

Gregory nodded, and motioned for her to follow him.

When they got to the shelter, Patricia saw that Uncle Steve was lying on his back in the snow. She crouched down next to him, peering through the darkness. His breathing seemed nice and steady, but he was definitely unconscious.

"*Fix* him," Gregory said urgently. "I mean, you know all that medical stuff."

Patricia sighed. "I just know a bunch of words, Greg — I don't know how to *do* anything."

He stared at her accusingly. "But — I thought you *knew* stuff. You always act like you know *everything*."

"Give me a break, I'm only *twelve!*" she said.

They glared at each other until Patricia finally took a deep breath.

"Look," she said. "We're really cold, and we're really scared, and we don't know how to help him. Let's try to be nice to each other, okay?"

"Be sweet," Gregory muttered.

Patricia smiled a little. That was what their grandmother always said to them right before she hung up the telephone, instead of "good-bye." "Yeah," she said. "Exactly."

Watching them, the dog paced anxiously and whined deep in his throat.

Patricia slipped her glove off and tapped her uncle's face lightly with her hand. "Uncle Steve?" she asked tentatively.

There was no response.

Gregory and Santa Paws were waiting for her to make everything all right, so she tapped his face again. Then she nudged his arm.

Finally, his eyes opened. He shook his head to

clear it, squinted at them, and then sat up partway.

"Sorry," he said hoarsely. "Got a little dizzy there." He rubbed his hand across his eyes and shook his head a few more times. "Okay." He frowned when he noticed Patricia's bare hand. "Hey, put your gloves on — it's cold out here."

If he was being authoritative, he must be okay. Or *better*, anyway. Patricia awkwardly wormed her hand back inside her glove. Just a couple of minutes of being exposed to the cold air had numbed her fingers pretty badly.

"Take it easy, I'm all right," Uncle Steve said to Gregory. "I overdid the lifting, that's all."

"You have to be careful," Gregory answered shakily. "That was way too scary."

Uncle Steve nodded. "I know. I'm sorry, pal."

While they were talking, Patricia glanced around the campsite. From what she could see, they had made a lot of progress. The wing was resting across the big tree trunk and a gigantic boulder to form the roof of a primitive triangular shelter. Someone — Gregory, presumably — had built up a snow wall to fill the open spot in the back. As a result, the shelter was fully enclosed, except for a wide opening in the front.

The snow had been trampled down to make a hard surface. Cushiony pine branches lined the bottom of the shelter to insulate it from the snow. In front of the opening, there was a neat semicircle made out of fairly big rocks and some jagged pieces of aluminum from the wing. They would form a firebreak. It would block the wind from the fire, and it would also help reflect the heat into their lean-to.

Smaller rocks were arranged together in front of the firebreak, as a base for their campfire. Otherwise, the heat from the coals would just melt all of the surrounding snow and the fire would go out right away.

"This is really *good*," Patricia said admiringly. "You're like, *nature guys*."

Uncle Steve's teeth flashed, so he must have smiled.

Gregory raised his fist in the air. "Airborne!" he said, trying to make his voice deep. Sometimes, he and his friend Oscar liked to pretend that they were in the Army, and they were always trying to chant infantry cadences.

"Okay, Airborne Ranger," Uncle Steve said, still smiling. "See if you can rip one more piece of metal off the end of the wing. We'll build the fire on it."

Gregory nodded, and climbed up on top of the fallen tree to work on the wing.

Uncle Steve shifted his position to one side and reached inside his jacket. His movements were extremely cautious. Finally, he came out with a small penlight. He flicked it on, and the bright beam cut through the darkness.

Now that they could see better, they all visibly relaxed. The campsite seemed friendlier, somehow. The black expanses of the wilderness were still surrounding them, but it felt as though they were in a safe haven.

Next, Uncle Steve dug painfully into one of the bellows pockets on his pants leg. He pulled out an ordinary plastic trash bag and then sliced open the two long sides with his Swiss Army knife.

"Here," he said, and handed it to Patricia. "Spread it out on the floor of the shelter. It'll help us stay dry."

Patricia nodded and carried the bag inside the shelter. Gregory had managed to tear another piece of fuselage from the wing, and he set it down on the bed of rocks.

Since everyone else had something to do, the dog looked at Uncle Steve expectantly.

"Santa Paws, why don't you just wag your tail and keep up morale?" Uncle Steve suggested.

The dog promptly lifted his right paw.

"Okay," Uncle Steve said agreeably. "That's good, too." Then he retrieved another garbage bag from his pocket. "Lay this one out on the ground, Patricia, and then we can inventory our supplies. And Greg, can you help me clear out my pockets?"

Gregory hesitated. "Will I hurt you?"

"No," Uncle Steve said, although it probably

wasn't true. "I just can't get to the ones on the left side very well."

Patricia watched as the two of them pulled out a surprising variety of objects. Between the flight jacket and the army pants, Uncle Steve had an *amazing* number of pockets.

"Are you maybe Mary Poppins in disguise?" she asked.

Uncle Steve nodded ironically. "Oh, yeah. I'm practically perfect in every way." He fumbled through the pile one-handed until he found a small plastic container of waterproof matches and a tube of fire-starter. "Here we go, Greg — it's show time."

Soon, a small blaze was glowing on the piece of fuselage. Following their uncle's instructions, Gregory carefully surrounded it with more kindling. Then, once the fire had caught pretty well, he added some thicker sticks. The wood crackled and snapped, and burned noisily away.

They all, including Santa Paws, gathered around the fire. No one spoke, so that they could just enjoy the luxury of starting to feel warm again. Or, at least, not quite as *cold*.

"Let's break out the brownies," Uncle Steve said finally. "I think we could all use a snack."

Patricia looked inside her knapsack until she found the foil-wrapped package. While she was at it, she took out the rest of the things from the picnic basket. There was a squashed meat loaf sandwich, the bag of carrot sticks, a can of Coke, a package of Santa Claus cocktail napkins, and a juice box. It might not be much, but it *seemed* like great riches.

There were six brownies in the package, and they each had one. Santa Paws gulped his down in one swallow, but the rest of them took their time. They wanted to savor every single bite. In the end, of course, Gregory ended up sharing the rest of his with Santa Paws, anyway.

"What else have you got in there?" Uncle Steve asked, indicating the knapsack.

"I don't know," Patricia said, and then she flushed self-consciously. *"Vogue."*

Uncle Steve grinned. "Well, see," he said to Gregory, "things were looking mighty bleak, but now we're going to be able to sit here, and get up-to-speed on the spring collections. Life is *good.*"

The thought of them all sprawling in front of the fire, reading *Vogue*, was a pretty funny image, and Gregory laughed.

"I didn't know we were going to crash," Patricia said defensively. "So I just brought vacation stuff."

Gregory started pulling things out of the knapsack. His face lit up when he saw her notebook computer.

"Hey, whoa!" he said eagerly. "We can send *E-mail*! Then they'll come rescue us!"

Uncle Steve and Patricia just looked at him.

"It'll be great," Gregory went on. "I'll send some to Gram, and to Oscar, and — " He stopped. "Why aren't you guys happy?"

Patricia moved her jaw. "I'm going to say one word to you, Gregory."

"Plastics?" Uncle Steve guessed.

Patricia and Gregory looked at him, perplexed. He shook his head. "Never mind."

Patricia focused on Gregory. "*Modem,*" she said. "The word is *modem.*"

Gregory's face fell. "Oh. Right." To use the modem, they needed access to a telephone line — and if they were near a telephone, they could just *call* for help.

"It was a good thought, though," Uncle Steve said kindly.

"Or we could just describe it as . . . a *thought,*" Patricia said, and winked at Gregory.

After unloading the knapsack, Gregory emptied his own pockets. He also helped Patricia with hers, since she couldn't move her arm very well. Then he unstrapped the bright orange life jacket. Two dark brown sealed bags fell out, along with a metal cup with a sturdy handle and a cylinder that looked like a firecracker.

"What's that?" Patricia asked.

"It's a flare," Uncle Steve answered. "We can use it for a signal, if someone flies over. Greg, slice each of the MREs at one end, and we'll see what we have."

The two Meals-Ready-to-Eat had vacuum-sealed food packets inside. Some of the packets were pliable, and the others seemed to be shrink-wrapped. The first meal was corned beef hash, with a pack of dry fruit mix. There was also an oatmeal cookie bar, crackers, a packet of apple jelly, a brown plastic spoon, an envelope of cocoa powder, and some Beverage Base powder — which was like Tang or Kool-Aid. There was also something called Accessory Packet A. It contained two Chiclets, water-resistant matches, a tiny bottle of Tabasco sauce, a Wet-Nap for washing, some tissues, coffee, sugar, salt, and cream substitute.

The other meal was very much the same, except that the main course was escalloped potatoes with ham, and it had a chocolate covered brownie, some applesauce, and a package of caramels to go along with its accessory packet.

"Fill the two bags with snow, and put them near the fire," Uncle Steve said. "Close enough so it'll start melting. Then we'll be able to heat up some water for cocoa."

It turned out that Uncle Steve had been carrying all sorts of useful things in his many pockets. There was an emergency space blanket, a squat white candle, a black watch cap, some

Chap Stick, his wallet, car keys, some stamps, a half-eaten roll of Tums, and a box of cough drops. He had also unearthed a nail clipper, a handkerchief, a notepad, two pens, another garbage bag, two packages of pocket heaters, needle-nose pliers, a roll of duct tape, and — of course — his Swiss Army knife.

"Adults have a lot of baggage, huh?" Patricia remarked.

"So I hear," Uncle Steve said dryly.

Along with *Vogue*, Patricia had brought the latest issue of *Entertainment Weekly*, the most recent J. Crew catalog, and a copy of *Wuthering Heights*. She had also packed extra sunglasses, her Walkman, some cassettes, her favorite pink sweatshirt, a Magic Marker, a hairbrush, some Lauren perfume, a blue ponytail holder, and vanilla-flavored lip gloss.

"It's good to look and smell your best when you're in a plane crash," Uncle Steve observed.

"Uh-huh," Patricia said. Dryly.

The only things Gregory had in his pockets were six more Milk-Bones, forty-two cents, half a candy cane, a cheap harmonica he didn't know how to play, an old ticket stub from a Bruins game, some sea shells, and a battered tennis ball.

Santa Paws had been overjoyed to see the tennis ball — to say nothing of the Milk-Bones.

Gregory shook his head. "Not now," he told

him as he zipped them back into his jacket pocket. "Maybe later."

Disappointed, the dog flopped back down by the fire. So Gregory relented and gave him a small piece of Milk-Bone. The dog wagged his tail and started crunching.

"Are you warm enough now to take your jacket off for a minute?" Uncle Steve asked Patricia. "I want Gregory to put a splint on that arm."

Patricia nodded, and awkwardly unzipped it. She was able to slip the jacket off her left side with no trouble, but the right side was a different story. The second she jarred her arm, she gasped and her eyes filled with tears.

Hearing the distress in her voice, the dog scrambled up. He watched her intently, his forehead furrowed with worry. He had never felt so helpless before!

"Okay, okay," Uncle Steve said quickly. "Greg's just going to ease it off for you. Hold my hand, and squeeze as hard as you want, okay?"

Patricia held his good hand with *her* good hand.

Gregory slowly peeled her jacket off. He *really* didn't want to hurt her. His sister had her eyes shut the whole time, but he could feel that she was shaking.

"You want to wear my down vest?" he asked.

"I've got way more layers on than you."

Patricia opened her eyes. "Won't you be cold?"

"Not as cold as *you* are," Gregory said. He took off his jacket, and unsnapped the down vest he was wearing underneath. Then he guided the right side over her broken arm, and helped her stick her left arm in, too. It was terrible to see her shivering so much, and he quickly fastened all of the snaps.

"From now on, long underwear," Patricia vowed. "Even in August."

Gregory had to laugh as he pictured her lounging on Crane's Beach in her bathing suit, sunglasses — and long underwear.

"Take her glove off, and feel her hand," Uncle Steve said, "I want to make sure she's getting enough circulation."

"It's nice and warm," Gregory reported.

"Now press one of her fingernails and release it," Uncle Steve told him.

"Her nail turned white, and then back to pink."

"Good. Now cut *Vogue* in half," Uncle Steve said. "Just go right down the binding. Then hold the pieces against her other arm to see if they'll fit. I think they're going to be too long, so you can just cut them down to size."

The magazine *was* too long, and Gregory sawed about three inches off. He rolled one half around her upper arm and taped it in place with some of the duct tape. Then he did the same thing to her forearm. He had to be very careful with the tape, so that the splints wouldn't be too tight.

The last step was making a sling. First, he wrapped his scarf just below her elbow, and then tied it around her neck. After that, he looped his belt around her wrist and fastened it around her neck, too. The most important part was for her wrist to be higher than her elbow. Gregory turned the penlight back on, and flashed it up and down her arm to make sure everything looked okay.

Patricia kept her eyes closed and held onto Uncle Steve's hand the whole time.

"How does it feel?" Uncle Steve asked.

Patricia managed a weak smile. "Like I have a broken arm."

Uncle Steve nodded, and gave her hand a sympathetic squeeze. "You did a good job, Greg," he said.

Gregory zipped her jacket back up, trying not to jostle her arm. Patricia mouthed the word, "Thanks," and he nodded.

Now it was Uncle Steve's turn!

10

Uncle Steve was so badly hurt that there wasn't really very much that Gregory could do to help him. They didn't have any bandages, so he pressed the whole package of Santa Claus cocktail napkins against the torn part of his shoulder. Then he tied it in place with Patricia's scarf and used Uncle Steve's belt for a sling.

Splinting his broken hip was even more complicated. Gregory searched through their woodpile until he found a stick long enough to reach from the outside of his uncle's ankle, all the way up to his rib cage. Then he selected another one to fit against the inside of his leg.

Next, he sliced the sleeves off Patricia's pink sweatshirt and set them aside. The Swiss Army knife was pretty much worth its weight in *gold*. After that, he cut the body of the sweatshirt into two pieces. He rolled each piece around one of the sticks for padding and started lightly taping them into place.

"Is that too tight?" he asked nervously.

Uncle Steve shook his head, gritting his teeth against the pain.

Gregory taped the two sticks, so that Uncle Steve's hip was immobilized as much as possible. Then he rezipped his flight jacket and tied his scarf for him. Finally, he used the Swiss Army knife to cut the discarded sweatshirt sleeves in half. He stopped before he reached the cuffs, so that they would hold together. Now he and Patricia would be able to use the sleeves as improvised scarves.

When all of that was done, Gregory let out an exhausted breath. He felt as though he could fall down right where he was and sleep for a *week*.

"Have another brownie, Dr. Callahan," Uncle Steve said, with a weary smile. "I think you've earned it."

Gregory was starving, but he hesitated. "Don't we have to ration them and all?"

"Right now, I think you need the energy more," Uncle Steve said.

Gregory glanced at his sister for confirmation. "Patty?"

"Fine with me," she said, sounding very tired.

Gregory was too hungry to argue, although he saved one bite for Santa Paws.

The dog snapped it down, and then leaned over to lick Gregory's face in thanks. The dog's stomach was rumbling, and he hoped that they would be able to eat some more food soon. It was way past his supper time! He remembered that when he had been on his own, living outside, he had *always* been hungry. So far, this situation was terrible in the same way. He wasn't sure why any of it was happening, but he knew that he would do whatever he could to help and protect his owners. His ribs still ached, and he moved around to try to find a more comfortable position.

Uncle Steve poured some half-melted snow from one of the MRE bags into the metal cup. While he boiled it over the fire, Gregory and Patricia took turns going behind the nearest boulder to go to the bathroom. It was scary to leave their warm shelter — even to walk just a few feet away — but they felt better knowing that their uncle and Santa Paws were right nearby.

Back at the shelter, Gregory unwrapped the emergency space blanket. The package was almost as small as his hand, but the blanket was surprisingly large. It looked like a huge, paper-thin piece of aluminum foil. The blanket seemed pretty flimsy, but it would help keep them warm during the night. When it was time to go to sleep, Uncle Steve wanted the two of them to snuggle up at the back of the shelter with Santa Paws. In the meantime, he would lie by the woodpile, so he could keep the fire going throughout the night.

After the water had boiled for a few minutes, Gregory stirred in one of the cocoa packets from the MREs. It wasn't safe to drink water from the woods without boiling, or purifying, it first. Fresh snow was safer than water from streams, but they still had to be careful.

Since they only had one cup, they took turns sipping the hot drink. For the first time in hours, Gregory and Patricia could feel themselves warming up inside. When the cocoa was gone, Uncle Steve melted some more water and let Santa Paws drink it up.

The dog finished the cup and then wagged his tail.

The only sounds were the crackling of the fire, and the whistling wind. The temperature had dropped at least fifteen degrees, and it felt like it might snow.

"It's so quiet out here," Gregory whispered.

"I could play some music," Patricia offered. Her Walkman was also a tape recorder. If she disconnected her headphones, they would all be able to hear.

"Don't tell me," Uncle Steve said. "All you have is Frank Sinatra."

Gregory and Patricia smiled, although it made them sad to think about their parents. By now, they had probably arrived in Vermont — and gotten the bad news.

Gregory poked through the small pile of cassettes among their supplies. "The BoDeans," he read aloud. "Memphis Slim, Nina Simone, Harry Connick, Jr., and — the Chipmunks?"

"Nothing personal, but that is a *really* weird mix," Uncle Steve commented.

As far as Patricia was concerned, when it came to music, variety was a good thing. "There's a Joshua Redman tape, too," she said.

Gregory made a face. "Can't we just listen to the Chipmunks?"

Uncle Steve and Patricia shrugged, instead of disagreeing. The Chipmunks tape was full of Christmas carols, and they sat close together to listen to them.

Santa Paws was very intrigued by the tape recorder. He sniffed it a few times, trying to figure out where the music was coming from. Once he even poked it with his paw.

"It's okay, boy," Gregory said, and put his arm around him.

The dog wagged his tail and sat down next to him.

Listening to the Christmas carols made Gregory and Patricia feel very homesick. Right now, they were supposed to be safe in their grandparents' cabin, surrounded by the whole family.

Uncle Steve probably felt pretty lonely and afraid, too, but he didn't say anything.

"Are the planes going to come find us tomorrow?" Gregory asked.

Uncle Steve didn't answer right away. "I hope so, Greg," he said finally. "I *really* hope so."

Gregory and Patricia were too exhausted to stay awake much longer. So they crawled under the space blanket, with Santa Paws snuggling up in between them. They were both wearing their makeshift scarves wrapped across the lower half of their faces. They had also pulled their hats down over their ears so that only their eyes showed. Their jackets were zipped, their gloves were on, and they were fully dressed. Despite all of that, they were *still* cold.

"Does your arm hurt a whole lot?" Gregory asked, right before they went to sleep.

Patricia nodded. It was throbbing horribly, but she didn't want to complain. She knew that Uncle Steve was in much worse shape than she was.

"They're going to rescue us tomorrow," Gregory said confidently. "I *know* they are."

Patricia nodded again.

Then they both closed their eyes.

It was a long, bone-chilling night, and Patricia kept having nightmares. Every time she woke up, she wasn't sure where she was — or why she was so cold. Then she would see Uncle Steve keeping watch over the fire, and remember what had happened. Thinking about it only made things worse, so she just made herself go back to sleep.

She woke up for good just after dawn. When she moved, Santa Paws opened his eyes. He wagged his tail under the space blanket, and rested his muzzle on her shoulder.

She reached up to scratch his ears, and his tail wagged harder.

"Good boy," she said softly. "Don't wake Greg up."

The dog wagged his tail, and lowered his head so she would scratch his ears some more. Since his ribs still really hurt, he was glad that she hadn't patted his side.

The wind seemed stronger, and she poked her head out from underneath the blanket to see that it was snowing. *Hard.* At least four or five inches had already fallen.

She heard low coughing, and quickly turned her head toward her uncle. He was lying next to the much-smaller pile of wood, looking even worse than he had the day before. His eyes were half-closed, and his face was brightly flushed. His wallet was open, and he was staring at a picture of his wife and baby.

Patricia crawled out from underneath the

space blanket, being careful not to wake Gregory up. She motioned for Santa Paws to stay. He wagged his tail, nestled closer to Gregory, and went back to sleep.

"Uncle Steve?" she whispered.

He looked up dully, and tried to smile at her. "Morning," he said, and then coughed some more.

She didn't ask him how he felt, because she was afraid of what the answer would be. So she looked out at the whirling snowstorm, instead. In the meantime, Uncle Steve closed his wallet and tucked it inside his jacket.

The storm wasn't quite a blizzard, but the flakes were coming down fast. There was almost no visibility, and the winds were gusting forcefully.

"They won't be able to fly in this, will they," Patricia said.

Uncle Steve shook his head.

"Do you think it's going to stop soon?" she asked.

He shook his head.

That meant that they weren't going to be rescued anytime soon. Definitely not today, and maybe not tomorrow, either.

"If it takes them a few days, will we be able to make it that long?" she asked.

Uncle Steve glanced over to make sure that Gregory was still asleep. "We're, um — " He hesitated. "The truth is, we're in kind of a tight spot here, Patricia."

In other words, *no*. Patricia nodded.

He reached over to take her hand. "I'm sorry. I wish I could do a better job of taking care of things here."

"It's not your fault you're *hurt*," she said.

"No," he conceded. "But I'm not exactly much help, either. Look, don't worry. When the storm stops, we'll put some signals out there, and — " He let out his breath unhappily. "We'll just do our best, okay?"

It didn't even seem possible that this was the way that they were going to celebrate Christmas Eve. It seemed even less possible that they could actually *die* out here. "Do you know where we are?" she asked.

He shrugged, and then winced from the effort. "I got a little disoriented by the crash, but — yeah, more or less." He looked around, and then pointed. "If I'm right, there should be a road about five or ten miles that way."

Only five or ten miles? "That's not far," Patricia said, feeling a flash of hope for the first time since the crash. "When Rachel and I were in the Walkathon last year, we went *twenty* miles."

Uncle Steve smiled sadly at her. "Those are pretty rugged mountains out there, honey. It would be a tough haul even without all of this snow."

Maybe so, but what choice did they have? "How much longer do you think you can hold out?" she asked. "If we wait until a plane *maybe* comes, it might be — " She didn't want to say "too late," so she stopped. "I don't want to just sit here. I think we have to *do* something."

Uncle Steve nodded reluctantly, and they looked over at Gregory and Santa Paws, who were still sleeping soundly beneath the space blanket.

"I don't want to leave you here, but I don't want to send my little brother out into the forest by himself, either," Patricia said quietly.

"No, we can't do that," Uncle Steve agreed. "Even with the dog, it's too dangerous for him to go alone." He indicated her sling. "Are you in good enough shape to walk? Tell me the truth, okay?"

Patricia wasn't sure, but she nodded. "It's not so bad. I'll just be really careful."

"It's going to be even tougher than you'd imagine," he warned. "You're really going to be tired, and cold, and — "

"Do you have a better idea?" she asked.

"No," Uncle Steve said, and then he sighed. "I wish I did."

11

Once the decision had been made, there were a lot of things they had to do to get ready. Patricia woke Gregory up, and they all shared the icy can of Coke. His eyes got very big when he heard that they were going to try to hike out.

"Is it safe?" he asked.

"Our plane crashed, Greg. *None* of this is safe," Patricia pointed out.

Since that was true, Gregory nodded amiably. If she and Uncle Steve wanted him to hike, he would hike. No problem.

The first thing they had to do, was to make sure that Uncle Steve had plenty of wood to keep the fire going until help arrived. He wouldn't be strong enough to crawl around on his own, and if he ran out of wood, he would freeze.

The driving snow made it that much harder to find wood, but at least there were a lot of dead trees around. They broke off as many branches as they could reach. Other branches had fallen down during the storm, and they dragged them back to the shelter to snap into more manageable pieces.

They also tied the rope to Santa Paws' harness again, so that he could help them retrieve some of the biggest branches. To try and keep the wood dry, they stacked most of it at the far end of the shelter where it would be under cover.

While they were working, Uncle Steve had been boiling water. He heated enough to fill the two empty MRE envelopes, and then divided an envelope of the orange-flavored beverage powder between them. The resulting, diluted orange drink tasted kind of weird, but it was nice and *hot*.

Then Uncle Steve melted more water in the empty metal cup and let Santa Paws drink from it.

The dog lapped down the lukewarm water gratefully. He was *very* thirsty, and eating mouthfuls of snow only made things worse. His side hurt so much, that he was having trouble breathing, too. He drank the water so fast, that Uncle Steve refilled it two more times to make sure that he had had enough.

When Santa Paws was finished, Gregory wiped out the cup with a handful of snow. "You

115

aren't going to make any cracks about dog germs?" he asked Patricia.

"Don't worry, I'm *thinking* them," she assured him.

While Uncle Steve gave them last-minute advice, they shared the meat loaf sandwich, some of the carrot sticks, and the last brownie. Santa Paws also had half of a Milk-Bone.

"Okay," Uncle Steve said, after drawing a crude map on his notepad. "This is approximately where we are. As nearly as I can figure, you want to head south, or southwest. There's a little compass on top of the case where the matches are."

Gregory examined the top of the little plastic tube. "The, um, needle points north?" he asked, just to be sure.

Uncle Steve nodded. "That's not going to be perfectly accurate, but it'll give you a general idea. Whenever you pass a distinctive landmark, you can write it down in the notepad. Or, if you want, you can even draw it."

Some of the advice he gave them was very complicated, and some of it was just common sense. For example, he told them that ice melted much more quickly than snow. So if they wanted to heat water, to save time, they should collect any icicles they could find. Another way to get water was to pack some snow into one of the garbage bags and put it inside their jackets.

While they walked, their body heat would start melting the snow. Then they could boil it, without wasting too much firewood.

"If you get too tired or cold, *stop*," Uncle Steve said, between bouts of coughing. "Find someplace out of the wind, light a fire if you can, and get your strength back. You want to stop *before* you get frostbitten, not the other way around."

Gregory and Patricia nodded solemnly. There was so much to remember that it was hard to keep track.

Uncle Steve wanted them to pack all of the remaining food into Patricia's knapsack, but they flat-out refused. He was going to need to keep *his* strength up, too. Finally, he agreed to keep the coffee, sugar, and cream substitute, one packet of crackers and jelly, the fruit mix, the tiny Tabasco bottle, the cough drops, and one of the packets of gum. He would also keep the empty Coke can to heat water in, while they brought the metal cup along.

They agreed that Uncle Steve would hold onto the penlight, while Gregory and Patricia kept the candle. Then Gregory wandered around the nearby trees until he found a really long sapling. He brought it back and strapped the orange life jacket to the end, so that Uncle Steve could wave it as a signal to any planes that might go by. In the meantime, he and Patricia would pack the flare.

117

"You kids bring the space blanket and the pocket heaters, too," Uncle Steve said. "The heaters only last a few hours, so save them until you *really* need them."

Gregory and Patricia exchanged glances, wondering if they should refuse. Wouldn't he need them more than they would?

"*End* of discussion," Uncle Steve said in a firm "hold it right there!" cop-voice.

"Yeah, but — " Patricia started.

Uncle Steve cut her off. "I have a nice, insulated shelter, and a fire going," he said. "I'll be *fine*. You two — excuse me, Santa Paws — you *three* are going to be out in the middle of it. What are you going to do, build a lean-to every time you need a break?"

The dog looked up alertly when he heard his name. They had all been talking so seriously that he thought they had forgotten him.

"How about my harmonica?" Gregory offered. "You could teach yourself to play."

"And you can read *Entertainment Weekly*. It's really good," Patricia said. "*Wuthering Heights*, too."

Uncle Steve laughed. "Okay. If you kids agree to take the Walkman, it's a deal."

Gregory packed the supplies they were bringing into Patricia's knapsack. It wasn't very heavy, and he didn't think he would have much trouble carrying it. He and Uncle Steve both put on extra pairs of Patricia's sunglasses to protect their eyes from snow blindness. Then Uncle Steve checked through the knapsack one last time, to see if they had everything they needed.

"Okay," he said, and put on a smile. "I guess that's it."

It was hard to say good-bye, and they all avoided each other's eyes. Santa Paws knew that something was happening and instinctively, he raised one paw in the point position.

"It's going to be fine," Uncle Steve said, sounding more confident than he looked.

Gregory and Patricia nodded, and kicked at the snow.

"Look, I'm going to be sitting here, and reading *Entertainment Weekly*, and having a grand old time," Uncle Steve said.

Gregory and Patricia nodded again. Patricia could feel tears in her eyes, and she quickly rubbed her glove underneath her sunglasses. Gregory just kept shifting his weight and blinking a lot.

"Come here," Uncle Steve said. He gave Gregory a quick, one-armed hug, and squeezed Patricia's good hand. "You're great kids, and I *really* love you."

"We love you, too," Patricia answered, her voice quavering a little.

"We'll go really fast, so help'll come right away," Gregory promised.

"Just be careful," Uncle Steve said. Then he reached up to pat Santa Paws. "Take care of them, boy. I'm counting on you."

The dog wagged his tail, and then barked.

"Hang onto the rope and let him break the trail for you," Uncle Steve told them. "And trust his instincts. He has better hearing, a stronger sense of smell — you name it. So, follow his lead."

With that, they all looked at each other again.

"See you soon," Uncle Steve said.

Gregory and Patricia nodded.

It was time to go.

The first few hundred yards were pretty easy. It was all downhill, and the trees protected them somewhat from the wind and snow. Santa Paws plowed along up ahead of them, the snow coming almost all the way up to his chest. His ribs felt like they were burning, but he forced himself to keep walking. Gregory and Patricia followed directly in his tracks.

With their sweatshirt-scarves wrapped across their faces, it was hard to talk. It didn't really matter, though, because they wanted to save their energy for walking. Every so often, they would pause long enough for Gregory to stick a small piece of duct tape on a tree. They wanted to mark their trail, so that any rescuers would be able to find Uncle Steve.

The ground suddenly got steeper, and they had to walk more slowly. Even though they were trying to be careful, they both kept slipping and sliding. Then Santa Paws stopped short.

"What is it?" Patricia asked.

Gregory waded forward through the snow to stand next to him, and saw that there was a ten-foot drop in front of them. There was enough snow down there so that it might be safe to jump — but it also might *not* be.

"What do you think?" he asked, when Patricia came up to join them.

She shook her head vehemently. "No way."

"It's going to take forever, if we go around," Gregory warned her.

"It's *really* going to take forever, if we both break our legs," Patricia said.

The dog waited patiently for them to decide what to do. This wasn't a very nice place to go on a walk, but if that's what they wanted, he was happy to cooperate. Even so, he would much rather be in their nice, warm house, napping underneath Mr. Callahan's desk.

His fur was covered with snow, and he shook violently to knock some of it off. The pain in his side sharpened, and he yelped once. A big chunk of snow had blown into his ear and he turned his head from side to side to try and dislodge it. His paws were also caked with snow. He lifted each one in turn and shook the icy particles away.

It was so windy on this exposed ledge that Patricia and Gregory were having trouble keeping their balance. The snow was swirling around them, and they couldn't see more than a few feet in any direction.

"Let's just keep going!" she yelled, and pointed off to the left, where the terrain appeared to slope more gently. "That way looks easier."

Gregory nodded, and turned Santa Paws in that direction.

"Come on, boy," he urged him.

The dog cocked his head, not sure where he was supposed to go.

"Find the car," Gregory told him. "Let's go find the car!" He had taught that phrase to Santa Paws to help him locate his parents' station wagon in crowded parking lots. But he could also use it here, because if Santa Paws couldn't find their *actual* car, he would always search until he found *any* car. If he knew that they were looking for the car right now, maybe he would be able to lead them to a road.

The dog sniffed the cold air and then looked at him, baffled. There definitely weren't any cars anywhere *near* here. The only scents he was picking up were things like pine trees and deer and decomposing timber. And — wait — a rabbit, maybe. Yeah, he could definitely smell a rabbit.

"Come on, Santa Paws," Gregory said. "Find the car. You can do it."

The dog wanted to make him happy, so he started making his way down the slope. The footing was very tricky, and he hesitated before each step. Gregory and Patricia were just as cautious. Sometimes, the going was so treacherous that they had to hang onto trees to keep from falling.

After a long time, they made it to the bottom of the mountain. They were in a valley now, and the ground was fairly level. But surprisingly, compared to stumbling downhill, it seemed like more work to navigate the flat terrain. Before, at least they had had gravity on their side.

It felt as though they had been walking forever. But when Gregory stopped to look at his watch after marking yet another tree with tape, they found out that it had only been an hour and a half.

"How far do you think we've gone?" Gregory asked, his breath warm against his scarf.

"Not very," Patricia answered grimly.

Gregory nodded. That was about what he had figured. He glanced up at the sky, but the snow was still coming down just as hard as ever.

Then he took out the match container and checked the little compass to see where north was. He wasn't still completely sure how it worked, but they *seemed* to be doing all right.

"We going in the right direction?" Patricia asked.

"I think so," Gregory said uncertainly. "Maybe a little bit too much east."

Patricia nodded. Either way, they were going to be heading *up*hill soon. This valley was pretty small, and mountains rose up all around them.

"Go for another half hour, and then we'll rest?" Gregory suggested. Uncle Steve had said that it was really important to pace themselves.

The thought of that was exhausting, but Patricia nodded. Somehow, they had to make it as far as they could before it got dark.

Their lives — and Uncle Steve's life — depended on it!

12

It was snowing so hard that most of the time, they couldn't really see where they were going. But Santa Paws kept plunging forward into the storm. They hung on tightly to the rope and let him lead them through the forest.

"Do you think he knows where he's going?" Gregory yelled.

"I hope so!" Patricia yelled back.

They forged on and on, through endless drifts. Sometimes the snow only came up to the tops of their boots. Other times, it was waist-deep. On top of which, they kept tripping over buried rocks and logs.

Except for the sounds of their labored breathing and the icy pellets of snow landing all around them, the woods were utterly silent. They hadn't even seen any *wildlife*.

After a while, Patricia was so cold that she was starting to stagger. Since she knew that she couldn't make it much further, she yanked on the rope to get her brother's attention.

"Greg, I have to stop for a while," she said weakly.

He was concentrating so hard on walking that the concept of doing something *else* seemed confusing.

"Just for a minute," she said. "Please?"

"Oh. Right." He looked around the dense forest, swaying slightly on his feet. "Do we just sit down where we are?"

Patricia gestured a few feet away. "Under that tree, maybe."

Gregory nodded and lurched over there.

Feeling the tug on his harness, the dog turned around. Gregory was going a different way now, so he reversed his direction and followed him. He loved his owners, but this was the *worst* walk he had ever been on. Too cold, too windy, too *everything*. And they still weren't anywhere *near* a car.

Gregory's hands were clumsy from the cold, but he unzipped the knapsack. He took out the space blanket and spread it on the ground. That way, they wouldn't have to sit directly on the snow. He started to flop down, but Patricia shook her head.

"Let's get some of this snow off first," she said.

Gregory nodded and started brushing her off.

He felt very uncoordinated and had to remind himself not to brush too hard where her arm was broken. Patricia used her free hand to knock most of the snow off him, too.

Bundled up with her face completely covered, his sister was unrecognizable. "You look like a really fat one-armed Eskimo," Gregory observed.

"*You* look like Charlie Brown's long-lost Canadian cousin," Patricia said, and paused significantly. "The *disturbed* one."

Maybe they were getting punchy, but they laughed a lot harder than either joke deserved. Then they stamped their feet over and over, trying to clear their snow-encrusted boots.

Just to be sociable, the dog shook a few times, sending a spray of snow in all directions.

Gregory and Patricia sat down on one end of the space blanket and Santa Paws squirmed in between them. Then Gregory pulled the ends of the blanket up around them. Now they were sheltered from the blowing snow, and might be able to warm up.

"I don't like nature anymore," Patricia said.

Gregory nodded. "If we make it out of this, I'm like, staying inside with Dad from now on."

They sat under the blanket, shivering. Santa Paws seemed pretty comfortable, and they both leaned close to him.

"Should we make a fire?" Gregory asked.

Patricia sighed. "That would mean we'd have to go look for wood, and figure out where to build it and all."

Right now, that sounded like *way* too much work.

"Next time we stop?" Gregory said, and Patricia nodded.

Santa Paws yawned and curled up into a tight circle. He was *really* tired. There wasn't much room, and he had to drape himself across their legs. Gregory and Patricia watched enviously as he drifted into a nap.

"He's lucky," Gregory said.

"Yeah," Patricia agreed. "We're going to have to take turns, if we sleep. Otherwise, we might freeze to death."

Gregory shuddered. After surviving all of this, that would be too awful.

Patricia changed the subject. "Let's drink our juice box. It might make us feel better."

Gregory lowered his scarf enough to grin at her. "When we sing 'My Favorite Things,' we *always* feel better."

Patricia looked right back at him. "I don't care if we *are* in the middle of nowhere. *Nothing* would convince me to sing 'My Favorite Things.' "

"I'm going to tell people you kept running down the mountains with your arms out, pretending you were Maria," Gregory said mischievously.

Patricia laughed. "Hey, if we make it out of this, you can tell people anything you want."

Gregory had been carrying the juice box inside the pocket of his hooded sweatshirt so that it wouldn't freeze. He poked the little straw inside, and they passed the box back and forth. The juice was actually fruit punch, and it was good and sweet.

"Can we listen to the Chipmunks for a minute?" Gregory asked.

Patricia nodded and fumbled for her Walkman. The batteries would probably run out pretty soon, but they might as well enjoy it until then.

They huddled under the space blanket, listening to music, and savoring every single sip of fruit punch. They weren't really warm, but at least they had stopped shivering.

Their hands and feet were so cold, that they broke down and opened one of the pocket heaters. The heaters looked like tiny white beanbags, and there were two in each package. They were about an inch and a half wide, and three inches long. The little bags were filled with some sort of minerals, which were activated when the bag was exposed to air.

Patricia put her heater inside her one exposed glove, while Gregory immediately dropped his into his left hiking boot. After a few minutes, he switched his heater to the other boot. Patricia also transferred hers to one of her boots. When that foot had warmed up, she changed it to the other one.

She couldn't retie her boots with one hand, so Gregory had to do it for her.

"We can stop again in a while, and switch them," he said.

"Okay," Patricia agreed, wishing that they had a *hundred* little heaters and didn't have to conserve them. "Are your hands warm enough?"

Gregory nodded. "They're all right. They just feel, I don't know, kind of *thick*."

"Take them out and blow on them a little," Patricia suggested. "Or put them under your arms for a minute. That might help."

Gregory did just that until he could move his fingers pretty well again. Patting Santa Paws made them feel warmer, too. The dog opened his eyes and thumped his tail a few times.

"Ready to go back out there?" Patricia asked finally.

Gregory put his gloves back on. "Guess we don't have much choice," he said.

Patricia nodded, and they climbed out of the space blanket to face the storm again.

They walked, and walked, and walked. Slipped, stumbled, and slid. Limped, and staggered, and limped some more. Sometimes they would make it partway up on a slope, only to fall back down and have to start all over again.

Then they heard a strange rumbling sound somewhere up above them.

Gregory squinted up into the falling snow. "What's that noise?" he asked.

Patricia shrugged, too tired to pay much attention. "I don't know. Sounds like some kind of engine or something, or — " Realizing what she had just said, she stared at her brother. "Greg! It's a plane!"

He stared back at her. "What? Are you sure?"

"They're searching for us!" she said. "We're saved!" Then she began looking around frantically, trying to locate the sound. "Where are they?! Greg, come on, we have to make sure they see us!"

They were surrounded by a thick cluster of trees, and it was hard to know which way to run. This might be their only chance for survival, and they had to guess right!

"This way!" Gregory shouted.

"No, *this* way!" Patricia said, pointing uphill. "Hurry! Before they leave!"

They scrambled through the snow as fast as they could, stumbling over rocks and branches. Sensing their excitement, Santa Paws barked loudly and raced up ahead of them.

As they ran, Gregory dug the signal flare out of the knapsack, and gripped it tightly in one hand.

"Should I set it off?" he yelled. "So they'll see us?"

"Set it off *where*?" Patricia yelled back. "We have to figure out where the plane is, first!"

The vibrating sound seemed to be louder now, and Santa Paws was staring up at the sky as intently as they were.

"Come on!" Patricia said urgently. "We need to get out in the open!"

There were trees everywhere, and no sign of a clearing or lake or any other open area. The plane's engine seemed to be off to the right, and they ran in that direction. The thought of being rescued gave them so much energy that they leaped over drifts that would have exhausted them a few minutes earlier. If they fell down, they would just pick themselves up and keep running.

They still hadn't seen anything, and now, the sound of the engine seemed to be fading away. One minute, it was there; the next minute, they could only hear the wind blowing.

"Wait!" Gregory yelled. "Come back!"

They both yelled, and waved, and jumped up and down, while Santa Paws barked wildly and ran around in circles. If someone really was out searching for them, why weren't they looking more carefully? Didn't the rescue people *want* to find them?

Patricia was the first one to give up. She sank

down into the snow, trying not to cry. Not only had they not been rescued, but now that the plane had searched this area, it probably wouldn't come back.

"Down here!" Gregory kept shouting into the storm. "We're down here!" He set off the flare, and peered hopefully into the driving snow. "Come back!"

Santa Paws barked some more, and threw in a couple of howls for good measure.

"Greg," Patricia said quietly. "Take it easy. Don't waste your energy."

"But — " He glanced down at her, still waving his arms to try and get the pilot's attention. "I mean — "

Patricia shook her head. "It's too late. They didn't see us."

Gregory slowly let his arms drop, so disappointed that he almost burst into tears. Then he slumped down miserably next to her in the snow.

The plane — if there had even *been* one up there — was gone.

The afternoon crawled by. It was still snowing, although maybe not quite as hard as it had been earlier. They were both so disappointed that the search plane hadn't seen them, that they barely spoke as they slogged through the drifts. Santa Paws seemed tired, too, and his tail dragged behind him.

After a while, they stopped to crouch under the space blanket and nibble on an MRE oatmeal cookie.

"I really thought that plane was going to come save us," Gregory said miserably.

Patricia reached over to put her arm around him for a minute. "If they didn't find us, maybe they'll find Uncle Steve. At least now, we know that they're looking."

Gregory was too depressed to find much consolation in that, but he nodded.

"You want to light a fire?" Patricia asked.

"Let's just wait until we set up camp for the night," Gregory said.

Patricia was too tired to argue, so she just shrugged and ate her share of the oatmeal cookie.

Then Gregory noticed that there were ice crystals caked all around the pads on Santa Paws' feet. He took his gloves off and gently cleaned the dog's paws out. Then he rubbed his hands together and stuck them inside his jacket to try and rewarm them.

Santa Paws thumped his tail against the space blanket. His paws were cold and sore, and it was a relief to be able to rest for a while. Resting helped ease the pain in his ribs a little, too. But it still hurt to breathe, and he had to take very shallow breaths.

They sat long enough to let their body heat fill

the enclosed blanket and listen to a few Nina Simone songs. Gregory and Patricia were both yawning, and they had to fight to stay awake. Santa Paws was already dozing.

"We're going to have to set up for the night soon, Greg," Patricia said. "Put aside some time to find wood and all."

Gregory lifted his jacket cuff enough to peer at his watch. It was almost two-thirty, so they probably had about two hours of light left. "One more hour?" he proposed. "See if we can get over this stupid mountain?"

They had been climbing for a couple of hours straight now, and Patricia didn't feel as though they had made any progress.

"Okay," she said, trying to sound confident. "Let's do it."

Then they staggered back to their feet and pushed on. The ground was so steep that Gregory and Patricia were gasping for breath and their legs trembled from the effort of climbing. Santa Paws was still in the lead, but he seemed to be very tired. His ears were drooping, and every few feet, he would stop and look back at them plaintively.

"He's really losing it," Gregory said. "I'll go up front and break the trail for a while."

Patricia nodded. "Okay. We can switch off every fifteen minutes."

Gregory bent down to hug Santa Paws and

then lead him back behind Patricia. Walking in the rear would take the least energy, since he could just step in their boot prints. The dog was so exhausted that he wagged his tail forlornly and was content to follow them for now. His paws were aching, his side was throbbing, and he was weak from hunger.

The snow came up to Gregory's knees. It took so much effort to plow through the untouched drifts that he was perspiring heavily after only a few minutes.

"You all right?" Patricia asked, when she saw him start to weave a little.

Gregory nodded, too tired to respond. They were approaching a ridge running along the side of the mountain, and the wind was picking up. So much snow was pelting his face that he could barely see an arm's length away.

The snow felt crusty under his feet. Because it was so much colder on the open ridge, a sheen of ice had formed quickly on the surface of the snow. Each time he took a step, his foot crunched through and it took a lot of effort to pull it free. No wonder Santa Paws had gotten so tired!

"Can you see anything on the other side?" Patricia yelled.

Gregory couldn't really see anything at *all*. "Snow," he yelled back. "Trees."

"No gas station?" Patricia asked. "No McDonald's?"

No *anything*.

Instead of going all the way up the mountain, Gregory decided it would make more sense just to cross over the ridge and start down the other side.

There was a wide slab of snow in front of him, and he climbed up on top of it. He was just turning to tell Patricia that everything looked safe, when suddenly, the entire slab gave way under his weight.

Then, he disappeared in an avalanche of snow!

13

"Greg!" Patricia shouted, completely horri-fied.

Before she had time to move, Santa Paws had already bolted past her. He galloped over the side and plunged down into the gigantic pile of snow below.

When Patricia made it to the top of the ridge, she saw no sign of Gregory anywhere below. Santa Paws was about thirty feet down the slope, digging frantically through the snow with his front paws.

Realizing that her brother had been buried by what might be tons of snow, Patricia almost screamed. As she ran to help Santa Paws, she fell halfway and started sliding. She rolled right past him and had to race back up.

Being able to use only one arm to dig made her cry in frustration. She kicked at the snow with her boots, too, but Gregory was nowhere in sight.

The dog's paws were a blur of motion and snow flew behind him as he burrowed deeper and deeper. Hoping desperately that he had found the right place, Patricia dug right next to him.

If they didn't hurry, he would suffocate!

The first thing they saw was a snow-soaked jeans leg.

"There he is, Santa Paws!" Patricia shouted. "His head! We have to clear his head!"

The dog scraped the snow away from Gregory's back, trying to dig him free. He was lying face down and very still.

"I see his hat!" Patricia said. "Right there!"

Santa Paws dug so hard that he pulled the hat right off. Seeing her brother's hair, Patricia reached into the snow pit to brush the last bits from his face. Then, while Santa Paws tugged on his sweatshirt hood from behind, she used her arm and both legs to try to push him over.

Working together, they managed to move him onto his back. Gregory's face was chalky-white and his lips looked blue. Patricia was terrified that he might have been smothered, but he moved one arm feebly. Then he started coughing and spitting out snow. Some of the color was coming back into his cheeks, and Patricia breathed a sigh of relief.

"Gregory?" she asked shakily. "Can you hear me?"

"I'm really cold," he whispered, his teeth chattering so much that he could barely form the words.

She was going to have to get him out of the wind and in front of a fire, *fast*. She scanned the slope rapidly. Snow, and trees, and more snow. A good ways down the side of the mountain, she could see what looked like a formation of rocks through the trees. It looked like their best chance.

Gregory was trying to sit up now. He moved his arms and legs experimentally, and shrugged his shoulders a few times. Santa Paws came over and licked his face joyfully, and Gregory did his best to give him a clumsy pat on the head.

"Be careful. Did you hurt anything?" Patricia asked.

"B-b-bruises and stuff," he said, stuttering from the cold.

"Okay." She was so glad to see him alive and talking that she hugged him with her good arm. "Rest here for a minute, and I'll go down to the rocks and see if I can make a shelter."

Gregory nodded, and leaned against Santa Paws to recover himself. Then, he sat bolt upright and the color drained from his face.

"What?" Patricia asked, scared all over again.

"The knapsack," he whispered, and looked around at the mammoth pile of snow around. "It's gone!"

* * *

Without the knapsack, they were in big trouble. Patricia started searching, but soon realized that it was a lost cause. Because the compass was attached to the top of the match container, Gregory had been carrying the matches in his jacket pocket. The only other things he had in his pockets were the Swiss Army knife and two Milk-Bones.

"I'm sorry, Patty," he said, shivering uncontrollably. "I didn't mean to — "

She hugged him again. "We'll be fine, Greg. We have the matches, so we can still build a fire. It's going to be okay." Then she held her hand out to help him to his feet.

When Gregory tried to put weight on his left ankle, his leg gave out. He gasped, and fell back into the snow.

"Is it broken?" Patricia asked, dreading his response.

"I think it's just twisted," he said weakly.

They looked at each other, both on the verge of bursting into hysterical tears.

Patricia didn't speak until she was pretty sure she could keep her voice steady. "Lift your arm around me, so I can help you down to those rocks," she said.

Gregory leaned on her heavily, unable to put much weight on his injured ankle. Then they started down the slope. Their progress was so slow that *snails* could have made it down there and back in the same amount of time.

Santa Paws moved ahead of them, thrusting his body through the snow to break a trail. Having a path to follow made it much easier to walk. Or, in Gregory's case, *limp*. Actually, Patricia was limping, too — and Santa Paws' gait wasn't all that steady, either.

Once they were inside the rock formation, the wind seemed to die down. Patricia swept the snow away from a small boulder. Then she eased Gregory onto it, so he could rest. He pulled his hood up over his head, wrapped his arms around himself, and tried to stop shivering.

Santa Paws was already climbing around the rocks and sniffing various crevices, his sides heaving from the effort of breaking their trail. He stopped in front of one and started barking.

Patricia walked over to see what he wanted to show her. She crouched down to peer into the crevice. It wasn't exactly a cave, but there seemed to be enough room for them to crawl inside. A few inches of snow had been blown through the opening, but much less than she would have expected.

"Good dog!" she praised him. "What a good boy!"

Santa Paws wagged his tail.

Gregory limped over to see what was going on.

"What do you think?" Patricia asked. "It looks safe."

Gregory nodded, shaking too hard to speak.

Patricia crawled inside first to clear aside as much of the snow as possible. It would be a tight fit in here with all three of them, but maybe they would be warmer that way.

There was a large crack at the furthest end of the crevice, and she kicked some snow over to block it. Once she was finished, she crawled back out.

"Go in out of the wind, okay?" she said to Gregory.

He was so cold that he didn't even try to argue.

Patricia decided to collect firewood first. Once Gregory was warmer, she would find some pine boughs for them to lie on. Doing everything one-handed took twice as long, but Santa Paws helped her by dragging the branches she tied to his harness. She even found a small, dead evergreen tree, and Santa Paws swiftly pulled it over to the rocks for her.

It wouldn't be safe to light the fire inside their shelter, because it would use up all of their oxygen. So Patricia doggedly kicked away the snow just outside until she reached bare rock. It wasn't very windy here, so she didn't take the time to build a firebreak.

Most of the wood was very damp, and she wasted three matches without even managing to light the tiniest twig.

"P-pine needles," Gregory said.

That was a good idea, and Patricia reached as far inside the dead evergreen tree as she could. She pulled out a thick handful of dusty needles, and scattered them around the twigs. Then, remembering the notepad Uncle Steve had given them, she reached into her inside jacket pocket.

The pages were nice and dry, and she crumpled several into tight balls of paper.

Gregory dragged himself over to the opening. "L-let me t-try," he said. "I can use both hands." His hands were shaking so much that he had trouble striking the match. But when it caught, he held the little flame to one of the wadded-up pieces of paper.

It immediately flared up, and then another one began burning. Patricia blew gently on the pine needles, hoping to make them ignite, too. At the same time, Gregory fed more wads of notepad paper into the blaze.

It took a while, but soon they had a small, steady fire.

"Can you keep it going, while I go find branches for us to sleep on?" Patricia asked.

Gregory nodded as he warmed his hands. He was still trembling, but not quite as badly as he had been before.

Patricia was in the middle of getting branches, when she realized that Santa Paws hadn't followed her.

"Santa Paws!" she called. "Come here, boy!"

When he didn't come bounding over, she assumed that he was in the cave with Gregory and went back to what she was doing. She had just dumped her second load of boughs outside the crevice, when Gregory poked his head out.

"Where's Santa Paws?" he asked, looking worried.

Patricia frowned. "I thought he was with *you*."

Gregory shook his head, and they stared at each other.

"What if he's hurt?" Gregory asked. "Maybe he fell down, or got lost, or — " Instead of finishing the sentence, he hauled himself outside. "Santa Paws! Where are you, Santa Paws!?"

They both shouted his name over and over and whistled for him. Any second, they expected him to appear, but he seemed to have vanished.

"Look, stay here," Patricia said, trying not to panic. "I'll go look for him, and — "

"If anything's happened to him — " Gregory started at the same time.

Just then, they heard the familiar sound of license tags jingling. A snow-covered shape trotted into the rock formation, his tail waving triumphantly. There was a canvas strap in his mouth, and he was dragging a bulky object through the snow.

Santa Paws had found the knapsack!

They patted, and hugged, and praised Santa Paws for a long time. Delighted by all of the attention, Santa Paws wagged his tail furiously and rolled over onto his back so they would rub his stomach.

It was getting dark now, and they were happy to be warm and safe inside their rock shelter. They sat with the space blanket draped over their shoulders, thankful to be alive — and together.

Patricia had placed a garbage bag with snow inside her jacket while she was gathering wood, and by now, most of it had melted. So Gregory took out their metal cup and began boiling water. They only had one packet of cocoa left, so they only used half of it. The thin chocolate liquid tasted delicious.

When the cocoa was gone, they heated more water in the cup. Then they squeezed the bag of escalloped potatoes and ham inside and boiled it for a while. When Gregory sliced the top of the bag open, the wonderful smell of hot food billowed out.

They waited for their supper to cool a little, and then spooned out Santa Paws' share. The dog gobbled the steaming food up. Then he wagged his tail to show how glad he was to have gotten something to eat.

The ham and potatoes tasted pretty salty, but Gregory and Patricia enjoyed every bite. Having some food in their stomachs made all the difference in the world.

"You think Uncle Steve's okay?" Gregory asked.

"Sure," Patricia said, making her voice sound more confident than she felt. "We got him all of that firewood, and — he's fine. And we'll be able to get him help tomorrow, I just know it."

Gregory nodded, although he knew she was just trying to make him feel better. Santa Paws seemed to be breathing a little funny, and Gregory frowned. "Is he okay?" he asked. "Do you think he's hurt?"

Patricia watched his side rise and fall erratically. "Maybe he's just tired," she said uneasily. "He had to work really hard today."

Gregory reached forward and patted the dog gently. "Are you okay, boy?"

Santa Paws opened his eyes for a few seconds, wagged his tail, and then went back to sleep. Gregory looked at Patricia, who shrugged, and then they both settled back uneasily.

For a long time, it was quiet.

Then Patricia let out her breath. "I can't believe it's Christmas Eve," she said in a low voice.

Gregory nodded unhappily, but then suddenly

turned to look at her. "Hey! What did you get me for a present?"

She grinned at him. "I'll give you one guess."

"Sunglasses," he said without hesitating.

Patricia's grin broadened, so he knew he was right. And he *liked* sunglasses, so that was fine. He had gotten *her* a blue felt hat with a little feather in the brim.

With luck, they would get to *open* those presents sometime.

Before lying down on their pine boughs, they listened to the Chipmunks tape of Christmas carols twice, until the Walkman batteries finally wore down. After that, it was quiet again, except for the crackle of their small fire.

The wind was blowing, and somewhere off in the distance, they heard the faint howl of an eastern coyote. Santa Paws was instantly on his feet, barking. Gregory and Patricia felt scared for a minute, but they knew that Santa Paws would protect them. After a while, he settled back down underneath the space blanket, and they knew that the coyote was gone.

They tried to take turns staying awake, but sometime during the night, they both fell asleep. When they woke up in the morning, the fire had gone out. But they were still pretty warm, because Santa Paws had moved to cover them with his body when the temperature started dropping.

It had finally stopped snowing outside. Under better circumstances, the landscape would have looked like a winter wonderland. The sky was bright and clear, and all of the branches on the trees glistened with snow.

"Well," Gregory said, and sighed. "Merry Christmas."

"Yeah." Patricia tried to smile. "You, too."

By poking through the ashes of the fire with a stick, they found some glowing embers. So they got the fire going again, and made another thin cup of cocoa. They ate some crackers and apple jelly, and fed Santa Paws one of the last two Milk-Bones. Then they melted enough water for him to drink, too.

Before leaving their shelter, they put the fire out. Patricia covered the ashes with snow, just to be extra sure. Then she found a crooked stick for Gregory to lean on while he walked. His ankle was better, but he was still limping badly.

They started downhill, with Santa Paws leading the way. Refreshed from getting some sleep, they made pretty good time. Then again, walking through deep snow in the sunshine was a lot simpler than trying to make their way through a near-blizzard.

When they got to the bottom of the mountain, the ground leveled off, and they could walk without stumbling. Santa Paws stopped every so often, and sniffed the air before going on.

Sometimes he would start off in one direction, only to turn and lead them a different way. Gregory and Patricia just followed him, no matter what he did.

There seemed to be more room to walk between the trees now. Before, they had been climbing over rocks and everything. But now, the way seemed fairly clear, although the snow was still knee-deep in most places.

Patricia glanced up to her right as they were walking, and then stopped short. "Gregory, look!" she said.

Gregory followed her gaze, and saw a wooden, official-looking sign nailed to a tree. It said RESTRICTED USE AREA, and the sign had been posted by the Appalachian Mountain Club and the United States Forest Service.

"Whoa," he said nervously. "Does that mean we're trespassing?"

Patricia shook her head as a huge grin spread across her face. *Now* she understood why the path seemed easier to follow. "No. It means we're on a *trail*," she answered.

14

"So, like, we'll be in a town soon?" Gregory asked eagerly. He was so excited that he even forgot to limp for a minute.

Being on a trail meant that *some* kind of civilization had to be nearby. "I don't know," Patricia admitted. "But it has to lead to a road — or a cabin, or — I don't know. But — it's good!"

There weren't any tracks in the snow, so no one else had walked on this trail recently. Then again, December wasn't exactly the prime hiking season.

Santa Paws forced himself forward through the chest-deep snow, doing his best to make a path for Gregory and Patricia. His ribs were hurting so much now that he was panting heavily, and sometimes he coughed, too. Each step was an effort, but he just kept putting one paw in front of the other.

Gregory and Patricia were so exhausted themselves that they didn't notice how much Santa

Paws was struggling. As they all waded endlessly through the drifts, they began to pass more small painted signs. There were arrows pointing them to different trails, and showing them how to get *back* to the mountains. Then they saw a sign that read KANCAMAGUS HWY., 1.2 MILES.

They were just over a mile away from the highway!

"Oh, boy," Gregory said, and put his arms around Santa Paws. "What a good dog!" He took the last Milk-Bone out of his pocket and gave it to him.

The dog wagged his tail and crunched his treat, still panting weakly. He wasn't sure what he had done that was so good, but the biscuit made his stomach hurt less. *Nothing* helped his ribs. He had started to catch slight whiffs of gasoline as they trudged along, but no matter how hard he tried, he *still* hadn't found the car.

When Santa Paws had finished his biscuit, he wagged his tail at Gregory and Patricia. Then he resumed his panting, unsteady trot down the snowy trail.

"Maybe we should take a turn," Patricia suggested, looking worried. "Let him rest for a while."

"Yeah," Gregory agreed. "He seems *really* tired."

First, Gregory tried to get up in front, and then Patricia tried. But each time, Santa Paws would gallop around the side until he was in the lead again.

"I guess he wants to go first," Gregory said, out of breath.

Patricia nodded, breathing too hard to answer. It certainly *seemed* that way.

They were all so exhausted that sometimes they would stumble off the trail. Then they would have to flounder around in the drifts until they stumbled back onto it. After a while, they found themselves in front of a wide area where the snow seemed somewhat grey and caved in. Santa Paws instantly stopped, and lifted one paw in the air.

"What's wrong with him?" Gregory asked.

"I don't know." Patricia limped forward to check. "Maybe he lost the trail, or — "

Before she could finish her sentence, there was a terrible cracking sound and the wet snow gave way beneath her feet! They had walked right on top of a snow-covered, partially frozen stream, and she had fallen through the ice!

The current beneath the thin crust of ice was very swift, and Patricia fought to stay afloat. Within seconds, she was so cold that her teeth were chattering and her legs and good arm were numb. Every time she tried to climb out, the surrounding ice would break away. The current was so strong that it was going to pull her underwater soon!

"Hang on, Patricia!" Gregory yelled. He started toward her, but then heard an ominous cracking underneath his boots. He froze where he was, and looked down at the ice sagging beneath his weight.

"Don't!" Patricia ordered through chattering teeth. "You'll fall through, too!"

Remembering that you were supposed to lie down and spread your weight evenly on thin ice, Gregory quickly flattened on the snow.

"Don't worry, I'm coming!" he promised.

Without hesitating, Santa Paws leaped over him and dove right into the freezing water. He swam over next to Patricia and dog-paddled in place. Patricia grabbed onto the seat belt loop on his harness, and hung on as tightly as she could. But her hand was so numb that she lost her grip and slipped underwater for a few seconds.

Santa Paws grabbed her jacket collar between his teeth and tugged her head up above the surface of the water. Patricia coughed and spluttered and gasped for air.

Gregory reached his arm out as far as he could. "Come here, boy!" he called. "You can do it!"

Santa Paws swam in his direction, dragging Patricia along behind him. She was still coughing and gasping, but she managed to grasp his harness again. Since she was hanging on now, Santa Paws released her jacket and just concentrated on swimming.

"S-s-sticks," Patricia gasped at Gregory, her voice shaking from the cold. "G-get some sticks!"

The ice sagged more as Gregory propelled himself backwards, pushing with both hands. Once the creaking sounds had stopped, he jumped up and ran toward the nearest tree. He ripped off several branches and carried them back to the ice. Then he spread them out, so that Patricia and Santa Paws would be able to grip onto something when they climbed out.

Santa Paws dog-paddled in a small circle so that Patricia would be closest to the edge of the ice. Then he pressed his body against hers, trying to push her to safety.

"Roll, Patty!" Gregory yelled. "Roll yourself up!"

Patricia tried, but she was so cold that she kept slipping back into the swirling water.

"Grab the end of a branch!" Gregory shouted. "Then I can pull you!"

With Santa Paws keeping her afloat, Patricia gathered up just enough strength for one last lunge. She was too weak to hang on, but she managed to wedge her arm around one of the branches. With Santa Paws pushing and Gregory pulling, she was able to crawl to safety. Then she lay where she was, struggling to catch her breath.

"Stay really flat!" Gregory warned her.

Patricia nodded, shivering so hard that she couldn't speak.

Santa Paws was trying to climb out of the stream, but his paws kept sliding on the ice and he would slip back into the water.

Quickly, Gregory swung one of the branches toward him. "Play tug, boy!" he yelled. "Come on!"

Santa Paws grabbed the end of the branch with his teeth in a viselike grip. Then Gregory pulled as hard as he could, until Santa Paws was able to scramble up onto the ice. He shook violently, but most of the water on his fur had already frozen into tiny icicles.

Patricia was so cold that she was having trouble standing up. Gregory helped her to her feet, and then guided her over to the nearest large tree.

"Sit down out of the wind, okay?" he said. "I'll make a fire really fast! Come here, boy! You stay, too."

Patricia nodded, hunching down into her jacket and shivering uncontrollably. Santa Paws was shivering almost as hard, and he leaned up against her. Patricia hugged him closer, trying to get warm.

156

Gregory piled up the driest branches he could find, and then squirted what was left of their tube of fire-starter onto the stack. There were only two matches in the match container, and the first one wouldn't light.

"What if this one doesn't work?" Gregory asked uneasily, looking at their last match.

Patricia didn't want to think about that, so she just shook her head.

Gregory took a deep breath, and then struck the match. After a tense second, it flared up and he cupped his hand around the flame so that the wind wouldn't blow it out. He brought it carefully to one of the globs of fire-starter, which sputtered, but then also started burning.

As soon as the fire was burning steadily, he began to heat a cupful of water. They didn't have any cocoa left, but he knew that it was a lot more important for Patricia to drink something *hot*, than it was for the water to taste good.

The fire was giving off a lot of heat now, but Patricia's face was very pale and she was still shivering.

"You'll feel better when you drink this," Gregory said, doing his best not to panic. "I *know* you will."

Patricia nodded feebly, and kept shivering.

Gregory was paying more attention to Patricia than he was to the tin cup, and by accident, he let his arm stray too close to the fire. His sleeve burst into flames and he looked down at it in stunned horror.

"Help, what do I do?" he yelled, close to hysteria. "I'm burning!"

Patricia and Santa Paws both lunged forward weakly and knocked him down into the snow. The flames went out right away from the lack of oxygen, but Patricia and Santa Paws stayed on top of him for a minute just to be sure.

"Y-you okay?" Patricia asked through her chattering teeth.

"I think so," Gregory whispered, his heart pounding so loud in his ears that he couldn't really hear. "Th-thanks." He sat up with an effort, and examined what was left of his sleeve. The fire had burned all the way through his layers and down to his forearm, leaving a red shiny spot behind. It hurt a lot, and he pressed a thick handful of snow against it to cool the burn.

The water from the cup had spilled and put their campfire out, too. The wet branches were steaming a little, and there was smoke everywhere.

Patricia and Gregory stared at each other in a daze.

"We don't have any matches left," Gregory said, trying not to cry.

Patricia nodded, feeling a few tears of her own trickle down her cheeks.

Santa Paws whined deep in his throat, and

started pacing back and forth. Then he paused, held his paw up, and sniffed the air curiously.

"With our luck, it's p-probably a grizzly bear or something," Patricia said grimly.

Santa Paws stood very still, his head cocked to one side. Then, suddenly, he galloped away from them.

"Santa Paws, come back!" Gregory shouted after him. "You'll get lost!"

Santa Paws kept running, until he had disappeared around a curve in the trail.

Patricia grabbed a low branch on the tree and used it to pull herself to her feet. "C-come on," she said. "We'd better go find him."

Gregory nodded, and lifted her good arm around his shoulders so that he could help her walk. They followed the trail of paw prints, stumbling along as quickly as they could. Santa Paws' tracks led right out of the woods and into an unplowed parking lot. There was a small, wooden information booth, but it was closed for the season.

Just beyond the parking lot, they could see the Kancamagus Highway. Only one lane had been cleared, but it appeared to be passable.

"He did it," Gregory breathed. "He saved us!"

Patricia nodded weakly, and sank down onto a snowy picnic bench to rest.

From somewhere up on the highway, they could hear frantic barking.

"Take it easy, boy," a deep male voice was saying. "Come here, okay? I'm not going to hurt you."

Santa Paws just kept barking and racing back and forth. After all their hours of walking, he had *finally* smelled a car! Now he just had to lead the driver back to Gregory and Patricia.

Realizing that Santa Paws had found help, Gregory and Patricia staggered over to the edge of the road. They could see a snowplow idling in the middle of the highway, and a burly man with a thick blond beard hurrying after Santa Paws. He was wearing a thick blue parka and a Lincoln Sanitation Department baseball cap.

Gregory sagged against Patricia, his legs so weak that he almost fell. "We made it," he whispered, hugging her as tightly as he could.

"I know," she whispered back.

Then, they both burst into tears!

After that, everything happened fast. The snowplow driver, whose name was Andy, helped them up into the warm cab of his truck and wrapped them up in a heavy wool blanket. He had a thermos of hot coffee and Gregory and Patricia took turns drinking from the plastic cup. They were both still crying, and shivering so much that they spilled almost as much coffee as they managed to drink.

First, the local police came, followed by some

state troopers and a paramedic. Gregory and Patricia told them everything, especially where they had left Uncle Steve and how they *had* to go search for him *right away*. They both talked so fast that they kept interrupting each other, and Officer Jeffreys, the state trooper who was in charge, had to keep telling them to slow down.

Soon, they were bundled up in the back of the state trooper's four-wheel-drive Jeep. It had been arranged that their parents were going to meet them at the hospital up in Littleton. They had left as soon as they got the call, and would be there as soon as possible.

The police officers were all very nice to them, and explained that rescue planes had already been up searching all morning. Now, at least, they knew *where* to look. Gregory and Patricia just prayed that their uncle was still okay.

The ride up to Littleton seemed to take forever. Trooper Jeffreys drove, and the paramedic rode in the passenger's seat. Gregory and Patricia were too exhausted to talk anymore, and Santa Paws fell asleep across their laps.

By the time they got to the hospital, Trooper Jeffreys had to wake all of them up. There were a lot of reporters in front of the emergency room, and plenty of television camerapeople, too. As soon as the paramedic opened the back door of the Jeep, the reporters started shouting questions. Bright lights on top of the cameras were flashing, and everyone started crowding around them.

"Tell us about your ordeal!" a reporter cried out.

"Did you ever think all hope was lost?" another wanted to know.

"Where's the hero dog?" a third demanded.

There were so many people that Gregory and Patricia hung back inside the car for a minute.

"Let's clear the way!" Trooper Jeffreys said in a commanding voice. "Back off now!"

Other police officers moved forward to control the crowd, and open a path to the emergency room entrance.

Santa Paws was the first one to get out of the car. He took one tentative step forward, and suddenly collapsed. He coughed weakly, and then closed his eyes.

"Santa Paws!" Gregory gasped, and rushed forward to help him.

The paramedic scooped Santa Paws up from the ground and rushed into the emergency room with him in her arms.

"The dog went down!" she shouted. "I think he's critical!"

"Bring him into Trauma One!" one of the doctors ordered. "And I want both kids in Trauma Two!"

"We can't leave Santa Paws!" Patricia said frantically. "We have to stay with him!"

"It's all right," another doctor said, in a very soothing voice. "It's going to be fine. They're taking very good care of him."

There was a curtain between the two trauma rooms, and Gregory and Patricia could hear voices yelling about "IVs *stat*" and "Taking chest films" and that someone should call in a veterinarian, *fast*.

Gregory and Patricia refused treatment until they were sure that Santa Paws was going to be okay. The X rays showed that he had broken several ribs in the crash, and that his right lung had collapsed. He was also badly dehydrated, and suffering from hypothermia.

"Is he all right?" Gregory asked repeatedly. "Is he going to be all right?"

"He's in intensive care now," one of the nurses explained. "Don't worry, he's a good, strong dog. He'll pull through."

But Gregory and Patricia *were* worried. All those hours, Santa Paws had been hurt, and they hadn't even *realized* it. But there was nothing that they could do about that now, so they just held hands tightly, and waited for news about him.

Then, they heard two very familiar, worried voices in the front of the emergency room. Their parents had arrived!

"Where are they?" Mrs. Callahan was asking. "Please, where are our children?"

"Right this way," a nurse answered, and led them to Trauma Two.

As soon as they saw their parents, Gregory and Patricia started crying again. Their parents were crying, too, and hugged them over and over. Aunt Emily had come along with them, and she was smiling bravely, but her lips kept quivering.

"Santa Paws is hurt," Gregory said through his tears, as Patricia was asking if the planes had found Uncle Steve yet. "Is Santa Paws okay?"

Unfortunately, there was nothing they could do now but *wait*.

It turned out that Gregory had torn some ligaments in his ankle. The doctors made him a soft cast, and he would need crutches for about six weeks. He also had a second-degree burn on his arm, and some minor frostbite.

Patricia was also slightly frostbitten, and she was still shivering from her fall through the ice. Her knee was sprained, and she had broken her arm in *two* places. The huge cast went all the way from her fingertips to her shoulder. It hurt so much that she just kept holding on to her mother's hand the whole time she was in the trauma room. The doctors had given her a painkiller, but the only thing it had accomplished so far was to make her very sleepy.

"We really didn't want to leave him," she whispered to her mother, struggling not to cry as they waited to hear about Uncle Steve. "But I didn't know what else to do."

Mrs. Callahan kissed her gently on the forehead. "You did the only thing you *could* have done, Patricia," she said, and kissed her again. "We're *very* proud of you. Both of you."

Just then, Gregory came swinging into the room on his crutches with a big grin on his face. Mr. Callahan walked next to him, resting his hand on his son's shoulder.

"Dad and I just went to see Santa Paws," Gregory said. "He's going to be okay! He wagged his tail and everything!"

Hearing that, Patricia started crying again and hugged her mother gratefully.

As a precaution, the doctors wanted all three of them to stay in the hospital overnight. Gregory and Patricia protested, but their parents insisted. In the end, they were put together in the same room in the pediatrics ward. Santa Paws was still in intensive care downstairs, being watched by a team of local veterinarians.

The nurses brought the family a late lunch, but none of them could eat it. They were too busy worrying. Gregory and Patricia's grandparents were driving down with Miranda, and could arrive at any time.

Then, at about three-thirty, the word came in that a rescue chopper had found Uncle Steve. He was very weak, but still alive, and they were air-lifting him directly to the hospital.

Aunt Emily went downstairs to the Emergency Room to wait for him. Soon, she sent word up that he was conscious, and talking, and wanted to know how *they* were.

For the first time since the plane had crashed, Gregory and Patricia relaxed. Uncle Steve was okay! They were *all* okay!

"I'm *really* tired," Patricia said to her parents. Over in the next bed, Gregory was already asleep.

They slept until about nine o'clock that night, with their parents watching over them the whole time. When they woke up, they drank juice and ate chicken soup and chocolate pudding.

"How's Uncle Steve?" Patricia asked. "Can we go see him? And Santa Paws, too?"

"Let me find out," Mr. Callahan answered. He went out to the nurses' station, and returned with a big smile on his face. "He's awake now, and they said it would be fine."

Gregory and Patricia rode down the hallway in wheelchairs, because it was a hospital policy. But since their parents were the ones pushing them, they didn't really mind.

In addition to his collarbone, Uncle Steve had fractured his pelvis and badly strained his back. He also had some frostbite and a severe case of bronchitis. The doctors had him on lots of antibiotics, so that it wouldn't turn into pneumonia.

Gregory and Patricia's grandparents were already in the room, with Aunt Emily and Miranda. The hospital dieticians had cooked a special holiday meal for everyone, and the nurses had set up a beautiful Christmas tree in the corner of the room. It was decorated with red and green bulbs and a string of brightly twinkling lights. Someone had also found a CD player, and Christmas carols were playing in the background.

When Uncle Steve saw them come in, he put down his spoonful of Jell-O and gave them a big grin. He looked tired and frail, but he also looked extremely glad to see them.

"Well, if it isn't two of my favorite heroes!" he said.

There was a lot of noise as they all tried to talk at once, and Miranda yelled, "Yay, Daddy!" over and over. Then there was a familiar low woof, and they all turned to look at the door.

It was Santa Paws, riding on a gurney!

Gregory and Patricia both limped over to hug him, and Santa Paws wagged his tail. He was still wearing an IV in his front paw, but he looked happy and alert. He would be back to normal in no time!

"*Here's* the hero," Gregory said proudly. "All we did was follow him."

Patricia nodded. "No matter what happened, he always took care of us."

Then Gregory laughed. "Yeah. We told him to find the car, and — he found the car!"

Everyone was still laughing, and talking at once, and Santa Paws took advantage of the confusion to bark some more. Hearing all of the noise, other patients from the floor had gathered around to share in the excitement. There were also nurses and doctors everywhere, and when Santa Paws barked again, they all clapped.

"Merry Christmas!" someone yelled.

"And a Happy New Year!" someone else added.

Santa Paws kept barking and wagging his tail as hard as he could. He was overjoyed to be together with the whole family again. Somehow, in spite of their grueling adventure, they were all warm, and happy, and *safe*.

It had turned out to be a *very* Merry Christmas, after all!

Santa Paws,
Come Home

Don't miss these other books about this lovable dog hero:

SANTA PAWS

THE RETURN OF SANTA PAWS

Santa Paws, Come Home

by
Nicholas
Edwards

AN
APPLE
PAPERBACK

SCHOLASTIC INC.
New York Toronto London Auckland Sydney
Mexico City New Delhi Hong Kong

ISBN 0-590-37990-9

22 21 20 19 18 17   1 2 3 4/0

Printed in the U.S.A.   40

First Scholastic printing, November 1999

For Zack

The best ever.

Santa Paws, Come Home

1

It was a cold December afternoon, and the dog was very happy. Actually, the dog was almost *always* happy, but today had been particularly nice. He had gone outside in the backyard a few times, he had eaten three Milk-Bones, and he had just finished the latest in a long series of naps. Even better, the family cat, Evelyn, had not hissed at him at all today!

The house was full of wonderful places to sleep. So far today, the dog had spent time curled up on the couch in the den, lounging in front of the fireplace, and sprawled across the freshly-made double bed in the guest room upstairs. He trotted out to the kitchen to get a drink of water from his dish, and then headed for the living room to sleep in front of the Christmas tree. He liked the smell of pine needles, and when he slept there, he always had good dreams about galloping around a beautiful forest. He had never understood why, when the weather got cold every

1

year, his family would suddenly bring a tree into the house. But, having the tree around seemed to make everyone feel especially cheerful and jolly. So that made him happy, too.

He had lived with his family, the Callahans, for a very long time now. Two whole years! Two *wonderful* years. When he was a puppy, he had been a stray. He had lived in the streets, scavenging for food and shelter. More often than not, he had gone hungry. It was a very sad and lonely time for him.

But then, one day, he met a boy named Gregory. The dog had been sleeping near a big brick building. Every afternoon, children would come running outside, and play noisy games on the grass or in the snow. They always had so much fun that the dog liked watching them. Gregory, along with his sister, Patricia, and his friend Oscar, started bringing him food and water. Then the dog went to live with Gregory and Patricia, and their parents, Mr. and Mrs. Callahan. And, of course, Evelyn, the cat. He had been happy ever since. The dog loved his new family very much, and he and Gregory and Patricia spent almost every waking moment together.

During the week, though, Gregory and Patricia would go off with their knapsacks full of books. Mrs. Callahan also left in the mornings, with a big canvas briefcase. She was a physics teacher at the local high school, and would drop

Gregory and Patricia off at the middle school on her way to work.

Mr. Callahan was a writer. So, every day, he would stay home, listen to music, and sit at his desk in the den. Sometimes he typed on a keyboard, but mostly he just sat there. The dog liked to sleep under the desk, and Mr. Callahan would rest his feet on his back while he worked. Mr. Callahan also liked to fix lots of snacks, which he always shared. Sometimes, he would spend all day lying on the couch and watching television and making phone calls. Today, Mr. Callahan had prepared a thick salami sandwich on whole wheat toast for lunch, along with a bowl of potato chips. The dog had enjoyed small tastes of each, but he preferred the salami. Evelyn did not like either, but she *did* stick her paw right into Mr. Callahan's glass of milk. Mr. Callahan was not thrilled about this, but he patted her and drank it, anyway.

Every weekday afternoon, the dog would start waiting for Gregory and Patricia to come back from school. Starting around three-thirty, he would keep one ear cocked in the direction of the kitchen door. Lots of times lately, they didn't get home until it was already dark outside! The dog would get very restless when this happened, and sometimes, he would pace around the kitchen endlessly until he heard the car in the driveway.

Today seemed to be another one of those long days. As the afternoon wore on, the dog would only nap for a few minutes at a time. Then he would get up, and lift his paws onto the front windowsill to look outside. Sometimes, he whined softly. Where *were* they? What was taking so long?

Finding him at the window yet again, Mr. Callahan patted him.

"Don't worry, Santa Paws," he said. "They'll be home as soon as practice is over. We have a couple of junior high jocks in the family now, that's all."

The dog wagged his tail when he heard his name. Although he had a lot of different nicknames, most of the people in town called him "Santa Paws." Gregory had originally named him Nicholas, but after months of hearing everyone else saying "Santa Paws," now the Callahans called him that, too. Patricia thought Santa Paws was a really dumb name — *beyond* not cool — but at this point, even she had given up and started using it routinely.

The dog was generally happy to answer to *any* name, but Santa Paws was his favorite. People always smiled when they said it, and he liked to see people smile. It seemed like a very merry name, indeed.

Finally, right after the sun went down, Santa

4

Paws heard the crunch of car tires on some frozen leaves in the driveway. They were home! His family! Back where they belonged! The world was wonderful again! Yay!

The back door opened, bringing a rush of cold winter air into the kitchen. Mrs. Callahan came in first, lugging a bag of groceries along with her briefcase. She usually had lots of homework papers to correct and lesson plans to prepare at night, so her briefcase was always full.

Gregory was next, also carrying a grocery bag in one arm. His knapsack was slung over his free shoulder. Gregory was twelve, and he was in the seventh grade this year. He was tall for his age, with dark brown hair and bright blue eyes. Underneath his ski jacket, he was still dressed in his basketball sneakers, grey sweatpants, a turtleneck with the sleeves cut off, and his favorite Phantom Menace T-shirt.

Patricia was the last one to come inside, weighed down by all of her hockey equipment. She looked a lot like Gregory, except that she always wore her hair in a bouncy ponytail. This year, the middle school had formed a junior high girls' hockey team, and even though Patricia was very small and thin for her age, she had been one of the first people to sign up. Hockey "appealed to her lower instincts," was her explanation. "What does *that* mean?" Gregory would always ask. Patricia, who had never lacked for confidence, would just sigh heavily and say, "If you have to ask, you'll never understand it." Gregory hadn't quite figured out a comeback for that yet — but he knew an insult when he heard one. Privately, he kind of wondered if, on her birthday this year, instead of turning thirteen, Patricia hadn't actually turned *thirty-three*.

Overjoyed to have the entire family home safe and sound, Santa Paws began barking loudly. He jumped on each of them in turn, managing to knock Patricia down in the process. He weighed more than ninety pounds, and didn't always realize how strong he was.

"Maybe you should take your skates *off* before you come in the house," Gregory suggested.

Patricia just grinned wryly, although their mother glanced over to check her feet, looking alarmed. Mrs. Callahan's expression relaxed when she saw that her daughter was actually wearing black cowboy boots.

"Did everyone have a good day?" Mr. Callahan asked. "How was practice?"

"I'm really tired," Gregory said. "Oscar kept making me laugh, so Coach had us run about a million laps."

Mr. Callahan winced, since he hated all forms of exercise. He had always said that playing chess was all the exertion he could handle. "How about you?" he asked Patricia. "Were you able to stay out of the penalty box?"

"Mostly," Patricia answered, and then she sighed. "They want me to be goalie, but I said no way."

"What's wrong with being the goalie?" Mrs. Callahan asked, as she unpacked milk and orange juice from her grocery bag. "It's a very responsible position."

"Let people hit a really hard puck *at* me, and I'm not even allowed to duck?" Patricia shook her head. "No way. I have orthodonture to think about."

"Besides, if you're stuck in the goal, you can't go around slamming people into the boards or anything," Gregory said.

"No," Patricia agreed, "and that's my favorite part."

Mr. Callahan looked at his wife. "Remember when she was four years old, and *lived* for ballet class?"

"Dimly," Mrs. Callahan said, with a grin.

As Patricia gathered up her hockey gear, Santa Paws grabbed one of her oversized gloves in his mouth and shook it playfully from side to side.

"Drop it, please," she said, holding out her hand. "Those are expensive."

Santa Paws was disappointed — he loved

7

games! — but he let the glove slip back to the floor. "Drop it!" was one of the phrases like "Down!" and "No!" which he knew, but was always sad to hear.

"Good dog," she said.

That made Santa Paws cheer up. "Good dog" was a wonderful thing to hear. Almost as good as "Suppertime!" and "Want a Milk-Bone?"

When Mrs. Callahan sent Gregory and Patricia upstairs to get cleaned up before dinner, Santa Paws followed them.

"I call first shower!" Patricia said.

"That's not fair — you *always* get the first one," Gregory protested.

Patricia shrugged. "That's because I'm older, and smarter, and faster."

He wasn't sure about "smarter," but she definitely had him on the other two. "Yeah, well — you're *short*," Gregory said.

Patricia laughed. "Is that the best you can do?"

Gregory nodded sheepishly. "Yeah, but only because I'm really tired. Otherwise, I could make fun of you for like, an hour straight. I'd be, you know, *merciless*."

"Oh," Patricia said, looking amused. "So, I should take pity on you, and give you the first shower?"

Gregory nodded again. "Yep. Also, because I'm

8

younger, and slower, and your very favorite brother."

Patricia pushed up the sleeve of her Oceanport Mariners jersey to show him a large dark purple bruise on her elbow. "See what happened when I checked Betsy Davenport? *I* should get the first shower."

Gregory promptly yanked his left sweatpants leg up far enough to expose a huge puffy red scrape above his knee. "See what happened when *I* dove out of bounds for a loose ball?"

Confused by these demonstrations, Santa Paws sat down and lifted one paw. From force of habit, Gregory reached over to shake it, and Santa Paws wagged his tail. If they were going to play some kind of new game, he wanted to be included.

"Did it bleed?" Patricia asked, bending down to examine the injury.

"Sure did," Gregory said proudly. "They even used one of those instant ice packs and took me to the locker room to clean it."

"Okay, you win." Patricia straightened up. "Don't use all the hot water."

"*If* you're lucky," Gregory said.

While Gregory showered, Patricia checked her e-mail. Then, while she was taking her turn, Gregory threw a tennis ball up and down the hallway for Santa Paws. Santa Paws joyfully retrieved it each time, his paws scrabbling against the polished wooden floor. Sometimes he gave the ball back, but sometimes, he was having so much fun that he kept it instead. Then Gregory would try to wrestle it free, with Santa Paws moving his head out of the way at *just* the right moment to avoid him. It was fun!

Once they had all trooped back downstairs for supper, Santa Paws alertly positioned himself right by the table. He never knew when someone might drop a piece of food, and he always liked to be ready for the possibility. Evelyn, the cat, was more subtle, and she just perched casually on a nearby counter.

Mrs. Callahan was serving the spaghetti when the telephone rang. Just as Mr. Callahan was saying, "Wait, let the machine pick up," Gregory was already racing across the room to answer it.

"Hello?" he said, and then saw his parents look at him sternly. "I mean, uh, this is the Callahan residence." He listened for a minute, and then covered the receiver. "It's the police, Mom. They want to talk to you or Dad right away."

Since Mr. Callahan's brother Steve was a member of the local department, he hurried over. He immediately asked the officer on the other end if Steve was okay, and then looked relieved.

"Oh, good, you had me pretty worried there," Mr. Callahan said into the phone. "So, what seems to be the problem?"

The rest of the family watched, as Mr. Callahan listened, and nodded, and said things like "Okay" and "I see." Finally, he nodded one last time, told the officer that they would come right away, and then hung up the phone.

"What is it?" Mrs. Callahan asked uneasily. "Is something wrong?"

Mr. Callahan nodded, his expression very serious. "It's an emergency," he said. "There's a missing child."

"Is it anyone we know?" Patricia asked.

Mr. Callahan shook his head, already reaching for his jacket.

Gregory felt just as confused as his mother and sister looked. "So — I don't get it. Why did they call us?"

"Why else?" Mr. Callahan said with a resigned shrug. "They need Santa Paws."

2

Hearing his name, the dog pricked his ears up. Santa Paws was well known throughout the town of Oceanport — and all over New England — for being very good to have around during emergencies. In spite of himself, whenever there was trouble, he always ended up right in the middle of the situation. He had never *meant* to become a hero, but somehow, it had worked out that way. For some mysterious reason, he was especially good at helping people during the holiday season. He had performed so many rescues during the last two years, that most of Oceanport thought he was a combination of Lassie, Underdog, and all 101 Dalmatians put together. A few of the more imaginative people in town might even have added E.T. to the list.

Santa Paws watched, baffled, as the entire family got up from the table *without even eating dinner*! What could they be thinking? It smelled so delicious!

In all the confusion, Evelyn snuck onto the table and stole a meatball. The dog hoped she might share it, but she just hissed at him and carried her treasure off to the living room to eat in privacy. He was afraid to follow her, in case she might scratch him.

"We don't *all* need to go," Mr. Callahan said, as he reached for the keys to the station wagon. "Why don't you kids wait here, and — "

"We want to help!" Gregory protested.

"We *know* we can help," Patricia said confidently. She zipped up her warmest Gore-Tex jacket, and put on her gloves and New England Patriots cap.

Mr. and Mrs. Callahan looked at each other.

"The longer we stand here discussing it, the longer that poor child is out there alone in the cold," Mrs. Callahan said.

Mr. Callahan nodded, and motioned for everyone to come along. His wife yanked him back, and pointed at his feet. Mr. Callahan blushed, since he was wearing Pink Panther slippers. Because he worked at home, he often forgot to change into proper clothing before he went outside.

"I'll start the car," Mrs. Callahan said, "while you get your boots."

It wasn't quite cold enough to snow, but an icy rain was falling and they would certainly all *need* their boots out there.

13

Santa Paws still couldn't figure out why nobody wanted to eat supper, but he barked happily when he saw Gregory holding his leash. He loved to ride in cars, and maybe they were going on a special adventure! He was always up for that!

On the drive over, Mr. Callahan explained the whole story. A family named the Jensens, who lived near the edge of town, had a two-year-old boy, Robert. No one was quite sure how, but Robert had wandered away a couple of hours earlier. His family had searched their house and backyard frantically, and then called the police. The police organized search parties immediately, but there was no sign of Robert anywhere. Most of the nearby neighbors had volunteered to help, with no success. Now it was dark, and getting cold enough outside so that everyone was starting to panic. If they didn't find him soon, it might be too late!

The Jensens' house was easy to locate, because there were police cars and other emergency service vehicles parked all over the place. There were even vans from the local television stations, reporting live from the scene. When the Callahans pulled up, a very young female officer came over to stop them.

"I'm sorry, ma'am," she said politely. "But this area is restricted right now. You'll need to take a different route."

"We were asked to come," Mrs. Callahan said.

14

"We have Santa Paws with us."

"Oh!" Now the officer looked very respectful. "Right this way. You'll need to report to Sergeant Callahan."

Mr. Callahan couldn't help grinning, since Sergeant Callahan was, of course, his little brother Steve. While recuperating from some severe injuries, Steve had had plenty of time to study for the sergeant's exam the previous spring. His score was the highest in the whole department, so he had been promoted, even though he was still mostly on desk duty. Steve had actually gotten hurt the Christmas before, when his private plane crashed in the mountains. All these months later, the hip he had broken was still bothering him. Patricia, Gregory, and Santa Paws had been flying with him that day, and — well, they still all felt very grateful to have survived.

None of them liked planes much anymore, either.

The Callahans and Santa Paws followed the female police officer down the street and across the Jensens' lawn. The entire atmosphere was tense and chaotic. The Jensens' house was surrounded by woods on three sides, so there were plenty of dangerous places for a tiny child to get lost. People were shouting orders and questions, and flashlight beams bobbed up and down through the trees as search parties worked desperately to find Robert.

"Hi, Uncle Steve!" Gregory said, as they walked up to the command post.

Uncle Steve was leaning on his cane and looked very tired, but he turned to smile at them. "Hi, guys," he said. "Thanks for getting here so quickly."

An officer wearing a uniform from one of the neighboring towns came over, looking discouraged. "Nothing in Sector Four. Sorry."

Uncle Steve sighed and marked the area off on a grid map. "Okay. Give your people a few minutes to have some coffee and warm up, and then have them double-check Sector Seven."

The officer nodded, and left.

Uncle Steven turned his attention back to his family. "We're not getting anywhere," he said in a low voice. "And no one's even sure if the kid had a sweater on, forget a jacket. We wanted to use dogs right away, but the nearest SAR team is still on a job out in the Berkshires right now. We sent for one of the Boston K-9 Units, but they're taking forever to get here. I'm sorry to drag you all out like this, but I thought Santa Paws could probably help."

"SAR?" Gregory whispered to Patricia. He had never heard those initials before, and wasn't sure what they meant.

"Search and Rescue," she whispered back.

He nodded. Since he was *almost* sure that

"K-9" was slang for "Canine," he decided not to ask about that one.

A burly man in a Massachusetts State Police uniform came lumbering over when he saw Santa Paws.

"Is this the hotshot dog?" he asked dubiously. "Well, let's get started." He extended his hand and indicated for Gregory to give him the leash.

Santa Paws didn't like the idea of going off with a complete stranger, so he sat down firmly.

"It's okay, boy," Gregory said, patting him.

Santa Paws wagged his tail briefly, but still didn't budge.

Gregory looked tentatively at the State trooper. "I, um, don't think he'll obey someone he doesn't know, sir."

The trooper, whose last name was Yeager, looked impatient. "Fine. Whatever." He turned to Steve. "We'll just have to wait for the K-9 team, then."

"But he'll go with *us*," Gregory assured him. "He's really good at finding things."

Trooper Yeager frowned at Uncle Steve. "The last thing we need is some kids and an amateur dog mucking up our search, Callahan."

"With all due respect, sir," Uncle Steve said, his voice both polite and testy. "This actually falls within my department's jurisdiction, and I'm giving the okay." He turned to a nearby Oceanport paramedic. "Ask one of the Jensens to come over here, please."

A very pale woman in her early thirties was led to the command post by the paramedic. Her hands were trembling badly and it was easy to see that she had been crying. The Callahans knew without asking that she must be Robert's mother. When she saw Santa Paws, her face fell.

"But — I thought he'd be a purebred," she said, her voice shaking. "Are you sure this is really Santa Paws? This dog looks like a *house pet*."

Gregory and Patricia both felt insulted, since they thought Santa Paws was beautiful. Dashing, even. At ninety pounds, he was mostly German shepherd, with some collie mixed in. He had thick brown fur, with black highlights on his face and tail. The American Kennel Club would be *lucky* to have such a fine dog in their organization.

"We're very sorry about your son, ma'am," Patricia said crisply, before anyone else could speak. "Could you please get us some clothes Robert wore recently, from his laundry basket, maybe? Whatever you think will have the strongest scent."

Mrs. Jensen seemed a little startled that a girl seemed to be taking charge of the situation — but no one who knew Patricia was ever surprised by things like that. She had always told people that she wanted to be a police officer, or a Supreme Court Justice — or the President of the country, when she grew up. Gregory, personally, had his money on President. Unless, of course, the United States switched to a monarchy, and then he knew Patricia would insist upon being the *Queen*.

"Yes, of course," Mrs. Jensen said, without arguing. "I'll be back in a minute."

Trooper Yeager — who had never met Patricia — put his hands on his hips. "You mind telling this kid we can run our own operation, Sergeant?"

"Actually, I do," Uncle Steve said mildly. "Instead of fighting, let's just try to find Robert, okay?"

"Well, I don't like it," Trooper Yeager said. "I don't want some *kid* — "

Mrs. Callahan, who had something of a temper herself, stepped forward. "This 'kid' is my daughter, mister, and I'd appreciate it if you didn't — "

"Here it is, here it is!" Mrs. Jensen said, rushing over with a tiny red shirt.

Everyone at the command post smiled tensely at her, and there seemed to be a silent agreement not to argue in front of the little boy's mother. Santa Paws just sat next to Gregory, completely perplexed. He could tell that everyone around him was very upset, but he wasn't sure what was going on.

"Thank you, ma'am," Patricia said, and handed the shirt to Gregory. "Don't worry about a thing. Santa Paws is *really* smart."

Since they fully agreed with that, her parents and Uncle Steve nodded.

Gregory held the shirt up to his dog's nose. "Smell that, okay, boy?"

Santa Paws sniffed cooperatively. He could smell a little boy, some slightly spoiled milk, and a faint odor of strained spinach. He sniffed again, and then wagged his tail at Gregory.

"Good dog!" Gregory praised him. "Now, find the boy!"

Santa Paws sat down again, puzzled. Find. He knew the word "find." He just wasn't sure *what* they wanted him to find.

"Oh, it's no use," Mrs. Jensen said, near tears. "We'll have to wait for the real dogs to come."

After the plane crash, Gregory had told Santa Paws to "find the car" — and he had led them miles across the White Mountains, through a blizzard, until they got to a highway. So he was sure that his dog could find anything, as long as he understood what they were asking.

Gregory held the shirt up to his nose again. "Come on, Santa Paws, you can do it!"

The dog sniffed for a long time, and then

sniffed the air again. There were so many people around, plus exhaust fumes from the cars, that it was hard to separate all of the different scents from one another. But now he had it! He jumped to his feet, and led them confidently towards the house.

"He's not there!" Mrs. Jensen groaned. "We've all searched over and over."

"Let's just trust the dog, ma'am," Uncle Steve said, very calm. "His sense of smell is much better than ours."

Santa Paws led them straight to the house, swiped his paw across the back door, and then sat down. Mrs. Jensen obviously thought this was a waste of time, but she opened the door. Santa Paws sniffed the air and headed straight for the garbage can in the corner of the kitchen. He banged his paw against the lid, and sat down again, wagging his tail. This search didn't make any sense, but he wanted to make them all happy.

Gregory looked more closely at the shirt in the bright indoor light, and saw the milk and food stains. He opened the trash can, and lifted out an empty milk carton, and a used Styrofoam plate covered with the remains of a meal.

"Oh, it's useless," Mrs. Jensen said, crying. "That's only what Robert had for lunch. This is just a waste of time."

"I agree," Trooper Yeager said grimly. "This

may be your jurisdiction, Callahan, but — "

"Did Robert spill any on his shirt?" Patricia asked.

Mrs. Jensen stared at her, and then stopped crying for a minute. "Actually, he *did*. Is that what your dog smelled?"

Gregory nodded. "He's not sure what we want him to find. Could you bring us some more clothes, so he'll know that we're looking for *Robert*, not food?"

For the first time, there was some hope in Mrs. Jensen's expression. She hurried into the laundry room and came out with more clothes. Gregory held each piece of clothing in turn up to his dog's nose.

"Find the boy, Santa Paws!" he said. "Find the little boy!"

The dog cocked his head.

"*Fetch* the little boy," Patricia said. "We want you to fetch the little boy for us."

The dog bounded to his feet. He *definitely* knew the word "fetch!" He ran over to the door, and barked twice. Once he was outside, he began sniffing around the steps and the driveway. There were traces of the very same human scent all over the yard, but some were more recent than others. He sniffed the ground, and then the air, trying to find the freshest one. The icy rain was washing away some of the smells — and also falling in his eyes — but he just kept sniffing. There it was, heading away from the house, only a couple of hours old! He barked and started along the trail.

A bright light beamed across the snow from the street, near one of the television vans. Apparently, a cameraperson was trying to film the search. Uncle Steve quickly sent two officers over to order the cameras turned off for the time being. He didn't want anything to distract Santa Paws right now.

The dog followed the trail as closely as he could, ignoring all of the chaos around him. It was strange, because the scent went back and forth and around in circles, with no logical pattern. But Santa Paws doggedly just kept following his nose.

"What kind of crazy path is *that*?" Trooper Yeager grumbled.

"Have you ever seen a two-year-old run around before?" Mrs. Callahan asked.

Trooper Yeager thought about that, and then closed his mouth.

The trail started leading downhill, towards the thickest part of the woods. Because of the rain, everyone was slipping and sliding on the icy grass. Since he had trouble moving quickly on his cane, and also had to run the search, Uncle Steve limped back to the command post. Mrs. Jensen had gone to get her husband, who was off searching in another sector.

Santa Paws veered back and forth, snuffling the ground every so often, but mostly keeping his nose in the air as he tracked the scent. He trotted into the forest, winding between trees in a crooked and unpredictable route.

"We searched this whole area already," one of the nearby police officers said softly. "It's clean."

"Shhh," someone else hissed. "The dog seems to know what he's doing."

Santa Paws plunged forward through the underbrush, and then he paused. He sniffed the air, turning his head from side to side. Then he pushed on deeper into the woods.

Ahead, there was a sound of water rushing. He followed the scent in that same direction, and soon came across a stream with a fairly strong current. He put his nose to the ground at the water's edge and inhaled deeply. The scent seemed to stop at the stream. Santa Paws sat down for a minute, not sure why he had lost the trail. How could it be there one second, and gone the next?

Gregory patted his head. "Come on, pal, you can do it. Find Robert!"

"If that poor little boy fell in the water, who knows how far it could have carried him downstream," Trooper Yeager said, his eyes dark with concern. "Tell the dog to hurry."

Just then, Santa Paws got up, and began to run back and forth along the side of the stream. He explored each direction, but was still stumped.

The little boy's scent had disappeared!

3

Now Trooper Yeager took charge. "All right, we don't have a minute to lose." He flicked on his walkie-talkie. "I want all the units in Sectors One through Three to assemble near the stream. We need some more manpower down here."

Suddenly, the dog's ears went up. Santa Paws turned his head to one side, and then jumped into the water. It was very cold, but he didn't even flinch as he started splashing his way downstream. He had picked up the scent again!

Gregory went into the water right after him, yelping when the freezing liquid bit into his legs. Patricia was only a couple of steps behind them. There were rocks under the water, and they both had a hard time keeping their balance. Their parents and all of the officers and volunteers followed closely.

Santa Paws stopped about ten feet away, and stuck his head into something below the overhanging bank. Then he turned towards Gregory and Patricia, and barked triumphantly.

"He found him, wow!" Gregory said. "What a good dog!"

Santa Paws barked, and wagged his tail as hard as he could. He was always so happy when they called him a good dog!

"Wait a minute," Mrs. Callahan called, as she and the others tried to catch up. "Why don't you two stay there, and let your father and me go first."

Gregory was already crouching down underneath the bank. In the dim light from the flashlights upstream, he could see the outline of a drainage pipe. The pipe was less than a foot and a half wide — too small for a normal person to fit through. But by squinting his eyes, he could just barely make out the shape of a small figure lying down about eight feet inside. The sight horrified him so much that he leaped backwards and ended up sitting in the water.

"Oh, no, we're too late," he gasped. "He's not moving!"

Patricia gulped, but pushed past him to see for herself. She was carrying a small penlight, which she flashed into the pipe. Then, she smiled.

"Relax, Greg," she said. "It's called *sleeping*."

Gregory picked himself up, not even noticing that he had gotten completely soaked. "Are you sure? Is he okay?"

Patricia nodded. "Absolutely. I can see him breathing."

More people were crowding around now, and inside the pipe, Robert woke up when he heard the commotion. He started crying when he saw all the unfamiliar faces, and then he retreated further into the pipe. Everyone seemed to be talking at once, which must have confused the little boy even more.

"Give us some room, kids, okay?" one of the Oceanport police officers asked. "We have to get him out of there."

Gregory and Patricia politely stepped aside. Santa Paws stood in between them, panting a little, but still wagging his tail.

"Good boy," Gregory said, resting his gloved hand on his dog's head. "You're very, *very* good."

Santa Paws wagged his tail. Yay! Gregory thought he was good!

"You're very, very *smart*," Patricia said, also patting him.

And Patricia thought he was smart! "Smart" was a good word, too!

"Come on, Robert," the Oceanport officer was saying in a soothing voice, as he extended one arm into the pipe. "Time to go home and see Mommy and Daddy."

Robert cried, and crawled further away, almost out of sight.

One of the paramedics tried next, but she

didn't have any luck, either. "He's too far in there," she said, standing up in the creek. "We're going to need the rescue equipment.

The diameter of the pipe was tiny, but — "Maybe I can fit inside," Gregory offered shyly.

"It's worth a shot," the paramedic said, and gave him a boost up.

Gregory did his best, but his shoulders were just too wide for him to be able to squeeze through. If he managed to climb in at all, he would get stuck immediately.

"All right," Trooper Yeager said from his position in the middle of the stream. "Let's get his parents down here, have them coax him out. Find out what sectors they're in. Come on, snap it up, people!"

A couple of officers hurried off to locate ropes and anything else they might need, while two others went to locate the Jensens. The total search area was very large, and they could be almost *anywhere*.

Patricia watched all of the excitement for a minute, and then let out her breath. "I'm a lot thinner than you are," she said to Gregory.

"Yeah," he conceded, "but you get way scared in small places."

Patricia nodded, but shrugged off her jacket and handed it to him. She *hated* small places. To make sure she would be as slender as possible, she took off her sweater and turtleneck, too.

That left her standing in the freezing rain in nothing but a T-shirt, as well as her jeans and hiking boots, and she started shivering.

"Patricia, put your jacket right back on," Mrs. Callahan said sharply. "The rescue squad will be able to get him out. They're trained for this."

Patricia looked at her. "Would you want them to come digging after one of *us* with ropes and chainsaws and all? If you could avoid it? And would you want to *wait* for all of that, if you didn't have to?"

Her mother hesitated just long enough for Patricia to know she had won the argument. So, Patricia went over and tapped Trooper Yeager on the arm.

He glanced down, looking annoyed, since he was passing some official communications along over his walkie-talkie. "Look, thanks, kid, your dog did a great job. But, we're really busy now, okay?"

"I can fit in there," Patricia said. "My brother's bigger than I am."

Trooper Yeager started to disagree, but then looked her over more carefully. "You know what, kid, you're right. You probably *can*." He glanced at Mr. and Mrs. Callahan. "It okay with you if we give it a go?"

Mr. and Mrs. Callahan nodded reluctantly.

"Why don't we wait for the ropes, at least," Mr. Callahan said. "And then — "

"Don't worry, Dad, I can fit," Patricia said, sounding very confident. "It'll only take a minute."

One of the paramedics taped a small flashlight to Patricia's forearm, so that she would be able to see where she was going, but still have her hands free. Then Patricia bent down and peered inside the tiny pipe.

"Whoa," she said, her voice trembling a little. "That's even smaller than an MRI!"

"Patricia — " Her father started, his voice worried.

But before she could let herself change her mind, Patricia pulled in another deep breath and started crawling into the pipe. It might make more sense to wait for the rescue crew — but, well, she had never exactly been a patient person. There wasn't much room to spare, and she could just barely guide herself forward. Her shoulders and hips were jammed against the cold cement on either side, but she forced herself not to think about how confined she was. Once she had gone about ten feet, she angled her arm so the flashlight wouldn't shine right in Robert's eyes. The little boy was so surprised to see someone coming in after him that he had stopped crying.

"Babysitter?" he asked, his voice sounding weak from being outside in the cold so long. His nose was running pretty badly, too.

The sides of the pipe seemed to be pressing even more tightly around her, and for a second, Patricia was afraid she wouldn't be able to breathe. But she forced a smile, so that Robert wouldn't be scared. Or, at any rate, not as scared as *she* was.

"Y-yeah, sometimes I'm a babysitter," she said. "Your mommy and daddy are waiting outside." She *hoped*. "Want to take my hand, so we can go see them?"

Robert's face lit up. "Mommy and Daddy?!"

"Robert?" a woman's voice called, her voice echoing through the pipe. To Patricia's relief, it sounded like Mrs. Jensen. "Bobby, please come here!"

"Mommy!" Robert said with a big smile. He laughed, and clapped his hands together a few times. "Where's Mommy?"

"She's right outside." Patricia reached out again. "Take my hand, okay? Then we can go see your mommy." Using her foot for leverage, she pushed herself forward a few more inches, and Robert crawled over to meet her. His hand was terribly cold, and she could see that his teeth were chattering. "Okay, good," she said, making sure her voice sounded hearty. "Come on."

It was slow going, but she gradually made her way backwards towards the opening of the pipe, clutching Robert's hand the entire time. If he pulled away, she might have to stay in here even longer! Then her feet hit a pile of old leaves, and she lost her momentum. Her legs kept slipping, and she couldn't get her free hand in position to help push them past the leaves. As far as she could tell, they were trapped!

"Dad, help!" she shouted, trying not to panic. "Dad! I think I'm stuck."

"It's okay, Patricia, we're going to get you out," Mr. Callahan said from the end of the pipe.

She could tell that he was reaching for them, but they were still too far inside.

"Patricia, you just hang on, okay?" he said. "They're coming with the ropes right now."

Patricia swallowed, suddenly feeling as though the pipe was squeezing against her with so much force that it was compressing her lungs. This maybe hadn't been a very good plan, after all. It was hard to get her breath, and she closed her eyes, forcing herself to count to ten. Twenty. Thirty. Robert must have sensed her fear, because he started crying again.

"Want to go *home*," he sobbed. "Want to go home *now*."

"You and me both," Patricia said shakily, doing her best to smile at him. She kicked at the leaves as hard as she could, but now wasn't sure if she could go forward *or* backwards. Where were the ropes? What was taking so long? Not that she was on the verge of hysteria or anything — but they really did seem to be stuck. Helpless. *Trapped.*

Could she stand it in here for another few minutes? Another few *seconds*? Forget the rescue squad — it was time to call in the cavalry. "Santa Paws!" she yelled. "Help!"

She heard him bark, and then he leaped out of the stream and squirmed inside the narrow space. It seemed impossible for such a big dog to be able to fit into the pipe, but he stubbornly wormed his way towards them. Then he grabbed her boot with his teeth and tugged her a few inches closer to safety, through the musty leaves.

"Good boy," Patricia said, some of her panic fading. If anyone could get her out of here, Santa Paws could. "You can do it, boy!"

Santa Paws kept pulling, until her boot came right off. He seemed surprised, but then dropped it and began wriggling towards her again. This time, he dug his teeth into her jeans leg and tugged with all of his might. As she hung onto Robert, Santa Paws dragged both of them all the way to the pipe's opening before scrambling free. He landed in the stream with a big splash, and barked a few times.

Working together, Mr. Callahan and Trooper Yeager carefully eased Patricia and Robert the rest of the way out. Mrs. Jensen quickly grabbed her son into a tight hug, while she cried and tried to thank everyone at once. Just then, Mr. Jensen, who had been off searching in the furthest sector, came running towards them. He was also crying, and hugged his wife and son as hard as he could.

"Thank you so much," Mrs. Jensen said over and over. "Thank you, you're all so wonderful! Thank you!"

Once again, Santa Paws had saved the day!

4

Everyone took turns shaking hands, patting Santa Paws, and congratulating one another. The icy rain was now just plain sleet, but no one even noticed. With Robert alive and well — and back where he belonged, the cold winter storm didn't seem very important. As soon as he got a chance, Santa Paws retrieved Patricia's sopping wet boot from where it had fallen in the creek and brought it to her.

"*You* are a really good dog," she said, and gave him a big hug. She was feeling much better now that she was outside — and her mother had helped her put her sweater and coat back on. If Robert ever got lost again, she hoped that he would pick a much *larger* tunnel next time.

"He's a *great* dog," Gregory agreed.

"For a house pet," Patricia said, and they both laughed quietly.

Santa Paws let his tail wave merrily. The cheerful mood of celebration surrounding them was contagious. It was almost like being at a party!

There were glaring camera lights everywhere, and lots of noise. Some of the television news crews had come down to film the joyful reunion of parents and toddler. The woods and stream were so crowded that it made everything seem that much more hectic and confusing. Although Robert seemed to be fine, his parents and the paramedics were taking him to a waiting ambulance. He would be whisked off to the hospital for a full checkup, just to make sure that he had survived his ordeal without any problems.

The Callahans and Santa Paws waded out of the water and climbed up the slippery slope through the woods. Now that the command post was being dismantled, Uncle Steve came to meet them. He was moving cautiously on his cane, but he had a huge grin on his face.

"Pretty outstanding work," he said cheerfully. "Any of you want to be deputized?"

Patricia thought about that. "Would we be given full arrest powers, and everything?"

"Truth is, all *I* really want is some supper," Gregory said.

Now Patricia realized that she was hungry, too. "Hey, that's right! We never had dinner!"

Both of their parents looked guilty. By now, their long-forgotten spaghetti would be too cold and stale to eat.

"Okay if we head home?" Mr. Callahan asked his little brother. "Fix them some dinner?"

"Absolutely," Uncle Steve said. "If we're lucky, you can escape the press, too."

But, he had spoken too soon. Since the ambulance holding the Jensens was pulling away now, most of the reporters swarmed over to shout questions at the Callahans. In the meantime, the cameras were all focusing on Santa Paws. This turned out to be rather poor timing, since he had just stopped to lift his leg against a tree.

"Film at eleven," Patricia muttered to Gregory, and they both laughed.

"What's it like to own a hero dog?" one reporter asked.

"Can you tell us how he knew where to find the little boy?" another one wanted to know.

"Is it true that he dove into a well, and saved the Jensen boy from drowning?" a third chimed in.

Mrs. Callahan raised her hands for silence. "I'm sorry," she said, with the particularly authoritative and dismissive tone that only platoon sergeants — and longtime teachers — knew how to use effectively. Nuns could sometimes do it, too. "But right now, we need to get our children home, and fed, and into some dry clothes. I'm sure Sergeant Callahan will be happy to answer any questions you have."

Uncle Steven grinned wryly. "Oh, yeah. Delighted." He summoned a few Oceanport officers over. "Clear a path, and escort my brother and his family to their car, okay?"

"Could we at least interview the *dog*?" one particularly persistent reporter asked plaintively.

Gregory leaned over to Patricia. "His — how you say in English? — verbal skills are not so good, no?"

Patricia gave him an affectionate shove. "You're an idiot, Greg, you know that?"

He nodded. "Well, yeah — since you tell me all the time."

Santa Paws let out a happy bark, and nudged Gregory's leg with his muzzle. Roughhousing was one of his favorite ways to spend time. If they wrestled here, they would be able to get nice and muddy, too!

"Could he just *pose* for a minute?" a cameraman asked.

Mr. Callahan rolled his eyes, but told Santa Paws to sit.

Santa Paws promptly sat down, as the cameras swung in his direction. He was blinded by all of the lights, and instinctively raised one paw. The reporters were thrilled, since it was the sort of thing Lassie would have done. His coat was still soaked from running around in the stream, and he stood up to shake off as much of the water as he could. Then he sneezed, looked surprised, and sneezed again. The reporters found this less exciting, but kept filming, anyway.

Gregory, Patricia, and their mother were already in the car by now. Santa Paws saw the open door and raced over to leap inside. It was too cold out in the sleet! Mr. Callahan quickly got into the driver's seat and started the car.

As they drove away, Gregory and Patricia watched the press turn around and move to surround Uncle Steve, instead. He seemed as blinded by the lights as Santa Paws had been.

"You know, tonight was a really weird night," Patricia said thoughtfully. "I mean, even weirder than usual."

Since it was hard to disagree with that, everyone else in the car nodded.

"Hey! Can we get pizza?" Gregory asked.

"Sure," Mr. Callahan said. "You can have anything you want. I'll drop you all off at home, and then I'll head back out. You want some ice cream, too?"

Gregory and Patricia nodded enthusiastically. They were very fond of ice cream.

Since they were obviously all happy, Santa Paws thumped his tail against the backseat. Their rainy, outdoor walk in the woods tonight had been much too congested and noisy for his taste, but he had still had a good time. He *liked* all of the adventures he and the Callahans had together, even if he didn't always understand what was going on. As far as he was concerned, he had the best family anywhere. And maybe there would even be some meatballs left, when they got home! Yay!

"How about you, Santa Paws?" Mr. Callahan asked, glancing at him in the rearview mirror. "Would you like an *extra*-large box of Milk-Bones?"

The dog's ears shot up, and his tail wagged even harder. Mr. Callahan had just said his favorite word in the whole world.

Milk-Bones!

Little Robert Jensen's dramatic rescue was the top story on all of the local newscasts that night. Each station used a different tag line, from "Hero Dog!" to "Santa Paws Saves the Day!" to "North Shore Nail-biter." One channel even played a few bars from the Underdog theme when they flashed Santa Paws' picture across the screen. Patricia was appalled by how wet and bedraggled she appeared on camera, which Gregory found very entertaining. His filmed image was just as disheveled, but he was pleased, because he thought it kind of made him look like an action hero. Mr. and Mrs. Callahan just kept shaking their heads, although they laughed when they watched Uncle Steve unenthusiastically reading the police department's official statement aloud. Uncle Steve liked *police work*, not public relations.

Throughout all of this, Santa Paws just sprawled on the rug in front of the fireplace and chewed energetically on the rawhide bone Mr. Callahan had brought home as a special prize for him. It was fun! His coat was damp, because right after Patricia and Gregory took baths, Mrs. Callahan gave him one, too. But, the fire in the fireplace was so nice and hot that it was helping him dry off. He wasn't cold at all anymore. And soon, it would be time for everyone to go upstairs to sleep. That would be fun, too!

The next day was Saturday, and it was exactly a week before Christmas. Mrs. Callahan still had a little bit of shopping left to do, and she decided to go to the mall. Patricia, Gregory, and Santa Paws piled into the car with her. They weren't planning to be gone very long, so Mrs. Callahan thought it would be just fine to bring Santa Paws along. It also wasn't very cold, so he would be perfectly comfortable waiting in the car. Mr. Callahan always said the mall made him too anxious, so he was staying home to blare Frank Sinatra CDs, and work on his new novel. In exactly that order, the rest of them suspected.

As they drove through the streets of Oceanport, almost everyone they passed waved and shouted things like "Way to go, Santa Paws!".

The people in cars all beeped their horns, too. The entire town must have seen the late newscasts, or else read the morning edition of the local newspaper. Now they wanted to congratulate their local celebrity. Santa Paws wasn't sure why the people were being so friendly, but it made him feel good.

Patricia slouched down in the front seat, and pulled her Red Sox cap over her eyes. She was still self-conscious about how silly she had looked on television. "I wish this could all be a little more low-profile," she grumbled.

Gregory grinned, and slung his arm around his dog. "Hey, it's tough living with a superstar."

Santa Paws leaned over to lick his face, and then turned to look out the window some more. For him, the best part about riding in cars was watching all of the scenery speed by.

The mall was very crowded, and they had to park in one of the furthest lots.

"Sure you can walk this far," Gregory teased his sister, "or should we send a special cart back for you?"

"Hey, when it comes to being a big baby, *you're* the one who — " Patricia began.

"No wrangling," Mrs. Callahan said instantly. "It's going to be hectic enough in there without the two of you fighting the whole time."

Patricia looked innocent. "Us? Fight?"

"Never happen," Gregory agreed.

"That's more like it," their mother said. "Now, come on. The sooner we go in there, the sooner we'll be finished."

Gregory lowered each of the back windows partway, and reached through the closest opening to pat Santa Paws on the head. "Be a good dog, boy. Guard the car!"

Santa Paws barked once, and wagged his tail. Then he settled against the backseat to wait for them to come back. He hoped that it wouldn't take too long.

Once they were out of sight, he snuck up into the front seat. The view was much better from there. He lounged on the driver's side, resting his paw on the steering wheel for balance.

A young man walking by gasped. "Look at that!" he said to his girlfriend. "He can even *drive*."

"Wow," the girl said, and shook her head with admiration. Was there *anything* the magical Santa Paws couldn't do? He had to be the smartest dog who had ever existed.

Santa Paws sat in the driver's seat for what seemed like a very long time. Then he decided he needed some fresh air, and he vaulted into the back again to stick his nose out the window. For variety, he jumped over into the far cargo area, too. But the roof of the car was too low for him to be able to stand up comfortably, so he returned to the backseat. Now what?

Oh, right. Fresh air. He stuck his nose out as far as he could, and breathed deeply. Because they were in a parking lot, he mostly just smelled gasoline, and exhaust, and other automobile smells. There was a Burger King nearby, and if he concentrated, he could pick out the odors of grease, french fries, and hamburgers. Well, that was more like it!

He sniffed and sniffed, until he got tired. Then he sat down to decide what to do next. Should he jump back in the front? No, he had already *done* that. Had he had a nap yet? He thought hard, but he couldn't remember. Besides, he wasn't *that* tired. He yawned a few times, just in case, but he was still wide awake. In fact, he was bored! Would the Callahans *ever* come back? This was *awful*.

Feeling very unhappy, Santa Paws flung himself down onto the seat and lay there miserably for a minute. He was so bored, and so lonely. How long had they been gone? It felt like hours. Years, even. He sighed loudly, and even whimpered once. He just felt horrible being alone like this. But, wait — he smelled a tennis ball! Where was it? He snuffled around the floor of the car until he located his quarry buried under the front seat on the passenger's side. It was jammed between an old box of Kleenex and a first aid kit. There were some maps blocking his way, too.

Using his front paw, he managed to dig the

ball out. The faded yellow cover was battered, and it smelled faintly of the ocean. Maybe he and Gregory had been playing fetch at the beach one time? It was hard to remember. Anyway, now he had a ball. He would *never* be bored now!

He shook his head from side to side, growling playfully, and pretending to defeat the ball in an epic battle. And — he won! The ball was completely at his mercy. What a good game! Now he stretched across the backseat, and dropped the ball between his front paws so he could admire it. The cover tasted too salty when he chewed it, so he let the ball fall from his mouth and land in front of him again. *This* was a good game, too!

So he spent a while picking the ball up, dropping it, and then repeating the cycle. Finally the ball bounced away and rolled under the front seat again. Santa Paws tried to retrieve it, but this time, the ball was too far underneath for him to reach. It was gone! No more ball! No more *fun*. Would Gregory come back and find it for him? The dog barked frantically, but he couldn't see his family, or even smell them.

He slumped down, feeling very sorry for himself. He was even too unhappy to take a nap. If *only* they would come back. He wanted his ball, he wanted a snack, and he wanted his family. Why were they taking so long?

Except that he actually *was* feeling a little sleepy. And his back itched. The itch was in one of the difficult spots to reach, and he had to twist his body in several directions before he could extend his paw to scratch just the right spot. *Ahhh.* Yes. While he was at it, he scratched up behind his left ear, too.

Now he felt *much* more comfortable. It was time for a little nap. He yawned widely, turned around three times on the seat, and plopped down. But the metal edge of a seatbelt buckle was pressing right against his ribs. Ow! So, he got up, repeated his three turns, and made sure he landed in a different spot this time.

Perfect! Now he could enjoy a nice, peaceful rest.

Santa Paws was sleeping soundly, when he suddenly sensed that something was wrong. He opened his eyes, not sure what had woken him up. Voices. Unfamiliar, coarse voices. There were people right by the car! *Strangers!*

His eyes flew open, and he leaped to his feet. Just as he started barking, a metal crowbar smashed against the window. The glass broke and showered all over him. These were bad, bad people. They were hurting the car! Just as he lunged towards them to defend the station wagon, the man in front shoved a thick wet cloth at him. The cloth was dripping with some sort of liquid and it smelled just terrible. His nose was filled with a sharp, unpleasant scent, like medicine at the vet's office.

For some reason, the overpowering smell made him feel very dizzy. He tried to bark and growl, but he could feel his legs crumpling. What was happening? Why did he feel so sick? The people — it was two mean-looking men — were opening the door now and reaching for him. Santa Paws gathered all of his strength to try and attack them, but his muscles didn't want to work. The scent on the cloth was just too strong, and all of a sudden, he fainted.

"Okay, good," one of the men said. "He won't give us any trouble now."

"We better hurry, Chuck," the other man said.

"Yeah, yeah, yeah," the first one, Chuck, answered. "Just get in the van and keep the motor running." The men were brothers, and their names were Chuck and Eddie Hawthorne. Chuck was the older of the two, but Eddie was both fatter — and meaner.

While Eddie got into the old grey van next to the car, Chuck reached into his jacket pocket. He took out a heavy leather muzzle and buckled it around the dog's nose and head. This was one dog who wouldn't try biting *him* again! Then, he unfastened Santa Paws' collar and let it fall cruelly onto the backseat.

"Hurry up!" Eddie yelled. "Before someone comes!"

Chuck lifted up the unconscious dog, grunting with the effort. This dumb dog was *heavy*. But he was worth a lot of money, and he and Eddie were going to get rich from this caper! The Hawthornes had grown up in a nearby town, and they had been in trouble with the law on and off for years. Mostly, they robbed and burglarized, although sometimes they liked to pass bad checks and do forgery, too. This time, they had been hired to steal the famous dog, Santa Paws, by a rich, greedy man down in New Jersey who was going to buy the dog and keep him as part of his collection of exotic animals. Fifty thousand dollars! Chuck and Eddie had never even seen money like that, and in a few hours, it would be theirs! For the two thieves, it was going to be a very profitable Christmas!

Chuck hauled the dog over to the van and dumped him inside. Then he climbed in after him, and slammed the door.

"Let's scram!" he ordered.

Eddie put his foot on the gas, and the van squealed across the parking lot. The cement was icy, and they skidded a little, but Eddie got the van under control. There was lots of traffic, and it made Eddie very impatient to have to wait in line. He muttered, and grumbled, and tapped on the steering wheel. Then he cut off two cars and steered the van away from the mall, going the wrong way through the entrance, instead of using the exit. He almost hit a minivan crowded with holiday shoppers, but he just laughed and drove faster. Along with their many other faults, the Hawthorne boys were really bad drivers, too. Soon, they would be on the highway and headed for New Jersey.

They had just pulled off the best robbery of their lives!

5

When they had finally finished their shopping, the Callahans came outside, loaded down with bags. The lines at the cash registers had seemed endless, and the whole excursion had taken much longer than Mrs. Callahan had expected. The sun was just going down, and a brisk winter wind was blowing. The sky had completely clouded over, and it felt as though it might begin snowing at any moment.

"I hope poor Santa Paws isn't too cold," she said, as they crossed the parking lot. "If I'd known we would be stuck in there for such a long time, I really wouldn't have let him come."

Gregory looked worried. "It *is* a lot colder than it was before. You think he's okay?"

"I'm sure he's fine," Mrs. Callahan said quickly. "His fur is nice and thick this time of year."

As they approached their station wagon, they could see a small crowd gathered around the car.

Patricia shook her head in disgust. "Boy, sometimes he must get really tired of all this attention."

"He's a dog," Gregory pointed out. "Dogs love attention."

Just then, an Oceanport police car pulled up near the crowd, and two officers got out. At a distance, it appeared to be Officers Bronkowski and Lee. Because of Uncle Steve, the Callahans knew just about everyone in the department pretty well. Officer Lee was speaking into his radio, while Officer Bronkowski was walking over to the station wagon. She had her flashlight out and seemed to be peering inside the back windows.

"Well, good," Patricia said. She was always pleased to see police officers on the scene. On *any* scene. It made life much more orderly. "We definitely need some crowd control here."

Then they heard a siren and saw a red flashing light as another squad car came roaring into the parking lot.

"Hey," Gregory said nervously. "They're acting like something's *wrong*."

Now, from a distance, they could hear another siren approaching.

"Hey," Gregory said again, as he started to get scared. The police cars wouldn't be using their sirens if they were just on a routine patrol of the mall.

Mrs. Callahan abruptly put her shopping bags down. "Would you two mind watching these for a minute? I'll be right back."

Patricia and Gregory looked at each other with wide eyes. Yeah, they minded! Something bad had obviously happened, and they didn't want to wait all the way over here before they found out what it was.

"Mom," Patricia started, uneasily.

"Just wait here!" Mrs. Callahan said, her voice sounding almost — fierce.

Their mother rarely got angry at them, and so Patricia and Gregory didn't argue. They just stood quietly by the shopping bags while Mrs. Callahan strode swiftly over to Officer Lee. In fact, she was walking so fast that she was practically running! She started talking to him, and then looked stunned by whatever he had told her. She pushed her way through the crowd, and joined Officer Bronkowski by the car.

"It's Santa Paws," Patricia said, practically whispering. "Something must have happened to Santa Paws."

"You think he *bit* someone?" Gregory asked, horrified. That was the worst thing he could imagine, because he knew his dog would never hurt anyone. Even if they were teasing him. But, why else would the police have come?

Patricia shook her head, feeling herself start

to tremble. She realized now that her mother wasn't angry — she was *scared*. That must be why she had spoken to them so sharply.

Gregory let his packages fall on the cement with a crash, even though a couple of them were fragile. "If it's about Santa Paws, I'm not waiting over here. *No way*."

Patricia grabbed his arm to pull him back. "Wait, Greg. Mom said — "

He shook her hand off roughly. "Since when do *you* do everything you're told? Leave me alone! I'm going over there."

The third squad car had arrived, and Uncle Steve and his lieutenant climbed out. Both men looked very solemn.

Patricia knew that when law enforcement *supervisors* showed up, that meant that things were serious. "Okay," she said, making up her mind. "Come on." She bent to gather up a few of her mother's bags, adding them to her own load. "Grab as many of the packages as you can."

Mutely, Gregory nodded, and they both hurried over to join the crowd of bystanders and police officers.

"What happened, Uncle Steve?" Gregory asked, able to feel his heart pounding inside his chest.

Uncle Steve turned away from the station wagon, carefully using his cane for balance. "We, uh — " He stopped. "We're trying to figure that out, Greg. Don't worry."

Gregory and Patricia stared at him. Had he lost his mind? How could they possibly *not* worry?

"I'll tell you what happened!" a boy in the crowd volunteered. "Someone stole Santa Paws!"

"Yeah, we saw it!" his friend said eagerly. "Two creepy men in a van! That's why we called the police!"

Unable to believe it, Gregory ran forward to see for himself.

"Don't!" Patricia ordered, as he reached out to open the back door. "There might be fingerprints!"

Gregory hesitated, his hand halfway to the door handle.

"She's right," Officer Bronkowski said. "Please don't touch anything, okay, Gregory? We're waiting for the crime scene unit to get here."

Gregory looked at the shattered windows, and gulped back tears. How could a "crime scene" involve *his* dog? "I-is there any blood? Did they hurt him?"

Mrs. Callahan put her arm around him. "No, they wouldn't hurt him," she promised. "It's probably just someone playing a joke on us. Don't be scared."

"It was no joke!" the boy in the crowd said,

seeming to enjoy his status as an eyewitness. "He was unconscious! We *saw* it!"

Gregory started crying then, covering his eyes with his hand. People had stolen and injured his dog! How could he ever have imagined that Santa Paws might have bitten someone? This was *so much worse*.

Furious that the boy had upset her brother so much, Patricia whirled to face him. She recognized him, and she was pretty sure he went to the high school. "Why didn't you stop them?" she demanded. "If you saw them, why didn't you do anything?"

"We called the police," the boy said defensively.

"They were *big*," his friend added, equally defensive.

Patricia glared at them. "*I* would have tried to stop them."

Uncle Steve's boss, Lieutenant Trent, was saying something in a low voice, and Uncle Steve nodded. He called over two other officers.

"Move the crowd out of here, all right, guys?" he said. "I want a hundred-foot perimeter, minimum."

"Sure thing, Sarge," one of the officers said, while his partner nodded. Efficiently, they guided the curious onlookers away. In the meantime, Officer Lee was setting up some yellow crime scene tape to keep the area as clear as possible.

As other shoppers left the mall and saw all of the commotion, they came over to see what was going on. So even though the crowd was now further away, it was bigger than ever.

Gregory, Patricia, and their mother stood about ten feet from the station wagon and unhappily watched all of the activity. Gregory wasn't making a sound, but tears were still streaming down his cheeks. Mrs. Callahan kept blinking, and had a handful of tissues clutched in one hand. Patricia's expression was blank, and the only sign that she was upset was how tightly her arms were folded across her chest.

"Did they set up roadblocks?" she asked Uncle Steve. "Barricade the highways?"

He sighed. "It wouldn't help much, Patricia — we have absolutely no idea which way they might have gone, and too much time had passed before we got the word."

Patricia nodded, her face even more expressionless now.

"We put out a BOLO, though, to the entire state, and we're going to extend it throughout New England," he said. "BOLO" was police slang for "Be on the Lookout." "Every cop in the state is going to be watching for them."

The two boys who had witnessed the crime had been interviewed several times now, but they hadn't been able to provide any new details. The thieves had been heavy men in their thirties, and both had unkempt, dirty-blond hair. The witnesses were sure that the thieves had been driving a van, but one boy thought it was grey, and the other one was sure it had been tan. They both agreed that there hadn't been any markings on the side, and — to Patricia's disgust — neither had noticed the license plate.

Mrs. Callahan had borrowed Lieutenant Trent's cellphone, and called Mr. Callahan to tell him the terrible news. About fifteen minutes later, he arrived in the family's other car, which was an ancient Buick sedan.

By now, the crime scene unit — consisting of a specially-trained officer and two lab technicians — was searching for evidence. Two spotlights had been set up so that they could see in the darkness. The lights in the parking lot weren't bright enough. They had located several clues, including a still-damp crumpled bandanna on the ground. Apparently, it had been soaked with chloroform, a drug which would have made Santa Paws pass out. One of the technicians cautiously picked the cloth up with a pair of sterile tweezers and dropped it into an evidence bag. The other technician was using special powders and sprays to try and locate fingerprints on the car. Later on, the Callahans would all have to give fingerprint samples to be used for comparison. In fact, anyone who might have touched the car — from family friends to the gas station attendant

— would probably have to be printed, too.

"What are they doing?" Gregory asked shakily, as he saw a technician running some kind of ultraviolet light over the inside of the car.

Uncle Steve didn't answer until the technician straightened up and gave the "All Clear" sign. "That's a way for us to see if there's any blood or other fluids," he explained. "Now we can be pretty sure he isn't hurt, because they didn't find anything."

Gregory nodded, and rubbed a fresh tissue his mother had given him across his eyes. At least he knew his dog wasn't bleeding, but they *had* drugged him. What if they had given him an overdose? Or, what if he was allergic to the drug, and it made him sick? Or maybe they hit him, or — Gregory shook his head, hard. He didn't want to think about anything like that. He didn't want to think about anything at all. He just wanted his dog back, safe and sound.

Patricia didn't start crying until she saw a technician sealing Santa Paws' collar into a plastic bag. But once she started, she couldn't stop. She got into her father's Buick and buried her face in her arms, crying and crying.

"Look, there's nothing more you can do here," Uncle Steve said to Mr. and Mrs. Callahan. "Why don't you take them home, and I'll call you the second we hear anything. We're also going to send Officer Bronkowski along, to set up a recorder on your telephone. The Lieutenant wants all of your calls monitored."

Mrs. Callahan looked shocked. "You mean, you think they might demand a ransom?"

"I *hope* so," Uncle Steve said frankly. "It'll make them that much easier to catch."

Gregory and Patricia didn't want to leave, but they were so upset that they didn't really want to stay, either. They put on their seatbelts and sat silently in the backseat, while their parents loaded all of the shopping bags into the trunk. None of them really cared about Christmas right now, but there was no point in leaving all of their packages behind, either. Once the investigation had been completed, one of the police officers would bring the station wagon to a garage so that the shattered back window could be replaced.

The family rode in complete silence. Losing Santa Paws was so awful that there really wasn't anything to say. Gregory and Patricia just kept crying quietly, and their parents were blinking and swallowing a lot. Mr. Callahan even had to pull over once, to clean his glasses because they had fogged up.

Gregory couldn't help hoping that all of this had been a mistake, and Santa Paws would be waiting at the front door when they got home. He didn't believe that it would really happen, but he wished with all of his heart that it would.

But, when Mr. Callahan pulled into the driveway, the yard was empty, and no one was waiting at the door. The first thing Mrs. Callahan did was check the answering machine, but no one had called them. They weren't even any hangups. If there was going to be a ransom demand, it hadn't come yet.

Gregory and Patricia went straight upstairs to their rooms. They didn't want supper and they didn't want to talk.

The only thing they wanted was their dog.

In the meantime, the beastly brothers, Chuck and Eddie Hawthorne, were speeding along Interstate Route 95 in their van. Santa Paws was still unconscious on the floor in the back.

"We're going to be rich!" Eddie gloated. "Man, I can't believe how easy this was!"

"Watch your driving, you dope," Chuck warned him. "You wanna get pulled over for speeding, with the merchandise in the back?"

"Yeah, yeah, yeah," Eddie mumbled, but he slowed down to about sixty miles an hour.

"That's better," Chuck said, and greedily crammed some potato chips into his mouth. They had only driven about fifty miles, and he was already on his second bag.

Eddie, on the other hand, had a sweet tooth. So he had been chomping on Twinkies and candy bars, and slurping Cokes the whole way.

"How long will that dumb mutt be out?" he asked, with his mouth full of M&M's.

Chuck shrugged. "I dunno, I never done that before. Couple hours, maybe. He wakes up and gives us any grief, we'll just dose him again."

Eddie burped, and reached for a peanut butter cup next. "He better be able to last 'til we get to Jersey. I'm not cleaning up after him — or taking him on no walks, neither."

"Hey, for fifty thousand bucks, we can afford some paper towels," Chuck said, "know what I mean?"

Both men laughed raucously at that. They slapped each other five, and then Eddie stamped harder on the accelerator. They were getting close to the Rhode Island border, and the sooner they got out of Massachusetts, the better. With each passing mile, Oceanport slipped further and further behind them.

If the Hawthornes had their way, Santa Paws would never see his home — or his family — ever again!

6

As the evening wore on, Mr. and Mrs. Callahan kept waiting by the telephone, but it never rang. Officer Bronkowski had connected a special recorder to their answering machine, and stayed long enough to make sure they knew how to run it properly. That way, if the dognappers called, the Callahans would be able to keep a copy of the conversation. Instead of just using *69, Officer Bronkowski had also set up a tracer line, which was connected to the switchboard over at the station house. Someone would be monitoring that line around the clock, ready to trace the location of any calls that came in. If the criminals tried to make contact, the Oceanport police were ready and waiting to respond!

As soon as Uncle Steve's shift ended, he came over to keep Mr. and Mrs. Callahan company. His wife, Emily, and little daughter, Miranda, would have joined him, but Miranda was only two and she was already in bed for the night.

There didn't seem to be much to say, so the Callahans and Uncle Steve just sat at the kitchen table and quietly drank cup after cup of coffee. The ticking of the clock on the wall seemed very loud.

In the meantime, Gregory and Patricia were still upstairs in their rooms. They had both changed into their pajamas and climbed into bed. Gregory had turned his light out, and was holding their cat, Evelyn, while he cried. Every time he tried to stop, he would think about his poor dog, and start up all over again. Evelyn purred, trying to comfort him. She wasn't sure where Santa Paws was, but she knew there must be a bad reason that he hadn't come home from the shopping trip. She liked to pretend that she hated dogs, but actually, she loved her friend Santa Paws very much. She hoped that he would be home soon, and that everyone would stop crying.

Over in her bedroom, Patricia had her stereo headphones on, but she wasn't actually listening to anything. She just wanted to be left alone. She tried reading for a while, but she couldn't concentrate. So she gave up and stared at her ceiling instead. She had cried for a while, but now she was almost too sad to do it anymore. All she knew was that she had never felt worse in her life.

Earlier, their parents had come upstairs with supper trays for them, but they just weren't hungry. Gregory drank his milk, and Patricia ate a couple of bites of butterscotch pudding, but that was all.

At about nine o'clock, the telephone finally rang once, but it was only Aunt Emily, wanting to know if they had heard anything yet. After that, a series of calls came in from reporters wanting statements, but whoever answered would just respond with a polite "no comment" each time.

Upstairs, alone in their rooms, Gregory and Patricia both knew that it was going to be a very long — and lonely — night.

The robbers continued speeding towards New Jersey in their van. Santa Paws was still unconscious, although the chloroform was starting to wear off a little. Eddie just cruised along the turnpike in Connecticut, switching lanes constantly. He also liked to keep his headlights at the brightest setting, to annoy the other drivers.

"Hey, man, I'm getting hungry," he complained, after a while.

"Yeah, right," Chuck said scornfully. "Give me a break — you've been pigging out on candy for hours."

"So what?" Eddie pointed at a sign for an upcoming rest area. "Let's stop there. We need gas, anyway, and we can get some extra value meals."

Chuck didn't want to take any chances, but his stomach was growling, too. He had finished his last bag of chips back around New London. "Yeah, okay," he said reluctantly. "But anyone sees that mutt, and I'll pound you!"

"You pound me, and I'll pound you right back!" Eddie warned him.

"Just shut up, and make sure you don't miss the exit," Chuck said, not very impressed by the threat. Eddie was mean, but when it came to fighting, he was *slow*.

They were about to go past it, so Eddie cut across two lanes of traffic. Horns blared all around them, and he howled with laughter.

"Gotcha, you chumps!" he yelled at no one in particular. Then he swerved into the rest area parking lot, knocking over a trash can on the way. This made him laugh even harder.

"Park away from everyone else," Chuck instructed him.

"Like I don't know that?" Eddie asked. "What, do I look stupid?"

Chuck studied him for a minute, then nodded. "Yeah. As a matter of fact, you do. *Unusually* stupid."

"Takes one to know one!" Eddie said, and cracked up again.

Before they got out, Chuck took the precaution of tossing an oil-stained piece of canvas over the unconscious dog. That way, no one would be able to see anything suspicious, if they happened to look inside the windows.

Santa Paws was dimly aware that the van had stopped, but he felt too sick to open his eyes. His stomach seemed to be spinning in circles, and it was hard to breathe. He tried to sit up, but he was so weak that he immediately lost consciousness again. The drug was still too strong for him to overcome.

The Hawthornes returned with several lottery tickets and enough food for at least half a dozen people. Big Macs, McChickens, milkshakes, super-sized orders of fries — if it was on the menu, they had ordered it. Except, of course, for the dumb salads. The Hawthornes *hated* salad. The only vegetable they liked to eat was onions, and they didn't even like those unless they were raw.

The brothers ate their food, and burped, and ate some more.

Under the oily tarpaulin, Santa Paws vaguely sensed the rich scent of meat. He opened his eyes briefly, then let them flutter shut again. For the first time in his life, the smell of food was actually nauseating. He was still too dazed to bother wondering where he was, or what was happening. All he knew was that he felt very ill, and that he kept passing out.

And with that, he fainted again.

Back in Oceanport, Mr. and Mrs. Callahan were exhausted from the stress of waiting for the ransom phone call that never came. Uncle Steve was going to spend the night, so he and Mr. Callahan set up the sofa bed. Uncle Steve insisted he was only staying because they were family, but the Callahans knew he also wanted to make sure they had some police protection on the premises.

Once the sofa bed had been prepared, Mrs. Callahan turned on the television in the living room. The news was just starting, and their beloved dog's disappearance was the top story. Her eyes filled with tears, and she quickly flicked it off.

"I know you don't want to see that," Uncle Steve said, "but the more publicity this gets, the better. People will be keeping an eye out for him."

Mrs. Callahan nodded, although she didn't believe that publicity would help. In fact, if Santa Paws had never gotten any publicity in the first place, he wouldn't have become so famous that someone would want to steal him. She would never share her fears with her children, but she was terribly afraid that they were never going to see Santa Paws again.

Gregory had long since fallen into a restless sleep, but just then Patricia came slowly downstairs. Her hair needed brushing, and her eyes were red from crying.

"I heard the phone ringing before," she said, without much energy. She knew that if there had been any good news, her parents would have raced upstairs to share it. "Has anyone seen him, or — or anything?"

Her father shook his head. "I'm afraid not, Patty. I'm sorry."

That was the answer she had expected, but it was still devastating to hear. "Okay," she said dully, and turned to go back upstairs.

"Would you like something to eat?" her mother asked. "It might make you feel better."

"No, thank you," Patricia said, and trudged towards her bedroom.

Her mother followed her, so she could tuck her in for the night. But first, she gave her a big, warm hug.

"Lots of people are looking for him, Patricia," she said. "I'm sure we'll have good news tomorrow."

Since her mother was just trying to make her feel better, Patricia forced herself to smile.

"Try to get some sleep," Mrs. Callahan said

kindly. "We'll talk about everything in the morning."

Patricia nodded, and closed her eyes without another word.

After Mrs. Callahan turned out the light, she went across the hall to check on Gregory. When she walked over to his bed, he woke up.

"Did they find him?" he asked eagerly. "Is he okay?"

"I'm sorry, Greg, but not yet," his mother said. "I didn't mean to wake you up."

Gregory sagged back down against his pillows. He had been having a terrible nightmare that Santa Paws was lost in the middle of a big city, and that no matter where Gregory searched, he couldn't find him.

"He's never coming back, is he, Mom?" Gregory said, fighting back another bout of tears.

Mrs. Callahan sighed, and reached over to brush his hair back away from his forehead. "I don't know, Gregory," she answered honestly. "We just have to hope, and pray, that everything is going to be all right."

Gregory hoped that with all of his heart — but he didn't believe it for a minute.

The next time Santa Paws woke up, he was relieved to find that he was much less dizzy and lethargic. But it was still hard to breathe, and he was very confused. He seemed to be in some

70

kind of vehicle which kept starting and stopping, and he could hear two harsh male voices arguing. And the constant back and forth motion was upsetting his stomach again.

He couldn't seem to see, or move, or — what was happening? Where was he? He tried to bark, but found that his mouth would barely open. Something uncomfortable was tightly fastened around his muzzle. Was it a new collar? But why would it be around his mouth? He brought a paw up to try and dislodge the strange object, but he had no luck. He was about to panic and whimper, when the strong human stench coming from the front seat made something in his memory flicker.

Now he remembered! It was the bad people! Had they taken him away in the Callahans' car? He must be in a car, because he could feel it moving, even though their progress seemed to be very herky-jerky. One minute, the car would be rolling forward, and the next, they would slam to a stop.

Santa Paws sniffed the air some more, trying to make sense of his surroundings. This wasn't his family's car, because everything smelled unfamiliar. Motor oil, car exhaust, and what seemed to be months' worth of fast food garbage. He must be in a car that belonged to the bad people, and they were taking him somewhere. Wondering if they might be driving him to the Callahans' house, he felt a flash of hope. But why was it taking so long? His limbs felt so stiff that he must have been lying on this cold metal flooring for *hours*.

Even though it was dark, he could tell that a coarse cloth which reeked of motor oil and axle grease was covering him. When the vehicle came to an especially short stop, the cloth slid off to one side and his head was exposed. The air inside the van wasn't very fresh, but it was much easier to breathe without being smothered by that suffocating canvas.

Where were Gregory and Patricia? Did they know where he was? Would they be coming to get him soon? What if the bad people had hurt them! He had to find them, right away! Keeping his family safe was the most important duty in the world!

He was going to jump up, but decided to stay where he was. Maybe he should try to figure out what the bad people were doing, first. Plus, what if they tried to make him smell that nasty medicine stuff again? He still felt very sick, and didn't want them to do anything to make him faint again. Fainting was too scary. Besides, the longer he stayed here quietly, the more strength he could feel slowly flowing back into his muscles.

Even so, it would be nice to jump up and bite both of the bad people, as hard as he could!

"You are so stupid," Chuck was complaining.

The van moved forward, then stopped abruptly, yet again.

"I am not," Eddie said, with a distinct whine in his voice. "Like it's my fault there's traffic? You think I'm, like, the Road God?"

Chuck shook his head with disgust as he stared at what looked like several miles' worth of an endless traffic jam ahead of them. At the moment, the highway resembled a parking lot more than anything else. "More like the Road *Hog*," Chuck said. "I *told* you to take the Merritt Parkway. But, did you listen to me? No. Do you *ever* listen to me? No. And now, look at this mess! We're going to be here for hours, and it's all your fault!"

"Yeah, well, the Merritt Parkway's too curvy," Eddie said, in his own defense. "And there's all those dumb trees. It doesn't have no McDonald's or nothing, neither."

"It *also* doesn't have any traffic," Chuck reminded him.

"I don't like parkways," Eddie said stubbornly. "And that one keeps changing names all the time. First, it's like, the Hutchinson, and then the Sawmill, and — it's just too hard. I figured, we stay on 95, and boom! Right over the George Washington Bridge, and then just another hour until we get our fifty thousand bucks. Then, hello, Atlantic City!"

"Look around, man," Chuck said, gesturing at

the cars surrounding them. The other drivers were also impatient, and many of them were leaning on their horns. "This is the Cross-*Bronx* Expressway, you bozo. You know what that means? We're *in* the Bronx! You know how dangerous that is?" Since he was from a small town, *anything* about a big city was frightening to him, even though the Bronx was really a very nice place.

"I'm not scared of nothing!" Eddie bragged. "Anyways, doncha read the paper? New York's got no crime anymore." Then he looked thoughtful. "Maybe we should move here. There must be good pickings, these days."

"Not me. City criminals got no class. Not like us." Then Chuck scowled and put his seatbelt on as his brother jammed on the brakes still one more time. "Watch where you're going, moron!"

"I am watching," Eddie insisted. "These dumb New Yorkers just don't know how to drive."

"Look who's talking," Chuck said.

Eddie slammed the van into "Park" so unexpectedly that they were almost rear-ended by the car behind them. "Okay, fine. You want to drive?"

"No, I don't want to drive, you big baby," Chuck said, mimicking his whine perfectly. "Just get moving."

"You're so smart, *you* drive," Eddie said, and unlocked his door. "I'm sick of your griping."

Santa Paws sat up partway, very alert. He knew that the sound of a car door unlocking usually meant that someone was about to open it.

"You'd better not get out of the van," Chuck threatened him.

"I quit!" Eddie said. "Unless you feel like walking the rest of the way, *you* can drive."

"Fine." Chuck unbuckled his seatbelt. "You want to switch, we'll switch. It'll be a lot better than listening to your moaning."

Santa Paws tensed all of his muscles, preparing himself for action. If the bad people were really going to open the doors, he might be able to run away. Then he could find his family and go home where he belonged. Where he was happy, and safe.

Eddie got sulkily out of the van, leaving his door ajar. Several nearby drivers beeped their horns, but he just made rude faces at them.

The door was open! This was his chance! Santa Paws silently rose to his feet, shaking the canvas off and getting ready to make his move. Then he dove for the exit with every bit of energy he had.

It was now or never!

7

Chuck must have heard something, because he turned around just in time to see Santa Paws lunging towards the driver's seat. Ninety pounds worth of determined, airborne German shepherd was an intimidating sight, and his first reaction was to cover his face with his arms and cower in his seat.

"Eddie!" he screeched. "Get back here! The mutt's trying to escape!"

Santa Paws vaulted right past the cringing man. Chuck recovered enough to make a grab for his back legs and he just barely missed. The dog plunged through the open van door and landed painfully on the highway below. He was slightly stunned by the fall, and had trouble getting up for a few seconds. The deadly chloroform was still in his system, and it had slowed both his reactions and his ability to think quickly. Santa Paws dragged himself to his feet, shaking his head to try and clear it.

Chuck had barreled out of the van right after him, and now Eddie ran to block his way from the other direction. Santa Paws looked back and forth, trying not to panic. He was trapped between the two bad men, and cars were hemming him in on the other side. He growled uneasily, although the sound was muffled by the leather muzzle.

Nearby cars started beeping their horns, since this tense man-dog confrontation was going to slow down traffic even more. Many of them were, after all, high-strung city people, and unnecessary delays made them irritable.

"Come on, nice doggie," Chuck said, with his cruel smile. "Come here, doggie! I have a bone to pick with — I mean, *give* you."

As both men charged towards him, Santa Paws leaped up onto the hood of the nearest car just in the nick of time. Chuck and Eddie promptly banged into each other, which made them twice as enraged at Santa Paws. The driver inside the car was startled to see a huge dog appear on her hood and she blared her horn, trying to scare this canine intruder away. Santa Paws had no idea how menacing the muzzle made him look. The piercing noise of the horn hurt the dog's ears, and he jumped off the hood and right into the middle of the slow-moving traffic.

Cars swerved right and left, trying to avoid

hitting the dog — and each other. But there was really no place for the cars to go in the heavy traffic, so there were several fender-benders. The traffic jam had become complete pandemonium. Santa Paws was aware that Eddie and Chuck were trying to chase him, but he was more afraid of getting run over by one of the cars or trucks. He had never seen so many automobiles in his entire life!

The combination of glaring headlights and a chorus of horns was very confusing. Santa Paws knew he had to get away, but he wasn't sure where to go. No matter where he looked, he could only see an endless parade of traffic. Where was the sidewalk? Where was the grass? Grass was always safe. He had to find some grass.

Finally, he turned left and started running. As he bounded up onto a concrete divider, he realized that there were even more cars on the other side of the highway. These cars were driving very fast, and coming from a whole different direction. Baffled and afraid, he turned to go the other way. He had lost track of Chuck and Eddie, although he could still hear them yelling.

"Get back here or you'll be sorry, you cur!" Chuck bellowed.

"Yeah!" Eddie agreed, although he wasn't sure what the word "cur" meant. "That goes double for me!"

Where should he go? What should he do? As Santa Paws stood uncertainly in the middle of the highway, one sports utility vehicle came so close to hitting him that he actually felt the tire brush against his side. It was time to get away from here!

Santa Paws ran as fast as he could, dodging traffic, until he came to a crowded exit ramp. Again, horns were beeping all around him, and cars and trucks were trying to steer out of his way. A Toyota crashed into the back of a BMW, and their drivers leaped out to yell at each other. Santa Paws raced towards the bottom of the ramp, his heart thumping wildly. This was so scary! He came to an intersection that seemed to connect hundreds of streets together all at once. Some of the streets led right underneath the highway, while others spread out in a confusing pinwheel in front of him.

What was this strange, alien, concrete place? Why weren't there any houses? Or trees? Or backyards? Where had the bad people taken him? He wanted to go home! *Now.*

The dog picked the street that seemed to have the fewest cars, and dashed down it at top speed. Soon he came across a sidewalk, and gratefully galloped along it, instead. Sidewalks were so much nicer than being in the middle of the road. He ran and ran, not sure if Eddie and Chuck were still following him. He turned corners, crossed streets, dodged down alleys, and raced below scary bridges and underpasses. Finally, he ran out of breath — and strength — and knew he had to stop and rest for a minute.

He saw a dark, secluded alcove next to a Dumpster and decided to hide there. He ducked inside, and then collapsed in the shadows, out of sight.

The dog had no idea where he was, but for now, at least he was free!

Once he caught his breath, Santa Paws slept for what felt like a very long time. During the night, the temperature dropped until it was only about twenty degrees, with a wind-chill that made it feel even more frigid. The dog began shivering so hard that it woke him up. Since he always took turns sleeping on Gregory's and Patricia's beds, he couldn't figure out why it was so cold. Usually, the blankets were warm and — wait a minute, where was he? This wasn't the Callahans' house!

Santa Paws looked around, blinking. Then the memory of his horrible experience with the bad people came flooding back. He sniffed the air nervously, to check and see if the men were anyplace nearby. No. His nose was overwhelmed by foreign smells, but the distinctive unwashed stench of the two bad men wasn't among them. Yay! He really had escaped!

Now his biggest problem was going to be trying to figure out exactly where he was. Or even *remotely* where he was. Sometimes, the Callahans went on outings to the city, but this place seemed different. There were lots of buildings and concrete, though, so this place must be *like* that. But, how was he ever going to find his way home?

Feeling lonely, he wanted to let out a little woof, but then he realized that he had another big problem. His mouth was strapped shut! He dug at the muzzle with both paws, whining in frustration. Then he rubbed his head against the chilly cement wall of his alcove. He rubbed so hard that his ear and cheek felt raw, but the muzzle didn't budge. He slumped down, whimpering quietly. Why had those men been so *mean*? He was used to people who *liked* him.

The wind was swirling around, and he pressed deeper into his narrow alcove. The alcove was really just a doorway, but it felt less exposed than lying out on the sidewalk. In a strange, spooky place, he knew he needed as much protection as he could get.

There was a scuttling sound over by a Dumpster, and Santa Paws saw some ugly little animals rummaging around. They had stiff dark fur, long yellow teeth, and pink naked tails. They looked sort of like cat-sized mice, but he was pretty sure he had never seen this kind of animal before. He didn't like them much, either. They seemed — creepy.

The little animals scurried, and squeaked, and rustled through bits of garbage in the street. One of them came near his alcove, and the dog growled at it. With the muzzle on, he wouldn't be able to bite them, but maybe the growl would be fierce enough to scare them away. The rodent flashed its sharp teeth in return, but then backed off.

Santa Paws wanted to move and sleep somewhere far away from those creatures, but he felt safer staying where he was for now. He would just have to stay awake to make sure none of them wandered over again.

Watching the animals fight over scraps of spoiled, discarded food from the Dumpster, the dog suddenly realized how hungry he was. And thirsty! When was the last time he had had any water? The drug had left a nasty taste in his mouth, and his tongue felt very dry. When the sun came up, he would have to go out and do some scavenging of his own. It had been a long time since he had been forced to survive on the streets — but he still remembered how to do it. Once he got rid of the painful strap around his mouth, he would be fine.

The small animals finally stopped fighting and snapping, and went scuttling off to find other trash to eat. Santa Paws was relieved to see them go. Maybe now he could get some more rest. Tomorrow he was going to start searching for the Callahans, and he would need as much energy as possible for that.

It was so cold that he curled into a tight ball and huddled against the doorway. He should have taken the time to find a park, or some other place like that where he could make himself a warm nest out of leaves. When he had been a stray before, he had spent most of his time sleeping in the woods. For a while, he had camped in a small cave, and he had also lived in an abandoned shed. It was when he had started sleeping up by the middle school that he had met Gregory and Patricia.

Thinking about his family made him start whimpering again. Did they miss him as much as he missed them? Were they worried? Were they *safe*? Would he ever see them again?

Feeling too miserable to try to sleep anymore, Santa Paws just huddled in his alcove to wait for morning.

When the sun finally came up, Santa Paws was so tired and cold that he wasn't sure he would be able to get up. His joints and muscles were practically frozen. When it came to being a stray, he was really out of practice! He staggered to his feet and stood there for a minute, until he felt steady enough to try walking. For the most part, the streets were quiet, although a few trucks drove past him as he wandered from street to street.

As the sun rose higher, people began to leave their apartment buildings to go to church, or work, or maybe do some shopping. Since it was a Sunday morning, the mood in the neighborhood was more leisurely than usual. The few people who noticed him seemed to think he was dangerous, because they quickly veered out of his way.

Santa Paws walked endlessly, with his head down and his tail dragging. No matter which way he went, he seemed to end up near yet another highway. He didn't like highways, so he would have to turn around and head off in a different direction. Once, when he was walking under some elevated tracks, a great thundering roar filled his ears. He flattened on the sidewalk, terrified. A great big machine pounded above him for what seemed like hours. It was bigger than a truck, or even a bus — and horribly loud. He didn't like this place *at all*.

Once the machine was gone, Santa Paws carefully got up. Would it come back? He wasn't waiting around to find out! He chose a new street to follow, wanting to put the monster machine as far behind him as possible.

He found a puddle in a street pothole and tried to lap up some water, but the muzzle was so tight that he couldn't open his mouth enough to drink. That meant that he wouldn't be able to eat, either. He would starve!

There was a low chain-link fence nearby, and he tried to hook the muzzle over one of the protruding wires to yank it off. The only thing he managed to do was scratch his already-raw cheek. By now, the muzzle felt like a vise! He was too hungry and thirsty to think clearly, so he started wandering aimlessly again.

Then he came upon a huge park, with tall fences and decorative stone walls. There were all sorts of intriguing smells coming from inside, and for a minute, he forgot how miserable he was. He stopped and sniffed the air. Animals! Lots of different animals! Some of the scents were familiar — he recognized goats, and birds, and rabbits, and squirrels. But what were all of those other animals? Was this a special home, just for animals? If it was, maybe he could rest here for a while.

The special animal preserve was surrounded by large parking lots. Happy families were leaving their cars and getting off big city buses to go visit the animals. Santa Paws watched wistfully, because the families looked so jolly and excited. They reminded him of the Callahans. He could see Christmas lights, too, which made him feel even more sad. He wanted to go inside and explore, but he couldn't see any other dogs, so maybe he wasn't supposed to go in there. It had never made sense to him that dogs were allowed to go into some places, and had to wait outside others, but he had learned to live with it.

He lurked at the edge of one parking lot, trying to stay out of sight. Along with the exotic animal scents, he could also smell food! Hot dogs, and popcorn, and other good things! There were trash cans here and there, and he knew that if it weren't for the hateful muzzle, he could fill his stomach with discarded food.

Some of the other animals might have been able to smell him, too, because he could hear various howls and screeches and roars. Santa Paws was wildly curious, but also a little afraid. Instinctively, he sensed that a few of those animals were downright *ferocious*. Maybe that was why they were all locked up in there?

The dog decided that this place made him nervous. He didn't want anyone to come along and put *him* in a cage. He also couldn't stand being able to smell so much delicious food that he couldn't eat. It was time to leave this mysterious park behind!

Santa Paws started running, and he didn't stop until he came to yet another wide highway. There didn't seem to be very many cars, but the ones he did see were driving very fast. Was there a way to cross this road safely, or would he have to go around it? That could take *hours*. He waited uncertainly by the side of the road, trying to make up his mind.

As soon as there was a break in the traffic, he tore across the highway to the grassy divider in the middle. Then he stretched out on his side to catch his breath. At home, whenever he walked anywhere near the street, Gregory always said, "No, no!" and shook his finger at him. So Santa Paws knew that cars could hurt him if he wasn't careful.

But right now, since he was in the middle of the highway, what choice did he have? He either had to go back — or go forward. The cars on the far side of the grass were coming towards him from the other direction, which was confusing. Why couldn't they all just go the same way on both sides? Santa Paws watched them pass for a long time, doing his best to judge their speed. He was fast, but those cars were a whole lot faster!

He waited until the road seemed clear, and then started across. But then a small delivery truck appeared out of nowhere! It was headed straight for him!

8

Santa Paws put on an extra burst of speed just as the driver of the truck slammed on his brakes. The truck squealed to a stop, leaving a terrible smell of burnt rubber in the air. Santa Paws could hear a man shouting at him, but he kept running. Boy, that had been a pretty close call!

He ran until he found a couple of trees to hide behind. His heart was pounding away, and he couldn't pant very well because of the muzzle. He *really* needed a drink of water. Worn-out from his already eventful day, he collapsed onto the ground to take a nap.

When he opened his eyes, he was less tired, but *more* hungry and thirsty. He rubbed the muzzle against one of the trees, but it stayed stubbornly attached to his face. By now he knew that he would never be able to take it off by himself. He needed to find a nice person who would help him. And if he was lucky, maybe the person would know Gregory and Patricia, and help him get home!

Back in Oceanport, the Callahans' house was much quieter than usual. Uncle Steve had gotten up early, so that he could go home and see his wife and daughter before his next shift. But before he left, he called the police station to see if any reports had come in. A few lost dogs had been located overnight, but none of them were German shepherd mixes. There was also no sign of a grey or tan van carrying two stocky men with straggly blond hair. An APB — which was an All Points Bulletin — had been sent to every law enforcement agency in New England by now, but so far, no one had called Oceanport with any information. Uncle Steve promised that he would be following up on every aspect of the investigation. He would call them right away if he got any news at all.

After Uncle Steve had left, the Callahans went to Sunday morning mass. Patricia and Gregory wanted to refuse, but their parents looked so tired and unhappy that they decided to go without voicing any objections. The church was decorated for Advent, and looked very pretty, but none of the Callahans were in a holiday mood. It would be awful to have their dog stolen at any time of the year, but the fact that it was almost Christmas made the situation seem even worse.

Right after the homily, Father Reilly offered a special intention for Santa Paws. He asked the entire church to pray for the dog's safe return, and reminded them of the many good deeds he had performed for the townspeople. He also announced that there was a sign-up sheet in the vestibule for anyone who wanted to volunteer to help look for Santa Paws.

Gregory had a hard time not crying, when he listened to all of the nice things Father Reilly was saying about his missing dog. It was nice to know that people all over town were sorry about what had happened, but that didn't make him feel any less sad. Patricia got so upset during Father Reilly's speech that she actually had to get up and leave the church for a few minutes.

After mass, everyone came up to the Callahans to pass along their sympathies and ask if there was anything they could do. One well-meaning woman even asked if they would like a little cocker spaniel from a litter her dog had just had. When Patricia heard that, she politely excused herself and went to wait in the car. Mrs. Callahan just thanked the woman for her kindness and tactfully changed the subject.

When they finally got home, Mr. Callahan tried to cheer everyone up by fixing homemade cornmeal pancakes and bacon. There weren't very many things he knew how to cook, but he was a champion at making breakfast. No one was hungry, but they all did their best to eat since he had gone to so much trouble.

Even Evelyn looked dejected. Instead of trying to snatch a piece of bacon when no one was looking, she just curled up sadly on the kitchen rug where Santa Paws usually slept. She missed him very, very much.

"Can we please go look for him ourselves?" Gregory asked. "Instead of just waiting around?"

"Of course," Mrs. Callahan said. "As soon as you finish eating, we'll go out driving, just in case."

Patricia looked up from her barely touched plate, her face brightening unexpectedly. "Hey, I know! We could offer a reward!"

Mrs. Callahan nodded. "That's a good idea, Patricia. Why don't you and your brother make up some signs, and then we'll get enough copies made to hand them out, and hang them in stores."

Feeling a little better now that they had something tangible to do, Patricia and Gregory quickly finished their breakfasts. Then they hurried upstairs to get to work on their computers. Hand-lettered signs weren't good enough for Santa Paws; they wanted these flyers to look *professional*.

While Mr. Callahan did the dishes, Mrs. Callahan pulled out the yellow pages. She looked up the phone number of every single animal shelter in the Greater Boston area, and wrote them down on a yellow legal pad. If necessary, she would call every animal shelter in the country! With each call, she reported that her dog was missing and gave whoever answered a detailed description of him. Almost everyone she called had heard of the famous Santa Paws, and they assured her they were already keeping watch for him. Many of them also gave her other numbers to call, belonging to animal rights organizations and any other people who might be able to help.

Upstairs, Gregory and Patricia used a scanner to copy several very flattering pictures of Santa Paws. They were careful not to look at the pictures too closely, so they wouldn't get too distraught to continue. Then, using a graphics program, they created three different posters. They tried to make the signs as eye-catching as possible by selecting lots of bright colors and dramatic fonts, as well as some clip-art with Christmas designs. At the bottom of each flyer, they typed in their phone number, as well as the main switchboard at the Oceanport police department, so people would know who to contact.

Then they printed out copies of each poster and proofread them for mistakes.

"I think we should put a thick border around the word 'Reward,'" Gregory said. "That'll get people's attention. Maybe around 'Missing,' too."

Patricia nodded, and added that to each of the

master copies. For good measure, she also created a border to emphasize the name "Santa Paws," too. "While I'm finishing up, why don't you go online," she suggested. "I know there are, like, dog rescue groups, and you can post messages there — and maybe some of the AOL bulletin boards and chat rooms and stuff. Plus, all your regular message boards and newsgroups, too."

Gregory nodded, and left the room to boot up his own computer. "I'm going to send out an e-mail to everyone in my address book, too, okay?" he called.

"Yeah, that's good!" Patricia called back. "Ask them to forward it, if they don't mind. I'll send one from my address book, too."

Neither of them had their own websites yet, but later today, they could maybe ask their friends who *did*, if they could post announcements on their sites. The more links they could set up, the faster they could get the word out. Their parents had never seemed too fond of the Internet, but as far as Gregory and Patricia were concerned, they just didn't appreciate all of the exciting possibilities. Sometimes their mother used it for research, or to correspond with other teachers, but that was about it. Their father had only tried going on the web once, had found it much too vast, and refused ever to attempt it again.

Maybe none of this would help them find their dog, but it certainly couldn't hurt!

Santa Paws was still resting under the two trees near the big highway he had crossed. Once he felt strong enough, he got up and began to walk again. He wasn't sure where to go, but he had to try and find some help. So he decided he would just wander around until he found someone very kind. Many of these streets had long rows of attached houses, with tiny fenced yards. The rest of the streets were crowded with small shops and fast food restaurants and beat-up old apartment buildings.

Smelling fresh, hot pizza, he stopped in front of one storefront. Santa Paws loved pizza, and it also reminded him of his family, since they enjoyed eating pizza, too. He waited in front of the door, hoping that someone would stop and help him with the muzzle. Maybe they would give him a bite of pizza, too!

He sat very politely, with his best posture. He waited for what seemed like hours, but no one even really paused. A few people spoke to him, but for some reason, he couldn't understand what they were saying. They were using words he had never heard before. Many of them sounded cross, while others just acted frightened. He knew he hadn't done anything wrong, so he wasn't sure why they didn't like him.

Finally, a plump bald man came out of the pizza place. He was wearing a tomato-stained apron and carrying a broom.

Santa Paws stood up, and wagged his tail. Finally! A nice person!

"Get out of here!" the man said, and shook the broom at him. "You're scaring my customers away!"

Santa Paws cocked his head. Why was the man so upset? And why was he swinging that broom? Then the bristles smacked him across the snout, and he leaped backwards, very startled. Had someone just *hit* him? Why? Was the world just suddenly full of mean people? What was going on?

"Get out of here, you mangy dog!" the man said, and aimed the broom at him again. "Before I have to call the cops!"

Santa Paws dodged the blow and retreated away from the store. Then he started running, with his tail between his legs. The broom itself hadn't hurt that much, but the idea that someone would want to hit him hurt his feelings terribly. He had always been a good dog. He *knew* he was a good dog! So why did all of these people think he was bad? It was very confusing.

He slunk along the streets, doing his best to avoid attention. A group of boys hanging around on a corner laughed when they saw him.

"Yo, pit bull!" one of them said.

The other boys laughed and started throwing bottles and soda cans at him. Most of them missed, but one of the bottles shattered on the sidewalk near his face and that unnerved him. Clearly, the best thing to do would be just to avoid people completely. For some reason, literally overnight, he had become their enemy. Was it like that when he was a stray before? It must have been, but he couldn't quite remember. He had never really *wanted* to remember those long, lonely months.

He passed a couple of dogs who were being walked on leashes, but their owners nervously pulled their pets away from the unfamiliar, scruffy German shepherd. In their experience, only vicious animals ever wore muzzles. An elderly woman with a tiny terrier paused as though she might want to help him, but by now, Santa Paws was too scared and he just ran away.

It was getting dark. He was alone, and miserable, and had no idea where he was. The wind was picking up again, and his paws ached from wandering so many miles on pavement and asphalt. He was also so weak from hunger and thirst that he knew he had to lie down for a while. But it was very hard, in the middle of the city, to find a secluded place.

Then he saw a huge pile of rags stacked on top of a metal grate. There was a dented grocery cart next to the pile, stuffed with grimy plastic bags and other worn objects. As he approached the rags, he felt a stream of hot air rising up through the grate. Heat! He could get warm! Yay!

He jumped happily onto the pile of rags. Then, to his horror, the rags *moved*! Then the rags let out a rumbling bellow!

The rags were alive!

9

Santa Paws was so shocked that he actually fell over in surprise. Finally understanding that the pile of rags was really a person dressed in lots of bulky layers of clothing, he scrambled to his feet. But as he tried to race away, a grimy hand wearing a torn work glove hauled him back.

"Hey, now, what's all this?" a raspy voice grumbled from inside the rags. "Can't a man get himself some sleep?"

The voice was actually rather pleasant, sounding more indignant than enraged. So Santa Paws relaxed a little, and waited to see what would happen next.

"What's the world coming to? Tell me that, will you?" the man asked, looking him right in the eyes. "Don't you know better than to wake a fella up?"

This man seemed odd, but at least he was friendly. His face was unshaven and his hair was badly tangled, so it was hard to tell what he really looked like, or how old he was. Santa Paws tentatively wagged his tail a few times.

"What's this here contraption you got on?" the man asked. "You a biter?"

Santa Paws wagged his tail a little harder. The muzzle was bothering him so much that, without thinking, he pawed at it again.

"I hear you, pooch. Don't much like being confined myself," the man said. "You gonna tear my hand up if I take that thing off?"

Santa Paws tilted his head, not sure what the man wanted to know. He recognized the tone of question, but that was as far as he could get with this one.

"*Sit*," the man said.

Finally! A word he absolutely knew! Maybe not one of his favorites, but nice to hear under the circumstances. Santa Paws wagged his tail again, and sat down.

"Are you a good dog?" the man asked.

The dog's eyes lit up. Someone had said "good dog" to him!

"Well," the man drawled, "I don't much figure you for a biter. And — serve me right if I'm wrong." He reached out to unbuckle the muzzle. His hands were very large, and the knuckles were swollen from the cold. It took him a minute to work the buckle loose, and then he pulled the restraint off. He examined the leather briefly, shook his head, and tossed it aside.

Santa Paws barked with joy. He could move his mouth again! It felt great! His jaw felt stiff from having worn the muzzle for so long, so he barked some more to loosen it up. It was lots of fun to bark, after so many hours of forced silence. Then he leaned forward and nuzzled his face against the man's hand.

"You got good manners, pooch, don't you?" the man asked.

Hearing the word "good," Santa Paws whipped his tail back and forth. He always *tried* to be good, so it was nice that this man had noticed.

"So. You get yourself lost, or you just down on your luck?" the man wondered aloud.

The heat wafting up through the gate was so enticing that Santa Paws squeezed next to the man, still wagging his tail. He loved people, he really did.

"It's right easy to get down on your luck," the man told him, with a sigh. "You make some stupid mistakes, maybe lose a job, disappoint your family — and if you have some bad luck, you can end up out on the streets, like me."

The dog's ears shot up. Had the man said "family"? Did he know the Callahans? How lucky he was to have found this person.

"Can't say I didn't get myself into this jam, but now, it's like nobody even *sees* me," the man went on. "They just walk on by, pretend I'm not here. Makes you feel pretty bad, I'll tell you. Especially this time of year."

Santa Paws watched him intently, trying to figure out what he was saying. All he knew for sure was that this man felt as lonely and sad as he did.

"You're a real good listener, pooch," the man said.

Santa Paws had never heard the word "pooch" before, but he liked it for some reason. It sounded — affectionate.

"Watch it now, little friend," the man warned. "I been on my own so long, I might just up and talk your ear off."

The warm grate felt so comforting that Santa Paws snuggled closer to the man. What a lot of clothes he was wearing! For all the dog knew, underneath the garments, the man was actually very thin. His *face* seemed thin, behind all those greying whiskers.

The man put his hand out. "I'm Roy. How's by you, pooch?"

Santa Paws lifted his paw, and Roy shook it, looking delighted.

"You know how long it's been since someone shook my hand, pooch?" he asked. "I tell you, friend, you almost make me feel human again." He dug through his layers of sweaters and shirts until he located the remains of a package of Saltines. "I don't got much, boy, but can I offer you some dinner?"

Hungry as he was, Santa Paws took the cracker gently from his hand. Gregory and Patricia had trained him to be very careful about not snapping by accident. He crunched it up, and thumped his tail gratefully.

"Well, all right then! Dinner is served!" Roy said cheerfully.

They finished all of the Saltines in no time. First Roy would eat one, and then he would offer one to Santa Paws. They took turns until the crackers were gone.

"Sorry, pooch," Roy said, crumpling the empty plastic wrapper. "Wish I could do you better, but that's all I got today."

Santa Paws wagged his tail. He *liked* this sad, nice man. He wanted to go find a puddle somewhere and drink, but he knew the man hoped that he would stay for a while. So he stretched out on the grate, using the man's knee for a pillow.

"Well, now, I like a pooch, doesn't eat and run," Roy said, pleased. "Glad to see you'll sit a spell."

It was dark now, and a light freezing rain was falling. Roy pulled some newspapers out of his shopping cart to cover them both up. The newspapers weren't a perfect shelter, but they helped protect them a little.

As the long cold night passed, mostly they both dozed. Sometimes, Roy would wake up and start telling him long stories about his life, and the adventures he'd had, and how he had ended up becoming homeless in the first place. How he wished he could start over, and do things differently this time. Whenever he spoke, the dog watched him intently. Then when Roy got tired of talking, he would just pat Santa Paws and tell him that he was a good dog. Hearing that made Santa Paws feel very happy. What a wonderful new friend Roy was.

It was — almost — like being back with his family again!

The Callahans had spent all of Sunday afternoon driving from town to town and putting up their signs. Mrs. Callahan had stopped at a copy store on Main Street, and had five hundred copies made of each flyer. So now they had a total of fifteen hundred to distribute. They hung the signs in stores, taped them to telephone poles, and handed them out to anyone who seemed interested. No one they asked had seen Santa Paws, but each person promised faithfully to keep an eye out for him. Some of them even asked for extra flyers to give to their friends. Mr. and Mrs. Callahan were quick to provide them with as many copies as they wanted.

It was a grueling way to spend the afternoon,

but posting the signs was more productive than sitting glumly in the house and waiting for the telephone to ring. Or *not* ring, as the case might be. Seeing Christmas trees, and menorahs, and houses decorated with wreaths and twinkling lights seemed very depressing, under the circumstances. It was a constant reminder that Christmas was less than a week away, and none of them wanted to think about that right now.

"Someone will see him, right?" Gregory said as he hung a sign in the window of a Laundromat. "With all these posters up?"

Mr. Callahan nodded, and rested his hand on his son's shoulder. "Someone's bound to, Greg. We just have to be patient."

Gregory didn't want to be patient — and neither did Patricia, but they managed not to say so. They knew their parents were only trying to make this terrible situation easier for them.

Since it was a school night, Mrs. Callahan wanted them to get home early enough to have dinner and get a good night's sleep. They still had some signs left over, but their father suggested that they bring them to school the next day and pass them out there. Mrs. Callahan was going to do the same at the high school.

When they got home, the red light on their answering machine was flashing wildly.

"It's good news!" Gregory said. "I know it is!"

Worn-out from the hours of driving and hang-

ing signs, Patricia was feeling much less optimistic about things. In fact, she was downright
cranky. "It's probably just a bunch of dumb reporters bugging us again."

"No, it's good," Gregory insisted. "It has to be."

Unfortunately, all of the messages turned out
to be from people who had called to say how
sorry they were that Santa Paws was missing.
The messages were very considerate — but they
weren't good news. The last one was from Uncle
Steve, reporting that they were still waiting for
results from the crime lab, but should have them
by the next morning.

Mrs. Callahan made tacos for supper, because
that was one of Gregory and Patricia's favorite
meals. The tacos were delicious, but there was
almost no conversation at the table. After dinner,
Gregory and Patricia helped with the dishes.
Then they headed upstairs to get ready for bed,
significantly earlier than usual. They didn't even
argue about who would go online first. Their parents had had an extra telephone line installed
when it was clear that their children were going
to tie up the main line for hours on end when
they were on the web. In return, Gregory and
Patricia had promised to take turns using their
computers. They had also promised that they
would never argue about it, either. Tonight was
probably the first time they had ever succeeded
in *keeping* that promise.

First Gregory downloaded his e-mail to read off-line. Then Patricia did the same. They had gotten lots of responses to their various postings and messages, but just like the answering machine, they were of the "sorry to hear about Santa Paws, hope someone finds him soon" variety. So far, none of the efforts to find their dog seemed to be helping at all.

After he had answered his e-mail, Gregory came into Patricia's room and sprawled unhappily across the bottom of her bed.

"You think he's okay?" he asked.

Patricia hesitated, but then nodded. There was no point in making her little brother feel worse than he already did. "They only took him because they think he's worth a lot of money. So, there's no way they'd hurt him."

Gregory had his own doubts, but he nodded, too.

Patricia got up from her desk chair to come over and sit next to him. "Look, Greg, the one thing we know for *sure* is that he's a survivor," she said. "I mean, we've seen what he can do, right? He's like — Superdog."

Gregory smiled weakly. "Underdog."

"Exactly," Patricia said, her smile just as feeble.

They sat there quietly. Evelyn came ambling in to keep them company and — without arguing — they took turns patting her.

"You think he misses us as much as we miss him?" Gregory asked.

She might not be sure of anything else, but Patricia *was* sure about that. "Definitely," she said.

The next morning, when Santa Paws and the man woke up, they both yawned and stretched. Roy stood up and stamped his feet to get the circulation moving. Then he checked his shopping cart to make sure no one had come along and stolen his stuff during the night. He had so few possessions that he treasured all of them.

Santa Paws gave himself a vigorous shake, and yawned a few more times. The rain had stopped just before dawn, and his fur was mostly dry now. The sun was shining, and even though he was terribly hungry and thirsty, he felt quite content. After such a good night's sleep, he knew he was ready to try and find his way back home to his family. Would Roy come with him, maybe? Santa Paws trotted down the street a few steps, then waited to see if Roy was going to follow him.

"Time to make my rounds, pooch," Roy explained. "If I find enough cans, I can make me a few dollars. And there's soup, over at the church today. You want to come?"

Come. That was another one he knew. Santa Paws trotted back over to Roy, even though he was eager to start his journey. He pawed his friend's leg, then ran ten feet away. He stopped and barked a few times.

Roy let out a resigned sigh, and smiled at him. "Looks like you got places of your own to go, hunh, pooch?" He crouched down and held his hand out. "Come here, and let me say good-bye, okay?"

Santa Paws returned and sat down in front of him.

"Well, there's a good boy," Roy said, and patted him. "I hate to see you go, but it sure was nice having you around last night."

Santa Paws thumped his tail on the sidewalk.

Roy looked at him for a long minute. "You want to know a secret, pooch? Over to the church one time, the Reverend told me he could get me into some kind of job-training. And I said, 'Rev, you won't catch me doing *that* until I see a sign.' You know? Something to show me my luck might change?"

Santa Paws tilted his head to the right, and then to the left. His friend was talking to him very seriously, and he wished he could follow the conversation better.

"Now, I don't believe in signs," Roy said. "Figured there was no such thing. And the Rev said, you just have to know where to look."

Santa Paws leaned forward and gave his hand a friendly lick.

"Now, see, there you go," Roy said, and smiled.

"Could be, the Rev was right, and it's a long time since I looked. Think I just might have myself a talk with him today, know what I'm saying?"

Santa Paws wagged his tail.

"Okay, then." Roy patted him one last time before straightening up. "You take care of yourself, y'hear, pooch? Good luck to you!"

The word "good" again! Santa Paws barked.

Roy went over to retrieve his shopping cart, then turned to wave at the dog. "See you around, pal," he said fondly, and began pushing his cart down the street. "Merry Christmas, little buddy!"

Santa Paws watched him go, wagging his tail non-stop. Then he stood up and sniffed the air in every direction. He sensed, somehow, that his family was north of here. Instead of being overwhelmed and afraid, from now on he was just going to follow his instincts. And his instincts were telling him to head north.

The rain from the night before had left lots of puddles, and Santa Paws drank until his throat was no longer dry. Then he began to trot up the street, heading directly — north.

He was on his way to find the Callahans!

10

Over the next few hours, the dog covered a lot of ground. He set a nice, steady pace, pausing only to drink from a puddle occasionally. By moving in an easy trot, he wouldn't get too tired. He did his best to head directly north, with maybe a slight tilt to the east. It just *felt* right.

Gradually, he left the city behind. It was a big relief to find himself in a more suburban setting. The streets were quieter, there were fewer cars, and he was able to cut through grassy backyards. Two days of constant contact with hard cement had really made his paws sore.

For a while now, he had been able to hear the noise of a crowded highway somewhere off to his right. He wanted to avoid it, but soon found that he had no choice but to cross. That is, if he wanted to stay on course. He whined uneasily, striding back and forth on the shoulder of the road. The traffic seemed very heavy and he was afraid to go anywhere near it.

Not sure what else to do, he continued along the side of the road for a while, even though it was taking him out of his way. The cars were driving so fast that he cringed almost every time one passed him. Then he came across a ramp, which led up to an overpass. A bridge! He could get across the highway!

There were some cars on the entrance ramp, but he soon found an opportunity to rush across to the thick underbrush on the other side. The overpass itself had a sidewalk, which made him very happy. From now on, if he needed to cross any more scary thruways, he would be sure to look for one of these special bridges! Soon, the highway was just a bad memory, and he was able to resume his determined trek through the suburbs.

The houses he was trotting by now were big and comfortable, sitting on large plots of land. The yards at home in Oceanport weren't usually quite this big, and there was no comforting smell of the sea. Even so, he felt confident that he was on the right path.

Every so often, he paused to drink from a small puddle. It was getting colder, and a thin film of ice was beginning to form across most of them. But the ice was easy enough to break with his front paws and then he could drink his fill. In one backyard, he even found a trash can filled with delicious leftovers! He knew it was bad to knock over garbage, but he was too hungry to worry about it. He gobbled down some cold potatoes and limp salad, along with a few pieces of stale bread. There were some pork chop bones, too, but most of the meat was gone.

The dog was just settling down for a nice chew when a man came out of a nearby house and looked angry when he saw the torn-up trash.

"Bad dog!" the man said. "Go home!"

Since he knew he *was* being bad, Santa Paws slunk away immediately. He didn't even remember to bring any of the bones with him. Further down the street, a large golden retriever boldly barked at him from behind a white picket fence. Santa Paws wagged his tail to show that he wasn't a threat and continued on his way. The retriever only barked a couple more times before losing interest and returning to her front porch for a nap.

Next, Santa Paws came to a golf course. Despite the chill in the December air and the grey overcast sky, there were a few die-hard sportsmen out there playing. Santa Paws stopped when he saw a small white object hurtling through the air towards him. What was it? Oh, a ball! How fun!

The ball gracefully arced down towards the ground, headed for a little hole with a flag sticking out of it. The ball landed directly inside the hole, with a small clatter against the sides of the cup. Santa Paws galloped joyfully over, knowing exactly what he was supposed to do with balls. People liked him to fetch them!

He nosed around inside the cup until he was able to grab the ball between his teeth. It was very small and hard — not nearly as nice as a tennis ball felt in his mouth. But he ran to return it to its owner right away.

Two men were hurrying across the brittle grass, hauling their golf bags on small wheeled carts. Instead of coats, they were wearing heavy sweaters, close-fitting leather gloves, and jaunty plaid caps.

"A hole in one!" the taller man was saying triumphantly. "I heard it hit the cup! I'm sure of it!"

"Could be," his friend agreed. "We'll see when we get there."

The tall man was terribly excited. "I can't believe this! I've been playing since I was nine years old, and I've never hit one. Wait until my wife hears!"

Since the men were coming in his direction, Santa Paws decided that it must be their ball. He ran up to them and dropped it at their feet. Then he wagged his tail proudly, and waited for praise.

The tall man looked shocked; his friend laughed.

"I can't believe it," the tall man said softly.

His friend was still chuckling. "Well, Keith, guess we'll never know."

Santa Paws was puzzled by their reactions. Weren't they happy? He had saved them the trouble of going all the way over to that hole to try and find such a tiny ball by themselves. Did they think he was bad? The very thought made his ears go down.

"I really want to yell at this dog," the tall man said finally, "but he thinks he did a smart thing, doesn't he?"

His friend nodded, laughing.

The tall man sighed, but then reached out to give Santa Paws a light pat. "Okay, good dog. I'm sure you meant well."

Santa Paws wagged his tail, pleased that they thought he was good. What a relief! Then he barked once, and resumed his steady trot north. The two men watched him go.

"I think my wife might find this story a little bit too funny," the tall man said.

"I think so, too," his friend agreed, and laughed some more.

A few minutes later, Santa Paws had crossed the outside edge of the golf course. Now he was back to traveling through peaceful neighborhoods, as well as a few commercial streets. A couple of people noticed him, and shouted, "Hey, dog!" or "Come here, pup!" Santa Paws wagged his tail pleasantly at each of them, but kept going. Soon he saw a good-sized lake and stopped for a nice long drink. The water was very cold, but it sure tasted good.

It was beginning to get dark now, and the dog was getting tired. Soon, he would have to choose a good place to sleep for a while. But every minute he rested meant it would take that much longer to find his family!

After crossing a fairly busy road — his legs stiff with tension the whole time — he found himself on another golf course. Or *was* it? Could he have gotten lost, and gotten in a circle? Santa Paws stood still to sniff the air, holding one paw up uncertainly. No, this was a different course, because there was nothing familiar about it. By now, it was too dark to play, so he didn't pass any golfers as he loped over the grass. There were small clusters of trees, then wide sections of winter-dry grass with sandy areas and small ponds here and there. He paused, trying to decide if he wanted to sleep in some of that sand. It would be nice and soft. But, no, he wasn't quite ready to stop yet.

Once he had left that golf course, he came to another — and then, another! What a strange town this was! There seemed to be more golf courses than houses! But maybe it would be fun to live around here, because there would be so many little white balls to chase.

Another highway was looming up on his left side, and Santa Paws slowed to a walk. Could he face trying to cross another scary road right now? After such a long day? Maybe it *was* time to rest. His stomach was rumbling, but he couldn't smell any food nearby. He would just have to go to sleep hungry.

He went back to find one of those sandy pits and dug a hole big enough to fit his body. Then he turned around three times, the way he always did, and curled up. At first, the sand felt chilly and he thought about moving. But he was too tired, and his body heat was starting to warm the hole up, anyway. It was easier to stay where he was.

Curled up alone in the darkness, Santa Paws thought about Gregory and Patricia. Would he find them tomorrow, maybe? He felt as though Oceanport was very far away, but he couldn't be sure. But he just missed them *so much*. And there was something particularly lonesome about being here on this deserted golf course, with nothing but the faint sound of speeding cars to keep him company.

The dog whined a couple of times, then closed his eyes. He knew that he was facing yet another cold, lonely night. The only good thing was that the sooner he fell asleep, the sooner it would be morning again.

At home in Oceanport, Uncle Steve had come over that afternoon with good news. The crime lab had gotten a "hit" — or match — on a couple of the unidentified fingerprints the technicians had collected from the station wagon. They belonged to a small-time thief named Chuck Hawthorne, who lived just north of Boston in the town of Revere. It turned out that he had a long history of committing crimes with the help of his little brother Eddie. They looked like even stronger suspects when a trace at the Massachusetts Department of Motor Vehicles showed that Eddie owned a six-year-old van!

The Revere Police were already on their way to the house where the brothers lived with their ill-tempered mother. They were planning to arrest the Hawthornes on suspicion of dognapping. If they were successful, the hoodlums would then be transferred up to Oceanport for questioning.

"Can I interrogate them?" Patricia wanted to know. "I know just what to ask!"

Uncle Steve glanced at Mr. and Mrs. Callahan, and then smiled. "Well — it's an idea, Patricia, but I don't think we should go that way. We have to be very careful with our procedures to make sure everything will hold up in court later."

"I would only ask questions," Patricia assured him. "I wouldn't, you know, physically threaten them."

Gregory nodded. "Yeah, you and Sipowicz."

Patricia flushed, since — okay, she watched more than her share of television. Especially police dramas.

"I appreciate the offer, Patty," Uncle Steve said, his eyes amused. "But you're just going to have to trust us to handle it ourselves, okay? We do this for a living." His pager went off, and he looked down to check the number. "That's my Lieutenant. I'd better check in."

Gregory and Patricia watched eagerly while he spoke on the phone. From his expression, it seemed as though he must be getting happy news. Uncle Steve hung up, looking elated.

"Okay, we're in business," he said. "Some state troopers spotted their van in a Wendy's parking lot near the Mass Pike, and arrested them when they came out." He pulled on his heavy police jacket and reached for his cane. "They're bringing them up now. I'd better get over to the station so I can meet them. I'll call as soon as I have more information."

Mr. Callahan clasped his brother's shoulder. "Thanks, Steve. We really appreciate how hard you're working on this."

"Hey, I wouldn't even be standing here right now if Santa Paws hadn't saved *my* life once,"

118

Uncle Steve said. "I don't just love that dog, I *owe* him."

"Don't let them lawyer up!" Patricia warned him.

Uncle Steve, who was halfway down the front steps, just laughed. Then, with a cheery wave, he left.

Gregory and Patricia exchanged huge grins. It was the first time they had felt happy since Saturday. They were trying not to get their hopes up too high, but it was almost impossible to avoid. Now that the police had apprehended the thieves, it meant that Santa Paws would be home soon. Maybe even tonight!

Santa Paws was sleeping restlessly in his sandy hole on the golf course. The combination of being hungry, cold, and sad made it very hard to relax. But he knew he needed to conserve his strength. Resting was the most practical way to do that.

Then, out of nowhere, there was a terrible sound of squealing car brakes, and he woke up with a start. What was *that*? He heard metal crunching, glass shattering, and tree limbs snapping. After a last dull crash, this was followed by complete silence.

Seeing that something bad had happened, the dog got up to investigate. The horrible sounds had come from the highway, and so he ranged off in that direction. Soon he came across the crumpled, steaming remains of a car. It had skidded off the road and down an embankment until it slammed into a tree.

The dog was very afraid of cars, but he knew he had to make sure everything was all right. He ventured closer, pausing to sniff the air every few steps. There was someone inside the car, but the person didn't seem to be moving. Santa Paws approached the driver's side and barked softly. The man inside was slumped against the steering wheel, unconscious. It wasn't good when people were very still like that! There was blood on his face, too. Blood was bad.

Very concerned now, the dog barked more loudly and pawed at the window. The man didn't respond in any way. Santa Paws tried a few more times, and then gave up. He knew that he had to go find help.

Fast!

11

The area seemed so isolated that Santa Paws wasn't sure where to go. He hated highways, but that seemed like his best chance. He scrambled up the embankment, and began barking at each car that passed. It was fairly late, so there actually weren't very many. None of them slowed down, so they must not have seen or heard him.

For a second, the dog considered standing in the middle of the road to attract their attention. He took two steps forward before changing his mind. It would be too easy for one of those cars to hit him that way!

No, he needed to find a house where nice people lived. Then maybe he could get them to come and help the man in the car. There were street lights up ahead, and he raced towards them. Good! There were houses here! Most of them had their lights out, though. He knew that meant that people were sleeping, and he shouldn't wake them up.

One of the houses *did* have lights on, and he dashed up the front walk. But then he heard what sounded like a ferocious Great Dane barking and growling inside. Not wanting any part of *that*, he wheeled around to go find a different house. He took shortcuts through yards, and heard other dogs bark at him. They were very *lucky* dogs, since they were safe at home with their owners. But, he didn't have time to think about that right now. Not with that man in trouble.

Around the next corner, he saw a house with plenty of lights on downstairs. He ran down the driveway and began pawing at the side door, barking frantically the whole time. He kept barking at the top of his lungs until someone came to the door to see what was going on.

It was a woman in her late forties with dark brown hair, wearing a flannel nightgown and slippers. She peeked outside, and then opened the door.

"What's wrong?" she asked.

Santa Paws wagged his tail, and barked.

"Whose dog are you, boy?" she asked curiously. "You don't look familiar."

Santa Paws barked, ran away a few steps, ran back, and barked some more.

Now a sleepy-looking man came to join the woman. "What's going on, Nancy?" he asked, putting on a pair of glasses so he could see better.

His wife shrugged. "I don't know. I can't remember seeing this dog around here before, can you?"

"No." The man yawned. "Look, I'm sure he'll calm down if we just leave him alone. If he keeps barking like this, he's going to wake the whole neighborhood up."

Seeing the man lift his hand as though he were about to close the door, Santa Paws barked more urgently. Didn't they understand? A man needed help, and they had to come, right away!

"Maybe he's lost," the man guessed. "I'll call the police, and they can send an animal control officer over."

"You'll do no such thing, George!" his wife Nancy said firmly. "If he's lost, we'll take him in for the night, and figure out what to do tomorrow."

George winced. "Oh, the cats are going to *love* that."

Nancy leaned down, snapping her fingers encouragingly. "Come here, boy. You can come in, it's okay."

Since she seemed to be receptive to him, Santa Paws grabbed her robe gently and tried to tug her outside. Then he let go of the cloth, and repeated his run up and down the driveway, barking.

"He's nuts," George said.

Nancy put her coat on over her nightgown. "Well, he's obviously trying to tell us something. I'm going out there to see what he wants."

"Dressed like that?" George asked.

His wife nodded.

"*You're* nuts," George said.

Nancy was already halfway down the driveway, following the frantic dog. George sighed and grabbed his own coat so he could go along.

Santa Paws led them back towards the highway. He stopped every few feet, just to make sure that they were still close behind. George grumbled about having to climb around the woods in his slippers, but Nancy plunged right in. When she saw the car, she caught her breath.

"George, call 911! There's been an accident!" she said. "Hurry, and I'll see what I can do until you get back."

George turned and ran to their house, his slippers flapping against the street with each noisy step.

"Don't worry, boy," Nancy said to Santa Paws. "We're going to get some help for your owner." She peered into the car at the unconscious man. The driver's side door was badly dented, but she was able to open the passenger's side. She climbed partway into the car to make sure the man was still alive. "Sir? Hello? Are you all right?"

The man didn't move, but the sound of his breathing was strong and regular. Nancy knew enough about first aid not to try to touch the man or move him. In a serious accident, it was always best to call an ambulance and wait for professional help. For now, she just took off her coat and used it to cover the man. It would help him stay warm until the paramedics arrived.

"Don't worry, mister," she said, even though she wasn't sure if the man could hear her. "The ambulance is on its way."

Outside the car, Santa Paws was too edgy to sit down, so he paced around. Was the man going to be okay now? Was this nice lady going to fix him? Had he done the right thing?

George came lumbering back from their house, out of breath.

"They'll be here any minute," he panted.

"Good," Nancy said. "I think this poor man's in pretty bad shape."

George nodded, and then gave her his coat since she was shivering. "The guy's lucky to have such a smart dog. You think he got thrown from the car?"

Nancy started to nod, then frowned. "Actually,

I don't know. The doors were all shut. The windows were closed, too."

"Well, he obviously got out *somehow*," George said.

Nancy nodded, and bundled her coat more closely around the injured man.

Santa Paws was the first one to hear the sirens, and his ears pricked forward. A minute or two later, George and Nancy heard them, too. George, who had brought a flashlight from the house, went up to the road to flag them down. It was actually the Hutchinson Parkway in Westchester County, which meant that Santa Paws had managed to travel pretty far that day. He was much closer to the Connecticut border than he had any way of knowing.

Then paramedics and police officers were climbing down the embankment. Santa Paws edged away a few feet. Seeing so many unfamiliar strangers all at once made him nervous. From their uniforms, he recognized that they must be people like Uncle Steve, but none of them looked or smelled familiar. So, he decided to play it safe and keep his distance.

The paramedics performed a quick examination of the injured driver. His vital signs were all strong, and they carefully fitted a supportive cervical collar around his neck to protect it. While they worked, the police officers interviewed George and Nancy. They were surprised to hear about the brave and loyal dog who had so cleverly saved his master's life, and they took detailed notes for their reports.

Just as the emergency medical technicians were strapping the driver to a backboard, he began to regain consciousness.

"Wh-where am I?" he asked. Then he groaned and tried to reach up and touch the bump on his forehead.

"Take it easy, sir," one of the paramedics said. "You've been in an accident, but you're going to be just fine." She did a few quick neurological tests and then nodded encouragingly at her partner. The man really *did* seem as though he would be okay.

"That's quite a dog you have there, sir," her partner said to the man. "He saved your life!"

The driver looked even more confused. "Dog? What dog?"

The paramedics looked worried, and repeated the series of neurological tests. Luckily, they got the same good results. Still, they couldn't help wondering if their patient might be suffering from some amnesia.

Now Nancy stepped forward. "Don't worry, sir, my husband and I will take your dog home for the night. We'll leave you our number, and you can pick him up as soon as you're feeling better."

"But I don't *have* a dog," the man said peevishly. "I don't even *like* dogs."

It was quiet, while everyone thought that over. Then one of the cops broke the silence.

"Well, maybe you should *start* liking them," he said, and everyone else nodded.

Nancy looked around to see where the dog was. If he didn't belong to the man, then maybe he really was lost. It was hard to believe that a stray would suddenly decide to rescue a complete stranger, but there was no other logical explanation. In any case, she wanted to make sure a great dog like that got home safely to his owners. And if he turned out to be an abandoned animal, then she and George would just keep him!

"Here, boy!" she called. "Where are you, boy?" She turned to her husband. "George, where did he go? We have to find him."

George shrugged. "I don't know. He was here a minute ago." He swung his flashlight back and forth, in case the dog was hiding nearby. "Come here, boy!"

The paramedics were carrying the driver up to the ambulance, so most of the police officers were now free to help search for the dog. They all fanned out into the trees, trying to catch a glimpse of the heroic stray. They searched, and called, and searched some more.

But, the dog was gone.

Wide awake from his adventure, Santa Paws decided to continue his journey north. If he got tired, he would just stop and sleep somewhere. But he might as well take advantage of this burst of energy. He *did* wish he weren't quite so hungry.

In some ways, it seemed much safer to travel at night. There wasn't much traffic, and if there were bad people around, they would have a hard time seeing him. Of course he was used to sleeping at night. Then again, he was also used to sleeping most of the day! Adapting to all of this running around was a big change for him.

He soon discovered that there was *one* small problem about being out after dark — most of the local wildlife was awake, too! He came upon a raccoon unexpectedly, next to a narrow creek, and they were both so flustered that they ran in opposite directions.

When he caught a whiff of skunk, he knew to give *that* animal a wide berth. Once he had gotten sprayed in the backyard at home, and Gregory and Patricia had given him about four baths in a row afterwards. Not only that, but they had used sticky tomato juice instead of water for two of them. Santa Paws hated baths, so he had vowed never to get near one of those black and white creatures again.

Later, he saw two deer in a small grove of trees, nibbling at some weeds. Then they bounded away on long skinny legs that were both elegant and also oddly awkward. The dog wasn't sure why he had made them so nervous, but he decided not to worry about it. Then, as he loped along through the darkness, he stepped on some broken glass by accident. It hurt a lot! Ow!

After putting weight on his right front paw, he realized that a sharp piece of glass was still stuck there. The dog stopped to see if he could pull it out. The glass was embedded deeply, and he had to gnaw at the piece for a couple of minutes before he could work it free. In the process, he cut his tongue a little bit, and whimpered. His paw was bleeding, and he licked the pads gently until the flow slowed down.

Then he stood up, cautious about putting his weight on that paw. It was painful, but not too bad. He didn't even really need to limp. So he started off again. From now on, though, he would try to be more careful about watching where he stepped. On a journey this long, he couldn't afford to injure himself. Things were difficult enough without adding *that* to his troubles!

Before long, the sky began to get brighter. The dog was getting tired and his trot had become more of a fast walk. His cut paw was aching, too. It was time to start searching for a nice, secluded spot to sleep. A spot *out* of the biting wind, if possible.

He noticed that there were folded newspapers in front of many of the houses he was passing. The newspapers had been dropped out near the street, which didn't seem right to him. At home, the Callahans' newspaper was placed neatly at the end of the driveway in the morning. Santa Paws always liked to be the one to bring it inside the house. Whenever he was awake, Mr. Callahan also let him go out to fetch the mail from the mailman, too. The dog felt good when he had special little tasks to do.

He was exhausted from his long night, but it still bothered him that these newspapers were in the wrong place. He should move them. So, at each house, he bent to pick up the newspaper on the sidewalk. Then he would run up to the front door, let it plop down nearby, and move on to the next house.

He was almost at the end of the road when he came to a small, well-kept white house with shiny black shutters. An elderly woman named Mrs. Steinberg lived there. Mrs. Steinberg was an early riser, and she enjoyed reading her morning newspaper with a cup of hot tea and some rye toast. Her paperboy, Todd, didn't have a very good throwing arm, so every day, her newspaper seemed to land in a different spot. Sometimes, she even had to dig it out of the bushes or from the flowerbeds. Luckily, Todd was extremely polite and likable, so this bad habit didn't bother her all that much.

Santa Paws grabbed Mrs. Steinberg's newspaper and ran up her cobblestoned front walk. He was just about to drop it on the welcome mat when the door suddenly opened. He and Mrs. Steinberg looked at each other in complete surprise. Then Santa Paws wagged his tail and deposited the newspaper directly into her hand.

"Well — thank you," she said, recovering from her amazement. She glanced around, but there was no sign of Todd — or anyone else, for that matter. "Good dog, I mean."

Santa Paws barked once, and then trotted towards the next house. He still had three more papers to redeliver.

Then, it would be nap time!

12

The night before, the Callahans had been very unhappy when they went to sleep. The news that the dognappers had been apprehended had seemed so promising, but it hadn't worked out that way. Over at the police station, the Hawthorne brothers were interrogated for several long, discouraging hours. They were kept in separate rooms, so the police could find out if their stories matched.

Chuck Hawthorne, the older of the two, just sneered a lot and kept demanding fresh cups of coffee and high-fat snacks. The only answer he gave to any question the police asked was, "I don't know." Luckily, Eddie was not as tough as his brother was. At first, he denied everything, but then he gave a complete confession. He even identified the eccentric millionaire who had hired them to commit the crime in the first place. The man's name and address would be faxed down to the appropriate police department in New Jersey, so that he could also be arrested.

When Chuck found out that his brother had caved in, he reluctantly confessed, too. This would have been wonderful news, except that both thieves said that Santa Paws had escaped from them on the Cross-Bronx Expressway. They had gotten off at the next exit, and driven around for a while to try and find him. When they had no luck, they gave up and came back home to Massachusetts. They were very mad that they had lost out on their fifty thousand dollars. And their trip to Atlantic City!

So Santa Paws was no longer in any danger from the criminals, but he *was* lost in a huge, often apathetic city. And — he was more than two hundred miles away from home!

When Uncle Steve had called with this updated information, at first, the Callahans were happy. Their dog had gotten away! Then, realizing what that meant, their happiness faded. In a city of more than eight million people, it would be close to impossible to find one lost German shepherd-mix.

"Are you *sure* we can't go to New York to look for him?" Gregory asked the next morning at breakfast.

The family had discussed this at length the night before, and Mr. and Mrs. Callahan decided that it just wasn't practical. New York was so big that they could search for *months* and never have any luck finding him.

"Your father's going to keep making calls this morning," Mrs. Callahan promised. "We'll get in touch with every animal shelter and police precinct in New York, to find out if anyone has seen him. And we'll just keep calling around, until we get some news."

Patricia and Gregory wanted to stay home from school to help call, but their parents didn't like that idea, either. They thought it would be better for them all to try and keep their lives as normal as possible. Patricia and Gregory weren't happy about this, but they just nodded glumly and pretended to eat their breakfasts.

Before it was time to leave for school, they went upstairs to check their e-mail yet again. Lots of people had been writing back to them, asking if they would send along a file attachment with a picture of Santa Paws. That way, their e-mail buddies — who lived all over the country — could print it out and make their own "Please Find Our Dog" signs. Patricia and Gregory were happy to do it, since they figured that there was no such thing as *too much* help in a situation like this.

"He doesn't know enough about cars," Gregory said unhappily. "How's he going to make it in a place like New York?"

Patricia had been thinking the exact same

135

thing. "I don't know, Greg," she said honestly.

Gregory didn't want to start crying, because then he would have to go to school with his eyes all red. So, he rubbed his sweatshirt sleeve across his face to try and keep the tears back. "You think he'll try to come home?" he asked, his voice muffled by his arm. "Dogs do that sometimes."

Patricia decided not to point out that dogs did that in the *movies*. She wasn't sure if it happened in real life. She sighed. "I just don't know, Greg. I sure hope so."

She knew that it wasn't very likely, but it was also probably the only way they would ever see their beloved dog again.

So tired that he was practically stumbling, Santa Paws finally curled up behind a stranger's garage to sleep. It was fairly well-protected from the wind, and he was able to burrow into an old compost heap for warmth. He slept all morning and into the early afternoon, without moving or even dreaming. He was just too exhausted for that. Running so many miles during the past three days had really taken a toll on his body.

When he finally woke up, his stomach was so empty that it was actually painful. He *hated* being on his own like this, he really did. He felt so sorry for himself that he had to whimper quietly for a while. And — his paw hurt, too.

With an effort, he dragged himself to his feet. Then he trudged out to the street and started on his way north again. Whenever he saw a trash can, he paused to sniff hopefully, but they always seemed to be empty. He had vaguely heard the noise of a big, grinding truck while he was sleeping. It must have been a garbage truck, picking up all of the nice, delicious trash.

He was so discouraged that he let his trot slow to a walk. Even at home, he was always hungry, but he needed extra energy to be able to travel. Right now, he didn't have any at all. He was even having trouble finding any puddles or brooks today. He walked along with his head slumped and his tail hanging down. He had gone so far, and there was still no sign — or scent — of his family. He was *never* going to find them. It was hopeless.

Soon, he came to a very tall chain-link fence. It was much too high for him to climb over, even if he hadn't been so worn-out. Besides, there were strands of nasty sharp wire at the top. But when he peeked through the fence, he could see that the ground of the other side was smooth and even. It looked much more comfortable than the streets and sidewalks he had been on most of the afternoon.

He wandered along the fence to see if there might be a hole. As soon as he found one, he quickly crawled through. There were two long metal tracks with smoothly-packed earth on both sides. The tracks ran as far as he could see in either direction. He liked the fact that there didn't seem to be any cars around, so he decided to give this route a try.

He wandered north along the train tracks for a while. Once he passed a cement platform with a small building behind it. There were people with suitcases waiting on the platform, but none of them even noticed him as he slunk by. That was fine with him!

He walked and walked and walked. Sometimes the embankment next to the tracks was too steep, and he found it easier to walk on the tracks themselves. But he liked the embankments better, because they were softer, and there were no metal bars to trip on.

He heard voices, and stopped short, all of his senses alerted. Was that danger ahead? Should he try and escape? Realizing that the voices were young, he relaxed. They were *boys*. Boys — and girls, of course — were his friends!

Feeling a little spurt of energy, he picked up his pace. It might be fun to walk with the boys. Besides, they might lead him to a place where he could find Gregory!

The three boys were friends from a nearby elementary school. Their names were Harold, Carver, and Jason, and they were all in the fifth grade. They weren't allowed to walk on the train tracks, but they did it almost every day, anyway. They had always heard that train tracks were very dangerous, and their parents had ordered them never to go near the area, but the boys didn't believe it. If no one was supposed to be on the tracks, how come the fences surrounding them had so many holes? Besides, they were sure nothing bad would happen to *them*. Unless, of course, their parents found out, and then they would all get grounded — probably for years!

Santa Paws caught up to them without much trouble, barking happily.

"Hey, check it out!" Harold said. "Pretty neat dog!"

They all gathered around Santa Paws to pat him, and see if he knew any tricks. Santa Paws cooperatively shook their hands, rolled over, and even played dead for a minute.

"*Cool*," Carver said. "Wonder whose dog he is?"

Jason felt the thick fur around the dog's neck. "No collar or anything. Maybe he got lost."

"Maybe his owners are really mean, and he ran away!" Harold guessed.

"So, let's see if he'll follow us," Carver said.

The boys continued along the tracks, with Santa Paws trotting right behind them.

"I know my mother won't let me," Jason said, "but maybe one of you guys can bring him home."

The other two boys looked at each other doubtfully.

"Well — maybe," Carver said. "I don't think my parents would want another dog, though. We already have two."

Harold just shrugged. His family had three rabbits, a guinea pig and some fish, so he wouldn't even bother asking for permission, probably. He knew they would say no.

"But it'll still be fun to play with him for a while," Jason said, and his friends agreed.

From somewhere down the tracks, there was a rumbling and a loud whistle. The boys didn't even seem to notice, but Santa Paws stopped right away. It sounded like a *really big* truck. It sounded bad. Maybe this wasn't a very good place to travel, after all.

"It's okay, dog," Harold said, and patted his back. "We always wait until they come pretty close before we jump out of the way."

"Yeah," Jason said enthusiastically. "Trains don't scare *us*. We think it's fun!"

What it was, was a very stupid and dangerous game. Trains were so fast and powerful that it took them a *very* long time to stop. Even if the engineer noticed a car or a person on the tracks, by the time the train would be able to stop, the obstacle would have long since been run over. There was no such thing as a *safe* way to walk across railroad tracks. The only smart thing to do would just be to stay away from them at all times.

The train chugged closer and closer. From a distance, it was impossible to tell how fast it was going. So it was easy to be fooled into thinking it was moving much more slowly than it really was. Santa Paws could feel the vibration of the railroad cars through the tracks and he moved nervously over to the embankment. He didn't like this place at all anymore, and wished he had never crawled through that hole in the fence.

"What a baby," Carver scoffed.

The boys waited on the tracks until the train was so close that its whistle was almost deafening.

"Okay," Harold shouted. "I count to three, and then we run!"

His friends nodded, grinning wildly. They liked "playing chicken" with trains. They had heard of other kids getting hurt, or even killed, that way, but they *knew* it would never happen to them. Not a chance.

"One!" Harold counted. "Two! Three!"

With that, he and Carver scrambled up onto the embankment and out of the way. Jason started to follow, but he slipped. He tried to get up, but found that he couldn't for some reason. He looked down and saw that his foot had slid underneath one of the railroad ties. He tried to yank himself free, but his ankle was too tightly

— and painfully — jammed between the hard-packed ground and the thick metal bar.

He was stuck, and the train was speeding directly towards him!

"Help!" he screamed. "Somebody help me!"

Santa Paws was terrified of the monstrous machine bearing down towards them, but he would never ignore a cry for help. He leapt off the embankment and down onto the tracks. Jason was trying to get up, but his lower leg was pinned in place by the railroad tie. He was so scared he started crying as he tugged helplessly at his rapidly-swelling ankle with both hands.

Up on the embankment, his friends began crying, too. The train was going to hit Jason, and if they went down there to help, they would be run over, too. Why hadn't they listened to their parents, and just walked home safely along the sidewalks? Now it was too late!

The train whistle was so loud that Santa Paws was having trouble thinking clearly. The engineer could see that there was something on the tracks, and put on the brakes. But the train had too much momentum, and it would be impossible for him to stop in time.

Jason cried harder and fought to get free from the rail pinning his sneaker. Santa Paws yanked on his jeans leg with his teeth, but the boy's foot didn't budge. So he fastened his jaw around the sneaker itself and shook his head back and forth fiercely. He would *make* that ankle come loose! The dog was able to tear away a few shreds of rubber, but it wasn't quite enough to set the boy free. So he dug fiercely at the cinder-packed ground under the railroad tie, using both paws.

The train was almost upon them now! There was an earsplitting metallic screech as the engineer pressed on the brakes with every ounce of strength he had. But the train just kept hurtling forward.

If Santa Paws jumped now, he would have just enough time to be able to save himself. Instead, he stayed on the tracks with Jason, still using his strong front paws and teeth to try and pry the boy's foot loose. The train was so close now that he could actually feel the heat from the engine. At the last second, he gave up and dug his teeth into the back of Jason's ski jacket, instead.

Using all four of his legs for leverage, the dog tugged backwards with one great, twisting wrench. Jason's foot popped right out of his sneaker and he fell backwards with a gasp of pain. Using more power than he knew he had, Santa Paws yanked him off the track and dragged him to safety, just in the nick of time!

Jason cringed as the train roared past them. Santa Paws was scared, too, but he kept his body protectively between the boy and the thundering machine. He yelped when rocks and hot cinders flung up by the train's speed struck against him, but he never moved.

Up on the embankment, Carver and Harold weren't sure if Jason had escaped because the train was blocking their view. They didn't want to look, anyway, because they were too afraid of what they might see.

About a hundred yards down the track, the train finally ground to a noisy halt. Immediately, conductors and other railroad workers jumped off. They ran back down the tracks, terrified that they had just run over a young boy.

Carver was the first one to be brave enough to peek at the spot where his friend had been. All he could see was — a badly mauled sneaker. Then he saw the big dog stand up from the space between the north- and southbound tracks. The dog shook his coat free of cinders and then nudged a weak and trembling Jason to his feet.

"The dog did it," Carver breathed. "He saved him!"

Jason just stood where he was, crying. He had sprained his ankle, but other than that, he was perfectly fine. Santa Paws ushered him firmly across the tracks and over to the relative safety of the embankment. He growled deep in his throat, because he didn't like it that the boys had been playing such a bad game, and wanted to warn them never to do it again. He knew now that railroad tracks were not a place for *anyone* to walk. Since the boys were still all crying, he hoped that they knew it, too.

There were lots of people racing towards them, and the dog didn't like *that*, either. They all seemed upset, and some of them looked angry, too. Since Santa Paws was feeling a little dazed and groggy himself, he didn't really want to be around yet another crowd of yelling strangers. He was *tired* of strangers.

The men and women from the train were overjoyed when they discovered that the little boy had somehow managed to escape. They had been *sure* that a terrible tragedy had taken place.

"Do you realize what a close call that was, young man?" one of the conductors asked sternly. "You could have been killed!"

Jason — and his friends — nodded meekly.

By now, the local police had been summoned and two officers were climbing down to the tracks from their squad car. When they heard about the near accident, they got angry, too.

"You boys are going to ride home with us," one of the officers said. "Each and every one of your parents is going to hear all about what happened here today!"

Jason and his friends nodded, looking guilty. They had been expressly forbidden from ever setting foot on these tracks, and their parents were not going to like hearing that they had been disobeyed. The boys would probably be grounded — and they knew that they deserved it.

"You're just very lucky you got away in time," the other officer said grimly.

"It wasn't luck," Jason mumbled. "The dog saved me."

The adults all frowned at him.

"What dog?" one of them asked finally.

"The German shepherd," Harold explained. "He pulled Jason free."

Now the adults looked puzzled, as well as annoyed.

"I don't see any dog," one of the police officers said, sounding very suspicious.

Confused by all of this, Jason and his friends looked around the embankment and tracks.

The dog had disappeared!

13

Santa Paws was very, very tired. He had taken advantage of the confusion at the train tracks to escape through a hole in the fence. Then he had run away until he couldn't go any further. Now all he wanted to do was collapse somewhere and get some sleep.

Many of the houses he passed were covered with bright holiday lights, and often, a cheery Christmas tree was visible through the front windows. Other than sadly noticing the appetizing smell of suppers being cooked, the dog didn't pay attention to anything else.

He found a small playground and limped inside. The sun had long since gone down, so the park was empty, of course. When he had been struggling to free the little boy, the cut on his paw had gotten much bigger. It was throbbing now, and he felt as though gravel had gotten stuck inside the wound. It hurt a whole lot.

The playground had a sandbox, and he wearily

climbed inside. Then he fell asleep almost before he had time to lie down.

It had been a very long day. He was glad it was over.

During the night, it began to snow. The dog moved from the sandbox to underneath the slide. Small flakes pelted him from both sides, but he was sheltered from the full force of the storm. Even so, it was very cold, and despite his thick brown fur, he could feel himself shivering.

By morning, at least six inches had fallen, and the snow was still coming down lightly. Santa Paws gazed out at the wind-blown drifts covering the playground. Normally, he liked snow, but today it just seemed like another burden. The thought of plodding along through all of those drifts made him feel tired all over again.

He licked up some of the snow to soothe his dry throat. Eating snow made him feel even colder, but it was better than nothing. Then he crawled out from underneath the slide. The snow was the light, dry kind, as opposed to the wet, sticky type. That made it easier to walk, but hard ice crystals quickly formed around his paws. He had to stop fairly often, to chew them away.

Most of the streets had been plowed, but road salt had been sprinkled everywhere. The salt made the cut on his paw burn — and his other paws began stinging, too. So Santa Paws avoided the roads as much as possible. That meant he had to climb over uneven drifts, which was very strenuous. In no time, he was panting.

When he turned a corner, he saw a McDonald's. He sniffed the air eagerly and his mouth began watering. Eggs, and bacon, and other wonderful odors! Forgetting his fatigue, he galloped over to the restaurant. One of the workers had just been emptying the trash, but he ran out of bags and went back into the restaurant to get more. In the meantime, he had left several sealed bags piled up near the Dumpsters.

Without worrying about whether it was bad, Santa Paws immediately tore one open. It was full of discarded food! He began gobbling the remains of Egg McMuffins, pancakes, sausages, and other breakfast foods. There were even some small cartons with milk left inside, and he slurped up as much as he could.

"Hey, you!" a voice called out.

Santa Paws wagged his tail pleasantly and went back to eating.

The young man, Wayne, who had been emptying the trash earlier, was frustrated to see that some of it was now strewn across the snow. But he liked dogs, and didn't really want to yell at this one.

"Come on, buddy," he said patiently. "I've got work to do here."

Buddy! Gregory sometimes called him Buddy! Santa Paws wagged his tail, and gulped down the remains of some hash browns.

Wayne had to laugh. *His* dog was a pig, too. "Go on home now, boy, okay? Good dog." Then he bent down to start cleaning up the mess.

Although there was still food inside the bag, Santa Paws stepped back politely. The boy didn't seem angry at him, and he wanted to keep it that way. But it was sad to see all of those tempting bags being tossed up into a Dumpster well above his head. It was *wasteful*.

Deciding that he wasn't going to get any more food, Santa Paws turned to go. He barked a friendly bark, and trotted away. Once he reached the street, he had to turn around a few times to get oriented. Then, once he was confident he was headed in the right direction, he started off. With a little food in his stomach, he was in a *much* better mood.

A family of five was just leaving the drive-thru window in their Subaru. They were the Kramers, and they were on their way to Rhode Island to visit their grandparents for Christmas. Mr. and Mrs. Kramer wanted to go up a couple of days early to help with the baking and decorating. They had three little girls. Janice was twelve, Gail was nine, and Susan had just turned four. For a special treat, their parents had decided to start their trip off with a quick stop at McDonald's.

Gail was the first one to notice the large brown dog moving steadily along the side of the road. "Look!" she said, so excited that she spilled most of her orange juice. "That's Santa Paws!"

Her father glanced at her in the rearview mirror. "Are you a sleepyhead this morning? You mean, Santa *Claus*."

"No, I don't," Gail insisted. "It's Santa Paws. He's magic!"

"Santa Paws!" Susan said happily, although she really didn't know what they were talking about.

Janice twisted around in her seat until she could figure out where her sister was pointing. Then she saw the dog, too. His ears made him look like the Flying Nun, so she recognized him right away. She had seen his picture in newspapers and on the Internet, and once on a cable news station. Even though this dog looked pretty scruffy, he was still very distinctive. "Hey, you're right," she said. "That *is* Santa Paws. Stop the car, Dad!"

Their father was utterly confused. "What on earth are you talking about?"

"Santa Paws," Janice repeated herself, speaking extra slowly. "The famous dog. The hero. *You* know."

151

"He's *America's* dog," Gail said solemnly.

"That's right," Janice agreed. "How can you not have heard of him, Dad?"

"I don't know," Mr. Kramer said defensively, and then he looked over at his wife. "Have you heard of Santa Paws?"

"Of course," Mrs. Kramer answered as she sliced a pancake into manageable pieces for Susan. "I thought everyone had."

"Yeah, really, Dad," Janice said. "You have to start spending more time online. He's all *over* the Internet."

Mrs. Kramer nodded, since she had seen a couple of messages about the famous lost dog, too. "It's also been in the papers since he got lost," she said. "Pull over, David."

Mr. Kramer shrugged and stopped the car at the side of the road. Janice and Gail unbuckled their seatbelts so quickly that Gail spilled what was left of her orange juice. Then they jumped out of the car, with their mother following close behind.

"Santa Paws!" Janice shouted. "Come here, Santa Paws!"

The dog stopped dead in his tracks. *Santa Paws?* Had he just heard his name? Puzzled, he lifted one paw out of the snow.

Gail clapped her hands a few times. "Come on, Santa Paws!"

Children. As always, he liked children. And if

these people knew his name, maybe they knew the Callahans! Santa Paws ran over, wagging his tail. The girls were patting him, and he raised his paw to shake their hands. They thought that was pretty cool, and they patted him some more.

Mr. Kramer stayed right by the car so he could keep an eye on Susan. Susan was interested in the big brown dog, but she was more interested in her breakfast.

Janice thought for a minute. "On the website I saw, it said to call the Oceanport Police Department. Up in Massachusetts."

"Why don't we bring him to RI?" Gail suggested logically. "Then his family can come get him."

The Kramers stood and debated all of this, since their car was quite crowded. Finally, Mr. Kramer was overruled, and it was decided that Santa Paws would come to Rhode Island with them. They would call the Oceanport Police Department on the way, and see what to do after that.

"He really needs a bath," Mr. Kramer said, still uneasy about all of this.

"Of course he does, Dad," Gail said. "He's been *lost.*"

"We'll just leave the windows cracked open," Mrs. Kramer decided. "Come on, Santa Paws."

When Santa Paws figured out that they wanted him to get into the car, his legs stiffened.

This family seemed very nice, but the *last* time he had gotten into a car with strangers, very bad things had happened to him.

"Santa Paws!" Susan said, and waved a little piece of sausage at him.

Santa Paws instantly forgot all of his reservations and leapt into the backseat. Sausage was one of his very favorites!

"All right," Mrs. Kramer said, once everyone was safely inside the car, and she was sure that her daughters were wearing their seatbelts. "Let's go find a telephone, and then get on the road. We have a long drive ahead of us."

Santa Paws wasn't sure what was going on, but it felt good to be with a family again. He would just stay here for a while, and wait to see where they went. Besides, Susan still had some sausage left, and she might share with him.

What he didn't know, was that he was on his way home!

Mr. Callahan heard the happy news from Uncle Steve about an hour later. He quickly called the high school and the middle school to let the rest of the family know what had happened. Santa Paws had been found!

Mrs. Callahan arranged to have someone else teach the rest of her classes that day. Then she drove over to the middle school to pick up Gregory and Patricia. The plan was for the whole family to drive down to Providence, Rhode Island, to meet the Kramers when they arrived. Then they would get their adored dog and drive him back to Oceanport. Santa Paws would be home for Christmas!

They were all so excited that everyone talked at once as they drove. A joyous reunion was ahead of them, and they could hardly wait.

"I knew the Internet would help," Gregory said with a huge grin on his face. "I just knew it!"

Patricia looked worried. "I hope he's okay. Did they say he was okay?"

Mr. Callahan shrugged. "According to Steve, the Kramers said he was just fine. They found him on a road in Connecticut, heading this way."

"So he *was* coming home," Gregory said proudly.

"He was certainly trying," Mr. Callahan agreed.

The family drove down Route 128 to connect to Interstate 95. None of them could stop smiling — or talking. In a few hours, their dog would be back where he belonged. All of their hopes and prayers had been answered, after all!

The further the Kramers drove, the more nervous Santa Paws got. Where were they going? Why was it taking so long? They kept patting him and saying words like "family" and "home."

He liked the Kramers, but he had his own family. The last thing he wanted was to live with a *new* family, no matter how kind they were. So he whined deep in his throat, and fidgeted around in the backseat.

The dog loved riding in cars, but he was feeling too tense to look out the windows. Every time he saw the scenery flashing by, it seemed as though his chances of finding the Callahans were becoming even more unlikely. This family could be taking him *anywhere*!

"He seems really nervous," Janice said. "Do you think he's carsick?"

"He's probably just tired," Mrs. Kramer guessed. "He must have had a pretty rough week."

"I guess so," Janice said, not quite convinced. "But — he's acting funny."

Gail patted the top of his head. "It's okay, Santa Paws. You'll be home soon."

Santa Paws managed a polite wag of his tail, but the word "home" sent another chill of fear down his spine. He only had *one* home. Going to a different one would be awful.

The car stopped once, so that Mr. Kramer could get gas and Mrs. Kramer could take Susan to the ladies' room. When the back door opened, Santa Paws tensed, getting ready to jump.

Gail put her arm around him to hold him back. "Sit, Santa Paws."

He obeyed automatically — but he didn't like it.

Soon, the family was back on the road again. Sometimes they sang Christmas carols, and sometimes Mrs. Kramer handed out snacks. Santa Paws felt so edgy that he didn't even eat the oatmeal cookie Gail gave him. He was much too worried to be hungry. Riding in the car made it too hard to keep his sense of direction, and he had no idea where they were going. With each passing mile, he felt more and more anxious.

After what seemed like years to the dog, they drove into the city of Providence. Seeing tall buildings and concrete, Santa Paws began to panic. They were in a city! They weren't supposed to be in a city. He didn't *live* in a city. He didn't want to hurt the Kramers' feelings, but there was no way that he was going to be able to stay with them. He was going to have to run away, the first chance he got.

The plan Uncle Steve had arranged was for the Kramers to meet Gregory, Patricia, and their parents in front of the Trinity Square Repertory Company in downtown Providence. It was a landmark both families knew well, and it was small enough so that they would have no trouble finding one another.

Mr. Kramer was driving towards Trinity Square when Susan announced that she needed to find another bathroom.

"Are you sure you can't wait?" he asked.

Susan was quite sure.

"It'll only take a minute," Mrs. Kramer said. "Besides, we're here a little early."

Feeling the car slow down, Santa Paws sat up alertly. Were they about to stop? He sure hoped so!

"That's right," Janice told him. "We're almost there."

Santa Paws wagged his tail absentmindedly as he watched the street outside. Yes, this was definitely a city. It also did not seem at all familiar. Where in the world had they taken him? This was just terrible!

Mr. Kramer stopped the car in front of a small, family-run restaurant. Gail was going to hold on to Santa Paws while her mother took Susan inside. But she changed her mind at the last minute.

"Wait, I'm coming, too," she said. She opened the back door and climbed out of the car.

In the split second before she closed it again, Santa Paws vaulted out after her. He needed to escape, so he could get back on the road and find his family. He looked at the busy street apprehensively, but then picked a direction at random and started running.

"Hey, wait!" Gail protested. "Come back, Santa Paws!"

Janice joined her on the sidewalk. "Come on, Santa Paws! Please?"

The family had been very sweet to him, and he paused just long enough to turn and wag his tail at them. Then, with a farewell bark, he loped gracefully away.

Mr. Kramer, Janice, and Gail tried their best to catch him, but the dog was too fast. Within a block or two, it was as though he had just melted away into the city. They kept running for several more blocks, but then regretfully gave up.

They had done a wonderful thing by finding Santa Paws — but now, unfortunately, he was lost again!

14

The Callahans had never met the Kramers before, but when they saw a sad-looking family waiting in front of the Trinity Square theater, they knew that something must have gone wrong.

"Where's Santa Paws?" Gregory asked nervously. "I don't see Santa Paws."

Mr. and Mrs. Callahan exchanged glances, both of them expecting the worst.

"Well, maybe he's in the car, Greg," Mr. Callahan said, trying to sound optimistic.

Since they could see that all three of the Kramer girls looked miserable, that wasn't very likely. Mrs. Callahan parked the station wagon, and they quietly got out. Gregory clenched his fists and Patricia kept swallowing over and over, as they prepared to hear bad news.

When the Kramers told them the unhappy story, Gregory and Patricia couldn't believe it. They had come *so close* to getting their dog back, and now he was gone. It didn't seem possible. Neither of them could think of anything to say, so they just smiled weakly at the Kramers and tried not to start crying.

Their parents thanked the Kramers profusely for everything they had done, and for trying so hard to bring their dog home. The Kramers felt very guilty about the way things had turned out, but Mr. and Mrs. Callahan assured them that it was no one's fault. After another few minutes of conversation, the two families exchanged subdued Merry Christmases, and went their separate ways.

"They should have kept a better eye on him," Gregory said grimly, once the Kramers were gone.

Mrs. Callahan put her arm around him. "They did their best, Greg. I'm sure he just got scared, because he didn't know where they were taking him."

Gregory only shrugged, and rubbed the back of his hand across his eyes. Patricia was so stunned and upset that she hadn't said anything at all the entire time.

"Let's get back in the car," Mr. Callahan said. "We still have a couple of hours before it gets dark, and we'll just drive around and look for him. Come on, everyone."

The rest of the family followed him without much enthusiasm. Santa Paws had gotten a big head start, and he could be anywhere by now. They knew that finding him in the middle of Providence would be a long shot, but they had to *try*.

Once Santa Paws was sure he had gotten away, he ran into an empty parking lot to catch his breath. He had to take the time to figure out which direction he wanted to go. He had a strange sense that the Callahans were fairly close by, but he couldn't imagine where that would be. Or why. He was *sure* he had never been to this place before, and there was nothing that reminded him of Oceanport. It wasn't as scary and crowded as that other city had been, but there were still too many buildings and too many cars for him to feel safe.

The parking lot had been plowed, but it was still very icy. The dog sat down in a small, soot-stained drift to think. He sniffed the air for a long time, searching for something — *anything* — familiar. There were lots of city smells, like car exhaust and garbage, but now he also noticed a distinct trace of the sea. He was someplace near the ocean! That was good!

His instincts felt very confusing, because part of him wanted to travel north, and part of him felt pulled back in the other direction. That didn't make any sense, and he rested his head on his front paws for a minute. Why did he feel so torn?

162

North. He *knew* he wanted to go north. As far as he could tell, the conflict he felt was probably that he was sorry he had made that nice family feel unhappy. He just hoped they understood that he lived somewhere else — not this city, and his real family *needed* him. It was time to be on his way.

Santa Paws stood up, shaking away some loose snow. He had had a good long rest in that car. Now his legs felt strong and powerful again. He gave the air one last long sniff, and then trotted out of the parking lot. He had to turn a couple of corners before he was sure he was going in the right direction.

Then, running with a comfortable, steady gait, he headed north.

Providence was smaller than he expected, and he soon found himself on the outskirts of the city. His journey took him down streets with three-decker houses, and through old industrial areas. He stayed well to the east of the big highway, but followed in the same general direction. There were some train tracks, too, but he knew better than to go near *them*. Once was more than enough!

Darkness was falling, and he liked the protection that gave him. Other than the Callahans, he didn't want anyone else to get a chance to recognize him. *Ever again.* It was much too dangerous. For all he knew, that nice little family had taken him *miles* out of his way. He wasn't going to risk having that happen twice.

Some of the roads had too much traffic, but he had learned a lot about using stop lights and overpasses to help himself safely avoid cars. The big streets still frightened him, but not as much as they had a few days earlier.

How long had it been since he had seen his family? He had no idea, but it felt like *years*. It would be so nice to curl up on his rug in front of the fireplace in the living room. He would be nice and warm, and someone would probably give him a Milk-Bone! Remembering what it was like at home made him feel so forlorn that his mile-eating trot slowed to a walk. Now all he wanted to do was go somewhere and lie down and lick his sore paw.

Mournfully, he pressed on. Tonight he was noticing happy Christmas lights and other holiday decorations. Being by himself at this time of year seemed even sadder, somehow. He almost stopped to howl for a while, but just whimpered quietly to himself, instead.

He noticed a car up ahead of him slowing down. Cautiously, he stepped into the shadows of a hardware store that had closed for the evening. Did the people see him? Was it the nice people? Was it the *bad* people? He waited against the side of the building, preparing to run away if necessary.

Someone on the passenger's side of the car opened the door and dropped what looked like a sack in the gutter. Then the door slammed shut, and the car drove away. Santa Paws didn't know what to make of that. How strange people could be!

When he was sure the car was gone, he ventured out into the street. He had a lot on his mind, but he was still curious to see what was in the sack. Maybe it was food! With that thought, he broke into a run. The nice family had given him lots of snacks, but that was several hours ago. Now, he was hungry again.

As he approached the sack, he saw that it was moving. He stopped. What if it was one of those nasty little animals with the bald pink tails? Yuck! He took a tentative step forward, then sniffed. Well, it didn't *smell* like one of those ugly rodents. In fact, it smelled — familiar.

The sack was an old pillowcase, with a knot tied tightly at the top. Whatever was inside was writhing around and making a small squeaking noise. No, wait, it wasn't squeaking.

The sound was more like — it was a *cat*!

Santa Paws woofed gently, hoping that the cat would relax. It would be much easier to free her if she weren't flipping around like that. Finally, he just rested a heavy paw on the squirming animal. That worked pretty well, and he began chewing a hole in the corner of the pillowcase. Once he got started, the cloth tore easily. He created a good-sized opening and then lifted his head out of the way.

After a short pause, a young black kitten stepped delicately out. The kitten took one look around and then swatted Santa Paws right on the nose. All of her tiny claws were extended, and the blow stung. But, more than anything, the dog's feelings were hurt. He had gone to all the trouble of saving this cat, and all he got in return was a vicious swipe across the face? It didn't seem fair.

Pleased to have established her dominance, the cat promptly sat down between the dog's outstretched paws. Then, with tremendous dignity, she began to wash. She was a beautiful kitten, about eight months old, with silky black fur and yellowish-orange eyes.

Santa Paws was dumbfounded. Even though he had lived with one for a long time, he didn't understand cats at all. As far as he was concerned, they were *mean*. His pride was so badly wounded that he got up to leave.

In a flash, the kitten switched from dignity to charm. She began to purr loudly and rub her head against the dog's legs.

Santa Paws wasn't fooled for a second. As far as he was concerned, this little cat was only *pretending* to like him. If Santa Paws relaxed, the cat would probably turn right around and smack him again. Anyway, he had saved the kitten's life already, so now he was free to go on his way.

Seeing him start up the street, the kitten fell into the gutter and began to mew pitifully. Santa Paws tried to ignore the crying, but he just couldn't. With a deep sigh, he turned to go back. The kitten stopped crying at once, and purred energetically.

Santa Paws knew that the kitten really *should* be upset. After all, some mean people had just tossed her out of a car and abandoned her on a dark, snowy street. Gently, he nosed her out of the gutter and up onto the sidewalk. She would be much safer there, out of the road. He was sure someone kind would come along soon and give her a new home.

As he straightened up, the kitten swung her paw back and — wham! — scratched him again. The dog growled at her just loudly enough to show that he was irritated. The kitten's orange-yellow eyes seemed to brighten with mischief, and then — whack! — she let him have it one more time.

Very annoyed, Santa Paws headed up the street. He didn't feel like spending the rest of the night getting scratched. As far as he was concerned, that little feline could just fend for herself.

The kitten let out a terrified squeak and scampered after him. The dog barked sharply at her and kept going. But it would take more than *that* to discourage this stubborn kitten. Every time the dog looked over his shoulder, he saw the little cat trailing along behind him.

Santa Paws was very tempted to break into a run, and see if he could leave her behind. But this kitten was cute, and brave, and he was starting to like her in spite of himself. So he paused long enough to give her a chance to catch up. Then they trotted down the street together.

Whether he liked it or not, Santa Paws now had a traveling companion!

Having the kitten along slowed the dog's progress a great deal. The little cat wasn't used to the cold and snow, and she was finding it hard to keep up. Also, some of the drifts were so deep that they were almost over her head. They had to stop and rest much more often than the dog would have liked. Each time, the kitten would snuggle up against his body for warmth. It was nice not to be alone anymore, but she certainly was making things difficult!

It had taken forever, but they were now out of the city and into the quieter suburbs Santa Paws preferred. The kitten was complaining with hunger, so Santa Paws tipped over a couple of trash cans for her. He was happy to eat anything that seemed edible, but the cat was much more particular. She picked through the garbage, tasting a morsel here and a morsel there. The dog had always figured that as long as it was food, it was just fine.

Every instinct in his body was urgently pulling him north now. Santa Paws had hoped to travel all night, but he wasn't sure the kitten could handle it. At home, Evelyn the cat never went outside at all. The dog wasn't sure, but maybe cats were only happy inside houses. This little kitten certainly seemed cold and tired.

He was able to urge her forward for another couple of hours. Then she plopped down in the snow and refused to go any further.

Except, they were right in the middle of the street! Did she really think they were going to sleep *here*? It was a pretty deserted road, but still. The houses were spread fairly far apart here, so it was more like the country than a suburb. Off in the distance, the dog could smell some barnyard animals like cows and horses and sheep. There were a few small farms in Oceanport, and he wondered if he might actually be near home. But he couldn't smell the ocean, so he knew that these were different farms. He wasn't surprised, but he *was* disappointed.

If the dog had been alone, he would have dug a deep hole in the snow and used it for a nest. But somehow, he knew the kitten wouldn't be satisfied with that. He could see what looked like a vacant building further down the road. If they were lucky, he would be able to find a way inside.

The kitten complained with a fierce meow when he used his paw to boost her to her feet. Santa Paws ignored that, already on his way down the plowed road. The kitten followed him cooperatively, although she was so tired she kept slipping.

The building turned out to be a small house that was under construction. The walls and roof had been completed, but the inside was an empty shell. It was pretty well boarded-up, but there were plenty of pet-sized openings. The dog led the kitten inside through some torn tar paper. He promptly stepped on a nail and yelped in pain. This time, he had injured one of his *back* paws.

The kitten had already found a comfortable place to sleep on some piles of insulation which hadn't been installed yet. Santa Paws yanked the nail out of his back foot with his teeth and then limped over to join her. The kitten reached her paw out, and he flinched instinctively. But, to his surprise, the kitten just patted him affection-ately on the nose. Then she curled into a tight little ball and went to sleep.

Now that they were in out of the cold, the dog realized that *he* was pretty tired, too. He yawned widely and turned around three times. Then he arranged himself carefully next to the kitten, and closed his eyes.

When he woke up some time later, he wasn't sure what had disturbed his peaceful sleep. He blinked his eyes in the darkness, waiting for them to adjust to the light. Was there an intruder? Were they in danger? The kitten was still sound asleep, all tucked up against his side.

The dog lifted his ears and listened for any unusual or disturbing sounds. *Something* was wrong, but he wasn't sure what it was. He could hear — crackling, and horses neighing. Then, as the smell of smoke filled his nostrils, he understood what the problem was.

Somewhere nearby, there was a fire!

15

Santa Paws sprang to his feet and dashed towards the ripped tar paper. The kitten mewed in protest, wondering why her new chum was leaving her so abruptly. Santa Paws just tore out of the house and began running towards the smoke.

For lack of a better idea, the kitten scurried after him. She really didn't want to be left alone in the middle of nowhere!

There was a burning barn across a field a couple of hundred yards away. Santa Paws vaulted over a snow-covered stone wall and into the field. He could hear panic-stricken horses neighing from inside the stable, and see the bright glow of flames burning through the barn's roof. He could also see a house, but all of its lights were off. The owners must be asleep.

At first, Santa Paws ran to the back door of the house and began barking. He scratched his paws against the door and barked, but no one came. Okay, if the people weren't going to wake up, he would have to try to save the horses by himself.

Santa Paws turned his attention to the barn. As far as he could tell from the mixture of scents in the air, there were four or five horses inside, and they all sounded terrified. The fire had started somewhere back in the area where the hay and oats were kept. It was spreading so quickly that the smoke was even thick *outside*.

The barn doors were closed and Santa Paws pushed against them with all his might. But they didn't move an inch. He moved back to give himself a running start, and then slammed his body against the doors. They *still* didn't move.

Then he felt the bite of small claws as the kitten ran right up his back. He was going to shake her off, but he could see that she was trying to reach something. He stood up on his hind legs, resting his front paws against the doors. Now she was high enough, and the kitten used her paw to flick the latch open. Then she jumped lightly to the ground.

With the doors unlatched, Santa Paws thrust himself forward again, pushing as hard as he could. When he backed off for a second, the kitten stuck her paw in the crack between the two doors and pulled one of them towards her. They were doors that needed to be *pulled*, not *pushed*.

Santa Paws took over now, using his body to

open the door she had loosened for him. Great gusts of smoke came billowing out at them. Santa Paws took one last deep breath of fresh air and rushed inside the inferno. Although he didn't notice, the kitten charged in right after him. Most of the barn's roof had burned away, and the flaming support beams were starting to collapse.

The horses were whinnying frantically and kicking at the stall doors with their powerful hooves. This time, there were no latches. Instead, the stalls seemed to be secured by heavy wooden bars. Using his front paws, the dog was able to knock each bar free, one after the other. At first, the horses were so scared that they didn't realize they could escape now.

Santa Paws used his muzzle to prod each stall open, and the horses began bursting out. So many hooves were flying around that he ducked to the floor to try and avoid them. In its panic, one of the horses kicked him right in the flank. It hurt so much that Santa Paws fell down. He picked himself up, keeping all of his weight off that leg.

A beam came crashing down right behind him, and he knew it was time to get out of this nightmare. It was *past* time. But as he staggered out of the fire, he heard a tiny meow coming from inside. He spun around and dove back into the fire to find the kitten. When she couldn't find a way to help Santa Paws, she had hidden underneath a small trough so that none of the horses would trample her. But then, when the burning beam fell down, it had blocked her escape.

The beam was on fire, but Santa Paws shoved his shoulder against it, anyway. He couldn't leave the kitten alone in the middle of the blaze. He moved the heavy beam just far enough for the kitten to scramble out from underneath the trough. Then the dog used his mouth to scoop her up from the ground. He carried her to the main doors, and then he lunged outside just as the rest of the beams came crashing down. The entire barn was on fire now, and the structure was already almost completely destroyed.

Santa Paws wanted to lie down in the snow to cool the burn on his shoulder, but he saw the horses racing back and forth like maniacs. If he didn't round them up, they would probably all run away. He dropped the kitten into a soft drift a safe distance away and then galloped after the horses. He barked his meanest, toughest bark to get their attention. It took a while, but he was finally able to herd them together.

Since the barn was a total loss, he wasn't sure where to *take* the horses. The house had a two-car garage and he decided to guide them over there. The horses were restless and frightened, but Santa Paws ran back and forth and barked whenever they tried to move away from the garage. So they stayed where they were and whinnied a lot.

There were headlights out on the road now, and he could hear sirens, too. His first thought was that it was *about time* some people had shown up. But then, he had to concentrate on the horses. One of them was trying to wander off, and since he was pretty sure it was the one who had kicked him, he snapped at it. The horse swiftly retreated to stand with the others. Santa Paws barked a more amiable bark in response.

The owners of the small farm, Mr. and Mrs. O'Neil, had been at a small holiday party at their neighbors' house. Someone had looked out the window at one point, and noticed the flames. The entire party had rushed outside to their cars and headed straight for the farm. One of them had used a cellphone to call the fire department, too.

Since it was obvious that the barn had been completely consumed, Mr. and Mrs. O'Neil were afraid that their beloved horses must have perished in the blaze. So, it was quite a happy shock when they swerved into the driveway — and saw all five horses right there waiting for them.

"Oh, thank God," Mrs. O'Neil breathed. "It's a miracle."

"No," her husband said, "it's a *dog*." He pointed at the large, smoke-stained shepherd

176

who was running from side to side, keeping the horses together.

Once all of the people started getting out of their cars, Santa Paws relaxed. It was *their* turn to worry about these wacky horses. The fire trucks were already setting up out on the road. Some of the firefighters sprayed water on the back of the house to protect it from catching fire. The rest of them concentrated on what remained of the barn. Satisfied that everything was under control, Santa Paws went to find the kitten. He was worried that she might get scared and run near one of the cars.

"Whose dog *is* that?" one of the neighbors was asking.

"Gotta be a farm dog," another guessed. "How else could he herd like that?"

"Here, boy!" Mrs. O'Neil said. No matter whose dog it was, she wanted to thank it for saving her beautiful horses. "Come here, you good dog."

Hearing "good dog," Santa Paws — naturally — wagged his tail. The black kitten had climbed out of her drift and tottered over to meet him. This whole incident had really been stressful for her. Santa Paws licked the top of her head, and she rubbed against his front legs. Then they both headed across the field to go get some more sleep.

177

"That was — strange," one of the neighbors remarked.

"That was — an *understatement*," one of the others said.

Everyone watched in disbelief as the dog and the kitten ran off together.

"Merry Christmas!" Mrs. O'Neil shouted after them, since she wasn't sure what else to do.

The dog wagged his tail, and that was the last thing any of them saw as the two animals vanished into the dark night.

Fighting the fire had been so strenuous that Santa Paws and the kitten had to spend the rest of the night, and most of the next day, sleeping to regain their strength. Some workers showed up at the construction site early in the morning. Luckily, the dog and kitten woke up in time and were able to slip out between two boards before anyone saw them.

So they rested in a small gully further down the road. Santa Paws dug down through the snow to make them a nest. The kitten was reluctant to lie directly in the icy snow, but finally she settled down. The snow felt very soothing to the dog, as it cooled the burn on his shoulder and the bruised lump on his leg where the horse had kicked him. Both injuries were painful, but he knew he was okay because he could still walk pretty well. He just wanted to get *home*.

They slept until almost dusk. Sometimes cars drove by, but they were far enough off the road so that no one saw them. Once it was dark, they yawned and stretched and climbed to their feet. The kitten shuddered as she shook snow off each paw. She really didn't like being outside like this. It was too cold, and too wet.

Santa Paws checked for traffic, and they stepped out into the street. When they passed the farm where the fire had been, they could hear the sounds of saws and hammers and other tools. During the day, much of the burned debris from the barn had been cleared away, but the whole area was still a charred mess. The horses were nowhere in sight, so they must be staying someplace else.

There was another small farm about half a mile down the road. The dog and the kitten snuck into a field where a few cows were, and drank some of their water. The cows seemed to be eating things like hay and grain from a wooden trough, which didn't appeal to the dog and kitten at all. Santa Paws tried a tiny bit of the grain, but then spit it out. It tasted like — cow food.

Santa Paws got the kitten as far as the next town before she started slowing down. He was never going to get home if she kept refusing to walk for very long! He tried to urge her forward, but she just mewed her most pathetic mew. They were behind a small strip mall and the dog could smell food. He sniffed each building until he located the source. It was a Chinese restaurant, and tantalizing odors were streaming outside through a metal vent.

The kitten parked herself in front of the vent, and made it clear that she planned to stay there indefinitely. Santa Paws decided to find her some food, so she might behave better. The lid of the closest Dumpster was too heavy for him to lift, although he tried several times. So he sat by the back door of the restaurant and barked.

The door opened, and a line cook wearing white looked outside. Santa Paws barked again, cocked his head to one side, and lifted both front paws in the air. The cook said something in a language he didn't understand, and then added "No!" and "Go home!" in English. Before he had a chance to close the door, the kitten strolled over and started purring and winding around his legs. Then she sat down next to Santa Paws, still purring.

The cook couldn't resist *two* begging animals. He shrugged and stepped inside for a minute. He returned with two paper plates, which were sagging with the weight of rice, beef, chicken, and even some shrimp. He set the plates down on the snow, shook his head, and went back to work.

The kitten instantly took charge of all the shrimp. Santa Paws didn't care, since he was happy enough eating everything else. Once he ate a hot pepper by accident, and *that* was a surprise. But he gulped down some snow, and soon his throat stopped burning. He resumed eating, but spit out any peppers or bits of orange peel he found.

The kitten gobbled her shrimp. Then she stuck her head in the dog's plate so she could nibble some chicken, too. Santa Paws was going to growl, but then just switched plates with her. She had left all of her rice and most of the beef.

When the kitten was full, she began playing with a stray pea pod. She batted it back and forth, and pounced on it once in a while. Santa Paws took advantage of this to lick both plates clean.

With her stomach warm and full, the kitten wanted to take a nap. But Santa Paws couldn't relax until they had gone at least a couple more miles. The kitten was sulky, but she followed him. Because she was taking her time, the dog had to keep checking to make sure she hadn't gotten lost. It seemed strange to him that she had no urge to hurry.

They came to a rest area near the big highway. The kitten scampered underneath a picnic table where it was nice and dry. She yawned one of her big yawns, curled up in some frozen leaves, and went to sleep.

After exploring the terrain to check for danger, Santa Paws joined her. The rest area had a wooden information booth, which was closed, and there was a long line of pay phones. Other than that, there wasn't much to see. Occasionally a car or truck would pull into the area. Sometimes a person would get out and make a phone call. Other times, the drivers seemed to be taking naps.

Feeling relatively safe under the table, Santa Paws decided not to worry about the infrequent visitors. There wasn't much chance that anyone would sit down for a picnic on a cold winter night! He kept watch for another hour or so, and then closed his eyes. Feeling responsible for another animal, not just himself, was really tiring!

The next morning was Christmas Eve. Santa Paws and the kitten, of course, didn't know this. The only difference they could see was that many more cars were driving in and out of the rest area. Lots of people seemed to be on trips today!

Santa Paws wanted to glide off into the woods, so they could avoid any trouble. Predictably, the kitten had other ideas. A pickup truck had parked near their picnic table. The man driving went to make a phone call, and his wife disappeared inside the information booth. The kitten took advantage of this to run and jump onto their rear bumper. She gave Santa Paws a wicked look with her bright orange eyes. Then she sprang into the back of the truck!

Santa Paws got very upset. Why would the kitten be that stupid? Obviously, she would rather ride than walk, but these were strangers! This was a *very bad* plan. Didn't she understand that this truck would take them someplace far away, and they would be even more lost than they were now?

The kitten poked her head up from the bed of the truck and blinked at him. Santa Paws knew the people might come back any second now. If the kitten was going to do something dangerous, he probably had to keep her company. But he was *not* happy that she was being so silly. At this rate, he would *never* find his way back to the Callahans.

The dog shot out from underneath the picnic table and sailed into the back of the pick-up truck. There was a loose tarpaulin covering the suitcases and other cargo stored there. The kitten had already climbed underneath, and he reluctantly did the same. He hid just in time, because the man had now finished his phone call and was walking towards them.

The man got into the driver's seat to wait for his wife. She came out of the information booth with two cans of soda and some packages of peanut butter crackers. Once she was in the truck, her husband started the engine. He flicked on his signal light, and then merged with the highway traffic.

Crammed next to an overstuffed duffel bag, Santa Paws couldn't stop worrying. The contented kitten was already asleep inside a bag of Christmas presents. Once again, the dog didn't know where he was going, or how long it would take.

The *next* time the kitten got any bright ideas, he was going to let her go by herself!

16

The truck sped up the highway for a long time. Riding in the back was very jouncy, and every time they hit a bump in the road, Santa Paws bounced against the truck bed. Soon, his whole body felt bruised and achy. When he felt the truck slowing down, he poked the kitten with his nose to wake her up. If the truck stopped, they were *absolutely* getting off.

The truck pulled into a parking place, and the engine died down. Then Santa Paws heard both doors open and slam shut. Good! They could leave now!

Just as he and the kitten popped out, they saw the driver of the truck staring at them. The man had noticed that the tarp in the back seemed loose. So he wanted to tie it down before going inside Howard Johnson's for lunch. Santa Paws wagged his tail at the man before he and the kitten jumped to the ground. Then he and the kitten trotted out of the parking lot.

Not sure what was taking her husband so long, his wife came back to get him.

"Come on, James," she said. "Our table is ready."

James looked at his wife, still feeling as if he might be seeing things. "A dog and a cat just got out of the back and ran off together," he said slowly.

"Boy, your blood sugar must be *really* low," his wife said. "Come get something to eat."

"But I *saw* them," James insisted. "Really."

His wife looked worried. "If you're that tired, I think I'll drive after lunch, okay?"

James nodded meekly. He looked around the parking lot, but there was no sign of any animals. It must have been his imagination — or low blood sugar.

By now, Santa Paws and the kitten were standing at the next corner, in front of a gas station. The dog was trying to get oriented to yet another unfamiliar place. He knew which direction north was, but it just didn't feel right anymore. For some reason, he wanted to go *south* this time. It didn't make sense. It seemed almost as if they had gone too far, and now he had to retrace their tracks.

The kitten was bored, so she started playing with her tail. It was fun to chase it in one direction, and then turn around and try to catch it from the other side. She was having a nice time.

186

Santa Paws took a few steps north, then paused. North had been the right way to go for *days*. Why did it seem wrong now? His instincts were telling him south, and east. It was cold, but the sun was out, and he looked up at the sky. Then he closed his eyes to think.

Okay, southeast. They would go southeast. He would just keep trusting what his instincts — and his heart — told him. The kitten had stopped playing with her tail, and now she was swatting *his* tail. The cars in front of them had stopped for a light, so it was safe to cross. Santa Paws used a paw to propel the kitten forward and lead her across the street. He wanted to cover as much ground as he could before she rebelled again.

They trotted, or walked, all afternoon. Santa Paws began to smell the ocean, which gave him some confidence. Maybe southeast really *was* the way to go.

He took the cat through vacant lots and back-yards as much as possible. They found some good leftovers behind a Taco Bell, and were able to drink at a small pond later on. When the kitten started yawning, he carried her by the scruff of the neck for a while. At first, she liked it. Then she began yowling, and he set her down. The snow was deeper here than it had been where they were before. He could understand why she was running out of energy, since he was losing steam, too. But the smell of the ocean kept getting stronger, and that made him feel good. He was *sure* that they were going the right way now.

In the early evening, they stopped for a nap. The kitten picked a spot underneath a pine tree. It was fairly dry and soft under there, and the dog liked the smell. He thought about the Callahans, and their funny habit of bringing trees into the house. Would they find his family soon? He was so tired and achy that he wasn't sure how much further he would be able to travel. And he *knew* the kitten couldn't handle much more. But he missed them — more than anything.

He and the kitten cuddled up together, and went to sleep. When an unusual sound woke him up later, the dog didn't want to open his eyes. He only wanted to rest. But then he heard the noise again. It seemed to be a woman, and she was groaning.

So the dog hauled himself to his feet and trudged off to find out what was going on. Seeing him leave, the kitten glumly went after him. She took her time, lagging about twenty feet behind.

Santa Paws followed the sound to a small ranch house. A woman with a huge stomach was sitting at the bottom of her front steps in a daze. She kept holding her stomach, and moaning.

The woman was Wendy Jefferson. She was

eight and a half months pregnant. Her husband had gone out to do a few last-minute errands before the stores closed. Right after he left, she went into labor, and she was afraid that her baby was going to arrive at any second. Her contractions were only a minute or two apart! She had called 911, but the ambulance was taking a very long time to arrive. So she went outside to try to get into her car and drive to the hospital. Now the contractions were so close together that she was having trouble getting up, so she was stuck here, alone, at the bottom of her steps. She was going to have to deliver her own baby!

Santa Paws woofed once, to let her know he was coming. The lady seemed upset, and he didn't want to scare her.

"Help," Wendy gasped, between contractions. "Please help me!"

Santa Paws certainly knew *that* word. As he turned to alert the neighbors, the kitten meowed curiously. The dog lifted her up and set her down next to the woman, to keep her company. Then he ran over to the house across the street. Christmas carols were playing loudly inside. He barked and barked, but no one seemed to hear him.

So he went on to the next house. A retired couple was home, watching "It's a Wonderful Life." The husband, Mr. Thompkins, came to the door. Santa Paws barked and pulled him outside.

"Careful there now, fella," Mr. Thompkins warned him. "I'm not too steady on my feet. What seems to be the problem?"

Santa Paws barked, and ran towards the pregnant woman's house. Mr. Thompkins was intrigued enough to follow. When he saw his neighbor lying on the ground, he was horrified.

"Lou, the baby's coming," Wendy said in a weak voice. *"Right now."*

Mr. Thompkins nodded and turned towards his own house. "Molly!" he bellowed. "Call an ambulance! Wendy's baby is coming!"

"Oh, my!" his wife responded. Then she ran to the phone.

Everything seemed to be okay now, so Santa Paws scooped the kitten up. They retreated to the edge of the property, just out of sight, to watch until the dog was *sure* it would be all right to leave.

Wendy's husband and the ambulance arrived at the same time.

"What happened?" her husband asked, looking worried. "Are you all right?"

"The baby's coming," Wendy answered, between the special breaths she'd learned at her natural childbirth classes. "A dog went and got help. At first, I thought it was Santa Paws, but he had a cat with him."

"Oh, it couldn't have been Santa Paws, then,"

one of the paramedics said authoritatively. "He works solo."

Everyone else nodded. That was a well-known fact about Santa Paws — who, before he had been stolen, had lived only a couple of towns away.

From the bushes, Santa Paws and the kitten sat quietly and watched all of the excitement. The baby was coming in such a hurry that the paramedics had to deliver him right there on the front steps! They didn't even have time to carry Wendy over to the gurney! It was a beautiful baby boy, and he cried a loud, healthy cry. Quickly, Wendy and her new son were bundled into the ambulance. Then her husband climbed in after them with a big grin on his face. The ambulance drove away, sirens wailing, and Mr. and Mrs. Thompkins went back inside to watch the end of their movie.

Now that the big event was over, the kitten yawned widely. She was ready for another nap! Santa Paws sighed, but then gave in. He wouldn't mind another couple of hours sleep, either.

So they returned to their pine tree and nestled together again.

It was late that night before Santa Paws could convince the kitten to get up. Every place they walked, people seemed to be sleeping. Except for Christmas lights, and street lights, it was very dark. There were no cars driving around, which made it very easy to get around. Santa Paws and the kitten wandered right down the middle of each street, where there was the least snow.

They walked until morning. Santa Paws steadily guided them southeast the whole time. The smell of the sea was very strong now, and he stopped to fill his lungs with the aroma. It made him feel very homesick. He was so tired that all he could concentrate on was placing one sore foot after the other.

The only thing that kept him going was the thought of seeing his family again.

At the Callahans' house, it had been a quiet Christmas morning. In fact, since their terrible disappointment in Providence, it had been a very quiet couple of *days*. Gregory and Patricia's grandparents had driven down from Vermont, and of course, Uncle Steve, Aunt Emily, and their daughter, Miranda, had come over, too. Gregory and Patricia didn't feel at all like celebrating, but they were trying to be good sports. All they said were things like "please" and "thank you" and "excuse me."

"Where's Santa Paws?" Miranda kept asking. She was so little that no one had really been able to explain it to her.

"Why don't you open this pretty red package?" Aunt Emily suggested, to change the subject.

Miranda happily tore off the wrapping, but then looked up at everyone else. "But *where* is Santa Paws?"

Gregory and Patricia took that as a cue to go to the kitchen and bring out a fresh coffee cake. Really, they just wanted to leave the room for a minute.

"We, um, we got some pretty nice presents," Patricia said.

Gregory nodded, since they *had* gotten lots of really terrific gifts. "You think Mom and Dad would mind if I went upstairs for a while?"

Patricia knew exactly how he felt. She wanted to do exactly the same thing. "We can't yet," she said. "Not with Grammy and Grand-dad here, and everything. Maybe after lunch."

Gregory sighed, but nodded again. He had never imagined that Christmas morning could be such an ordeal. Even with lots of guests, the house just seemed so — empty.

Patricia put on a pot holder and took the warm coffee cake out of the oven. She slid it onto a plate, and Gregory carried the cake out to the living room.

"You know, your mother and I were thinking," Mr. Callahan said, from the rocking chair near the fireplace.

Gregory and Patricia both froze. Their parents

weren't going to suggest getting another dog, were they? They didn't *want* another dog. *Ever*.

"Maybe we could drive back up with your grandparents and do some skiing this week," Mr. Callahan went on. "Would you like that?"

Gregory and Patricia loved to ski, but the idea didn't sound as exciting as it normally would.

"That sounds great," Uncle Steve said, his voice extra-enthusiastic. "You can try out that new snowboard, Greg, and you've got those great glacier glasses, Patricia."

"Sure," Gregory said, making an effort to smile. "That would be fun."

"Yeah," Patricia agreed. "I mean — thank you."

Their parents smiled, but their eyes looked very sad. Uncle Steve had only been trying to cheer them up, so he just shrugged helplessly and drank some coffee.

Gregory and Patricia sat back down on the couch. They still had lots of unopened presents left, and Patricia hadn't even touched her stocking yet.

Miranda stopped banging on her new toy drum for a second — which was a relief to everyone in the room. "Why is the cat crying?" she asked.

They all looked over at Evelyn, who was sound asleep by the fireplace. Then everyone looked at Miranda, with some confusion.

"Well, sweetpea," Grand-dad said. "She's fine. See how she's sleeping?"

Miranda shook her head firmly. "She's *crying*. The cat is very sad."

Thinking about why Evelyn might be sad made Gregory and Patricia feel even worse. She probably *was* sad. And — she wasn't the only one.

"Daddy, help the cat," Miranda said to Uncle Steve.

He was just as perplexed as anyone else, but he bent over to pat Evelyn. Before he touched her, Evelyn suddenly sat up straight, with her ears flicking forward.

"Hey, that's weird," Gregory said, hearing a pathetic little meow. "There *is* a cat crying." The sound seemed to be coming from the front door, and he got up to check. He opened the door, and saw a small black kitten on the welcome mat. Her legs were tangled, and it looked as though she had been plopped straight down from the sky.

The kitten stopped crying at once, and stood up with a big stretch and a yawn. Then she ambled past him, and into the house.

"Hey, whoa," Gregory said, stepping out of the way. "Weird."

"Is that your black cat?" Miranda asked Mrs. Callahan.

"Well — apparently so," Mrs. Callahan answered, with a small smile.

Miranda smiled, too. "Pretty cat."

The little kitten was marching straight to the kitchen. She found Evelyn's bowl right away and helped herself to some tunafish. She purred happily, and drank some water, too.

Gregory looked at Patricia. "That's totally weird. A cat just like, *showing up*."

"Maybe some elf left it," Patricia said wryly.

Gregory thought about that. After all, they hadn't heard a car or anything. But, no, even on Christmas, that would be unlikely. He started to close the door, but then stopped and stared outside.

"What?" Patricia asked.

"I don't know," Gregory said, feeling his heart begin to beat faster. "I just — for a minute, I thought — "

They looked at each other and then threw the door all the way open. Their dog was running towards the house, wagging his tail, and holding the morning newspaper in his mouth!

"Santa Paws!" they said together, and then they raced outside to meet him.

Santa Paws was so excited that he dropped the newspaper. He began barking, and jumping, and trying to kiss them — all at the same time! Gregory and Patricia started patting and hugging him, and they all ended up sprawled in the snow together. Gregory and Patricia weren't sure if they were laughing, or crying — or doing a little bit of both.

"Mom, Dad, he's back!" Gregory yelled. "Santa Paws came home!"

Everyone in the house ran to the front door to see the joyous reunion. Mr. and Mrs. Callahan started crying when they saw their beautiful dog, and soon everyone else had tears in their eyes, too.

"There's Santa Paws," Miranda said, smiling broadly. "Santa Paws brought the cat for a present. Santa Paws *always* comes on Christmas."

Under the circumstances, none of the adults were about to disagree.

"It's a Christmas miracle," Grammy said softly.

With all of the hugging and the barking and the tears, it took a while before anyone was ready to go inside. Hearing the commotion, their neighbors up and down the street had come out to see what was going on. Realizing that Santa Paws — everyone's hero — had come home, they all started clapping.

"Welcome home, Santa Paws!" someone yelled.

"Merry Christmas, everyone!" Mr. Callahan said, waving to them. "Come on over! We're about to have a *very* big celebration."

The whole neighborhood thought that was a wonderful idea, and they all came trooping towards the Callahans' house. Someone started singing "Joy to the World." The rest of the neighbors — and Miranda — joined in.

Mrs. Callahan, Aunt Emily, Grammy, and Grand-dad went to make coffee, tea, and hot chocolate. They also filled plates with homemade cookies and brownies for the group to enjoy. The neighbors filed into the living room, still singing. Uncle Steve was on the phone to the police department, so he could pass on the good news. Mr. Callahan was putting fresh logs on the fire to keep the room nice and warm. All in all, it couldn't have been more festive!

Santa Paws sat on his rug in front of the fireplace, right between Gregory and Patricia. He smelled like smoke, and motor oil, and who knew *what* else, but they were so happy to see him that they didn't mind at all. The only thing that mattered was that their dog had come home! The black kitten, who was already feeling like part of the family, lounged in front of them and purred. Evelyn examined the kitten, decided that she approved, and sat down nearby to wash.

Patricia and Gregory couldn't stop patting and hugging their dog. Santa Paws wagged his tail as hard as he could, and took turns shaking hands with them. Over, and over again.

"Hey, boy," Gregory said suddenly. "Do you want a Milk-Bone?"

Santa Paws barked with delight. *Yes!* He

wanted a Milk-Bone! He wanted a Milk-Bone *very much*.

The room was filled with laughter and excitement and jolly conversations. Santa Paws couldn't believe that after so many long, lonely days, he was back on his rug, with Gregory and Patricia patting him. He looked at his family, his two cat friends, and the roomful of nice visitors. What a great time he was having! It was Christmas, and he was home safe and sound.

He had never felt so happy in his entire life!

And — he hadn't even eaten his Milk-Bone yet!

Santa Paws
to the Rescue

by Nicholas Edwards

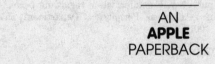

AN
APPLE
PAPERBACK

SCHOLASTIC INC.

New York   Toronto   London   Auckland   Sydney
Mexico City   New Delhi   Hong Kong

For Buddy, my pal
and
For Maggie, sweet as can be

No part of this publication may be reproduced in whole or in part, or stored in a retrieval system, or transmitted in any form or by any means, electronic, mechanical, photocopying, recording, or otherwise, without written permission of the publisher. For information regarding permission, write to Scholastic Inc., Attention: Permissions Department, 555 Broadway, New York, NY 10012.

ISBN 0-439-20849-1

Copyright © 2000 by Ellen Emerson White. All rights reserved. Published by Scholastic Inc. SCHOLASTIC, APPLE PAPERBACKS, and associated logos are trademarks and/or registered trademarks of Scholastic Inc.

12 11 10 9 8 7 6 5 4 3 2 1   0 1 2 3 4 5/0

Printed in the U.S.A.   40

First Scholastic printing, November 2000

1

The dog was having a great day. His three main requirements for this were lots of food, naps, and fun. Just now, when he was sleeping in front of the fireplace, he even had a dream about playing a game which involved hunting for hidden Milk-Bones! Of course, his whole family was in his dream, too, all of them smiling and helping him find the biscuits. He *loved* the Callahans more than anything, and felt very lucky that he was their dog. Unfortunately, he woke up from his nap when his cat friend, Abigail, jumped down on top of him from the mantlepiece. She pretended that it was an accident, but the dog was pretty sure she had been *aiming* for him. That was still okay, though, because it gave him a great excuse to chase her.

The dog was a little off balance as he jumped up to run after her, and he knocked several ornaments off the Christmas tree with his tail. They raced out into the front hall, through the den and dining room, up and down the stairs twice, and then straight into the kitchen.

Mr. Callahan was standing at the counter, making himself a roast beef sandwich for lunch. "Hey!" he said, mildly, and pointed a table knife covered with low-fat mayonnaise at them. "No, no, no! That is very bad."

The dog stopped short. Bad? Mr. Callahan thought he was *bad*. He sank down to the floor, instantly very discouraged.

"She leads you into wicked ways, Santa Paws," Mr. Callahan told him. "It's really not good."

The dog's ears went up and he wagged his tail, when he heard the word "good." He *enjoyed* the word "good." It was one of his favorites.

Abigail leaped onto the kitchen table, where the other family cat, Evelyn, was already sitting. Evelyn hissed at her, and jumped over to the counter, instead.

"All right, all right," Mr. Callahan said. "Will you three be good, well-behaved animals, if I give you each a treat?"

The dog loved treats, and he was delighted to sit and accept a chunk of roast beef. Yay! It tasted great! Evelyn took her piece into the dining room, so that she could eat by herself. Abigail, who never liked to cooperate, used her front paw to push her tidbit lazily back and forth across the table. Then she pounced on it, growled softly, and batted it away again.

2

"She's an oddball, Santa Paws," Mr. Callahan said, as he recapped the mayonnaise jar and spread some lettuce leaves on top of two slices of homemade rye bread. "That's all I have to say."

The dog thumped his tail against the floor, alert for the possibility of more roast beef. He was tempted to steal Abigail's share of meat, but she would probably scratch him across the nose if he did. He watched her very carefully, though, in case she might drop it. Then, as far as he was concerned, it was his.

Mr. Callahan finished preparing his lunch by placing three dill pickles on his plate, along with his sandwich and some taco chips. He also poured himself a glass of skim milk, and then carried his tray out of the kitchen.

Santa Paws followed him into the living room and took a strategic position near the couch. He knew it would be rude to beg, but he still liked to be within easy range of food. *Any* food. Just in case.

Sharing lunch with Mr. Callahan was always fun. Of course, he enjoyed *everything* he did with the Callahans. They were the best family in the world! He had lived with them for almost three whole years. Wow!

When he was a puppy, he had been a stray on the streets of Oceanport. He hated being by himself, and he was always very hungry and cold.

Then, one lucky afternoon, he met a boy named Gregory Callahan on the elementary school playground. Gregory, and his big sister Patricia, brought him wonderful meaty cans of food to eat, and the dog ended up going to live at their house. Ever since then, he had always been happy. He *loved* Gregory and Patricia! He also loved Mr. and Mrs. Callahan — and Abigail and Evelyn. They all had lots of exciting adventures together.

Mr. Callahan was a writer, so he stayed home every day and worked on his new computer. He was still learning how to use it, and the dog hurried out of the room whenever he heard Mr. Callahan shout, "Oh, no! Come back!" at the disappearing file on his monitor screen. The dog liked it much better when Mr. Callahan spent hours lying on the couch, reading books or watching old movies on television. For some reason, this always seemed to make him very tired, and he and the dog would both take long naps.

Mrs. Callahan taught physics at Oceanport High School, which meant that she was gone during the day. She was very nice, and almost always remembered to feed him at exactly the same time every evening. The dog got very nervous if his supper was late for any reason. Mrs. Callahan also brushed his fur regularly with a set of fancy brushes, and she even made sure that his nails were never too long! Recently, she had bought him a brand-new royal blue collar and told him that he looked very handsome, indeed. "Handsome" was a happy word, and the dog wagged his tail enthusiastically whenever he heard it. "So, we have a blue-collar dog now," was Mr. Callahan's only comment.

Gregory was thirteen years old, and in the eighth grade this year. He was tall for his age, and very good at sports. Both he and Patricia had brown hair and blue eyes, just like their parents. Patricia was a year older than he was, and Mr. Callahan often said that she was "fourteen going on thirty." "Make that *forty*," Mrs. Callahan would say. Patricia's only response to this would be to lower her sunglasses — she almost *always* wore sunglasses, even indoors — for a second or two and look at them with benevolent pity.

Evelyn, who was a plump grey tiger cat, had lived with the Callahans even longer than he had! The dog was *pretty* sure that she loved him. Most of the time, anyway. Abigail was the newest member of the household. She was all black, with yellowish-orange eyes. When the dog had been lost the year before — mean, bad people *stole* him on purpose! — he had come across a tiny, abandoned kitten during his long journey home. He wasn't sure that he wanted a traveling companion — but she didn't leave him much choice in the matter. In fact, she gave him no choice whatsoever.

"Would you like a bite, Pumpkin?" Mr. Callahan asked suddenly, holding out part of his sandwich.

Mr. Callahan was the only one in the family who ever referred to him as Pumpkin. The dog wagged his tail and happily gulped the sandwich section down. He didn't like lettuce very much, but the rest of it was delicious. Even the mayonnaise.

Gregory had originally named him Nicholas, and everyone in the family had at least one special, private nickname for him. But mainly, they just called him "Santa Paws." All of the people in Oceanport seemed to know who he was, and they would always wave and shout "Hi, Santa Paws!" whenever they saw him in town. It was great to have so many friends!

After lunch and another long nap, the dog went out to the backyard for a run. It was snowing, and he had fun skidding through the one or two inches that had already fallen. But his paws got very cold, so he barked at the backdoor until Mr. Callahan came and let him into the house. The dog ate a Milk-Bone, drank some water from his red dish, and then crawled underneath Mr. Callahan's desk for a rest.

As the afternoon wore on, something terrible

happened. Mr. Callahan *left the house*. Alone! The dog had followed him out to the kitchen, waiting to hear the magic words, "Want to go for a ride in the car?" He wagged his tail tentatively, and held one front paw up in anticipation.

"You be a good dog, Santa Paws," Mr. Callahan said, as he put on a green plaid wool coat and a Bruins scarf. "Stay and guard the house."

Stay? The dog's tail dropped and he slowly sagged down to the floor. He had to stay home? By himself? This was awful!

Mr. Callahan smiled and bent down to pat him on the head. "It's okay, we'll all be back soon. Don't let Abigail break too many things."

Was *Abigail* going to get to go in the car instead of him? Oh, this was terrible. And unfair!

Mr. Callahan opened the door, glanced down at his feet, and sighed. He was still wearing his Tasmanian Devil slippers. He changed into his boots, gave Santa Paws another Milk-Bone, and then went outside.

The dog was so unhappy that he completely ignored his Milk-Bone. He kept his gaze on the door, hoping that Mr. Callahan would change his mind and come back. Abigail wandered over and gave one of his ears a light swat. The dog wasn't allowed to growl at cats — ever; for any reason — but he lifted his lip enough to show her one tooth. Abigail ignored this and kept whacking his ear.

The dog waited and waited and waited. And waited. The kitchen floor wasn't very comfortable, but he was determined to stay where he was until his family came home. It was his duty! He did eat his Milk-Bone, though.

After a while, Abigail got bored. She headed upstairs to take turns lying on everyone's pillows, although she stopped along the way to knock three round shiny ornaments off the Christmas tree, and to dash up and down the piano keyboard a couple of times. Evelyn just stayed on the loveseat in the den, sleeping.

The dog did his best to maintain his vigil, but he kept dozing off. When he heard the family station wagon — the Callahans thought SUVs were extremely silly, especially in the suburbs — and Mr. Callahan's old Buick sedan pulling into the driveway, he started barking joyfully. They were home! Yay!

Upstairs, there was a distinct thud as Abigail jumped off some bed or other, on her way downstairs. Evelyn would also probably join them, but the dog knew that she would take her time doing so.

The backdoor opened and Gregory came in, his hair and jacket covered with snow.

"Hey, boy!" he said. "You have a good day, pal?"

Good. Yes! The dog lifted his front paws so that he and Gregory could do their usual ritual of dancing around the kitchen together. Santa Paws was mostly German shepherd and weighed almost ninety pounds, so if he wasn't careful about jumping gently, he sometimes knocked people over by accident. Luckily, whenever it happened to Gregory, he just thought it was funny.

"Well, okay," Mrs. Callahan was saying to Patricia, as they entered the kitchen. "But I can't help thinking that maybe it would be better if you took it a little easier out there. It's only a game."

Patricia shrugged as she carried her hockey sticks and the heavy equipment bag over to the corner where the family stored their sports gear. "It's not my fault girls' hockey has so many dumb rules about body-checking. That's why I like playing co-ed better." In addition to being on the junior high girls team, this season Patricia had also joined a local Bantam hockey league.

"I know," Mrs. Callahan said, setting her briefcase and Patricia's book-crammed knapsack on the table. "It was just a little embarrassing to be sitting next to Mrs. Lewis when you plowed right through poor Harriet."

"She's much bigger than I am," Patricia said defensively. "And I didn't do it on purpose — I was just going for the puck."

Gregory laughed. "Yeah. Sure."

Patricia put her hands on her hips and turned

to glare at him. "I have just two words for you, Gregory. Hat. Trick."

"I have two words for *you*," Gregory said. "Penalty. Box."

"I really hope you two aren't fighting," Mr. Callahan said, as he lugged in an armload of snowy logs from the woodpile.

Gregory and Patricia liked to argue almost constantly, and it really got on their parents' nerves.

"Who, us?" Gregory asked. "No way."

"Never happen," Patricia agreed.

"Well, good," Mr. Callahan said. "Not exactly the holiday spirit." The wind was so strong outside that he closed the door with an effort. "It's really starting to come down out there."

Gregory looked worried and stopped dancing with Santa Paws for a minute. "Hey, whoa, what if they cancel school?"

"We'll spend the morning celebrating?" Patricia guessed.

"Yeah, but we have a game with Eastman on Friday," Gregory said. "I don't want to miss it." He was a starting forward on the Oceanport Junior High basketball team, and even though he wasn't as competitive as Patricia was, he still liked to play.

"It's two days away, Greg," Mrs. Callahan said. "Don't worry about it now."

There was a small television on the counter,

10

and she flipped it on to the Weather Channel. A gleeful reporter talked about the current snowstorm sweeping across southern New England, and promised unusually cold temperatures for the next week or so. He also pointed at a swirling cloud formation down near the Carolinas and predicted that New England might well be battered by a winter nor'easter once the storm had made its way up the coast. "Bundle up, folks! It could be quite a blustery Christmas!" he proclaimed with great enthusiasm.

Mrs. Callahan glanced at her husband. "Maybe you'd better bring some more wood in tonight, just in case."

"Oh, come on, Mom," Patricia said. "They *always* predict terrible storms, and then get all disappointed when they head out to sea, instead."

"Well, it can't hurt to be prepared," Mr. Callahan said, and put his coat back on. "Why don't you two come out and give me a hand?"

On their way outside, Gregory grabbed an old canvas tote bag from the row of hooks where they always hung their coats. Santa Paws liked being able to help, and by carrying the bag's handles, he could manage at least two small logs.

There were three or four inches of snow on the ground now, and more was falling steadily. The dog was so happy that his family was home, that he galloped around in circles.

While Mr. Callahan lifted the tarpaulin covering the woodpile, Gregory and Patricia started to gather kindling. Seeing the sticks, the dog got very excited — were they planning a game of fetch? He pranced over and grabbed one of the sticks, shaking it back and forth.

"Okay, pal," Gregory said, and threw it across the yard for him.

"I wish we could teach him to *collect* the sticks for us," Patricia said.

Their father looked up from the stack he was piling together for them to carry inside. "And chop and split the logs, while he's at it."

Gregory shook his head. "No way. Dogs should just have fun."

Santa Paws chased the stick down in the snow and ran back towards Gregory. Then suddenly, he stopped short, and let the stick drop out of his mouth. He listened and sniffed intently, as the hair rose up slightly on his back.

Something — somewhere — was very wrong!

2

Santa Paws had no idea *why* he could always sense when people were in trouble, but over the years, he had learned to listen to his instincts. In Oceanport — and all over New England, for that matter — he had the reputation for being a hero. He never exactly planned to rescue anyone, but it just seemed to work out that way.

Once he had located the source of this particular problem, he ran towards the gate and sailed over it into the driveway. Then he raced down the street at top speed.

"Hey, whoa," Gregory said uneasily. "Santa Paws! Come back!"

Patricia sighed. "Here we go again."

They ran after him, with Mr. Callahan lagging only a few steps behind. Inside the house, Mrs. Callahan glanced through the kitchen window just in time to see her entire family tearing down the street in the middle of the snowstorm. She

13

shook her head, and went back to throwing together a hamburger casserole for supper.

Santa Paws headed directly towards the Robinsons' house. Every year, the Robinsons liked to decorate their roof with dozens of strands of Christmas tree lights. Tonight, Mr. Robinson had noticed that some of his lights seemed to have burned out. So, he had come outside to fix them. Unfortunately, his ladder had slipped in the snow and fallen out of reach. Now Mr. Robinson was dangling helplessly from his roof! He had been shouting for help, but no one inside his house could hear him over the noise of the wind.

Santa Paws stopped directly below him and began barking.

"Oh, thank goodness, Santa Paws," Mr. Robinson said weakly. He wasn't sure he could hang on much longer! "Please, go get help!"

Santa Paws ran over to the front door and jumped against it, barking the whole time. His front paw grazed the doorbell by accident, and it rang loudly. After a moment, Mrs. Robinson opened the door.

"What is it, Santa Paws?" she asked curiously.

Santa Paws barked, and dashed around the side of the house. Mrs. Robinson followed him, and got there just as Gregory, Patricia, and Mr. Callahan arrived.

"Hang on, George!" Mr. Callahan said. He

quickly grabbed the ladder and raised it against the side of the house.

Mr. Robinson grabbed the rungs gratefully and slowly eased himself down to the snowy ground.

"Whew," he said, letting out his breath. "That was close." He smiled at the Callahans. "You really have a mighty fine dog there."

Gregory and Patricia were very pleased to hear the compliment, since *they* thought Santa Paws was the best dog in the world.

Mrs. Robinson looked quite annoyed. "George, I thought you were upstairs. Did you really have to come out here in the middle of the storm?"

"The lights were broken," Mr. Robinson said meekly.

Gregory noticed that the extension cord was dangling free, and showed it to Patricia. She shrugged and then plugged the cord back in. Instantly, all of the strands lit up with a bright, festive glow.

Mr. Robinson's face flushed. "Gosh, I think I'm just going to head on in for some supper now." He reached out to give Santa Paws a quick pat. "Good dog."

Santa Paws barked enthusiastically. Mr. Robinson was one of his friends!

"Thanks again, everyone," Mrs. Robinson said.

After exchanging goodnights, the Callahans walked back up the street, with Santa Paws in the lead.

"That was smart, Santa Paws," Gregory said proudly. "Way to go."

Santa Paws wagged his tail, because "smart" was yet another word that he liked very much.

When they carried their load of logs and kindling into the house a few minutes later, Mrs. Callahan looked up from the evening newspaper she was reading. Her casserole was already baking in the oven.

"Good rescue?" she asked.

"Average," Patricia said, as Gregory said, "*Excellent* rescue."

Mrs. Callahan looked at Mr. Callahan for confirmation one way or the other.

"George Robinson was about to fall off his house," he said.

Mrs. Callahan thought about that, nodded, and resumed reading the newspaper.

"Want a Milk-Bone, boy?" Gregory asked.

Santa Paws dropped his log-filled tote bag so that he could bark. Yes! A Milk-Bone would be just great!

What fun he was having!

After dinner, Gregory and Patricia had their nightly fight about whose turn it was to do the dishes and, as usual, Patricia won. She relented slightly, though, and agreed to dry the pans and set the table for breakfast.

When they were both finished, Patricia sat

down on the kitchen floor to clean and organize her hockey equipment. Since their favorite television program didn't come on for another twenty minutes, Gregory sat nearby to brush Santa Paws.

"Rachel thought it was really nice of you to keep crashing into the boards right near us today," he said.

Rachel was Patricia's best friend, and even though she was blind, she still always came to Patricia's games. "Well, she doesn't have a frame of reference for hockey," Patricia said, as she carefully wiped down her skate blades with a chamois cloth. "So I like to give her good sound effects."

Gregory laughed. "And make Mom and Dad nervous."

Patricia grinned sheepishly. "Maybe a little, yeah." She began unwinding the frayed black tape on her stick so that she could replace it with a fresh layer. "Rachel says you give really good color commentary."

"Hey, yo! A career!" Gregory said cheerfully.

"What happened to being a veterinarian?" Patricia asked.

"That'll be my *day* job," Gregory explained. He liked science — and animals — so he had always figured that being a vet was the way to go. As far as he knew, Patricia was still deciding among being an FBI agent, a Supreme Court

Justice — or a Vampire Slayer. Preferably a *rogue* slayer, of course.

When Patricia dropped the ball of old tape on the floor, Santa Paws promptly picked it up and gave Gregory a pleading look. He liked fetching *much better* than he liked being brushed.

"Okay," Gregory said, and threw the tape-ball down towards the pantry.

Santa Paws tore off to retrieve it, his paws skidding on the linoleum.

"How do you think he knows all the stuff he knows?" Gregory asked.

Patricia lifted an eyebrow. "What, you mean, *fetching*? Or the stock tips he gives me?" For her most recent birthday, their grandparents had opened a small online trading account for her — with the strict rule that she do absolutely *no* margin trading, under any circumstances. Patricia assured them that this would be no problem for her whatsoever, because she was purely "buy-and-hold" by nature. For some reason, her grandparents had found that hilarious.

Gregory shook his head and tossed the tape-ball again. "You know I mean the rescue stuff. How does he know?"

"Magic?" Patricia guessed.

That was actually Gregory's theory, but he would have felt dumb saying it aloud. "Well, it's pretty cool," he said.

Patricia nodded. "Yeah, it's definitely cool."

18

Mrs. Callahan came out to the kitchen, presumably to check on their cleaning efforts. She stepped smoothly to one side as Santa Paws careened past her on his way after the tape-ball again.

"Do you think Santa Paws is magic, Mom?" Gregory asked.

Mrs. Callahan edged further towards the wall as Santa Paws narrowly avoided her on his way back. "Actually, I think he's a little on the clumsy side, Greg," she said, with a smile.

"Okay," Gregory said, "but none of the *other* dogs in town do, you know, hero stuff."

"That's true," Mrs. Callahan conceded. "But I kind of hope he takes Christmas *off* this year, don't you? Wouldn't it be nice to have a quiet holiday for once?"

Gregory and Patricia nodded. It had been several *years* since they had had anything resembling a quiet holiday. Somehow, Santa Paws always seemed to be involved in unusually difficult adventures every Christmas. With luck, this year would be different.

They *hoped*.

By the next morning, the snow had stopped, leaving a picturesque six inches on the ground. A traditional holiday singing performance was going to be held on the village green that night, and the Callahans were planning to attend. The town of Oceanport was very conscious of its diverse population and multi-cultural background. During the month of December, there was always a special exhibit in the park called "The Festival of Many Lands." That way, everyone's heritage could be celebrated, instead of simply focusing on Christmas. Oceanport took the notion of America's being a melting pot *very* much to heart.

When Gregory and Patricia got home from their respective team practices, they heard a familiar — and dreaded — sound as they walked into the kitchen. Off in the den, their father was playing Frank Sinatra. IIe *always* played Frank Sinatra when he was working. Seven days a week, fifty-two weeks a year, rain or snow or shine — the house was filled with the sounds of Frank, Frank, *Frank*.

Mrs. Callahan was sitting at the kitchen table, correcting papers to hand back before the holiday vacation. Once they had told her about how their days had gone, and spent a few minutes patting Santa Paws, Gregory gestured towards the den.

"I guess, um, Dad's working, right?" he asked.

"Either that, or singing to himself," Mrs. Callahan said.

Gregory and Patricia nodded grimly. Mr. Callahan did a lot of singing to himself. It was usually

20

a sign that he had writer's block and was in a very foul mood.

"You know, Frank did Christmas songs," Patricia said. "Couldn't he at least play Frank's Christmas CDs?"

"You would think," Mrs. Callahan agreed, concentrating on her papers.

Gregory and Patricia decided to take this as a no. Besides, they had snacks to eat, television to watch, and email to check. On top of which, over the years — no matter how much they complained — they had actually grown rather fond of Frank.

For a special treat, Mrs. Callahan ordered take-out from one of their favorite restaurants, Nuestra Casa del Taco. After dinner, they were going to meet their Aunt Emily and her three-year-old daughter, Miranda, at the municipal park. Their Uncle Steve was on duty tonight with the Oceanport Police Department, but he was in charge of crowd control at the concert, so they would see him, too. Uncle Steve was Mr. Callahan's little brother.

Since the celebration was being held outdoors, Santa Paws could come, too. He leaped into the backseat of the car with great excitement, wondering what sort of adventure was ahead of them. They *always* went someplace interesting and fun!

"Dad, you're going to have to listen to *ordinary* singers," Patricia said, as Mr. Callahan parked the station wagon on Main Street. "Think you can handle it?"

"Brought my Walkman, just in case," he said cheerfully.

Mrs. Callahan stared at him. "Tell me you didn't."

Instead of answering, Mr. Callahan just grinned.

It was very cold, but the sky was perfectly clear and filled with stars. Holiday lights reflected off the fresh snow, and as they walked towards the park, they could already hear the Oceanport Amateur Brass Band tuning up. The band would be accompanying the Village Adult Choir — whose star soloist was a nine-year-old boy named James.

Lots of people said hello to the Callahans, but *everyone* they passed had an enthusiastic greeting for Santa Paws. The dog happily wagged his tail, shook paws with anyone who asked, and posed for pictures with small children.

Gregory watched him, shaking his head. "He could run for Mayor," he said to Patricia. "He could *win*."

"Sure," Patricia agreed. "As long as he held down property taxes."

Gregory wasn't quite sure what that meant, but his parents seemed to find it very funny.

22

The park was so crowded that they had a hard time making their way over to the Bodhi Day Buddhist exhibit, where they had planned to meet Aunt Emily and Miranda. But first, they ran into Uncle Steve, who was giving several other local police officers their sector assignments. Right now, he was a Sergeant, but he was hoping to move up to Lieutenant after the next promotional exam.

"Traffic control is going to be our main issue," he was saying, "but — "

"Hi, Uncle Steve!" Gregory yelled in his direction.

Uncle Steve looked over and waved. He had the same dark, thick hair Mr. Callahan had, but he was much more muscular and didn't wear glasses. "Hey, everyone," he said, and nodded towards Santa Paws. "Glad to see you brought the canine ESU. You never know when we might need him." ESU stood for "Emergency Services Unit."

Mr. Callahan shook his head quickly. "No, he's taking the holidays off this year."

"Very much so," Mrs. Callahan agreed.

"Well, I'd say he's certainly earned the vacation time," Uncle Steve answered. Two years earlier, Santa Paws had saved *his* life — along with Gregory and Patricia — after their private plane crashed, and that was something that Uncle Steve would never forget. "Emily took Miranda over to look at the Father Christmas in Lapland exhibit, but she said she'd be right back."

"As you were, then," Patricia said, to the great amusement of all of the police officers.

Uncle Steve gave her a salute. "Yes, ma'am."

Patricia grinned and saluted back. She had always thought that she just might end up being a police officer someday — except that she wanted to get her PhD, first. "Carry on."

While Uncle Steve continued briefing the officers, the Callahans headed for the Buddhist exhibit. It had been sponsored by the Oceanport Zen Center, and honored the Buddha's Day of Enlightenment. The Festival of Many Lands included every form of holiday celebration imaginable. The exhibit next to the Buddhist one was about the Frost King legend in Scandinavia, and displays honoring Kwanzaa and Germany's St. Thomas Day were right across from them. Gregory went to look at the Kwanzaa exhibit, because that was the holiday his best friend Oscar celebrated. In fact, Oscar's mother was a graphics artist, and she had been the head designer of the booth this year. As far as Gregory could tell, she had done a really good job.

Miranda came toddling over, wearing a bright red wool coat and eating a candy cane. Aunt Emily, looking very weary, was hurrying after her. Aunt Emily worked full-time at an advertising agency in Boston, and since she was seven months pregnant, she was feeling pretty harried lately.

"Merry Christmas!" Miranda said. "We saw reindeer!"

"You did? Wow," Mr. Callahan said, and swung her up into his arms. "Can you show them to me, buttercup?" Then he carried her back towards the Lapland exhibit, which had been designed by Oceanport's Finnish-American Society.

Aunt Emily sat down gratefully on a nearby bench to rest. "She *never* gets tired," she remarked to Mrs. Callahan.

Mrs. Callahan smiled wryly, and glanced at Gregory and Patricia. "And they *never* grow out of it."

Gregory and Patricia did their best to look innocent — and remarkably well-behaved. Then Patricia noticed her friend Rachel standing near the *Feliz Navidad* display with her mother.

"Rachel, over here!" she called. "Your eight o'clock." Because Rachel was blind, she could get around much more easily if she used the concept of a clock to help herself navigate.

Rachel started towards them, using her cane. She had desperately wanted a guide dog for years, but none of the training schools would let her attend until she turned sixteen. Since she had expected to be allowed to go when she turned *twelve*, the idea of waiting so much longer had been terribly disappointing to her. Like Patricia, she was only fourteen now, so she still had two years to go. But she always moved quite gracefully on her cane, and lots of times, people never even noticed that she couldn't see.

Since it was so crowded, Patricia moved out to meet her halfway.

"Do you think this concert is going to be even *remotely* cool?" Rachel asked.

"No," Patricia said instantly. "But we can stand around and be, you know, quietly sarcastic and all."

Rachel nodded. "Okay, good. We can make fun of Greg, too, if we get bored."

"Hey!" Gregory protested. "I heard that!"

But before the conversation could escalate into a quarrel, the choir began to file up onto the bandstand. Seeing this, the entire crowd quieted down instantly. Just as the choir burst into a rousing version of "Hark the Herald Angels Sing," Mr. Callahan brought Miranda back over to join the rest of the family.

The dog sat next to Gregory, leaning heavily against his leg. Gregory reached down and rested a gloved hand on top of his head. The dog always liked that, especially when Gregory rubbed his ears gently. It was also nice to be outside, surrounded by so many smiling people. The music was making him feel sleepy, so he yawned widely and decided to take a nap.

"You can't look bored at town functions, Santa Paws," Patricia said. "You just blew the election."

Santa Paws wagged his tail at her, and then closed his eyes again. He was having a really happy dream about being given *three* whole dishes of food for supper, when his eyes suddenly flew back open.

There was trouble in the air!

3

The dog jumped to his feet and cocked his head to concentrate on all of the different scents nearby and decide which one was bothering him. There were *so* many people around. It was confusing! Then he let out one sharp bark, and began running towards Main Street.

"Oh, no," Gregory groaned, and his parents both sighed deeply.

"What is it?" Rachel asked, hearing the commotion.

"Santa Paws just took off," Patricia said. "Something must be going on."

Surprisingly, almost no one nearby noticed any of this, although a couple of people cheerfully said, "Bye, Santa Paws!" as he dashed away. Gregory was trying to follow him, but he was making much slower progress through the crowd. Since Mr. Callahan was still holding Miranda, Mrs. Callahan went after them this time.

Police Officers Lee and Bronkowski were stationed near the park entrance. When Santa Paws tore past them, they exchanged glances.

"That's not good," Officer Lee said thoughtfully.

"Not good at all," Officer Bronkowski agreed, and she reached for her radio to report this alarming development.

Santa Paws headed directly for Main Street. He wormed his way around parked cars and scrambled through thick drifts of plowed snow. There were bad people on the loose, and he had to stop them! He really didn't *like* bad people, especially after the horrible time when he had been stolen.

Just up Main Street, there were three boys from the high school who were trying to break into the parked cars. They were taking advantage of everyone being at the concert to steal CD players and radios, plus any Christmas presents they could find. Lots of people had gone Christmas shopping on Main Street before the concert, and left the bags in their cars. The boys didn't *need* any of these things — they just thought it would be fun to take them. Oceanport was such a quiet little town that many people regularly forgot to lock their cars, even though they should probably know better. On the other hand, the three boys — Michael Smith and his friends

Luke and Rich Crandall — also enjoyed breaking windows, so they didn't even *care* if the cars were locked.

Michael was flipping through a stack of CDs on the front seat of a Volvo, while Luke tried to get into the Jeep Cherokee behind it. Rich was shaking up a can of red spray paint, so that he could vandalize a Toyota. The Callahans' car was parked only two cars away!

Santa Paws loped up behind the boys and let out a low growl. He *knew* these boys, because he had had to chase them away from the Nativity scene in the park a long time ago, when he was a lost puppy.

Michael turned to see who was growling at them, and then sighed. "Look out, guys. It's that stupid Santa Paws."

Rich pointed the spray can at him. *"Bad dog! Go home!"*

Bad? He was *not* bad. The dog growled and took a menacing step closer.

"You know what? I really don't like this dog," Luke said. "There's no way to have fun in this town with him around." Luke had been using a crowbar to try to pry car trunks open, and he raised it to swing at Santa Paws.

Just then, Gregory finally caught up to Santa Paws.

"Hey!" he said, out of breath. "Leave my dog alone!"

"Who's going to make us?" Rich asked with a sneer.

Even though the boys were a lot bigger than he was, Gregory wasn't afraid. But he *did* kind of wish Patricia had come along, since she was really good at acting fierce. He, personally, hadn't had much practice. "*I* am," he said, clenching his fists tentatively.

Luke laughed. "Oh, yeah?" He swung the crowbar in the dog's direction, and Santa Paws dodged out of the way. "You, and what army?"

Santa Paws growled deep in his throat and moved to stand protectively in front of Gregory. Luke and Rich looked at each other uncertainly, and then retreated a couple of steps.

"Come on," Michael said, trying to encourage them. "We really going to let some *kid* and a dumb dog scare us off?"

"Well, boys, as it happens, *I'm* part of their army," a very calm voice said.

They all turned to see Mrs. Callahan standing a few steps away, with her arms folded across her chest. She was clearly *not* amused by the situation.

"Um, we were just kidding, Mrs. Callahan," Luke mumbled. He dropped his crowbar and tried to kick it underneath a car, out of sight.

Seeing this, Rich quickly shoved his spray can into a snowbank. All three boys knew Mrs. Calla-

31

han from the high school — and knew her quite well, since they had each stayed back a year.

"Yeah, we, uh, we like dogs," Michael said.

"And kids," Luke added. "We like kids."

"We *love* kids," Rich said. "*All* kids."

Uncle Steve and two other officers arrived now on foot, while Officers Lee and Bronkowski pulled up in their squad car. Mrs. Callahan frowned at Uncle Steve and looked pointedly at her watch.

"I know, it wasn't the world's greatest response time," he said sheepishly. "We had a little communications problem." Then he grinned at her. "I have to say, though — I had no idea you could run that fast."

"Yeah, really," one of the other officers chimed in, as he struggled to catch his breath. "She's got *wheels*."

"Yes, well, I was in a hurry," Mrs. Callahan said, and looked a little self-conscious. "Is it all right if we go back to the concert now?"

Uncle Steve nodded, as Officer Lee ushered the three boys into the backseat of the squad car. "Sure thing — we'll take it from here."

"So, wait, I'm like, an eye-witness," Gregory said uncomfortably. "Am I going to have to testify?"

Uncle Steve grinned again. "Don't worry about it. I think we'll start off by calling their parents down to the station for a nice, long talk."

"I'm willing to testify," Gregory assured him. "For, you know, civic responsibility."

Uncle Steve looked at Mrs. Callahan. "Exactly how much television do you let them watch?"

Mrs. Callahan chose to ignore that. "Come on, Greg, come on, Santa Paws. Let's go back to the park."

The dog wagged his tail. Were they going for a walk now? Yay!

A few minutes later, they rejoined the rest of the family.

"Heroism run amuck?" Mr. Callahan asked his wife quietly.

"More or less," she said. "Be nice if he *could* take a little vacation."

Overhearing that, Patricia nudged Gregory. "So, should they — " she indicated the choir — "start singing, 'He knows when you've been bad or good, so be good for goodness sake?' "

"*Definitely*," Gregory said, and patted Santa Paws fondly.

Instead, the choir began a lively rendition of "I Have a Little Dreidel." Santa Paws turned around three times, settled comfortably against Gregory's leg, and closed his eyes.

After all of the excitement, he *really* needed another nap.

The concert concluded without further incident — much to the Callahans' relief. By the time they got home, everyone was hungry. So they had a late night snack of grilled cheese sandwiches, hot chocolate, Milk-Bones for Santa Paws, and some tuna fish for the cats. After that, since they were really tired and tomorrow was the last day of school before winter vacation, Gregory and Patricia headed upstairs to go to sleep. Santa Paws had already conked out, sprawling across the crocheted quilt on Gregory's bed.

"So many rescues, so little time," Patricia said.

Gregory nodded. No *wonder* Santa Paws rested almost constantly. Then again, the cats also slept about eighteen hours a day — and had very little excuse. Then he shook his head. "Boy, you should have seen her — Mom was going to *pound* those guys."

Patricia laughed, doing her best to imagine the scene. "Well, you'd better believe I'm going to remind her next time she yells at me for being too rough at hockey."

"The next time I foul out, too," Gregory said. Although he usually fouled out due to *clumsiness*, not because he was aggressive. Whenever he fell over his own feet, his father said not to worry about it, that he was just growing too fast right now — and the same thing had happened to him when he was thirteen. Then again, his father was *still* a klutz, which Gregory figured might not bode too well for his own future.

"See you tomorrow," Patricia said, as she went into her room.

"You need protecting in the middle of the night, you just call me," Gregory advised.

"I think I'll call *Mom*," Patricia said.

They both laughed, and headed off to bed.

The next morning, the temperature was near the freezing level, and the sky was covered with thick, grey clouds. Both Gregory and Patricia had overslept, so breakfast was very hectic. Today was the last day of school before vacation, and the next day was Christmas Eve! Mrs. Callahan was trying to get everyone organized, while Mr. Callahan talked on the telephone to his early-rising editor in New York.

"No, I really don't want to change that sentence," he said, and then listened briefly. "Well, because it's crucial. Losing it would destroy the entire narrative drive of the book." Then he listened some more. "Oh, no, I don't think so. I like *that* sentence, too, frankly."

Gregory shook his head, as he grabbed a Pop-Tart to eat in the car. "Writers, man. *Way* too uptight."

Mrs. Callahan was waiting impatiently by the door, because she didn't want to be late. "Do you have your history homework?" she asked him.

"No, I forgot," he said, and turned to go back upstairs.

"What about your uniform?" she asked when he returned.

Gregory winced. "Right. Okay." He went upstairs again.

"And get a sweater!" Mrs. Callahan called after him. "You might need it later." She looked at Patricia, who was finding this whole exchange pretty funny. "Algebra assignment?"

Patricia nodded.

"Lunch money?" Mrs. Callahan asked.

Patricia nodded.

"Book report?" Mrs. Callahan asked.

Patricia started to nod, then blushed slightly and rushed upstairs. Mrs. Callahan sighed and leaned against the backdoor to wait for them.

"*That* sentence, too?" Mr. Callahan was saying. "I don't understand. Don't you like *any* of them?"

Once Gregory and Patricia were back in the kitchen, they all said good-bye to Mr. Callahan, who smiled and gave them a distracted wave. Then, Mrs. Callahan opened the door and ushered Gregory and Patricia outside.

"Car keys?" Patricia asked, once they were all in the driveway.

Mrs. Callahan grinned wryly. "Right," she said, and went back to get them.

So far, they were all having a rather stressful day.

* * *

36

Throughout the morning, the winds picked up, until the windows of the house began to rattle. Santa Paws and the cats were getting increasingly edgy, and they all kept pacing nervously from room to room. Sometimes thunderstorms frightened them, and this winter storm seemed to be having the same effect so far.

Mr. Callahan was trying to work, and this endless animal activity was distracting him.

"Come on, lie down," he kept telling them. "Good dog. Good cats. Please lie down."

They would obey for a few minutes — and then start prowling around again. By midafternoon, a hard, sleety snow had begun falling. Ice was clattering against the windows, and Santa Paws whined softly.

"It's just a storm," Mr. Callahan said reassuringly. "Nothing to worry about. Who wants a snack?"

A gust of frigid wind came rushing down the chimney, and Evelyn streaked upstairs in dismay. She hid deep inside the linen closet and curled into a tight ball to try and sleep. Abigail examined the dish of chicken catfood Mr. Callahan fixed for her, but then ignored it. Santa Paws accepted a Milk-Bone politely, but he just carried the treat around, instead of lying down to eat it the way he normally would. All of this was starting to unnerve Mr. Callahan a little, and he decided that he wasn't hungry, either.

The lights flickered every so often, indicating that the power was probably going to go out soon. Mr. Callahan quickly saved everything to disk, and shut his computer down. He wasn't going to take any chances of losing his latest revisions! Then he turned on the television to see delighted weather announcers discussing "the real corker of a nor'easter currently slamming into the New England coast." They were predicting a small accumulation of snow, lots of ice, and very dangerous road conditions. For the time being, there was a Winter Storm Advisory being issued.

"Maybe you should go out now," Mr. Callahan said to Santa Paws. "Before it gets any worse."

The dog shrank down on his rug, as though he were trying to make himself invisible. He didn't like storms — *any* storms. He especially didn't like *this* storm.

"Come on, Pumpkin," Mr. Callahan said heartily. "I'll go with you and bring in some more wood."

The dog slowly dragged himself to his feet and slogged reluctantly after him. When Mr. Callahan pulled the door open, more cold wind blew into the house. The dog shivered and retreated back towards the den.

"Okay," Mr. Callahan said. "I'm not going to make you, Santa Paws."

There were already lots of branches strewn

around the yard, and the footing was very slippery. Mr. Callahan walked carefully as he carried several loads of wood inside. He put the logs in the back hall, where they could dry off without dripping water all over the house.

The dog bravely joined Mr. Callahan on his fourth trip out to the wood pile. But just as he stepped outside, a huge branch snapped off a nearby tree and came crashing to the ground about ten feet away from him. The dog yelped and ran to huddle against the backdoor.

This storm was scary!

4

Mr. Callahan gathered up one final armload of logs and brought them, along with Santa Paws, into the house. He forced the backdoor shut, fighting against the powerful winds, and then locked it.

"I really hope we don't lose any trees out there," he said, looking concerned. There had been a pretty strong hurricane a few months earlier, and many of the trees in the yard — and all over Oceanport — had been badly damaged. It would not take very much wind to knock some of them over. He reached down to pat Santa Paws on the head. "Anyway. How about a Milk-Bone, boy?"

The dog took the bone without much enthusiasm and slunk into the den to lie underneath Mr. Callahan's desk. Abigail, who was also feeling jittery, crawled in next to him. The lights flickered again, but then came back on. Every instinct the dog had told him that this was a *terrible* storm

—and he wanted it to be over. Until then, he just felt like hiding.

People who lived in New England were accustomed to ferocious storms. In fact, most of them *liked* bad weather. Mr. Callahan — along with his wife and children — was no exception to this. Whenever there was a huge storm in Oceanport, the first thing everyone liked to do was run down to the seawall to see how big the waves were. But he still couldn't help wondering why Santa Paws and the cats seemed so unnerved. After all, animals were usually very good at sensing things that human beings didn't even notice. Could this storm be worse than the typical winter nor'easter?

First, he tried calling the junior high school to see if classes were going to be dismissed early. The number was busy, so other parents were probably doing the same thing. He watched a few more weather reports, ate a blueberry muffin, and unloaded the dishwasher. The sleet still seemed pretty heavy, but not particularly alarming. Finally, for lack of a better idea, he put a call in to the Oceanport Police Department and asked to speak to Sergeant Callahan.

"What's up?" his little brother asked cheerfully, when he came on the line.

"Have you heard anything about this storm?" Mr. Callahan asked.

"Not really," Steve said. "The last report we

got said that it was probably going to blow out to sea."

"Hmmm." Mr. Callahan frowned. "The last report *I* heard said that it was going to intensify."

"Well, we'll probably have a few fender-benders," Steve said. "So we'll be out there on the roads making sure people slow down tonight."

Mr. Callahan kept frowning as he looked at Santa Paws hunched underneath his desk. "Okay. I was just — okay."

"Since when does a little sleet make you nervous?" Steve wanted to know.

"It's not me," Mr. Callahan said, somewhat defensively. "But — well, the animals have been acting very strange today."

"Your pets are all *extremely* strange animals," Steve pointed out.

"Well, yeah," Mr. Callahan conceded. After all, it was hard to argue with that. "But I don't think I've ever seen Santa Paws this tense."

"It's probably just the wind that's bothering him," Steve said. "I think it affects their ears."

Mr. Callahan wasn't quite so sure about that, but after talking for a while about their various Christmas plans, he hung up. Then he went over and crouched down next to his desk. He hadn't realized that Abigail was hiding there, too, and he patted both of them.

"Take it easy, okay?" he said. "There's no reason to be scared. Everything's going to be fine."

Then he sat back down in front of the television to keep an eye on the latest weather reports. Santa Paws and Abigail climbed up next to him, and Abigail tucked her head underneath his elbow. Mr. Callahan frowned again. Granted, they might not be the world's most ordinary animals, but this was *still* very peculiar behavior.

Santa Paws snuggled very close to Mr. Callahan. The dog was very glad to be indoors, where it was *safe*. He just hoped that this storm would be over soon.

Over at the junior high school, school had just ended for the day. Gregory had been afraid that his basketball game would be canceled because of the weather, but so far, they were still scheduled to leave on the team bus promptly at three o'clock. Home games were more fun, because then his family always came to cheer him on. It was kind of interesting to play in other gymnasiums, though. Somehow, even though the courts were regulation size, each one felt very different, and changed the energy of the game.

Gregory and his best friend, Oscar, went straight to their lockers to get their coats and their gym bags. They would change into their uniforms at their opponent's school. They were playing the Eastman Junior High School Sharks — a team that was both better, and *taller*, than the Oceanport Mariners were.

"We're going to lose today, Greg," Oscar said glumly. Oscar played point guard on the team, and he and Gregory had been best friends since kindergarten. They both liked basketball, but they spent much more time talking about football, which was their favorite sport. "We're going to lose *big*."

Gregory thought so, too, but he didn't want to admit it. "Well, Coach gave us all those new plays. Maybe we'll get lucky."

"Hey, I'm just hoping we don't get embarrassed," Oscar said, and paused. "Can you *remember* any of the new plays?"

"Um, not really," Gregory confessed. "I kind of get confused when he writes all that stuff with the Xs and the Os."

Oscar nodded. "Me, too. And I'm the one who's supposed to be reading the other team's defenses and all."

Gregory had to grin, since whenever he got nervous on the court, Oscar inevitably forgot everything he knew about basketball and started shouting out football terminology. When he would yell something like "nickel defense!" or "look out, flea-flicker!", *both* teams would usually stop what they were doing and look at the sidelines for an explanation.

Suddenly, his locker-door slammed shut right in front of his face. Gregory flinched, but it was only Patricia's way of saying hello.

"Just wanted to wish you children good luck at your game," she said, her voice very chipper.

Gregory opened his locker again and wedged the door open with his knee, so she couldn't slam it again. "Thanks, old lady. Are you going right home?" he asked. Her hockey practices weren't scheduled to resume again until after the holidays.

Patricia made a face. "No. I have to stay after and wash Mrs. O'Leary's blackboards, first."

"You volunteered for that?" Oscar asked, sounding skeptical.

"No, I guess you'd call it — a command performance," Patricia said.

"That a code word for 'detention'?" Gregory asked, checking to make sure he had everything he needed in his knapsack.

Patricia nodded wryly. "Yeah. She says she doesn't like my attitude. Or my handwriting." She paused. "Or my sunglasses."

"Go figure," Oscar said.

Patricia magnanimously decided to overlook that remark. "So I'm supposed to 'think it over,' while I clean up her classroom." She glanced at Gregory. "Don't tell Mom and Dad, okay?"

"They'd probably think she was a grinch for making you do it on the last day before vacation, anyway," Gregory said.

"Well, they'd be right." Patricia checked her watch. "Oh, great. Now I'm even late showing up."

Gregory leaned over so that he could see the time, too. "Whoa, so are we. Come on, Oscar, we don't want to miss the bus. Tell Dad I'll call from Eastman when we're on our way back here so he can pick me up, okay?"

"Okay," Patricia said. "Hope you guys have a good game."

As they ran off, she sighed and headed towards the eighth grade wing. Because she was late, Mrs. O'Leary was probably going to make her wash all of the *desks*, too.

At the high school, Mrs. Callahan had to attend a mandatory teachers' meeting before she would be able to go home for the day. Then she was going to stop at the mall and pick up some last-minute Christmas presents. Every year, she planned to get all of her shopping done early — and every single year, she ended up still having presents left to buy on Christmas Eve.

When she called home to check in, she wasn't at all surprised to hear that the animals were behaving oddly, but the fact that there was a major storm going on *did* come as news. The high school building was only one story high, and had been designed with very few windows. Anyone who was inside could go all day without getting anywhere near a window. This atmosphere was supposed to promote good concentration, but mainly, it just caused claustrophobia.

"Are Gregory and Patricia home yet?" she asked.

"No, but I'm expecting them any minute," Mr. Callahan answered. "I'm sure Gregory's game was postponed, but I'll call the school and make sure."

"Do you think they'll be okay walking home?" Mrs. Callahan asked.

"Sure," Mr. Callahan said. "It's not that bad yet. The dog has just been making me nervous, that's all."

Mrs. Callahan laughed. "Better the dog, than your manuscript."

"Well, now that you mention it . . ." Mr. Callahan said, letting his voice trail off sadly, and Mrs. Callahan laughed again.

Before they hung up, Mr. Callahan promised that he would get dinner started and warned her to drive extra-safely.

"Maybe you should pick up some milk and bread, too," he said.

That was an old Southern New England joke, since whenever there was even a *hint* of bad weather approaching, many people often rushed out immediately to stock up milk and bread. No one was exactly sure why those two specific items had been singled out for special attention over the years — but it happened without fail during every storm.

"I was thinking more along the lines of plenty of chips and Twinkies," Mrs. Callahan answered. "But I'll get a half gallon of skim, if that would make you happy."

"That would be peachy," Mr. Callahan said. He was very fond of chips.

Once she was off the phone, Mrs. Callahan automatically looked around the windowless teachers' room.

"Did you know that there's a terrible storm going on outside?" she asked Mr. Jarvis, one of the French teachers.

Mr. Jarvis also looked around at the painted cement block walls, and then shrugged. "If you say so."

Mrs. Callahan wanted to go check outside, but it was time for the teachers' meeting, which was being held in the — windowless — library. If anyone brought up new business at the meeting, maybe she would suggest that they try to find enough money in the budget to put in some *sky-lights*.

When Mr. Callahan finally got through to the main office at the junior high, he was very upset to hear that Gregory and the rest of the team had already left for their game. Eastman was about twenty miles away, and he didn't like the idea of Gregory being out on the road with such icy conditions. Actually, he would feel a lot better when the *whole family* was back home, safe and sound.

All of the television stations were now officially issuing Winter Storm Warnings and Traveler's Advisories. The latest radar indicated that the storm was gathering strength, because of a low-pressure system. High winds and sleet were predicted to continue for the rest of the afternoon and throughout the night. The coastal areas north of Boston — in other words, Oceanport and the other nearby towns — were expected to be especially hard hit by this nor'easter. People were being instructed to stay inside and wait for further updates.

It always got dark early during the winter, but the storm made it seem as though dusk had already fallen. A light sheen of ice was covering all of the trees in the backyard, and the patio also had a visible layer of ice on top of the shoveled snow.

As he peered out the kitchen window, Santa Paws came over and nudged Mr. Callahan's leg anxiously with his muzzle. He could tell that Mr. Callahan was troubled, and he wondered if they were *both* worrying about the storm.

"Good dog," Mr. Callahan said, almost as a reflex. "It's okay, everyone's going to be home soon."

The dog whimpered quietly in response. Where was Gregory? Where was Patricia? Why weren't they here yet? When would they come?

Mr. Callahan let out his breath. He was finding Santa Paws' distress extremely contagious. "Well, it's not going to help if we stand around here and stare out the window," he said aloud. "Come on, we'll go do something constructive."

There were plenty of storm preparations that he could make. The faucets should all be turned on slightly to prevent the pipes from freezing, the bathtubs and kitchen pans could be filled with fresh water, and it would also be a good idea to gather up as many spare candles and batteries as possible.

Besides, Mr. Callahan knew that the best strategy to keep from worrying was to stay busy!

Mrs. O'Leary had been very cross when Patricia arrived ten minutes late for detention. So she told Patricia to wash the blackboards and desks in the adjoining classrooms, too. With a very mature effort, Patricia managed not to ask her if she should scrub the floors with an old toothbrush while she was at it — or drop and give her twenty push-ups.

When she finally finished and had rinsed out the sponge and bucket, Mrs. O'Leary was waiting behind her desk and tapping her foot impatiently. She was young and blond and very fashionably dressed, but somehow, her rather cranky personality did not fit her chic appearance.

"*Well?*" she asked.

"I'm all finished, ma'am," Patricia said politely.

"I see." Mrs. O'Leary looked her over with a very critical gaze. "Am I going to have to speak to your parents again, Patricia, or are you going to come back to school with a better attitude?"

"I'm going to mend my ways, ma'am," Patricia said, with enough sweetness to hide any potential sarcasm. "I have a whole new outlook."

Mrs. O'Leary wasn't buying *that* for a second, but after a long pause, she nodded. "Very well," she said. "You may go home now. Do you have a ride?"

"Um, yeah," Patricia answered. "I'm all set, thank you." Actually, she was afraid that she would get in trouble if she called home and admitted she'd had detention, so she would just walk. It was only about a mile and a half to her house from the school.

Once Patricia got outside and saw the ice everywhere, she almost turned around and went back to call her father. But he might still be in a bad mood about his book revisions, and she didn't want to bother him. Naturally, she *also* didn't want him to yell at her. Besides, if she hurried, she might be able to get home before he even noticed how late she was. As a rule, he lost track of time when he was working.

So she pulled up her hood, zipped her Patriots jacket, and started walking. The ground was very slippery, and it occurred to her that maybe today hadn't been the best day to wear shiny-soled cowboy boots. Still, she only fell once during the first block and a half, and figured that was a pretty good average.

The sleet felt more like hail as it pounded down. Everything was covered with a glaze of ice, and it actually looked kind of pretty. The trees were iced right down to the smallest twigs, as though they had been sprayed with a fine covering of glass.

As headlights came down the street in her direction, Patricia instinctively moved away from the curb and closer to a nearby hedge. The car slowed as it approached, and Patricia saw that Mrs. O'Leary was behind the wheel. Unfortunately, when she stepped on the brakes, the car skidded on the ice. Mrs. O'Leary pressed harder on the brakes, and the car began to spin out of control.

For a perplexed second, Patricia just watched the car skid, and then she realized what was happening.

It was coming right towards her!

5

When Patricia saw that the car was hurtling right over the curb, she tried to jump over the thick hedge out of harm's way. She managed to get partway over, but then landed in the middle of the bushes. Mrs. O'Leary was frantically trying to steer out of the way, and the car finally came to a stop against a snowdrift on the sidewalk.

At first, the only sound Patricia could hear was her own heart beating. Then she tried to sit up, without falling even deeper into the brittle hedge. Mrs. O'Leary's car door flew open, and she leaped out. Her face was very pale and she was trembling all over. She was trying to say something, but seemed to be too upset to speak.

"You know, I really *was* going to improve my attitude," Patricia said.

Mrs. O'Leary just stared at her.

Few things in life disappointed Patricia more than having a joke fall flat. With an effort, she pushed herself the rest of the way out of the hedge, hearing a tearing sound as she scrambled free.

"Well, shoot," she said, looking at a small rip in the sleeve of her Patriots jacket. She was very *fond* of her Patriots jacket.

"Patricia, I-I'm so sorry," Mrs. O'Leary stammered, her voice shaking. "Are you all right?"

Patricia nodded, wondering if her mother could discreetly sew the tear, or if a piece of blue electrical tape might do the trick.

"I-I was just going to offer you a ride home," Mrs. O'Leary stuttered. "I really didn't mean to — the ice — oh, this is terrible!"

Patricia grinned then, since it occurred to her that this narrowly-avoided accident probably meant that she wasn't going to get yelled at in class again anytime soon. That was an unexpected fringe benefit, which might almost make ripping her jacket worthwhile. "No, it's okay," she said. "Really. Is your car all right?"

Mrs. O'Leary blinked, and looked at her car. It was on the sidewalk, with the motor still running, but seemed to be undamaged. "Are you *sure* you're not hurt?" she asked.

If she made any sort of joke here, it would just be unkind. "Yes, I'm fine, thank you," Patricia said. "I'm pretty late, though, so I'd better head home now."

"Well then, please let me give you a ride," Mrs. O'Leary offered. "I'm really so very sorry."

The idea of getting into that particular car a minute or two after it had fish-tailed wildly across the street wasn't enticing. "Thank you, but I'm just going to go back and call my father," Patricia said, and gestured towards the school. "He's going to be wondering where I am."

"All right, but I'm going to come back with you," Mrs. O'Leary said. "I'll wait until I'm sure you're all set."

Patricia started to protest, but Mrs. O'Leary held up her hand.

"It's the least I can do," she said.

It didn't seem to be worth arguing, so Patricia just nodded. She stood *well* out of the way — poised to leap to safety again, if necessary — as Mrs. O'Leary moved her car off the sidewalk and parked very cautiously. Then they headed back towards the school entrance.

Patricia just hoped that her father would be able to come right over to pick her up. Somehow, it felt as though it had been an *unusually* long day.

Back at the house, Mr. Callahan had finished every storm preparation task he knew — and still, Patricia wasn't home yet. He immediately called the school, but the office assistant who answered assured him that all of the students had left for the day and that no student activities were scheduled in the building.

When he hung up the phone, Mr. Callahan looked at Santa Paws. "Okay, I am now officially worried about *both* of my children," he said.

Hearing the concern in his voice, the dog contributed a sympathetic woof, since he wasn't sure what else he could do to make Mr. Callahan feel better.

Mr. Callahan thought for a minute, scanned the list of frequently called numbers Mrs. Callahan had placed on the bulletin board, and dialed Patricia's friend Rachel's house. He let it ring at least eight times, but there was no answer. So he set the phone down and tried to remember if Patricia had made plans to go Christmas shopping, or anything else he might have forgotten.

In case she was walking home, he would go out and drive along her usual route. It wouldn't take long, and the sooner he found her, the better. The *last* thing he wanted was for her to be wandering around alone in an ice storm — especially after dark. Once Patricia was safe at home, he would only have to worry about *two* people, instead of three.

The dog watched uneasily as Mr. Callahan picked up his car keys and put on his coat and boots. This was very bad. Mr. Callahan should stay. The whole family should come home and they should all *stay*. That would be good.

The lights dimmed for a minute in a brown-out, and all of the kitchen appliances stopped running. Then, slowly, the electricity came back on, and the refrigerator kicked into its normal hum again. Mr. Callahan shook his head. People in Oceanport were *used* to having the power go out briefly during storms, but that didn't mean that it was ever *convenient*.

"I'm just going to go look for Patricia," he told Santa Paws. "I'll be right back, okay? Good dog."

Santa Paws had already started pacing apprehensively before Mr. Callahan even left the house. He went from room to room, cringing every time an especially hard gust of wind and ice pounded against the windows. Abigail came out from underneath the desk and mewed sadly at him.

Then, there was a sharp cracking sound outside as a huge tree limb crashed to the ground. They were both so startled that Abigail ran right back under the desk, and Santa Paws followed her.

When nothing else frightening happened, the dog ventured out — and resumed his restless patrol around the house.

If there was any trouble, he wanted to be ready to do anything he could to help!

* * *

Over at Eastman Junior High School, Gregory's team was playing surprisingly well against the Sharks. In fact, they had a two point lead at half-time! This probably had something to do with the fact that the Sharks' star power forward was home with the flu, but it would still be nice to win for once.

Gregory and his teammates were having trouble executing their new plays correctly, but their defense was strong and they scored a lot of points on fast-breaks. Oscar forgot and traveled a few times, because he would fade back like a quarterback waiting to pass, instead of remembering to dribble. "Hit the open man in the key, Oscar!" Coach Yancey kept telling him during time-outs. "Before the zone collapses on him." When Oscar finally gave up and looked at Gregory for a translation, Gregory said, "Throw me a slant pass when I cut across the middle." That made perfect sense to Oscar, who smiled and started doing just that.

The second half had just started when an official time-out was called, and the coaches and referees all huddled together.

"Sorry, boys," Coach Yancey said, when he returned to the sideline. "They're calling the game."

Oscar looked outraged. "Because we're *winning*?"

58

"Because the storm's really picking up out there, and they want us to head home before it gets any worse," Coach Yancey said. "We'll reschedule the game for sometime after the holidays."

"We'll pick up right where we left off, right?" Philip, the team's center, asked. "The score, I mean?"

Coach Yancey shook his head. "Sorry. It'll be a whole new game."

Gregory and the other Mariners were very disappointed by the news. They had been playing so well, and what were the odds that they would manage to do that again? Especially against *this* team. But they slouched off to the visiting team's locker-room, changed into their street clothes, and assembled back on the bus. Coach Yancey counted heads to make sure everyone was there, and then the driver, grouchy old Mr. Monroe, put the bus into gear with a harsh, grinding sound. Mr. Monroe was a retired Marine, and he thought that all students — no matter how old they were — should behave like well-trained, highly-motivated military recruits at all times. As a result, life as a junior high school bus driver was a constant letdown for him, and he spent most of his time grumbling and mumbling to himself.

"I can't believe it," Oscar said glumly. "We were going to *win* this one." Then his face brightened, and he waved to get Coach Yancey's attention. "Hey, Coach, can we stop at McDonald's?" That was the normal team tradition after games, win or lose.

"Not this time, Oscar," Coach Yancey said. "I'd rather just get you all back to the school."

"Even if we're really hungry?" Nathan, the scrawny team manager, asked. He was so small that he ate *constantly* in an attempt to grow. So far, it hadn't worked.

"Even if," Coach Yancey said. "Sorry."

The entire team sat in dejected silence. The only sounds were the windshield wipers beating back and forth, and the icy sleet hitting against the bus.

"Hey, wait!" Abdul, the second-string shooting guard, said, as he dug through his knapsack. "I've got band candy!"

"All right!" someone yelled. "Band candy!"

At least half the team exchanged high fives, and there was a general atmosphere of celebration.

"Let's have some quiet, ya little weevils!" Mr. Monroe bellowed. "I'm trying to drive here."

They were all — including Coach Yancey — a little bit afraid of Mr. Monroe, so everyone immediately began whispering instead of yelling. Abdul passed out overpriced and undersized bags of chocolate-nut candy.

"Don't you have to account for all of that candy later on, Abdul?" Coach Yancey asked in a low voice.

"Probably, yeah," Abdul said without much concern.

"Well, maybe you should have everyone write their names down first," Coach Yancey suggested, "or — "

"We're a team, Coach," Abdul said. "I trust my *team*."

Instead of arguing further, Coach Yancey just helped himself to some candy. Besides, he was hungry, too.

Gregory looked at the small piece of chocolate in his hand. Band candy *was* always amazingly expensive — and usually sort of stale and odd. "What do you think, is this about five dollars worth?" he asked Oscar.

Oscar nodded, and ate three dollars worth in one bite.

"Would you like some candy, Mr. Monroe?" Abdul asked politely. "To help you concentrate?"

Mr. Monroe glared at him in the rear view mirror. "Whatsa matter? Can't you see I'm driving, kid?"

"Yes, sir," Abdul said. "No excuse, sir."

Since that was an excellent imitation of a gung-ho military recruit, most of the team laughed.

"The power lines look pretty cool," Oscar said, pointing out the window at the icicles forming on the wires.

"Yeah, but I hope they don't break." Gregory crunched another two dollars worth of candy. "Remember the hurricane that time? It was like, four days before we got the power back."

"That was really boring," Oscar said. "I thought my brother was going to die without his video games." He paused. "I actually wasn't so happy, either."

Gregory hadn't liked it much himself, for that matter. "You should see Patricia if she can't get on the Internet for a couple of hours. She turns into this total maniac."

"That could be scary," Oscar said thoughtfully.

Gregory nodded. Patricia was nothing, if not addicted to being online. Their parents had finally had to break down and put in a second phone line, so that they could occasionally *receive* telephone calls.

"The worst Delia and Todd — " who were Oscar's little sister and brother — "ever do is stamp their feet and maybe cry a little," Oscar said.

Gregory tried to remember if he had ever seen Patricia stamp her foot. Mostly, she just narrowed her eyes and looked threatening. Since Gregory was bigger than she was now, their fights were never physical anymore, because Gregory liked to play fair — and Patricia was no fool. If she really got on his nerves, his current strategy was to look annoyed and say, snidely, "Oh, you're too *thin* to hit." Even though Patricia really liked being thin, that always infuriated her for some reason. Which, as strategies went, made it a superior weapon!

In the end, though, he was mainly happy that he had a sister who was so totally, irrefutably *cool*. He figured that it helped improve his own reputation, considerably.

Oscar gazed out the window as the sleet fell even harder. "Boy, I'm glad I'm not driving."

"Me, too," Gregory said. "It's looking really icy out there."

From where they were sitting, they could hear Mr. Monroe grumbling away, but he didn't sound any more crabby than usual. The road they were on was full of curves and Mr. Monroe seemed to be holding onto the steering wheel very tightly. The storm was so fierce now that there wasn't any other traffic on the road, so at least they didn't have to worry about other cars. The old Kenyon Bridge was just up ahead, rising over a deep watery channel leading inland from the ocean.

"Want to hear a science fun-fact?" Oscar asked.

"Not really," Gregory said. He enjoyed science, but still. "I mean, like, we're on *vacation*."

The bus wheels clattered as they started over the bridge.

"No, this is a good one," Oscar assured him. "I saw it on the Discovery Channel. When it's cold out, bridges freeze a whole lot faster than — "

Before he could finish his sentence, the bus suddenly began gliding off to the right. The side scraped noisily against the steel bridge supports, and then the bus bounced off and veered sharply in the other direction. Mr. Monroe tried to get control of the wheel, but the bus seemed to have a mind of its own.

Gregory and Oscar exchanged scared looks, and then braced themselves against the back of the seat in front of them.

It didn't seem possible, but they were about to crash!

6

Everyone started yelling at once. The bus swerved back and forth, first careening off one side of the bridge and then, the other. Equipment was flying all over the place, and people were being thrown out of their seats. It seemed to take forever, but Gregory didn't have time to think about anything more complicated than trying to hold on.

The bus skidded off the end of the bridge, burst through the guardrail, and rolled down the icy embankment. They landed in the frozen marsh below with a loud crunch. Then, as the bus finally came to a stop in the mire, it was absolutely silent inside.

Gregory found himself lying in the aisle, somewhere in the middle of a pile of his stunned teammates.

"Everyone all right?" Coach Yancey asked hoarsely. "Anyone hurt?"

There was no answer at first.

"Are we hurt?" Oscar asked Gregory. "I can't tell."

"I can't, either." Gregory carefully pulled his legs free and tried to climb onto the nearest seat.

The bus had landed at a steep angle, although luckily, it hadn't tipped all the way over. Gregory braced his foot on the side of the seat to keep his balance. His other foot slipped and knocked against Philip's shoulder.

"Hey, watch it, Callahan!" Philip protested.

"Sorry," Gregory said, and adjusted his position.

Looking around in the very dim light, he could see that everyone else seemed to be moving, which he figured was a good sign. A fair number of his teammates were groaning, though, or saying, "Ow." *That* seemed like a bad sign. And Mr. Monroe, up front, was holding one hand to his forehead.

"Is anyone *hurt*?" Coach Yancey asked again, sounding almost frantic.

Everyone started answering at the same time, so it was hard to understand what they were saying.

"One at a time, ya maniacs!" Mr. Monroe bellowed. Then he winced and brought his other hand up to his head, too.

Gregory moved his arms and legs experimentally, turned his head to the left and the right, shrugged his shoulders, and then decided that he was fine. "I'm okay, Coach," he said. "You okay, Oscar?"

"Yeah," Oscar answered, sounding a little uncertain.

It turned out that they were all mostly just shaken up and bruised, but Nathan, Kurt, Harry, and Jethro each had more serious twists and strains, some of which might involve fractures. Kurt almost definitely had a broken ankle, and Jethro's elbow was dislocated. Coach Yancey fished around through the jumbled pile of knapsacks and equipment bags, looking for the team's first aid kit.

"They call the game *and* we crash?" someone — maybe Abdul — said gloomily. "That really stinks."

Since Mr. Monroe hadn't volunteered anything yet, Gregory made his way up front to find out if he was not hurt. He was muttering something grim about being surrounded by "demented munchkins." Gregory would have been worried about a serious head injury, but that was the sort of thing Mr. Monroe *always* said.

"Sir?" he asked, making a point of sounding extra-polite. "Are you okay, Mr. Monroe?"

"Banged up my noggin some, but no problem," Mr. Monroe said grumpily. "Now, give me some space, kid — I gotta go check the vehicle." He started to stand up, looked dizzy, and abruptly sat back down.

"We'll take care of it," Coach Yancey said. "I'll just go flag a car down, and — " His voice trailed off when he looked up at the deserted, icy road. In order to flag a car down, one had to drive *by*.

"Oscar and I can go find a house and use their phone," Gregory suggested.

"Who you going to call?" Philip asked. "Triple A?"

Gregory and Oscar gave that some thoughtful consideration. It sounded like a sensible choice.

"911," Coach Yancey said firmly. "We want to call 911. But I really don't feel right about sending you two — "

Kurt looked up from his swollen ankle. "You feel right *leaving* the rest of us here, Coach? With broken bones and all?"

"Well, no," Coach Yancey conceded. "But — "

"Coach, I've *done* this before," Gregory said. "And this is only the suburbs."

Everyone in town knew about the plane crash he had been in, and how he and Patricia and Santa Paws had been forced to cross miles over the White Mountains in the middle of a blizzard to find help for their injured Uncle Steve. Gregory never brought it up — he didn't like remembering the experience, and it also felt like bragging — but this was a good time to make an exception.

"Yeah, I guess you have," Coach Yancey said. "Okay, you two head out and find a telephone.

There are a few houses just up the road there. But, please be *very* careful." Then he sighed. "Frankly, I wish that dog of yours was here right now."

Gregory wished the exact same thing.

Patricia had called home from the main office at the junior high school, but the answering machine picked up. She left a message saying where she was, and asking one of her parents to come pick her up please whenever they got home.

"I'm happy to give you a ride, Patricia," Mrs. O'Leary said.

Patricia still wasn't eager to get into a car that did *quite* that much skidding. "It's okay. I honestly don't mind waiting."

Mrs. O'Leary put her hands on her hips. "Well, now, really. What happened outside was a fluke. I'm a perfectly competent driver."

"Oh, I know," Patricia said. Anyway, she *hoped* so. "But they're going to be coming over here soon to pick up my brother, anyway, so no problem."

When the vice principal, Mr. Weingarten, said that Patricia could wait in the office until her ride came, Mrs. O'Leary finally gave in. With one last profuse apology — and a stilted "have a happy holiday" exchange, she left.

"Well, now! It's certainly nice to have you here in this office for a reason unrelated to discipline,

Miss Callahan," Mr. Weingarten said with a big smile.

Patricia didn't get sent to the principal's office very often, but when it happened, it was usually quite complicated and unforgettable — for everyone involved. She didn't mention that she wouldn't still be at school in the first place, if she hadn't gotten detention today. "Yes, sir," she said. "It makes for a nice change."

From force of habit, she automatically sat in the row of metal seats designated for problem students, and then took a book out of her knapsack to pass the time.

"I'm guessing that's one of those Harry Potter books you kids enjoy so much," Mr. Weingarten said with his wide, hearty smile. He was a nice man, but sometimes he had a tendency to try just a little too hard to be "hip."

Patricia held up her book — *The Sound and the Fury* by William Faulkner. She was also reading a book about the Salem witch trials and another about strategies for the small investor, but she had left them both at home.

Mr. Weingarten's face fell. "Oh. Well — enjoy."

Patricia nodded and opened to the page where she had left her bookmark. She had been reading for ten or fifteen minutes when she heard her father's voice out in the hallway. She closed her book and went out to meet him.

Mr. Callahan looked very relieved when he

saw her. "There you are, Patricia! Where have you been?"

Her parents liked it when she and Gregory were honest. "Well, I sort of had, um, detention," Patricia said.

Mr. Callahan lifted his eyebrows. "Sort of?"

"It was pretty minor detention," Patricia said, in her own defense.

"Mrs. O'Leary again?" he guessed.

Patricia nodded, and then looked at him uncertainly. "Are you going to yell at me?"

"No," Mr. Callahan said, after a lengthy and pointed pause. "I'm going to give you a life lesson."

Patricia — almost — repressed a shudder. "This isn't going to be the 'honesty is the best policy' one, is it?" Her father had an endless supply of Life Lessons, which he sometimes referred to as "thematic arcs."

"No. This is the 'go along to get along' one," Mr. Callahan said. "Okay? It saves a lot of time."

"Like you and your editor this morning?" Patricia asked.

Mr. Callahan elected not to answer that question. "Why don't we just head home before that ice gets any worse," he said.

Patricia stuck her book back into her knapsack to protect it from the sleet. "Is Mom going to pick up Greg when his bus gets here?"

Mr. Callahan moved his jacket sleeve up so he

could look at his watch. "No, it's late enough so that we might as well wait for him." Seeing Mr. Weingarten come out of his office, Mr. Callahan motioned to get his attention. "Hi, Mark. When are you expecting the basketball team back?"

"About half an hour ago, now that you mention it," Mr. Weingarten said. "They ended up canceling the game because of the weather."

"*After* they got all the way over there?" Mr. Callahan asked.

Mr. Weingarten nodded. "And to make matters worse, they were *winning*."

"No wonder the other team wanted to cancel the game," Patricia said with a grin. Then she noticed her father's worried expression. "What's wrong, Dad?"

"Oh, I'm sure they just got held up," Mr. Callahan said, looking distracted. "Do you know what time they started back here, Mark?"

Mr. Weingarten was also looking concerned now. "No, but let me go find out."

"Do you think something happened?" Patricia asked, beginning to feel pretty uneasy herself.

"No," Mr. Callahan said quickly. "I'm sure they're perfectly fine."

But Patricia could tell that he really wasn't sure at all. "It's only two towns over. And Mr. Monroe's a really good driver."

"Absolutely," Mr. Callahan agreed without any

hesitation. "I'm sure they'll be here any second now."

Since he was avoiding her eyes, Patricia knew that he was just trying to keep her from worrying. However, if that was his goal, unfortunately he was already too late.

When Mr. Weingarten came back out, his hearty smile was completely gone. "They, uh, they left over an hour ago," he said.

"But, wait, that means — " Patricia stopped in the middle of her sentence. She knew perfectly well what it meant.

Gregory's bus was missing!

Back at the house, Santa Paws was still roaming restlessly from room to room. Abigail sprawled out on the living room rug, hoping that he might roughhouse with her, but the dog ignored her. He had other things on his mind.

He stood at the backdoor for a while, alert for any sound which might mean his family had come home. But all he could hear was the howling wind and tree branches snapping off all over the neighborhood.

Abigail joined him in the kitchen. She found an empty paper cup on the counter and knocked it onto the floor. Then she rolled it away, pounced on it, and swatted it across the linoleum again.

Santa Paws was so busy concentrating on

what was going on outside that he didn't even notice her energetic game. A draft of cold air was blowing in through the tiny gap at the bottom right corner of the door frame. He couldn't smell anything unfamiliar, but the odor of the ocean was much stronger than usual and the snapped tree limbs were adding a distinct fragrance of fresh sap to the air.

Feeling lonely and bored, Abigail came over and rubbed against the dog's front legs, purring loudly. Santa Paws didn't encourage her, but he didn't show his teeth or move away, either. He loved Abigail, but he wished she would stop being so silly, with such a horrible storm going on outside. This was a very bad time for playing games! He just couldn't pay attention to her right now.

He could hear a strange squeaking sound, which seemed to be coming from the old maple tree in the front yard. He dashed out of the kitchen towards the living room. The tree was right outside the bay windows, and he wanted to check that squeaking more closely.

It was too dark to see clearly, but the branches of the tree seemed to be whipping wildly from side to side. No, the entire *tree* seemed to be moving. It was bending back and forth as though it might fall right down!

The dog could feel strong pressure in his ears from the growing power of the storm, and the bay windows were shaking so hard that he was afraid that they might burst open. He whimpered a little in spite of himself, and shook his head and lowered his ears to try and reduce the pressure inside them. It hurt!

Abigail's ears must have been painful, too, because they were bent back along the side of her head, and she wouldn't even come *in* to the living room. She was also meowing unhappily. The dog decided that she had the right idea, and he began backing out of the room. He stayed low to the floor, almost crawling.

There was a terrifying, shrieking crack out in the yard, and the dog stopped short in alarm. What was *that*? What a loud noise! Why didn't it stop?

The oak tree, weakened from decades of nor'-easters and hurricanes, had just splintered in half. And now one huge section was crashing straight towards the house!

The branches scraped across the windows, and then the glass shattered from the force of the falling tree. Part of it landed on the roof with a loud crunch, and the rest of the tree came plunging right into the living room!

The dog yelped in fear, and leaped backwards into the hall. He landed on top of Abigail, who had flattened on the floor to protect herself. She meowed in protest and squirmed free. In a panic, they both ran into the den as fast as they could.

A tree! It had come right into their *house*. It almost seemed to be attacking them!

The dog wanted to hide under Mr. Callahan's desk, but he could feel the wind and cold air seeping inside from the destroyed windows in the living room. He panted nervously for a minute, and then ventured back out to the hall. He peeked around the side of the doorway, and was very upset to see that the tree was still there. Trees weren't *supposed* to come into the house like that. Not ever. The Callahans were going to think that he was a very bad dog.

The branches were filling most of the space left by the broken windows, so not much sleet was falling into the house yet, but the temperature in the room was dropping quickly. The dog was afraid that *another* tree might come down on top of him, but he forced himself to move a few steps closer and investigate.

Something brushed against his back leg, and he jumped in fear. It was only Abigail, and she gave him a little whack with her paw to show her displeasure at his dramatic reaction. The dog felt scared and shaky, so he sat down to do some more panting. Once he felt calmer, he got up again.

He approached the tree and nosed at the ice-covered branches. They didn't move, and he relaxed a little.

Abigail thought trees were fun, so she started climbing on the branches. But the ice was so slippery that she fell off and landed in a jumbled heap on the rug. She rolled to her feet, shook her fur disdainfully, and then retreated out to the hall to wash — and attempt to recover her wounded dignity.

Evelyn had crept cautiously downstairs to see why there had been such a terrible crash. She took one look at the tree and went right back up to the linen closet. It was very warm in there, sleeping all curled up in a nest of clean towels, and she had *no* intention of coming out again until the storm was over.

The dog was still in the living room. He sat back on his haunches, perplexed. Should he stay here on guard? Should he go back out to the kitchen and wait? It would be much easier if the Callahans were here, because they would say things like "Stay" or "Come," and then he would know what he should do.

But where *were* the Callahans? It was much too scary for them to be outside right now. What if they were hurt? What if they *needed* him? What if they were lost? They *must* be lost, if they weren't home yet.

The dog got up and paced anxiously in front of the smashed windows. He wasn't supposed to go outside unless the Callahans said it was okay.

Most of the time, one of them even came outside *with* him. Sometimes he even wore a leash! Leaving on his own was against all of the rules.

But he knew that he could wiggle past those branches and get out of the house. It might be bad if he did that, but they should *be* here. He was *sure* that they should be home by now. He should check on them.

The dog stayed in the living room for one last indecisive second. Then he vaulted up onto the branches and began to make his way clumsily towards the windows. He lost his balance a couple of times, but finally managed to shove through the opening and jumped outside into the roaring storm.

He was going to go find his family!

7

The dog stood by the fallen tree for a minute to think. The storm had already done a lot of damage, and the yard was so strewn with huge branches that it looked completely different. In fact, he felt a little disoriented. Had the whole *town* changed this way, or was it only happening at the Callahans' house?

There was a thud — and a small squeak of dismay — as Abigail landed on the ice behind him. Abigail *always* arrived on *noisy* little cat feet. When the dog jumped out the window, she had concluded that whatever Santa Paws was doing, she wanted to do, too. But now that she was actually outside in the sleet and freezing rain, she was having second thoughts.

The dog was very upset to see her. First of all, she was too small, and the storm was too dangerous for her to be out here. And if she *did* come, she would just get in his way. For one thing, she was a big baby about cold weather, and started shivering and complaining if she felt even an imaginary chill. She also tired easily, wouldn't be able to keep up — and had an *incredibly* short attention span, so she would lose interest in what they were doing before they even got a block away from the house.

He barked sharply at her in an attempt to encourage her to go back inside through the broken windows.

Abigail paid no attention to this. Instead, she started practicing how to keep her balance on the ice-crusted snow. It was hard, but she liked a challenge, even if the ice felt unpleasant against her paws.

The dog growled softly, and tried to herd her in the direction of the tree — and the safety of the house. Abigail just turned her back on him, twitched her tail in his face, and continued delicately picking her way across the ice.

The dog gave up, since he had never — not even once! — won an argument with a cat. *Any* cat. He decided to go to the driveway, and see if he could trace the scent of Mr. Callahan's Buick from there. Cars were very hard to follow, because they all smelled so much alike on the roads, but he could at least give it a try.

He sprang over the gate and went into a controlled slide when he hit the ground. Abigail attempted to do the same thing, but she crashed right into a snowbank with another alarmed squeak. She struggled to her feet, and then gave each paw in turn a persnickety shake. The dog hoped that she would come to her senses now and go back inside, but he also knew that she was too stubborn for that. So he just pretended that she wasn't even there.

The sleet was swirling around violently, and each little ice pellet *hurt* when it hit them. The dog was feeling less sure about his idea to go off searching for his family in this terrible weather, but the thought that they might *need* him was uppermost in his mind. That was much more important than his own comfort.

All he could tell for sure was that Mr. Callahan's car had turned right when he pulled out of the driveway. Beyond that, there wasn't much of a trail. Still, it was a place to start.

He began trotting down the street, hoping to catch even the faintest familiar scent. The road was covered with ice, and tree branches had landed in unexpected places. It was a winter obstacle course!

Behind him, Abigail allowed herself one mournful, self-pitying mew. Then she puffed up her fur to make herself feel brave, and scampered after him.

The dog was determined to keep looking for his family until he had found every single one of them. No storm, no matter how fierce, was going to be enough to stop *him*.

* * *

The school bus was so badly tilted at the bottom of the embankment that Gregory and Oscar couldn't get the front door open. Coach Yancey and a couple of their teammates helped them climb through the emergency exit in the back. They both jumped out, landing knee-deep in the only partially-frozen marsh. Actually, in Oscar's case, it was more like *hip*-deep.

"Maybe he should have sent someone taller," Oscar said, looking down.

"I could go by myself," Gregory offered, even though the idea of braving the storm alone was pretty intimidating.

Oscar shook his head vehemently. "What, and let you get all the glory? Not a chance, bud."

Gregory grinned, and they began trudging towards the steep slope leading to the road. The water smelled strongly of the sea, and was incredibly cold. Every step was an effort, because they kept sinking into the icy muck. The marsh grass was rigid with ice and broke off whenever they tried to use it to pull themselves along.

"I wonder if rice paddies felt like this," Oscar said, his teeth chattering a little. His father had served in Vietnam, and Oscar had always been intensely curious about what that must have been like. His father was proud of his service — but he didn't talk about it very often.

"It was really *hot* there, though," Gregory said, shivering. "Right?"

"Far as I know, yeah." Oscar yanked one high-top out of the partially-frozen mud with a loud sucking sound. He had to pull so hard that it almost came right off his foot! "I guess this is totally different."

"No war going on, either," Gregory pointed out.

"So far," Oscar said, sounding very pessimistic.

They both fell about six times on their way up the steep embankment. By the time they made it up to the road, they were wet, frustrated, and *cold*. It would have been nice if a car had been conveniently driving past, but the road was empty in both directions.

Oscar glanced down at the stranded bus. "You know, crashing was really scary and all, but I'm kind of thinking we were *really* lucky."

Gregory wasn't sure he *wanted* to think about it. There were just too many scary possibilities. "Um, yeah," he said, looking away. "But let's just, you know, hurry up and find a house or something."

They had only gone about a hundred feet down the road when all of the streetlights blinked out at once. It was a shock to find themselves in complete darkness.

Gregory felt a second of panic, but then took a

deep breath. "Whoa. Okay. Okay, no big deal."

"Power must have gone out," Oscar said.

"Yeah," Gregory agreed. It wasn't really a surprise, considering how bad the storm was, but it *was* pretty spooky.

Their eyes were starting to adjust a little, and they started walking again. Being in the dark made it that much harder to keep from falling on the ice every other step.

"Made you think about the plane, didn't it," Oscar said unexpectedly.

The crash. "Yeah," Gregory admitted. "It sort of freaked me out, a little."

"Don't worry, Greg — it freaked *all* of us out," Oscar said. "I mean, you know, it was *scary*."

"We could have flipped over," Gregory said, hearing his voice shake. "We could have fallen into really deep water, we could have — all kinds of awful things. And we could have really gotten *hurt*." Or worse.

"But we're okay," Oscar said. "Mr. Monroe did a good job keeping us from turning over or anything."

Gregory nodded. Yes. They were lucky. No question about it. But it had still scared him pretty badly.

"Do you think about the plane a lot?" Oscar asked curiously.

Gregory shook his head. "Not really. Especially since Uncle Steve got off his cane and all, so we don't have to remember the whole thing every time we look at him. I just — have dreams about it sometimes." *Bad* dreams.

"I wonder if — " Oscar slipped and landed hard on the street, his hands taking the brunt of the fall. "Ouch."

Gregory helped him back up. "You all right?"

"Yeah." Oscar brushed off some of the ice and snow. "You think Patricia has nightmares about it, too?"

"Probably," Gregory said. Did she? He had no idea, really. Mostly she claimed that she only dreamed about George Clooney — and sometimes, a younger version of Gene Hackman. "Although I can't see her *telling* anyone, if she did. Except for Rachel, maybe." He shrugged. "I don't know. Sometimes I'm not sure if all *girls* are weird, or just Patricia, know what I mean?"

Oscar laughed. "Yeah, she's probably not the best test case, for figuring out girls in general. After growing up with her, either they're *all* going to want to date you, or else *none* of them are."

Gregory had to laugh, too. "Thanks, Oscar. That makes me feel a whole lot better about things."

"That was the plan," Oscar said cheerfully.

There were three houses off to the side of the road, but with the power out, it was hard to tell if anyone was home.

"What do you think?" Gregory asked.

Oscar pointed at the middle house, where there seemed to be a bobbing light moving past one of the upstairs windows. "That one. Unless, you know, it's just *haunted*."

Gregory laughed again. "You really *do* know just what to say. You've got the gift, man."

"Well, hey," Oscar said, and ducked his head modestly.

They made their way up the treacherously slick front walk, and Oscar pushed the doorbell. They waited for a minute, and then Oscar tried the doorbell a second time.

"I guess the ghost doesn't want company," he said.

Gregory gave him a playful push, but with the ice underfoot, Oscar promptly fell down.

"Oh." Gregory looked guilty. "Sorry."

Oscar climbed to his feet with a long-suffering sigh. "No problem. Keep trying and I'll let you know when I break something." He reached out for the doorbell again, and then stopped. "Are doorbells electric?"

Gregory closed his eyes. *Boy*, were they stupid. "Yes."

"Thought so," Oscar said, and took his glove off so that he could knock on the door instead.

After a minute, the door opened and a flashlight pointed at them.

"Um, hi," Gregory said, lifting his hand to

block the brightness of the beam. Because of the light in his eyes, he couldn't even tell if the person who had opened the door was a man or a woman — or, for that matter, a *ghost*. "Our bus just crashed over by the bridge, and we were wondering if you could please call the police for us?"

The flashlight beam lowered enough so that they could see an elderly man with white hair and thick glasses. "Sure, boys," he said. "I think my telephone's still working. Is anyone up there hurt?"

Gregory nodded. "I'm pretty sure our driver has a concussion, and Kurt broke his ankle and everything. I guess we need ambulances, too."

The man walked over to an end table in his front hall and picked up a portable telephone. Just as he started to dial, he paused, looking curiously at Gregory. "You seem awfully familiar, son. Do I know your parents?"

Gregory squinted at him in the glow from the flashlight, and then remembered when they had met. Last spring, this same man had been fishing off the town pier when he dropped his wallet in the water by mistake. Without even being asked, Santa Paws had promptly jumped in and fetched it for him.

"Not really, sir," he answered, "but I think you know my dog, Santa Paws."

The man nodded with recognition. "Of course!

Wonderful dog, that Santa Paws. A credit to us all." Then he remembered something else. "Is your father that nice writer fellow who always shows up at the diner in his slippers?"

There was no way around it — Oceanport was a *small* town. "Yes, sir," Gregory said.

"Well, how about that," the elderly man said, sounding pleased. "Nice to meet you." Then he dialed 911. "Hello?" he said when the dispatcher picked up. "I want to report an accident."

Gregory and Oscar exchanged triumphant smiles. They had done it! Now help was only minutes away.

Patricia and Mr. Callahan were still sitting in the main office at the junior high school, waiting for news. Other parents had arrived, expecting to pick up their sons, and they were just as upset when they discovered that no one knew where the bus was — or if the team was okay. Some of them were making panicked phone calls, some were planning to go out and search for the bus, and everyone else was either just sitting glumly in the row of disciplinary chairs or pacing up and down the corridors. Mr. Callahan had already called the police station to make sure that sector cars would be looking for the missing bus while they patrolled. Things at the station were starting to get so hectic because of the weather, that he hadn't been able to speak to Uncle Steve directly.

Patricia kept trying to think of something distracting to say, but her mind was a blank. Her brother was probably fine — but what if he *wasn't*? She liked to give him a certain amount of grief, but that didn't mean that she still wasn't crazy about him. Gregory was so steady, and dependable, and easygoing, and — he was just about her favorite person in the world. If anything bad happened to him, she wouldn't know what to do.

"I'm getting cellphones for the whole family," Mr. Callahan said decisively. "That way, we can actually keep track of one another."

Under any other circumstances, Patricia would have been elated to hear that idea — her own cellphone! — but right now, she was too worried.

"Maybe beepers, too," Mr. Callahan said, thinking aloud.

Patricia decided to break the tension with a little joke. "We also could have microchips implanted." After they had recovered Santa Paws last year, their veterinarian, Dr. Kasanofsky, had put one in the loose skin on his neck — just in case.

To her horror, Mr. Callahan actually seemed to be *considering* the idea.

"Joke, Dad," she said.

He looked startled, but then nodded. "Right. I suppose that would be — impractical."

"Just a little, yeah," Patricia said.

They sat silently after that, waiting to hear the office telephone ring with some news — or for the bus to pull up in front of the building as though nothing unusual had happened.

"So," Mr. Callahan said brightly. "How was school?"

Patricia had to check his expression first, to make sure that he was serious. "Oh. It was, um, swell."

Her father nodded, apparently wanting her to elaborate.

"Uh, I learned a great deal," Patricia said. "Things that I can probably apply throughout the rest of my — " From where she was sitting, she could see a police car arrive in front of the school, followed by a second, and then a *third*.

Her father saw the police cars too, and slowly stood up as though he were expecting bad news.

The back door of the first car opened and someone stepped out, almost losing his balance on the icy curb.

It was Gregory!

8

Not that she was glad to see him, but Patricia was the first one out the door to meet the police cars. She maybe even *ran*. Mr. Callahan and the rest of the parents — and Mr. Weingarten — were quick to follow her.

"Everything okay?" she asked. "What happened?"

Gregory shrugged casually. "The bus crashed," he said. "So the police had to drive us back."

"Yeah, you should have seen it — we went right off the side of the bridge! Totally out of control!" Oscar said, and then waved at his mother. "Hi, Mom."

"That bus is *toast*," Abdul added, and then smiled at his father hurrying to greet him. "Hey, Dad, I sold all my band candy!"

Gregory and Oscar exchanged guilty looks.

"Um, Dad, can I maybe borrow some money to pay for all the band candy I ate?" Gregory asked.

"Me, too, Mom," Oscar said meekly to his mother.

"Better make that a blank check," Patricia advised, as her father blinked and reached for his wallet.

The parents whose children had been taken straight to the hospital were very upset when they heard that their sons had been hurt in the crash, but relieved when they were assured that none of the injuries appeared to be serious.

As Gregory, Patricia, and their father headed for the Buick, Gregory was still acting very nonchalant. But once he got inside, his face began to look a little green.

"Busy being cool in front of the guys?" Patricia asked.

Gregory nodded, snapped on his seatbelt, and slumped down in the backseat with his eyes closed. Now that it was all over, he just wanted to go home and lie down for a while. There was part of a leftover apple pie in the refrigerator — if his father hadn't eaten it already — and a piece of that might be nice, too.

"Well, I'm just grateful that you're here, and in one piece, and — well, 'grateful' pretty much covers it, actually," Mr. Callahan said.

As he turned on the engine, the CD player immediately began to blare Frank Sinatra belting out "Fly Me to the Moon." Patricia and Gregory groaned and put their hands over their ears.

"Sorry," Mr. Callahan said, and turned the volume down. "But, that was an alternate take, you know. Very rare."

Gregory and Patricia had absolutely no sensible response to this.

Mr. Callahan drove extremely slowly, but the car still lost traction a couple of times. Whenever it happened, Gregory sucked in his breath, and Patricia reached back over the front seat to pat his arm.

"If it makes you feel better, Mrs. O'Leary almost ran me over before," she said.

Her father turned to stare at her.

"Oops," Patricia said, and faced forward again.

Gregory shook his head. "I know she doesn't like you, but — wow."

"Why didn't you think to mention this to me, Patricia?" Mr. Callahan asked.

Patricia smiled sweetly at him. "Mention what?"

When they drove up their street, they could see that the power was still on — but a tree had fallen onto the roof, and seemingly inside the house, too.

Gregory gasped. "Whoa! Look at *that*!"

"Well — " Mr. Callahan stopped, as though he might have been about to swear. "Gosh. Darn. Shucks."

"What's your deductible, Dad?" Patricia asked.

He just looked at her, and then parked the car.

Patricia fell as she opened the gate, and Gregory and Mr. Callahan almost did, too, when they tried to help her up.

"I don't like this storm," she said, rubbing her bruised elbow. "I don't like anything about it."

Gregory went ahead to examine the splintered trunk of the old oak. He shook his head sadly. "I used to *climb* this tree."

"Used to fall out of it a lot, too," Patricia said.

That was true, but it had still always been a great old tree. Then Gregory thought of something. "Hey, Santa Paws and the cats must have been really scared! We'd better go make sure they're okay."

To their horror, once they got inside, they couldn't find *any* of the animals. Gregory hadn't cried when the bus crashed, but he was *very* close to crying now.

"They didn't just steal Santa Paws this time," he said miserably. "They came and stole *all* of them."

The two thieves had actually been arrested long ago — and convicted of dog-napping and assorted other criminal charges. "They're both still in jail, Greg," Mr. Callahan said, resting a gentle hand on his shoulder. "No one came in here. The cats are probably just hiding somewhere, and Santa Paws — " Santa Paws was too *big* to hide successfully, so there was no way of pretending that they had just conveniently overlooked him

94

during their frantic search of the house. "I'm sure he's just — well — "

"I know where he is," Patricia said quietly.

Gregory and Mr. Callahan stared at her, their expressions somewhere between skepticism and hope.

"He's out looking for *us*," she said.

Her brother and father didn't bother arguing with that — because once she had said it aloud, they knew she was right.

Santa Paws and Abigail had ranged about a mile away from the house as Santa Paws explored each and every street thoroughly. Abigail's paws were cold, so she was getting sulky and lagging behind him. The dog was not sympathetic, since he had not exactly invited her along on this expedition. Mainly, he was upset that they had found no sign of the Callahans so far. Where *were* they? Should they go home and check again, or should they keep looking? He just didn't know what to do.

They were trotting down Hawthorne Street, when the dog heard unhappy whimpering. He stopped short, and Abigail bumped right into him. She hissed and gave his hip a hard swat with her paw. Since the dog's coat was fairly frozen, he didn't even feel her claws — and didn't bother reacting in any way. Abigail seemed disappointed by his lack of response and hauled her paw back to take another shot at him. The dog sensed the blow coming and neatly side-stepped out of the way just in time. Disgruntled about having swung and missed, Abigail sat down and began to wash the paw as though that had been her original intention.

The whimpering seemed to be coming from the mailbox on the street corner. Santa Paws rushed over and found a small, quivering puppy crouched down underneath it in an attempt to avoid the sleet. The puppy was a young spaniel mix who belonged to a family who lived about two blocks away. He was very mischievous and liked to squeeze under the fence surrounding his yard whenever possible. Then he would romp joyfully around the neighborhood until someone in his family came and found him. The storm had frightened him, though, and he was convinced that this time, he was lost forever.

Santa Paws barked a quick greeting, and the puppy wagged his tail shyly. Abigail came over and hissed at him, but neglected to scratch him since he looked so bedraggled and pathetic. Santa Paws had seen this puppy before while he was on walks with Gregory, so he knew exactly where he lived. He firmly nudged the puppy to his feet and began to escort him home.

A car drove down the street at one point, and the dog ushered both the puppy and Abigail safely out of the way until it had passed them.

Then he resumed leading the puppy home. The hole in the fence was too small for Santa Paws to crawl underneath, but the puppy squirmed through happily and began to gambol around his backyard.

The dog knew that he couldn't just leave, because that goofy puppy would probably run right out again ten minutes later. He really didn't like it when he had to perform the same rescues *twice*. So he ran over to the fence's gate and began to bark as loudly as he could. Abigail was beyond bored by this entire episode, but she ambled vaguely after him.

The backdoor of the house opened, and an older woman came outside. She wasn't wearing a coat, and she started shivering immediately.

"Well, there you are, Nelson!" she said, ecstatic to have her puppy back home in one piece. She scooped him up into her arms and gave the top of his head a big kiss. "We were *very* worried about you."

Santa Paws barked a few times, hoping she would understand that the puppy had to *stay* inside until the storm was over. In fact, as far as he was concerned, maybe the puppy ought to learn how to stay in *general*.

The woman walked over to the gate to see who had barked. "Well, hello, Santa Paws," she said, with a wide smile. "Did you bring Nelson home for us? Thank you! What a good dog you are!"

Good! Yay! The dog wagged his tail.

The woman noticed Abigail lounging around behind him, and beamed at her, too. "And who's your little friend, I wonder? Well, you're a good, smart cat, whoever you are."

Abigail yawned and turned to look in the opposite direction.

"Well, you two hurry home now," the woman advised them. "This weather is just frightful!" She turned to go back into the house. "Good night, Santa Paws — and thank you again!"

The dog waited until he saw the door close before starting down the street to continue his search for the Callahans. Abigail looked deeply apathetic, but then gave in and darted after him. They had only gone another few blocks when they heard a faint voice calling out from someplace close by.

"Help!" the voice wailed. "Someone, please help me!"

The dog stopped in his tracks. It was going to be very hard to find his family, if he kept having so many interruptions! But he spun around at once and followed the sound of the voice. If there was one word he knew well, it was the word *"Help."*

After her teachers' meeting, Mrs. Callahan had driven directly over to the mall, which was on the outskirts of town. She noticed that the roads were, indeed, a tad slick, but she was too busy thinking about what was left on her Christmas list to give the weather conditions much attention.

The mall was crowded with other last-minute shoppers, and Mrs. Callahan waited in line after line, in store after store. At this rate, she would be lucky to get home in time to *eat* supper, forget helping prepare it.

Once or twice, the lights in the various stores dimmed, and everyone in the lines would make jokes about wishing they had completed all of their shopping on the Internet weeks ago. The general consensus was that the weather was no match for the power of determined consumers and the holiday shopping season.

Mrs. Callahan thought about calling home to let the family know that her excursion was taking much longer than she had expected, but each payphone seemed to have a very long line. In any case, she assumed she would be done soon.

An hour and a half later, that assumption seemed overly optimistic. After waiting in one final line with two pairs of wacky slippers she couldn't resist buying for a certain eccentric writer, she decided that she would just have to finish the rest of her shopping the next day. She disliked shopping on Christmas Eve, but yet again this year, she would be doing so.

The parking lot was so slick that people were

having trouble getting to their cars without falling. Mrs. Callahan copied the idea she saw a couple of other people using, and stood on the back of a shopping cart like a ten-year-old in order to glide over to her car. This technique was quite successful, and in all honesty, entertaining enough to make her want to do it again. However, she was running late enough as it was.

The station wagon was encased in a thin layer of fresh ice, which she had to chip away with her keys in order to open the door. Then she had to run the car heater for a while, so that the windshield would defrost enough for her to be able to scrape *that* sheen of ice away, too. It was beginning to seem like a terrible night to have to be out on the road, and she wished that the mall were closer to her house. But it wasn't, so she just took a deep breath and put the car into gear.

She saw two fender-benders happen up in front of her before she even got out of the parking lot. There were also cars sliding all over the place on the main road, no matter how slowly people tried to drive. One car coasted helplessly right through a red-light, and smashed into a pick-up truck coming from the other direction. Neither driver was hurt, but both cars were badly damaged and blocking the road.

Traffic began to back up as everyone waited for tow trucks to clear away the disabled cars, and for the police to arrive to direct traffic. After ten minutes, Mrs. Callahan began to get impatient, so she turned off onto a side road. It would be much faster to detour around all of the main routes, and avoid other cars as much as possible.

The ice was treacherous, but the car's snow tires maintained reasonably good traction — which came as a relief. Unfortunately, she didn't have any chains, but they would have helped, too. Mrs. Callahan drove through a couple of neighborhoods which were completely dark, so the power must be starting to go out in various parts of town. She hoped that her house hadn't been affected by the outages, and her first worry was about all of the Christmas food in the refrigerator and the possibility of its spoiling. It would be a shame to waste all of the food — and have to do even more shopping to replace it.

There was a huge branch blocking the street in front of her, and she had to divert to yet another back route. Maybe this *was* a pretty serious storm! The wind was howling so loudly that she could even hear it inside the car with all of the windows shut, and her windshield wipers could barely keep up with the violent gusts of sleet. There was no traffic on the back roads, but somehow that isolation made the driving seem even more stressful than it might have been otherwise.

Looking for a pleasant distraction, Mrs. Callahan flipped the radio on, but every single station seemed to be exclusively airing dire weather bulletins and travel advisories. So much for happy holiday tunes. Since she already *knew* that the weather was terrible, she turned the radio off again and drove in silence.

The neighborhood she was passing through now was a brand-new housing development. Most of the homes hadn't even been completed — or sold, and no one had moved in yet. Even an endless traffic jam seemed more appealing than such a lonely road, so Mrs. Callahan started to turn around and make her way back to one of the main routes.

There was a strange shattering sound off to her right, and she couldn't imagine what it might be. But she put her foot gently on the brakes, just in case. There was a huge dark shape coming towards her, and Mrs. Callahan realized that it was a giant tree falling. She pressed her foot down on the accelerator and tried to swerve out of the way, but it was too late.

The tree landed right on top of her car!

9

Santa Paws had very little trouble tracking the call for help to a driveway halfway down the block. A man was lying on his back, gasping for breath and clutching his chest. It was Mr. Spiegel, who had come out to shovel a path behind his car before the ice got any thicker. As a rule, he never exercised, so the stress and the strain of shoveling had been too much for him. There was a terrible crushing pain in his chest, and he was almost sure that he was having a heart attack.

Mr. Spiegel looked up blearily to see a large German shepherd mix and a small black cat standing above him.

"You're Santa Paws, aren't you," he said, his voice weak. "Please help me. I need a doctor."

Santa Paws knew that *something* was wrong with this man, but he didn't know what it was. But he had learned long ago that whenever he was stuck for an answer, he just had to find a nice person to help him out. He pawed the man's shoulder gently, woofed once, and then trotted off to locate someone to take care of this situation for him.

When Abigail started to accompany him, the dog used his paw to propel her back in the direction of the man. He should *not* be left alone. Abigail meowed angrily, but she *was* feeling tired. Maybe she could stay next to this man and have a brief rest, while they waited for Santa Paws to come back. She liked naps a lot better than officious little errands, anyway. In her opinion, Santa Paws could be rather irritating and single-minded when he was off on a mission. She would just as soon skip the usual hectic sprint around the neighborhood, frankly.

Mr. Spiegel did his best to take deep breaths. He was very frightened by the symptoms he was having, and it was hard not to panic.

The freezing rain was so chilly that Abigail burrowed up underneath Mr. Spiegel's coat for warmth. Then she curled up and went to sleep, purring quietly. Mr. Spiegel was surprised that such a small sound could be so comforting, and he made an effort to concentrate on the warm rumbling of the little cat's purr. It made him feel a tiny bit better, although he was still extremely scared.

The dog ran to three different houses, barking his deepest bark in front of each one. There didn't seem to be anyone home, and he had to sit down for a few seconds to think of a better plan. That nice man back there was sick, and needed his help right away! He couldn't waste time!

Santa Paws shifted his weight indecisively. When he barked at doors, people almost always came outside to see what was wrong. He *depended* on that. But this time, he would have to — *make something up?* If only Gregory and Patricia were here with him. They were very smart.

Maybe he should run back home, or — wait! An idea! He would go see the friendly men and women who drove the cars and trucks with the sirens and the flashing lights! Yay! He had a plan!

Happily, the dog jumped up and dashed towards the fire station. It was only about a quarter of a mile away, and the police station was located in the building next door. He had been there many times with the Callahans when they stopped by to say hello to Uncle Steve. Uncle Steve would *absolutely* help him, and the other officers probably would, too. Lots of times, when he was involved in adventures around town, the men and women in uniforms would mysteriously show up to assist him at some point. They were very good helpers.

When he ran up to the public safety complex, one of the rescue ambulances was just returning to headquarters. There had been so many car accidents during the last few hours, that the firefighters and paramedics had been extremely busy. This ambulance was being driven by paramedic Fran Minelli, and her partner, Saul Rubin. They had had an exhausting shift so far, and were looking forward to having a few minutes to relax and sip some hot coffee before being called out again.

The dog waited until they had parked the ambulance, and then he barked an energetic, but respectful bark.

Fran saw him first, and tapped her partner's arm. "Better hold off on that cup of coffee, Saul."

Saul looked over, and then groaned. "So much for our break. Think there's any chance he's crying wolf?" He bit his lip thoughtfully. "Or — crying shepherd?"

"Not a chance in the world," Fran said.

Saul felt the same way, but he had been hoping that she would disagree with him. "What's up, Santa Paws?" he asked, sounding resigned.

The dog barked, ran towards the street, then ran back to them.

"Okay." Fran hauled an aid bag out of the ambulance. "I'll follow on foot in case it's right nearby, and you drive."

Saul nodded, and slid behind the wheel of the rescue vehicle.

Santa Paws was so fast that Fran soon realized she didn't have a hope of being able to keep up. She motioned for Saul to pull over, and then climbed into the passenger's seat. It seemed clear from the dog's urgent behavior that there was a *serious* emergency waiting for them somewhere.

Santa Paws led the ambulance efficiently to Mr. Spiegel's house. Then, once they had parked, he stepped aside to let them take over.

" 'Crying shepherd,' " Fran muttered to Saul, when they saw Mr. Spiegel lying in his driveway in obvious distress.

Saul shrugged defensively, and grabbed some supplies and a cardiac kit from the back of the ambulance.

"Hello, Mr. Spiegel," Fran said, as she bent over him to take his vital signs. "Don't worry, you're going to be just fine now."

Abigail poked her head out from inside Mr. Spiegel's coat, and Fran jumped in surprise.

"Oh, my," she said. "Is your cat friendly?"

"Yes, my cat is extremely friendly," Mr. Spiegel answered.

Fran reached down to lift Abigail out of the way. Annoyed by having been so rudely awakened, Abigail hissed at her and slashed a warning paw in her direction. Fran swiftly withdrew her hand.

"I, uh, thought your cat was friendly," she said.

"Well, yeah, *my* cat is," Mr. Spiegel told her.

Fran and Saul finally caught on to the joke, and they both laughed. *This wasn't his cat.* If Mr. Spiegel could kid around — and make a reference to a Pink Panther movie, no less — then his prognosis had to be pretty good.

Pleased by her power to intimidate, Abigail jumped off Mr. Spiegel and flounced over to the side of the driveway to wash her face.

"Did the cat just show up out of nowhere?" Saul asked curiously, as he did a quick EKG, glanced at the results, and rechecked Mr. Spiegel's vital signs. Fran was on her mobile unit, calling ahead to the hospital to let them know that they were about to be transporting a probable cardiac arrest victim.

Mr. Spiegel shrugged, although it was somewhat difficult for him to move with the small monitor and IV hooked up to him. "No idea. She showed up with Santa Paws."

Fran and Saul looked at each other.

"Strange," Saul said. "He's always been a loner."

Fran nodded. "Classic hero archetype."

Santa Paws waited a few feet away, until he was sure that everything was under control. Then he barked once, and headed towards the street. Afraid that she might be left behind, Abigail hustled after him.

"Thank you, Santa Paws!" Mr. Spiegel shouted weakly.

The dog wagged his tail and trotted away. Now that he had done his job, he could go back to looking for the Callahans!

At the house, Gregory and Patricia were trying to help their father deal with the tree in the middle of the living room. First they had carried all of the Christmas presents, and anything else that might be damaged by exposure to the elements, into the den for safekeeping. Now it was time to figure out what to do with the actual *tree*.

"Maybe we should just leave it there," Patricia suggested. "So there's, you know, evidence of wrongdoing."

"Actually, I think this falls more into the category of an 'act of God,' Patricia," Mr. Callahan said.

Gregory had been extremely upset when Mr. Callahan vetoed the idea of their going out into the storm to search for Santa Paws and the cats, so cleaning up the mess was a good way for him to take his mind off things. "Should I go get the camera?" he asked. "So you have like, a photographic record for the insurance company?"

Mr. Callahan considered that, and then nodded. "Yeah, actually. That's a very good idea."

They took pictures of the tree from every possible angle. Then Mr. Callahan began to snap off branches, with the idea of gradually breaking the tree into manageable pieces.

"This is going to take forever, Dad," Patricia said, after a while. "I think we need someone with a chainsaw." All they had accomplished so far was to create a large pile of branches on the floor — while the tree still seemed to be just as big as when they had started.

"Yeah, really," Gregory said. "Maybe we should just close the door and worry about it tomorrow. Besides, I'm kind of getting hungry."

Mr. Callahan looked at his watch, blinked, and took a second look.

"What?" Patricia asked uneasily.

"It's just later than I thought," Mr. Callahan said. "I wonder where your mother is."

"Christmas shopping," Gregory reminded him.

"I know," Mr. Callahan said, "but — "

Frowning, he walked over to the telephone to make sure that there was a dial tone. The lights were flickering or fading every so often, and the phones might be on the verge of going out, too. But the dial tone sounded normal.

He hung up, frowning harder. "I'm surprised she hasn't called to tell us to go ahead and start dinner without her, that's all."

Considering how badly things had been going today, Patricia got nervous. "You don't think there's anything wrong, do you? I mean, it *always* takes her forever when she goes Christmas shopping."

"Absolutely," Mr. Callahan said, his voice a shade too jovial to be entirely convincing. "Let's go make some supper, so it'll be ready by the time she gets here."

Quietly, Gregory and Patricia followed him out to the kitchen. They were sure that their mother was all right, but they were still concerned.

Where *was* she?

Mrs. Callahan was in trouble. The large tree had smashed into the station wagon, crushing the hood and badly cracking the windshield. To make matters worse, it had hit some power lines on its way down and knocked over a telephone pole, too. The telephone pole had landed on the back end of the station wagon, hemming her in.

The accident had happened so quickly that it left Mrs. Callahan stunned. The force of the crash had slammed her into the steering wheel, and while she wasn't quite unconscious, she wasn't exactly *alert*, either.

She wasn't sure how much time had passed before she tried to sit up. When she finally moved, there was such a sharp pain in her ribs that she gasped. She had been wearing her seatbelt, but the station wagon was so old that it didn't have air bags.

Slowly and cautiously, she eased herself back against the seat. It was painful, but she didn't feel any severe pain until she tried to take a deep breath. So, for lack of a better idea, she resolved not to take any more deep breaths.

The dashboard had collapsed from the weight of the tree, but Mrs. Callahan was able to pull her right leg free without any trouble. Her left leg seemed to be stuck — *and* to be broken. It was twisted at an odd angle, and it *definitely* hurt a great deal.

"This is not good," she found herself saying aloud.

The engine seemed to be releasing steam, but it was hard to tell through the thick sleet. She turned the ignition key experimentally, but nothing happened. Afraid suddenly that she was doing something dangerous, Mrs. Callahan turned the ignition off. She couldn't smell any gas leaking, but she didn't want to take any chances.

The windows were up, but it was already starting to get cold inside the car. The windshield was cracked in so many places that frigid air was leaking steadily inside. Since the windows were automatic and didn't have handles, they wouldn't work if the engine was dead. So while she might freeze to death, at least the damaged windshield meant that she wouldn't *suffocate*.

Trying to find a short-cut home had unquestionably been a mistake. On a normal night, with no storm, the police department might send a cruiser on a routine patrol through this part of town. But with the horrible weather, tonight they would be concentrating their efforts in the areas where people actually *lived*.

She could walk to a populated street without much trouble, if she hadn't injured her leg. She could also beep the horn endlessly, but who would hear it? If *only* she had had the good sense to buy a cellphone, long ago. But — she had never really needed one before. Putting off that particular purchase was a decision she certainly regretted now!

She couldn't think of a solution to this situation, so she closed her eyes and took several — shallow — breaths. Her leg was hurting so much that it was difficult to think clearly. But she knew how worried her family was going to be if she didn't get home soon, so she *had* to think of something sensible to do.

Taking a couple of ibuprofen would be a good start. Mrs. Callahan fumbled around in the darkness until she found her purse. Teaching all day sometimes gave her headaches, so she always carried a bottle of aspirin or some other pain reliever. She located the bottle and swallowed two of the pills. They tasted terrible dry, and she felt around inside the bag for something to get rid of the bitterness. There were a few cough drops floating around at the bottom, and she put one in her mouth. Neither of these actions were a solution, but they were better than just *sitting* here.

It was very cold. She was already wearing her gloves and a knitted hat, and now she buttoned her coat all the way up to her neck. Maybe, if she was lucky, instead of freezing, she might just get — chilly.

Maybe.

But, like Patricia, she was not a very patient person. Even though it would be horribly painful, she should probably just walk, or limp, her way to the nearest occupied house. It was really the best way to handle this.

"Okay, then," Mrs. Callahan said aloud, to give herself confidence.

Using both gloved hands, she tugged on her pinned leg. It hurt even more than she had expected it would, but to make matters worse, it also didn't *budge*. She reached down with her left hand to move the seat back, which set off such a strong jolt of pain in her leg that she was afraid she might faint. Having the seat further back gave her more room to maneuver, but her leg stayed at the same sickening angle. She had a sinking feeling that the only way she would be able to free herself was if she used a *blow-torch* on the dashboard and steering column.

Unfortunately, she did not have a blow-torch handy.

Maybe opening the driver's side door would help. She could turn more easily that way, and it might result in her leg slipping free. Even if it didn't work, it was certainly worth a try.

As Mrs. Callahan reached for the door handle, she became aware of a strange crackling sound, above and beyond the howling of the storm. She listened intently, noticing for the first time that there seemed to be tiny flashes of light around and near the car at unpredictable intervals. Not only that, but the light flashes were *blue*. Crackling and blue flashes meant only one thing.

She was surrounded by live wires!

10

Mr. Callahan fixed roast beef sandwiches for Gregory and Patricia's supper, but he didn't bother making one for himself.

"Aren't you hungry, Dad?" Gregory asked with his mouth full.

"Late lunch," Mr. Callahan said. He was looking out the window with a pensive expression, which was probably better than his staring at the telephone as though that would *make* it ring.

Gregory and Patricia wanted to tell him not to worry — but he might get mad, and besides, they were worried, too. So they ate their sandwiches without much conversation, and even voluntarily chose nutritious fresh apples for dessert, instead of ice cream or cookies. Evelyn had made an appearance halfway through the meal, meowing for her own dinner, and they were glad to discover that *one* of their pets was at home where she belonged. Abigail might be lurking somewhere, too, but they hadn't seen her yet.

"Um, you could call Uncle Steve, maybe," Patricia said.

Mr. Callahan turned away from his post at the window, in an attempt to make his concern less obvious. "No, I think they probably have their hands full over there. I'm sure she'll be here any minute now."

Many minutes had already passed, but Gregory and Patricia simply cleared the table and cleaned up the kitchen without arguing. Mr. Callahan was so distracted that he didn't even seem to notice any of this.

"Can I ask again if we can go look for Santa Paws?" Gregory whispered.

Patricia shook her head. "He's too upset, and he's *never* going to let us go outside," she whispered back.

Gregory knew she was right, so he stayed silent.

If anything, the storm seemed to be getting worse. The winds sounded as though they were reaching hurricane force, and there were regular loud cracks and snaps as tree branches gave way from the weight of the ice.

It was time for a television show they liked, but none of them was exactly in the mood to watch a situation comedy right now.

"Do either of you know *where* she was going to shop?" Mr. Callahan asked. "Was she just going to go downtown, or was she heading all the way out to the mall?" The center of Oceanport was small, but had a surprisingly wide variety of stores crammed together within the space of a few blocks. Some of the shops, like Mabel's Five and Dime, were notoriously well-stocked, with all sorts of fun and interesting potential gifts tucked away on tall wooden shelves.

Gregory and Patricia looked at each other, and shrugged.

"She was buying presents, Dad. If she told us which stores she was going to, we could guess what she was getting," Gregory said logically.

Mr. Callahan checked the clock one last time, and then went over to get his coat. "I'm going to take a quick ride over there, see if I run into her."

Gregory looked eager. "Can we come, too? And maybe look for Santa Paws along the way?"

"No," Mr. Callahan said. "You two stay here. No point in *all* of us being out there in that mess. If your mother gets back here before I do, just tell her where I went, and that I'll be home soon."

"Yeah, but if we came, we could — " Gregory started.

"*No*," Mr. Callahan said firmly. "Really. I won't be gone long. Please just stay put, okay?"

It probably wasn't necessary to point this out, but Patricia said it, anyway. "Drive carefully, Dad."

118

"*Extremely* carefully," Mr. Callahan said, and headed outside.

Once the door had closed behind him, Gregory and Patricia looked at each other.

"Now what?" Gregory asked.

"I don't know." Then, Patricia sighed. "We could go check our email, I guess."

That seemed like a reasonably good way to kill time, so Gregory nodded and they started upstairs.

It really wasn't that late yet, but they had had such an eventful day, that it already *felt* like the middle of the night!

Santa Paws and Abigail were down near Main Street. So far, they had not seen, heard, or smelled any sign of the Callahans. Abigail was cold and exhausted — and the dog was starting to run out of enthusiasm, too. It had been *hours* since he had eaten, and his supper was long overdue.

Most of the stores had closed early because of the storm, and the street was almost completely deserted. Every so often, a car would creep past them, with an anxious driver behind the wheel. Other than that, they were pretty much alone.

Out of the blue, Abigail abruptly sat down in front of Sally's Diner and Sundries Shop, and refused to move another step. The dog used his paw to try and force her to start walking again, but Abigail wouldn't budge an inch. She wanted to go home *right now*, and that was all there was to it!

The dog considered leaving her, but the truth was, he was tired of this endless search, too. And maybe the Callahans had come home by now! It would be worthwhile to go back and check.

The minute he turned to face in the direction that led back to the house, Abigail sprang to her feet. She was always pleased when the dog saw things *her* way. Luckily, he was very easy to manipulate.

They had only made it about fifty feet when the dog paused. Abigail smacked him indignantly across the muzzle, but Santa Paws didn't even flinch. He just spun around and ran back down Main Street.

Once again, duty called!

Less than twenty minutes after Mr. Callahan left the house, the power went out. The multiple windows on Patricia's computer screen blacked out in an instant, and the television show Gregory was watching disappeared right in the middle of a punch line. They each sat very still, waiting for the power magically to return. Naturally, it didn't, and so they got up to go find each other — and some flashlights.

They met on the landing at the bottom of the stairs. In fact, they banged into each other.

"Power's out," Gregory said.

Patricia gasped. "No. Really?"

Since it was pitch black, he knew she couldn't see him blushing. "Yeah, well, you're the oldest," he said. "What do we do?"

"Light a big bonfire in the middle of the den and dance around it," she said.

Gregory took a step backwards and slammed right into the wall. "Whoa. And — *ow*," he added. "That seems like a totally bad idea, Patty."

Patricia nobly overlooked that extraordinarily gullible response. "Dad left all those flashlights in the kitchen. Let's go get them."

They ended up sitting at the kitchen table, so that they would only have to use one of the flashlights and could conserve the batteries. Even with the beam of the light brightening the room a little, it still seemed almost oppressively dark — and kind of scary.

"I hope they get back soon," Gregory said.

"They will," Patricia reassured him. "Mom just lost track of time, I bet. And — the lines at the stores were probably really long." That was the answer they both wanted to hear, so that was the one she gave.

"Yeah, that makes sense." Gregory shifted in his chair restlessly. "How come the furnace went off? We don't have electric heat."

"No, but the motor needs electricity to run," Patricia said. "Or a generator or something."

"Oh." Gregory started to open the refrigerator to get something to eat, but then paused. "We should probably keep this closed, right? Until the power comes back on?"

"Yeah." Patricia stood up. "You know, maybe I'll give Rachel a call. This might be flipping her out."

"Why? How would she even know the lights went out?" Gregory asked curiously.

"She'll know that the heat stopped, and that her computer isn't working or anything," Patricia said. "Besides, her mother was going down to the city to pick up her father at the airport, so she's the only one home."

Gregory shrugged. "All the flights were probably canceled."

"Maybe," Patricia said, and dialed her friend's number. When no one answered after a dozen rings, she hung up. "I wonder if their phone's out. I mean, I *know* she's supposed to be home right now."

"Maybe they went somewhere," Gregory guessed.

Patricia shook her head. "In the middle of this? No way." Then she looked very thoughtful, nodded once to herself, and went to get her coat.

"What are you doing?" Gregory asked suspiciously.

"I'll just run over there and make sure everything's okay," Patricia said, pulling on her jacket.

"I'll be back before Mom and Dad even know I left."

Gregory frowned at her. "That's totally stupid."

"Yeah," Patricia agreed, "so?"

Gregory couldn't think of a good retort for that. "Well, then, I'm coming with you."

"No, you have to stay here in case they *do* get here first," Patricia said.

Gregory hated being put in the middle of things like that. "What do I tell them, that you just took off and I couldn't stop you? They're going to be really mad."

Patricia nodded. "Yeah, say I overpowered you and then made my escape."

"You're too *thin* to overpower me," Gregory said grimly.

Patricia grinned and sat down on the floor to lace on one of her pairs of hockey skates.

Gregory stared at her. "Are you nuts?"

"With all that ice out there, this'll be easier," she said, knotting her bootlaces together and slinging them around her neck. That way, if she needed to walk at some point, she could change out of her skates. "I can make much better time."

He kept staring.

"It's not like I'm using my good game skates," she said, in her own defense.

Since it was impossible to talk Patricia out of something once she had her mind made up,

Gregory didn't bother trying. "You might as well wear your helmet, too."

Patricia's eyes lit up. "Good idea!" She used the wall for support as she stood up, since linoleum was not exactly the ideal surface for skate blades.

"Mom's going to be mad if you scratch up the floor," Gregory warned her.

"I know, I'm being careful." Patricia stepped delicately over to the backdoor, and then eased herself out to the patio. She took a couple of experimental glides forward, and while the surface was uneven, it still worked pretty well. "See?" she said triumphantly. "I'll be back in about twenty minutes."

Watching her skate down the back walk and out to the street, Gregory came to the conclusion that while it *was* a dumb plan, it just might work. He went back inside, rehearsing exactly what he was going to say if his parents happened to arrive home first.

The one thing he knew for sure was that Patricia was really going to *owe* him one.

He sat in the kitchen for a while, eating graham crackers and reading *People* magazine by flashlight. Mysteries and horror books were his favorites, but he didn't want to read anything creepy while he was here alone, in the dark.

Then it crossed his mind that since he *was*

stuck here by himself, this was the perfect opportunity to go out and look for Santa Paws and — possibly — Abigail. If human beings weren't supposed to be wandering around in this storm, pets weren't, either. He could at least walk around the block and call them a few times. If his dog heard his voice, Gregory knew that he would come running right away.

So Gregory bundled up, wrote a note for his parents explaining where he and Patricia had gone, and left the house.

Call him crazy, but he had elected *not* to wear skates.

When Santa Paws had sensed danger on Main Street, he had run straight to Harold's Happy Hardware Store. Harold had closed up for the night two hours earlier and let his employees go home, but he had stayed in the back office to work on inventory paperwork. Since he could walk home from his store, he wasn't worried about driving through the sleet.

Abigail trudged after him, so tired that her paws kept slipping on the ice. They should have been halfway home by now, but, *no*. The dog was running off to someone's rescue again. With every step, she planned some fiendish ways to take her revenge. Once they were home, she was going to eat from the dog's dish — whenever she wanted, scratch him a few times when his back was turned, and meow *really* loudly in his ear when he was asleep.

Harold was locking the front door of his store and double-checking to be sure that everything was secure. He had considered nailing plywood across the front windows to protect them from the storm, but that was really more suitable for hurricanes. There was a creaking sound coming from somewhere, but when he looked around, he couldn't locate the source. So he shrugged and put his keys into his pocket.

Out of nowhere, a large dark shape came barreling out of the night towards him. It looked like some kind of wild and vicious animal! Harold screamed and threw his arms up to protect his face.

He was about to be attacked!

11

There was no time to waste, and Santa Paws launched himself powerfully into the air. There was a parked car in his way, so he vaulted right over it. He slammed into Harold at chest-level, using all of his strength to knock him down. Harold groaned as he landed flat on his back on the ice. When he recognized his silent assailant, he was shocked.

"Santa Paws, what on earth do you think you're doing?" he demanded angrily. "That really — "

Just then, the heavy metal sign above his store tore free from its supports and came crashing down onto the exact spot where Harold had just been standing. The sign probably weighed more than two hundred pounds, and it hit the ground with such force that it actually dented in several places.

"Oh," Harold said. "Never mind." If Santa

Paws hadn't come along at just the right moment, he would have been crushed!

The crisis was over, so Abigail meowed sulkily. It was time to *go home* already.

The dog instantly turned and loped over to her. Whenever possible, he liked to avoid letting cats get into snits. And — his work was done here.

"Thanks, Santa Paws!" Harold called after him. "I'm going to give your family permanent discounts!"

The dog barked in his direction, without pausing in his steady trot. Then he and the cat disappeared into the stormy night.

While Mr. Callahan drove out to the mall, he saw numerous cars that had slid off the road, crashed, or run into other forms of trouble. Each time, he slowed down to make sure that his wife's station wagon wasn't there.

Despite the Christmas rush, the mall had closed half an hour early on the advice of the Oceanport Police Department. The road conditions were just too hazardous for their customers and employees. By now, the parking lots were almost empty.

Mr. Callahan cruised through each of the lots, looking for their station wagon. It was nowhere in sight, so he stopped his car for a minute to decide what to do next.

Had she passed him on the way home? Quite possibly, they had just missed each other. With that cheering thought, Mr. Callahan began to look for a payphone. There were several near the main entrance of the mall, and he parked right in front.

When he dialed the house, the phone rang, and rang, and *rang*. His first instinct was to panic, but then he realized that the storm could easily have knocked their telephone service out. So, except for a brief spin through downtown Oceanport, he would go directly home.

With luck, the entire family — pets and all — would be there waiting for him!

Patricia was finding her skating strategy surprisingly successful. Every so often she would hit a rough patch, and take a spill. But, for the most part, it was smooth sailing all the way. With the power out, the streets seemed somewhat unfamiliar, and she had to be careful not to skate into fallen branches. More than once, she ran into a parked car, but she wasn't skating fast enough to get hurt.

The wind was so cold that it seemed to be whipping right inside her jacket, and the pounding sleet made it that much harder to see where she was going.

In the darkness, she almost glided right past Rachel's house. Fortunately, it had a distinctive wooden fence. Patricia used one of her skate blades to feel for the curb, and then stepped onto the sidewalk. She skated up to Rachel's front steps, and carefully made her way up the stairs. The house was completely dark, but Rachel wouldn't have had any reason to turn on a flashlight or light a candle.

Patricia took one of her gloves off and rapped loudly on the door with her bare hand. With the storm, the sound would be muffled, but Rachel had better hearing than anyone she knew. She let about a minute go by, and then knocked again.

"Hey, Rachel!" she yelled. "Open the door, okay?"

Once she was sure that no one was there, Patricia side-stepped down the stairs to the front walk. Either Rachel and her parents had gone somewhere, or Rachel was staying at a neighbor's house, waiting for her parents to come home. Patricia knew that Rachel's favorite neighbor was Mrs. Kravitz, who lived around the corner. If Rachel had gone *anywhere* by herself, that was the direction she would have taken. So it wouldn't hurt to go knock on Mrs. Kravitz's door, and see if her friend was there.

Patricia was at the end of the street, making a sharp right turn on her skates, when she heard something — or some*one* — moving along the sidewalk.

"Hello?" she said tentatively.

There was a pause, interrupted only by the howling whistle of the winds.

"Patricia?" a voice answered, sounding just as uncertain. "Is that you?"

Rachel! Patricia skated towards the voice, feeling very relieved. For one thing, she was pleased to have located her friend; for another, she was even *more* pleased that the person lurking nearby hadn't been an odious criminal or something. "Yeah. Are you going down to Mrs. Kravitz's?"

"I *was*," Rachel admitted. "But — well, I kind of got turned around. There's like, all these branches and stuff on the ground, and — everything's *different*. I'm not really sure where my house is." Since she didn't have a guide dog yet, Rachel had to depend on nothing more than her cane — and her memory — when she wanted to go somewhere. Whenever the desks got rearranged at school, or anyone she knew redecorated their house, it was a real challenge for Rachel to get around until she memorized the new layout.

"It *is* different," Patricia said. "I've been pretty disoriented, too."

"Why do your shoes sound weird?" Rachel asked.

Patricia grinned. "Because they're hockey skates."

"Figures," Rachel said, and laughed. "How'd

you know I'd be dumb enough to be walking around in the middle of all this?"

Patricia shrugged. "Takes one to know one."

"That's for sure. I'm really glad they did, but I can't *believe* your parents let you come over here," Rachel said.

Thinking about how they would react if her parents got home before she did, Patricia felt guilty. "They didn't. My mother's late coming back from shopping, and my father went to look for her, so I — snuck out."

"Looks like *you'll* be grounded for the rest of vacation," Rachel said wryly. "But, then again, *I* probably will be, too."

Once they had established that Rachel's parents hadn't come home yet either, Patricia sat down on the curb to change into her boots. Then Patricia guided her back to her house so that she could leave a note saying that she was at the Callahans.

"I've been out there for a pretty long time," Rachel confessed. "I could have gone up to a house, but I was too embarrassed to tell whoever answered the door that I was lost. I figured I'd find my way home eventually."

Patricia laughed. "Well, I guess when it comes to the Seven Deadly Sins, you've got *pride* nailed."

"It's better than greed or gluttony," Rachel said.

"Yeah," Patricia agreed, "but sloth kind of appeals to me."

Once they were back outdoors, they picked their way carefully across the ice. They were making good progress until a ferocious blast of wind tore some already sagging power lines down right in front of them.

"What?" Rachel asked, when Patricia stopped.

"A bunch of telephone wires and stuff just came down," Patricia said. "You think it's safe to go by them because the power's out?"

"No way," Rachel said instantly. "They could still be charged somehow."

Since it wasn't worth risking their lives to find out — it was important to avoid *any* downed power line, no matter what — they went a couple of blocks out of their way, instead. That put them right by Patricia's aunt and uncle's darkened house. Since Aunt Emily had a cellular telephone, it seemed like a good idea for them to go in and have Patricia make a quick call home — just in case.

When Aunt Emily opened the door, Miranda was yelling and bouncing around in the background. There was a small camp lantern giving off an orange glow in the living room. Aunt Emily looked tense and exhausted — and surprised to see them.

"What are you two doing out on a night like this?" she asked. "Come on in." She looked at Pa-

133

tricia's helmet curiously. "Nice hat, Patricia."

"Patty, Patty, Patty!" Miranda shouted exuberantly. "Merry Christmas! Did you bring me any presents? And tomorrow is my birthday, too!" She smiled widely at Rachel. "I'm going to be a big girl."

Miranda had been saying "Merry Christmas" to everyone she met for about three months now. "Merry Christmas, Miranda. We're really sorry to just show up, Aunt Emily," Patricia said, "but I think I need to call home and let my parents know where I am. Could I use your cell phone?"

Aunt Emily shook her head. "I'm sorry, the battery's dead. I was just going to recharge it when the power went out." She rubbed one hand wearily across the back of her neck. "I'm afraid that the regular telephone isn't working, either."

Patricia was about to apologize again for their showing up unannounced, and say that they would just head home, when she noticed how gingerly her aunt was moving across the room. "Is everything okay?"

Aunt Emily waved that aside, as she lowered herself onto the couch. "Just some minor contractions, no big deal."

Contractions certainly *sounded* like a big deal. "Um, but you still have two months left," Patricia said.

Aunt Emily nodded. "I know. It's probably just

false labor. So Miranda and I have been trying to keep quiet, right, Miranda?"

"Yes!" Miranda said, as she pounded away on her tiny piano keyboard. "I am a *very* good girl."

"Don't mind me, girls, if I just lie down here for a minute," Aunt Emily said. She stretched out on the couch, resting her legs up on two pillows.

"Does Uncle Steve know?" Patricia asked.

Aunt Emily shook her head. "No, it started after the phones stopped working. He's supposed to be off at midnight, but I'm guessing he'll have to pull a double-shift tonight."

"But you'd rather he knew about it," Patricia said.

Aunt Emily hesitated. "Well — I mean — "

"Got it," Patricia said, and sat down on the floor to put on her skates.

It looked as though a quick trip down to the police station was in her immediate future.

The sleet was coming down so hard that Gregory made a point of staying within a block or two of his house. He wanted to find Santa Paws and Abigail, but that didn't mean he had to be *stupid* about it. He had brought along a flashlight, so that it would be easier to see where he was going — and if there was anything dangerous in his way.

The storm was probably drowning out the sound of his voice, but he kept calling out, "Santa Paws! Come here, Santa Paws!" Every so often, he threw in a shout for Abigail, too, even though he knew that she went out of her way *not* to answer to her name. But the click of a catfood can — or any can, really — opening could wake her up from the deepest sleep in about a second and a half.

The sleet seemed to be freezing onto his jacket and hat, and Gregory wondered if this was just a waste of time. He was starting to get *really* cold. Besides, Santa Paws had found his way home before, and he would have no trouble doing it again. But that didn't mean that Gregory wasn't worried about him.

"Santa Paws!" he yelled. "Come here, boy!"

To his delight, he heard a faint, and very familiar, answering bark! He stayed right where he was, aiming the flashlight beam down the murky street. It was hard to see through the sleet, and he held one hand above his eyes to try and sharpen his vision.

Santa Paws kept barking, and after another minute, he came galloping towards Gregory at top speed. He jumped on Gregory so joyfully that they both tumbled onto the ice. But they were so glad to have found each other, that neither of them minded.

"Oh, good boy, you're very smart," Gregory said. "Let's go get some Milk-Bones."

The dog barked and wagged his tail energetically. A Milk-Bone would be fine, but it was more important that he had found his family! Part of his family, anyway. He was so happy! To celebrate, he leaped on Gregory again, and they both fell over a second time.

Gregory was just getting up when a small black shape streaked towards him and sprang right into his arms.

"Well, hi, Abigail," Gregory said, and patted her with his frozen glove. "What a pretty girl."

Abigail liked being called pretty, and she started purring. From her perspective, it was all well and good that she had found Gregory, but better than that, now she would get to be carried home!

Mrs. Callahan was still trapped in her car. It was incredibly frustrating not to be able to go for help, but with the wires snapping and crackling in the wind, she was frankly afraid to *move*. Staying in the car was the safest choice. Of course, with her leg pinned, it was really her *only* choice.

It was so cold that her teeth had started chattering. For some reason, she also felt terribly sleepy and kept dozing off. The pain from her injuries was pretty intense, but she was still having trouble staying awake. She was not what you would call an outdoors person, but she knew enough to realize that falling asleep in freezing temperatures was the worst possible thing to do. A lot of people who did that never woke up again.

She turned the key backwards in the ignition to see if she could get the radio to work. Unfortunately, the electrical system seemed to be dead along with everything else, because nothing happened when she turned the dial. Her hazard lights also wouldn't go on. That would have made it much easier for someone else to see her, but the weight of the tree must have crushed the engine almost completely.

The evening newspaper was on the front seat, and she tucked a couple of sections inside her coat for extra insulation. She also moved her arms and good leg to help get her blood flowing.

Staying warm — and awake — might be a matter of life or death!

12

Using one of Aunt Emily's flashlights to guide her path, Patricia was able to skate quite quickly. The surface was still rough and unforgiving, but she was nothing if not an aggressive athlete. She glided up to the public safety complex just as Fran and Saul were returning from taking Mr. Spiegel, the heart attack victim, to the Emergency Room. The doctors on duty had said that Santa Paws had gone for help just in time, and that Mr. Spiegel would make a full recovery.

Saul recognized Patricia and waved cheerily. "Hi, are you looking for your dog? You just missed him."

"Really?" Patricia said. "What was he doing?"

Fran unloaded the kit they had used from the back of the ambulance, so that they could restock the supplies. "Rescuing a cardiac case along with some cat. Kind of a *mean* cat."

That wasn't the answer Patricia had expected

to hear, but it was good to know that Abigail was safe, and up to her usual tricks. And if Santa Paws had completed his rescue, they were probably on their way home now.

"Well — that's good," she said. "Good for them. Um, I think *I* might need your ambulance, too."

Tired as they were, Saul and Fran snapped to attention.

"Not for me," Patricia assured them. "My aunt is having some contractions, and she isn't sure if it's, you know, Braxton Hicks" — which was a form of false labor — "or if she should go to the hospital."

"You're right, we'd better get over there." Fran turned towards a patrol officer just heading out of the station to get into his squad car. "Hey, Timmy! Is Steve Callahan around anywhere? His wife's having some premature contractions."

"Let me raise him on the radio," Timmy responded. "I think he's out at that big accident on Fairfax. Should he go home, or meet you at the hospital?"

"Patch him through on our frequency," Saul said. "We'll update him once we know more." He motioned Patricia over. "Come on, you'll ride with us."

Patricia skated to the passenger's side door, noticing that her skates blades were starting to get *very* dull and unresponsive. They might not

140

have been exposed to ideal conditions tonight — but they had really come in handy when she needed them!

The paramedics drove her back to Aunt Emily's house. Earlier that evening, they had paused to put chains on their tires, so the ambulance handled the roads with very little skidding. Aunt Emily wasn't eager to go to the hospital, but after talking to Uncle Steve over the handheld radio, she agreed.

In the meantime, a squad car arrived to take Patricia, Rachel — and Miranda — to Patricia's house. The police officers were pleased to see Rachel, because her mother had just gotten in touch with the Oceanport station house from Boston, to say that she was stuck in the city because of the weather, and could they please send someone over to check on her daughter and see if she needed anything. Apparently, Rachel's father's flight had been grounded in Baltimore, so he wouldn't be home anytime soon, either.

To keep Aunt Emily from worrying, Patricia went upstairs to pack a few of Miranda's favorite stuffed animals, her pink "grown-up lady" purse, and a Little Mermaid nightgown. It looked as though the Callahans would be doing some unexpected babysitting tonight!

When Mr. Callahan drove up his street, he was alarmed to see a police car stopping in front of his house. He jumped out of the Buick almost before he had a chance to turn off the engine.

"What's going on?" he asked nervously.

Patricia was holding Miranda's hand to help her out of the car. Her cousin was a little confused by all of the activity. It was also past her bedtime and she had yawned the whole way over. "Hi, Dad," she said. "We're just — " She wasn't sure where to begin. "Miranda and Rachel are spending the night. It's kind of a long story."

Rachel knew the Callahans' house very well, so she had no trouble finding her way across the driveway to the back gate. She lifted her cane in a little wave. "Hi, Mr. Callahan. Thank you for having me over."

Hearing all of the commotion, Santa Paws started barking inside the house. Gregory peeked out the window, saw the cars, and went out to see what was happening.

"Merry Christmas, Gregory!" Miranda shouted.

"You, too, Miranda," he said, looking a little confused. "Hi, Rachel."

Rachel waved her cane in his direction this time.

"Well, if you're all set here," Officer Bronkowski said, "we'd better get back on patrol."

While everyone else was thanking Officer Bronkowski and her partner, Officer Lee, for

142

their help, Gregory was looking around for the station wagon.

"Um, Dad?" he asked. "Where's Mom?"

When Mr. Callahan realized that his wife *hadn't* returned while he was gone, his face went completely pale.

"You kids go inside now, okay?" he said, once he was sure he could keep his voice reasonably steady. "Make sure Miranda's nice and warm. She could get a chill, being out in this."

Gregory and Patricia caught on at the exact same time, and they exchanged scared looks.

"Go on," their father insisted. "We'll talk in a few minutes."

Gregory and Patricia looked at each other again, and then Gregory reached for Miranda's free hand to help lead her across the ice. Rachel came along right behind them, just as quiet and uneasy as they were. Only Miranda was still chirping away about Christmas and her birthday, what fun it would be to play with the cats, and when would her mommy come to get her.

Once Mr. Callahan was sure they were out of earshot, he turned to Officers Bronkowski and Lee.

"I'm afraid we need you two to stick around for a few minutes and take a report," he said quietly. "It looks as though my wife is missing."

* * *

Once they were inside the house, Patricia busied herself with taking off Miranda's coat, hat, and mittens, while Gregory went to get her a cookie. Rachel sat down at the kitchen table, absent-mindedly patting Santa Paws.

"It's dark," Miranda said, sounding as though she was close to tears. "I don't like it. I want to go home."

"Okay, but first we're going to have fun here playing games," Patricia said. "So don't cry, Miranda."

Gregory held out the cookie. "You *can't* be sad when there are chocolate chips in the room."

Miranda's face brightened, and she took the snack from him. "Can we go play with Abigail?" she asked.

"Well, we can try," Gregory said doubtfully. Abigail was on the unpredictable side, as far as her moods were concerned. He lifted a small flashlight from the table and handed it to her. "Let's go look for her."

"Yay!" Miranda said, and directed the beam crazily around the room.

Rachel was sure she had already guessed what was going on, but once Gregory and Miranda were gone, she still had to ask. "When was your mother supposed to be home?"

"*Hours* ago," Patricia said, suddenly close to tears herself.

"She could just have a flat tire," Rachel said. "It doesn't have to be anything *bad*."

Patricia nodded. "I know." Her mother could also have tried to call and not been able to get through, or leave a message on the answering machine. But Patricia had a terrible feeling that something *awful* must have happened. Otherwise, her mother would have found a way to get home already.

When Mr. Callahan came in, it was obvious that he was so worried that he couldn't quite think straight. He sat down across from Patricia and Rachel, then brought both hands up to rub his forehead.

"Dad — " Patricia started.

"When did the power go out?" he asked.

"Right after you left," Patricia said.

Mr. Callahan nodded, and sucked in a deep breath, his hands still covering his eyes. Then he exhaled heavily and lowered his hands. "Okay," he said. "They're starting an official search. Can you three handle Miranda while I go and help them?"

"Of course," Patricia said, while Rachel was saying, "No problem, Mr. Callahan."

"Okay, good." He shook his head as though he'd lost his train of thought. "Bring all the sleeping bags to the den — that'll be the warmest room for now. You all can camp out in there.

And please don't light any candles. I'm afraid Miranda — or Santa Paws — might knock one over by accident. Just stick to the flashlights, we have plenty of batteries."

Hearing his name, the dog came over and rested his head on Mr. Callahan's knee. He could always tell when his family was upset, but he almost never knew *why*. His stomach was rumbling, and he wished that Mrs. Callahan would come home and give him his supper.

"Any questions?" he asked, giving Santa Paws a light pat.

Patricia had lots of questions, but all of them involved her mother, so she just shook her head.

"Okay." Mr. Callahan stood up. "In case I can't get back here right away, I'll make sure Steve has a car sent by to check on you every so often. Just sit tight, and — " His voice broke. "And, um, I'm sure everything's going to be all right."

There wasn't much else to say, so Patricia just hugged him and stuck an apple in his coat pocket in case he got hungry later. Then, as he plunged into the storm, she looked at Rachel.

"Guess we'd better go get those sleeping bags," she said.

Rachel nodded, and they headed upstairs to the attic.

It was way past her bedtime, but Miranda had no interest in going to sleep. Abigail had made it very clear that she did not want to play, so Miranda settled for throwing a tennis ball for Santa Paws to fetch. The dog was happy to cooperate, no matter how wildly she threw the ball. Patricia finally bribed her into a sleeping bag, by promising that they would use a flashlight to make shadow puppets on the wall for her.

At one point, Police Officers Littlejohn and Nichols knocked on the back door. They had no news about Mrs. Callahan yet, but they reported that Aunt Emily was feeling better, and had been admitted for overnight observation as a precaution. The only thing they knew about the search was that it was "ongoing."

Gregory thanked them and returned to the den. He shook his head in answer to Patricia's unasked question. Patricia's face fell, but she nodded.

She handed him a pair of scissors and some construction paper. "Here. Miranda wants you to make Santa Claus and *all* of his reindeer."

Gregory's mouth dropped open. "What?" The only shadow puppets he could really manage were simple things like rabbits, and cats.

"Don't forget Rudolph," Patricia said. "Go to it."

Gregory gritted his teeth and started cutting the paper.

After what felt like an infinite number of shadow puppets, Miranda finally fell asleep. Patricia and Rachel were also having a hard time staying awake, although they were trying their best.

The dog came over to nudge Gregory's leg, and Gregory knew he needed to go outside. That gave him an idea and he walked softly out of the room, being careful not to disturb anyone. He put on his still-damp jacket, and then took a sweatshirt of his mother's out of the laundry basket in the pantry.

"I want you to find Mom," he whispered, and then held the sweatshirt out for Santa Paws to smell. "Okay? *Find Mom.*"

The dog obediently sniffed the sweatshirt, and cocked his head to one side. What did Gregory want? Didn't he know that that was Mrs. Callahan's shirt? What was he supposed to find?

Gregory tucked the sweatshirt into his jacket and scrawled a fast note, in case Patricia woke up. It read: "Took the dog out. Back soon." Then he put on Santa Paws' leash, found a dry pair of gloves, and slipped outside.

The temperature had dropped enough so that the freezing rain was more like hard snow now. It was well below freezing, but the light covering of granular snow made it easier to walk without slipping. Once they were in the driveway, Gregory held the sweatshirt out again.

"Concentrate, Santa Paws," he said. "I want you to *find Mom.*"

The dog sniffed the sweatshirt, and held his paw up uncertainly.

"Find Mom," Gregory said. "Find the car."

The dog knew all of those words, but following cars was so hard! He had already tried — and failed — to do that once tonight.

Gregory also wasn't sure where to start. There were so many different ways to drive home from the mall, and his mother could have taken any one of them. That is, if she had *gone* to the mall in the first place. She could have done her shopping down near Main Street, or in one of the neighboring towns, or — there were too many possibilities. But he had to make a guess, and the mall seemed to be her most likely choice. All he could do was start leading Santa Paws in that general direction, and then just hope that they got lucky.

"Good boy," he kept saying, to encourage him. "Find Mom. *Fetch* Mom."

The dog walked steadily forward, tilting his nose in the air, and then running it along the snow in a regular pattern. If there was a scent *anywhere*, somehow he would locate it.

They were covering more ground than Gregory had expected, and he wondered if it might be time to turn around. If he was gone too long, Patricia might wake up and get really upset. But as long as there was a chance that Santa Paws could find his mother, how could he not try?

No matter what he did, the dog couldn't seem to pick up a scent. It was upsetting not to be able to do what Gregory had asked, and he whined a few times.

"It's okay, you're good," Gregory said, hoping to console him. Maybe he shouldn't put so much pressure on his dog, especially when they were both so tired after such an incredibly grueling day. It might be better if he just left this up to the police.

Santa Paws kept forging ahead. If his nose wouldn't help him, he would have to rely on his instincts, instead. And his instincts were telling him to keep going forward. They also seemed to be pulling him — west. He was focusing so hard on the task at hand that he almost forgot that Gregory was at the other end of his leash. And he didn't even *notice* the thick layer of snow starting to coat his fur.

Gregory had no idea where they were going, but trusting Santa Paws had never once been the wrong choice. His dog seemed so preoccupied that Gregory just trailed after him without another word, not wanting to interfere in any way. He was caught off-guard when Santa Paws halted, and it took a fancy bit of coordination to keep from falling right over him.

"What is it, boy?" he asked.

Santa Paws stood very still, concentrating intently. For a second, he thought he might have caught the tiniest whiff of — wait, there it was again! The dog turned his head to catch the wind just right, and try to confirm what he already sensed. Yes, the scent was distinct now.

He knew where Mrs. Callahan was!

13

Gregory understood his dog well enough to recognize the moment when he finally honed in on a scent. And Santa Paws had unquestionably tracked something down!

"Good boy," he said, trying to hold back his own excitement. "Find Mom!"

That was all the coaxing Santa Paws needed, and he bolted forward in the direction of the smell. Gregory tried to hang on to the leash, but Santa Paws wrenched it right out of his hands. The dog was so eager to follow the trail that he was a block away before he realized that he had left Gregory behind. He waited impatiently for Gregory to catch up.

"Slow down a little, okay?" Gregory said, breathing hard.

He retrieved the end of the leash, and Santa Paws set a more manageable, but still very rapid, pace. The dog was taking him towards a part of town where nobody lived, which seemed weird, but Gregory wasn't about to contradict him.

There was lots of debris, mainly branches, lying all over the ground. The flashlight helped a little, but the beam was too weak to light more than a short, narrow path. Santa Paws took several turns, leading him down curved, icy streets. There was plenty of construction going on around here, and Gregory could see the skeletons of houses silhouetted dimly against the sky. Someday, this would be a really nice suburban neighborhood, but right now, it just felt abandoned and creepy.

Further up ahead, Gregory thought he could make out the outline of a huge tree lying across the road. As they got closer, he saw that it *was* a tree, and it seemed to be lying on top of a car. A station wagon!

"Hey, Mom!" he yelled. "Are you in there?"

He dropped the leash and started running as fast as he could, terrified of what he might find. Then, when he was about sixty feet away, Santa Paws came racing over and slammed into his legs. Gregory lost his balance and fell painfully onto the ice and gritty snow.

Gregory shook his head, dazed by the unexpected spill. "Santa Paws, don't do that! You're right in the way."

To his complete astonishment, Santa Paws *growled* at him when he tried to get up. Then the dog stepped on his chest, pushing him back down. At first, Gregory's feelings were hurt, but then he was just angry.

"*No*," he said. "Bad dog!"

The dog's tail went between his legs, but he kept growling whenever Gregory made an attempt to move forward.

"Okay, okay," Gregory said, and cautiously slid back a few feet. That didn't earn him a growl, so he edged a little further away.

The dog seemed calmer now, but still looked wary.

Gregory took his time standing up, still stunned by what had just happened. Santa Paws was the most gentle dog in the world! Had the stress of the storm made him *completely* lose his mind?

The dog came over now, his head lowered in apology, and wagging his tail. Gregory patted him hesitantly, and the dog leaned against him, his tail whipping back and forth. Since everything seemed okay now, Gregory lifted his leg to take a tentative step. Santa Paws pressed firmly against his legs and forced him backwards.

"Okay, okay," Gregory said. He understood that his dog was trying to tell him something — and to *help* him, not hurt him. "You're a good boy."

Santa Paws wagged his tail in relief. He hated frightening Gregory, but how else could he warn him? The stench of burnt electricity was so strong that he couldn't figure out why Gregory didn't smell it, too.

"Take me to Mom," Gregory said. "Okay? Find Mom."

The dog whined softly. He didn't want to go near the car. The car was *bad*.

"Come on, Santa Paws," Gregory said, while he wrapped the end of the leash tightly around his hand and wrist. "Take me to the car."

The dog had to think. What should he do? Finally, he veered to the right and herded Gregory off the road and into the woods. He kept his body between Gregory and the bad car every step of the way. He led Gregory through the trees in a wide detour, so that they could approach the car from the other side. He brought him to within about forty feet of the car and then stopped, keeping them both well off the road.

Gregory gulped, and then flashed his light at the station wagon. He could see a figure slumped in the front seat, and he instinctively lunged towards the car. Santa Paws blocked his way firmly, and kept him right where he was.

Mom!" Gregory shouted at the top of his lungs. "Mom, are you okay?"

The figure stirred and looked groggily in his direction. In the thin beam of light, he could see that it was his mother — and she was alive!

"Mom, it's me!" Gregory said.

Mrs. Callahan was half-asleep, and she felt tired and confused. She thought she had heard her son's voice, but she must be hallucinating. However, the light shining at her face convinced her, and now she was wide awake. Her power window still wouldn't open, but she pried her fingers underneath the rubber guard and forced it down a couple of inches with more strength than she knew she had.

"Gregory, stay where you are!" she ordered through the crack. "Don't come anywhere near the car!"

"Why? I don't — " He thought he saw a bright blue light flicker, and he pointed the flashlight at the top of the car. "Oh, wow." Those were *live* power lines. No wonder Santa Paws had snarled at him! They could have been electrocuted!

"Where's your father?" Mrs. Callahan asked.

"With the police, looking for you," Gregory said. "I'm just here with Santa Paws. Are you okay?"

"I'm fine," Mrs. Callahan said briskly. "Make sure you don't come any closer. Can you go over to Sycamore — " which was a few streets away — "and call for help? There's a payphone at that convenience store."

Gregory had a better idea, especially since he didn't want to leave his mother alone. There was also a good chance that the phones were out on Sycamore Street, and the power might be, too.

He bent down and put his hands on either side of his dog's face.

"Santa Paws, *go find help*, okay?" he said. "We need *help*."

Help! Finally, an easy one! He knew how to find *that*. The dog barked, and then sprinted away into the darkness.

"He can go ten times faster than I can, Mom, but do you want me to start walking?" Gregory asked. "Or — is there something I can do to help? Like, keep you company, maybe?"

On the one hand, Mrs. Callahan didn't want Gregory within a *mile* of these wires. On the other hand, there could be other wires down elsewhere, and it wouldn't be safe for her son to be walking around without Santa Paws to protect him.

"Okay," Mrs. Callahan said finally. "But please don't move from where you are, no matter what."

Gregory nodded, although if the wind blew one of those wires in his direction, he would probably run like crazy. Even from here, he could see that his mother was shivering, and that worried him. She had been trapped in that car for hours now! "Are you sure you're all right, Mom?"

"Well, I may spend Christmas on crutches," she answered casually. "But let's talk about something else, okay?"

Crutches! "Um, sure," Gregory said. "Definitely."

This was followed by a long silence, since they were both tired, upset, and not thinking very clearly at this point.

"So," Gregory said, finally. "Nice weather we're having."

His mother's laugh sounded genuine, which made him feel much better.

"You're right," she said. "Couldn't be nicer."

It was quiet again.

"We trust Santa Paws implicitly, don't we?" Mrs. Callahan asked.

"*Totally,*" Gregory said.

The dog knew that he couldn't maintain a full sprint all the way to the building where he had gone to see the nice, uniformed men and women earlier that night. It was *far*! So he settled into a smooth, steady lope. That way, he could cover a great deal of ground without having to stop and rest.

He had to slow down once, at an intersection, when a big, heavy truck rumbled past him. It was leaving a dense trail of small white crystals behind. When Santa Paws crossed the street, the crystals made his paws sting. He remembered that feeling from other winters. It was salt! Yuck!

He had to limp a little from the burning pain, before he resumed his regular gait. He was glad he only saw one or two cars, because it was much easier to run in the middle of the road. Having to dodge traffic always made rescues much more difficult. And this was *Mrs. Callahan* he was trying to help!

The thought of Gregory and Mrs. Callahan back on that cold, lonely road waiting for him gave the dog a burst of extra adrenaline. He picked up speed, bounding over drifts of snow, and branches lying in front of him. He dashed around one final corner and ran up to the fire station. The public safety complex was equipped with generators, so their power was still on at a reduced level.

There was no one in sight, and Santa Paws barked urgently at the main entrance. Everyone on duty, except for the dispatcher, was out tending to one emergency or another — or helping search for Mrs. Callahan. Santa Paws barked his very loudest bark, hoping that someone would hear him.

He stood up on his hind legs to paw at the door, and it opened! Whoever had left last hadn't closed it completely. The dog ran into the police station, barking frantically. The dispatcher, Eric Martinez, was busy coordinating all of Oceanport's emergency service workers simultaneously. The near-hysterical barking was bothering him, and he looked up from his combination switchboard and radio relay system. When he saw a panting and snow-covered Santa Paws, he grabbed his receiver to make a system-wide announcement.

"All units, this is Dispatch," he said. "We have a probable canine 10-13 emergency here. Be advised that Santa Paws has just arrived at my location. Unit Ocean-Charles-Niner, are you available to respond?"

The squad car in question answered with an official 10-1, that they were now en route to quarters, with an ETA of approximately six minutes.

"Is Unit Ocean-Charles-Two still out of service?" Eric asked. Ocean-Charles-Two was Uncle Steve, although when he worked earlier shifts, he was either Ocean-Adam-Two, or Ocean-Bravo-Two. After receiving confirmation of that, Eric quickly switched gears to handle a call from another unit about a 10-40, Code 2, which was a car accident with a nonserious classification.

Santa Paws whined nervously, not sure why the man was talking on the telephone, instead of coming over to help him. He moved indecisively towards the exit, hesitated, and came back.

"All personnel should be aware that the male canine is in a highly agitated state at this time,"

Eric reported. "The subject's owner may want to 10-6 — " which was "stand-by" — "for possible assistance."

Santa Paws barked in an attempt to get his attention. Eric motioned for him to come over, and then patted him.

"Good dog," he said, covering the receiver with one hand. "They're on the way."

The dog didn't relax until he heard sirens outside. Yes! Help was here! He raced to the door, barking the whole way.

Officers Hank Littlejohn and Tracy Nichols were Unit Ocean-Charles-Niner.

"I hope those kids are all right," Hank said to his partner. "We should have been checking on them more often."

"We've been checking on the whole *town*," Tracy pointed out.

The dog barked at them, ran to the door where the ambulances usually were, barked again, ran to the street, and barked a third time.

Hank sighed. "It would be so much easier if someone could teach him how to talk."

Tracy watched intently as Santa Paws performed the exact same ritual again. "He's trying to tell us that this is big," she said. "That he needs more than one unit."

Hank was skeptical. He had always preferred cats to dogs. To his way of thinking, cats were

161

sensible. "Does he mean he needs a fire truck or an ambulance?"

"How should I know?" Tracy asked. "I'm only making an educated guess."

Hank picked up the radio and requested immediate backup, including a "bus" — or ambulance — for the previously broadcast 10-13. The nearest rescue vehicle was the unit being driven by Saul and Fran. Only a couple of minutes passed before they pulled up in front of the station.

"Looks like you're having a hectic night, too," Saul said to Santa Paws.

Yay! People he knew would help him! The dog barked, ran out to the street, and waited for them to follow him.

Since Fran and Saul were already comfortable with the technique of following Santa Paws to an emergency scene, they went first. Hank and Tracy rode behind them, driving their squad car slowly.

The dog was pretty worn out by now, and he lost his footing a couple of times. Fran was so worried that she might hit him by accident, that she finally stopped the ambulance.

"He's had it," she said. "Either one of us needs to walk with him, or we should put him in here, and see if that works."

Since the dog *did* seem exhausted, Saul opened his door and whistled for him. The dog looked back over his shoulder wearily, but kept trotting forward.

"Come here, boy!" Saul called out. "We're going to try an experiment."

The dog loved to go for rides, but this did not seem like a good time. What did they want? Didn't they know that they had to hurry?

"Come on," Saul insisted.

Reluctantly, the dog obeyed. Saul patted the front seat, so that Santa Paws would know to jump inside. Then he climbed in after him and shut the door.

"Okay," he said. "Now what?"

Fran shrugged. "Trial and error, I guess. Whenever I miss a turn my dog expects me to take, she gets really upset. Maybe he'll do the same thing."

"Worth a try," Saul said.

Santa Paws wasn't very happy about being in the ambulance, and he squirmed around uncomfortably. But he stayed quiet as the ambulance continued up the street. Only then it went too far! They were going the wrong way! Help! He jumped up and started barking.

Fran had already radioed the squad car about what she was doing, so Hank and Tracy weren't surprised when she backed up and turned onto the street she had just gone by.

Yes! This was right! Santa Paws relaxed against the seat. But now it was time for another turn! What if they went past it? That would be bad! He got up and barked again, in anticipation of the intersection ahead of them.

Fran did her best to read that cue, and started to turn right.

Oh, no! This was wrong! What was she *doing*? Santa Paws kept barking, hoping that he could make her understand.

Fran stopped, backed up, and turned left this time.

Yes! That was good! The dog slouched back against the seat to rest for a minute. This was *so* stressful.

Slowly, but surely, he managed to guide them back to the street where Gregory and Mrs. Callahan were. This required a lot of barking, and a few episodes of flinging himself onto the seat in despair.

Since his view wasn't blocked by a huge tree, Gregory saw the flashing lights first.

"Mom, here they come," he said happily. "He did it!"

Once again, Santa Paws had saved the day!

14

Soon, more emergency vehicles arrived, followed by some workers from the local electric company. They were the only ones who knew how to shut down the power and remove the wires safely. Even the police and firefighters weren't trained to approach downed power lines — and had the good sense to keep their distance whenever they encountered them.

As the scene got more crowded and chaotic, Officer Littlejohn brought Gregory and Santa Paws over to his squad car. Gregory would rather have been able to keep an eye on his mother, but everyone else preferred the idea of his staying securely out of the way. But when Mr. Callahan finally arrived, Gregory jumped out of the squad car to meet him.

After hugging him fiercely, his father made only one remark to the effect of "Weren't you back at the house getting ready for bed the last time I saw you?" Then he hugged Gregory again, hugged Santa Paws for good measure, and rushed over to the cleared area near the station wagon.

The electric company had disconnected the transformers by now, and followed the other technical procedures for handling downed power lines. That gave the fire department an opportunity to move in and free Mrs. Callahan from the car. The dashboard and steering column were so badly crushed that they actually had to use the Jaws of Life to get her out. Gregory knew that all of the tools the firefighters used were designed to *help* people, but hearing the harsh sounds of metal rending and tearing apart was awful.

When the paramedics carefully moved her from the car to a gurney, Gregory saw several people quickly avert their eyes. That scared him, too. After all, emergency service workers were *accustomed* to seeing accident victims. Santa Paws was sitting on the seat next to him, and Gregory found himself clutching his dog for comfort. Santa Paws *liked* to be hugged, so he didn't mind at all.

Officer Nichols walked over and picked up her logbook. She stayed by the car to write notes, and Gregory could tell that she was doing it deliberately. Taking notes probably wasn't a top priority right now. Even though he didn't know her very well, he was glad that someone had come over to keep him company.

"Why did they all look away when they saw Mom?" he asked shakily.

Officer Nichols hesitated, as though she was debating whether to edit her response. "She'll be fine, but her leg is pretty badly broken, and sometimes that can be hard to look at."

Gregory immediately got a vivid image in his mind of a couple of terrible football injuries he had seen on television, and he shuddered. It was horrible to picture his *mother* looking like that.

"Can I go talk to her?" he asked. "Is it okay?"

Officer Nichols put her logbook down. "Sure. The EMTs are just making her comfortable right now." She caught the eye of the fire captain supervising the operation, and indicated Gregory. The fire captain nodded, and Officer Nichols opened Gregory's door.

"Stay, Santa Paws," Gregory said. With so many cars and trucks around, he didn't want his dog outside in the middle of all the confusion.

The dog wagged his tail, and sat down patiently to wait for him.

For a second, Gregory was afraid to look inside the back of the ambulance. But when he took a peek, he saw his mother bundled up in blankets, with a huge balloon splint around her left leg — and *smiling* at him.

"Give your mother a kiss before I have a couple of officers take you and Santa Paws home," Mr. Callahan said. He was grinning broadly, too, looking so relieved that he seemed about ten years younger than he had earlier that evening.

Gregory stared at him. "I can't go to the hospital?"

His father ruffled his hair, and then gave him another big hug. "It's three in the morning, Greg. Your mother and I want you to go home and get some rest."

Gregory would have preferred going along to the hospital, but he *was* really tired. Maybe even exhausted. He climbed up into the back of the ambulance, doing his best not to jar the gurney in any way.

"Hi, Mom," he said, feeling almost — shy.

His mother reached out and took his hand, holding on tightly. "Thank you," she said.

Now he felt *really* shy, somehow.

Mrs. Callahan winked at him. "Has Miranda been out pounding the pavement, too?"

Gregory relaxed then, and smiled back at her. "Yeah. Patricia assigned her the seawall patrol."

"You know, I wish I couldn't quite picture that," Mrs. Callahan said dryly.

The idea of plucky little Miranda toddling along the icy seawall above the crashing waves and rocks below *was* pretty daunting. The idea of Patricia *assigning* her to do it, was even more so. "Are you okay, Mom?" he asked. "Your leg and all?"

"Oh, please," Mrs. Callahan dismissed that with a wave of her hand. "I've been through childbirth. *Twice.*" Then her voice softened. "Lucky for me."

Gregory ducked his head, a little embarrassed, but also very pleased.

"All right now." His mother pulled his hand over and gave it a light kiss. "I want you to go home, get some sleep, and *promise* not to worry. Okay?"

"Okay," Gregory said. He would certainly do his best — even about the worrying part.

Once the ambulance had left, with Mr. Callahan riding in the back, Gregory went to join Santa Paws. The dog leaned up to lick his face, and then curled up on the seat again. Officers Littlejohn and Nichols must have sensed how tired Gregory was, because they didn't try to engage him in much conversation on the way home. The only real sound was the windshield wipers squeaking as they swept fresh snow away with each pass.

"Um, thank you very much," Gregory said, when they pulled up in front of his house. "Can you thank all the other officers and firefighters and all?"

"Sure thing," Officer Nichols promised.

Gregory was surprised when both officers got

169

out of the car with him. "Um, I have Santa Paws with me. I'll be fine from here."

"Well, we're just going to hang out for a while," Officer Nichols said. "Keep an eye on things."

Now Gregory got it. This just might be their *assignment*. "You mean, until my parents get home."

"Something like that," Officer Littlejohn agreed.

The thought of having some adults around in case something *else* went wrong was kind of reassuring. Maybe it meant that Santa Paws would feel as though he could take it easy for a while, too.

"Okay," Gregory said. "Thanks."

When they got inside, Miranda and Rachel were still asleep, but Patricia was waiting tensely at the kitchen table. She had been using a flashlight to read her book about investing and — apparently — highlighting many sections. Gregory and the police officers gave her the whole story, speaking softly so that their voices wouldn't carry into the den. Patricia took it all in, asked a couple of pointed questions, and then stood up.

"Because of the power and all, we can't make you any coffee," she said to Officers Littlejohn and Nichols, "but would you like some cookies?"

The two police officers looked at each other. After all, they had had a long night, too.

"We would *love* some cookies," Officer Nichols said.

Once the officers were pleasantly occupied at the kitchen table, playing cards and eating cookies, Gregory and Patricia left the room to get ready for bed. Santa Paws wasn't so sure about having people he didn't know in the house, but since Gregory and Patricia didn't seem to mind, it must be okay. He followed them, wagging his tail and carrying a Milk-Bone.

The house was chilly, with the heat off, but at least there were plenty of blankets and sleeping bags. Gregory was about ready to fall asleep standing up, but they sat on the stairs to talk for a minute. Abigail meandered in from the den, where she had been sleeping at the bottom of Miranda's sleeping bag. She looked Gregory and Santa Paws over critically, twitched her tail once or twice, and went back to the den.

"Mom's really okay?" Patricia asked.

Gregory nodded. "Yeah. Dad was all smiling."

Patricia relaxed a little. If their father was happy, then everything must be all right. She gave Gregory's arm a small shove. "So, Mr. Hero. You *had* to go running outside in the middle of the storm like a big jerk?"

"Santa Paws was the hero," Gregory said. "I was just along for the ride."

Hearing his name, the dog looked up from his bone long enough to thump his tail against the floor.

"Anyway, you're just mad *you* didn't get to go," Gregory said.

Patricia grinned. "Yep. You've got that right."

Suddenly feeling exhausted, Gregory leaned forward to rest his head on his arms.

Since no one was around who might make fun of her for displaying affection towards a family member, Patricia patted him on the back.

"Come on," she said. "You need some sleep."

Gregory nodded, using the stair railing to pull himself up. "What time is it, anyway?"

Patricia looked at her watch. "Almost four." Then she remembered something. "Hey, Greg, you know what? It's Christmas Eve."

Gregory had to laugh when he realized that so far, this had been a *typical* Callahan holiday experience.

"So it is," he said.

Mr. Callahan came home around nine o'clock in the morning, with the news that Mrs. Callahan was feeling fine and would be able to come home either that afternoon, or early the next morning. He had fresh coffee for Officers Littlejohn and Nichols, and pints of cold milk and warm soup he had gotten from the hospital for everyone else. Miranda thought this was the funniest thing she had ever seen.

"Soup, for *breakfast*?" she kept saying to Mr. Callahan. "You are so, *so* silly."

Officers Littlejohn and Nichols gave everyone cheery goodbyes and left to return to the police station. Officer Littlejohn *did* grab a few more cookies for the road.

Evelyn had emerged briefly from the linen closet to eat some catfood. Abigail joined her, but was far more interested in having some soup. So far, no one had shared with her, though. Santa Paws gobbled down his first can of food so quickly that Gregory opened another and gave him half. It was more than he usually ate in the morning, but after the night before, he was extra hungry!

Once Abigail was finished nibbling her meal, she sat down a foot away from the dog and gazed at him with her big yellow eyes. Being stared at like that made him very nervous, and that was why she always did it. Santa Paws kept glancing over in the hope that she would have lost interest, but so far, she hadn't even *blinked*. So he let out an unhappy little whine and took shelter behind Gregory's chair. Abigail's eyes gleamed with victory, and she helped herself to a bite of the food left in his dish.

"Very, *very* silly," Miranda said to herself.

Then she looked at Mr. Callahan seriously. "I like the party, but can I go home now?"

"Actually, we're going to keep having a Christmas slumber party *here*," Mr. Callahan answered. "Your father and mother are coming over here in a little while, and your mother will stay for a nice rest, while your father brings some more things from your house."

Miranda's expression was uncertain, and maybe slightly tearful, as she thought about all of that.

"It's going to be lots of fun," Mr. Callahan assured her. "We get to start celebrating Christmas a whole day early! Plus, it seems to me that *someone special* has a birthday today."

Miranda beamed about *that* particular concept. While she was occupied by playing with the crackers floating in her soup, Patricia leaned over to talk to her father quietly.

"Aunt Emily needs to stay off her feet, and Uncle Steve's going to be working a lot, so she's coming here?" she guessed.

Mr. Callahan nodded. "We can keep the sitting room pretty warm with the fireplace, and it's much better than her trying to run around after Miranda by herself."

Patricia grinned. "So *we'll* be running around after Miranda."

"Looks that way," Mr. Callahan said. "And as long as the pipes don't freeze, we're still in pretty good shape here, for cold water, at least. They've opened a shelter over at the high school, but I think we can avoid that."

"Why won't they let Mom come home right away?" Gregory asked.

"Well, they're not too excited about sending her back while the power's out," Mr. Callahan said, "but I think she'll talk them out of that pretty soon."

Gregory and Patricia sure *hoped* so.

The dog was ready to go outside now, and he scratched at the backdoor with his paw.

"Okay, boy," Gregory said. When he opened the door, he was amazed by the sight of their backyard. *"Wow."*

Patricia came over to join him. "What?" Then she stared, too. "Double wow."

"How bad is it?" Rachel asked.

"Looks like a bomb went off," Gregory said.

The storm was over, but it had left a great deal of damage behind! There were broken branches lying in every possible place, and a section from one of their other trees had sheared off. Part of the fence had fallen down, too. Long icicles hung from the roof, and every branch and tree glistened with its own coating of ice. The snow had been blown into uneven drifts, and their next-door neighbor's car was so heavily encased in ice that it seemed to be frozen to the ground!

The dog explored the yard to get used to the

new terrain. He had liked it *much* better before. He felt very ill at ease, and he moved around skittishly. All of his instincts seemed to be churned together into one big knot of anxiety. He just knew that Oceanport was a town *full* of problems today. He was tempted to run back inside and take shelter underneath Mr. Callahan's desk, but that wouldn't be right. People counted on him to help! But he could sense so much trouble, in so many different places, that he wasn't even sure where to *start*.

"Oh, no," Gregory said, when he saw his dog's rigid posture and fidgety pacing. "Santa Paws has that look."

Mr. Callahan sighed. "You'd better get him back indoors. We really don't want a repeat of yesterday."

Gregory yanked the door open, but his shoulders slumped as he saw Santa Paws gracefully hurdle the fence and race down the street in a blur of speed.

"What is it?" Patricia asked.

"There he goes again," Gregory said glumly.

The dog felt so conflicted about which problem to address first, that he stopped at the end of the street to think for a while. Who needed his help the *most*? Or, if he couldn't figure that out, who was the closest?

"Hello, Santa Paws," someone said. It was

Jane Yates, who he had helped a long time ago when she and her three children were temporarily homeless. Now they lived in a nice apartment, and Jane had a great job delivering the mail. In fact, that was what she was doing right now! It didn't matter that there had been a bad storm, and it was Christmas Eve — she was still going to complete her route. Her coworker Rasheed was busy doing the same thing on the other side of town. It would take more than sleet, snow, and lethal ice to stop *them*.

The dog wagged his tail at her, even though he was distracted.

Jane always carried dog biscuits in her pocket to feed the many pets on her route. She took one out and handed it to him. "Here you go, little chum." Then she went merrily on her way.

Santa Paws crunched his bone while he pondered the possibilities. Then he heard an ominous rumbling sound, followed by a loud cry for help coming from a backyard down the block.

Yay! Now he knew what to do!

15

Santa Paws tore down the street, leaped over a stone wall, dodged past a fallen birch tree, and cut behind two houses. Finally, he found a man lying beneath a lot of wood! Oh, no! That looked *terrible*. The dog barked with great concern.

The man was Rabbi Gladstone, who presided at the Oceanport Synagogue. He had come outside to get some firewood to help heat his house. But when he pulled a couple of logs from his neatly-stacked woodpile, they were so icy that most of them toppled right on top of him!

"Good morning, Santa Paws," Rabbi Gladstone said, sounding a little winded, but very composed. "Could you get me some help, please?"

The dog whirled around and ran to the Gladstone's backdoor. Rabbi Gladstone's teenage daughter, Lisa, came out at once to see what was happening. She gasped and ran back into the house to get her mother.

The dog was perplexed when she left. But he returned to Rabbi Gladstone, and used his front paws to pry away as many logs as possible.

Drawn by the sound of the barking, Jane Yates had come running.

"Oh, no, look at that," she said in dismay. "Are you all right, Rabbi?"

"I think so," Rabbi Gladstone answered. "But, gosh, they're, um, really heavy."

Before pitching in to help Santa Paws remove the logs, Jane whipped out the cellphone from her coat pocket. She dialed 911 and reported the accident. The dispatcher — it was Eric, still on duty! — promised to have an ambulance and one of the ladder trucks from the fire department sent over at once.

When the paramedics arrived, the dog didn't recognize either of them, but they certainly knew who he was! They worked together with a squad of four firefighters to clear away the wood. The dog sat about twenty feet away, with Rabbi Gladstone's worried family and Jane.

Once the emergency service workers had freed Rabbi Gladstone, the only serious injury they could find was a badly crushed right hand. Other than that, he was mostly just bruised. But if he had been there for much longer, the pile might have shifted and caused much worse injuries. The paramedics bundled him into the ambulance for a trip to the Emergency Room. Just as the doors shut, Rabbi Gladstone waved at Santa Paws and shouted a quick "Thank you and Seasons Greetings!"

The dog barked back in a friendly way. Rabbi Gladstone was a nice man.

"That was good," Jane said, and handed Santa Paws another treat. "You're a good dog."

The dog wanted to be on his way, but it wouldn't do to waste a biscuit. *Ever*, under *any* circumstances. Once he was finished, he licked his chops. What a great aftertaste bones left! *Yum*. Then, witn one last wag of his tail, he returned to the task — *many* tasks — at hand.

It was going to be a very full day!

Back at the Callahans' house, Gregory and Patricia were trying to talk their father into letting them go after Santa Paws.

"And what will Miranda be doing during all of this?" he asked them, since he was going back to the hospital to see if Mrs. Callahan could be discharged yet.

Just then, Rachel's mother arrived to pick her daughter up. She had been so pleased the night before when it was relayed to her from the police station that Rachel was staying with the Callahans. The highways from Boston were still not really passable, but she had been able to get on a commuter rail train that stopped in Oceanport, and took the town's one cab directly over to the Callahans' house.

"How many hours has it been since we've been able to get online?" Rachel asked, when she and Patricia were saying good-bye.

"At least fourteen," Patricia said, and shuddered. "Are you getting the shakes yet?"

Rachel nodded. "Total withdrawal. It's ugly."

During all of this, Abigail seized her opportunity to slink off to the living room. The door was shut to keep the cold out, but *that* was no problem for her. She easily forced it open by wrapping her front paws firmly around the knob. Then she scampered onto the section of tree lying on their floor, slipped out through the broken window, and went outside.

She needed to go join Santa Paws, and do him the favor of sharing her wise counsel and advice. How was he ever going to be able to save people *by himself*?

The dog was cruising up one street, and then down the next, pausing to sniff the air and listen for anything suspicious every block or two. Out of nowhere, Abigail suddenly appeared and jumped onto his back. The dog was so startled that he yelped and tried to shake her off. Abigail clung on stubbornly, and once the dog had calmed down, she batted him once across the back of the head to indicate her disapproval. Did he *always* have to overreact?

The dog promptly sat down, and Abigail slid right down his back and landed in a small heap in the middle of the street. The dog was amused by this, and used his paw to knock her playfully onto her side. Abigail was much *less* amused, so she hissed at him and rolled out of the way.

Suddenly remembering that he had things to do, the dog picked up his methodical patrol where he had left off. Abigail was welcome to join him, but she would have to keep up!

They covered a lot of ground, only having to pause for minor incidents. A man named Mr. Gustave had dropped his keys through a wide crack in his porch floor, and Santa Paws crawled under the house to retrieve them. Abigail sat on the porch swing the whole time, sneering at the notion of doing something as undignified as squirming around underneath a *house*. *She* would never dream of such a thing.

After that, they helped get Mr. Corcoran's cat, Matilda, down from a tree. She had run outside when he went out to get his mail, been horrified by the ice, and darted up into a tree to demonstrate her utter consternation. Santa Paws barked helpfully up at her, but Matilda only retreated two branches higher. Her footing was precarious with all of the ice, and now she was too afraid to go up *or* down.

Abigail observed all of this without much interest. But the cat's owner was very upset, so she grumpily climbed the tree herself. Santa Paws didn't like watching this, because he was afraid she might fall. Abigail jumped boldly from branch to branch until she was only a foot or two away from Matilda. Then she gave her a long, unblinking stare. Matilda stared back. They stared, and stared, and stared.

Finally, Abigail got so bored that she hissed and pretended that she was going to pounce on the other cat. Matilda was frightened enough to race down the tree and fling herself into the safety of Mr. Corcoran's arms.

"Thank you so much, Santa Paws," Mr. Corcoran said as he carried his adored pet back to the house. "And your friend, too!"

Abigail bounced around on the branch, enjoying the sensation of rocking. The dog barked sharply at her, but she paid no attention to him. Giving up on being able to get her to behave, the dog started down the street. Abigail scurried down the tree trunk and ran to catch up. She had been enjoying her game, but not enough to risk being left behind. She might miss something!

The dog could hear a cow bellowing somewhere in the distance. He tracked the sound to Meadowlark Way, and found a miserable black and white Holstein standing in the middle of the road. She had gotten separated from the rest of her herd during the storm, and now she wasn't sure what to do. Naturally, she hadn't been milked because of this, so her udders were swollen and she was very uncomfortable.

When she saw the dog and cat, she mooed pathetically and stamped her hooves on the icy road in frustration.

With one look at those sharp hooves and that big body, Abigail spun around. It was nice to hang out with Santa Paws, but she was no fool. A large, angry farm animal was *her* cue to go home — and stay there.

Besides, she was getting hungry. And it was nippy out.

The dog turned in time to see Abigail bound away in the general direction of the Callahans' house. He was somewhat disappointed that she had left, but now it would be easier for him to concentrate. Whenever he was around Abigail, he spent most of his time bracing for whatever awful thing she might do to him next.

He didn't want to get anywhere near those hooves, so he kept his distance as he herded the cow down the road towards the nearest farm. He knew where she lived, because he had brought home one or more of the Jorgensens' cows many times before. In fact, he had become an expert cow retriever!

When Santa Paws guided the cow back to the barn, Mortimer Jorgensen looked up.

"Yolanda!" he said. "It's for you!" Their water pump had frozen, so he was busy hauling buckets from the creek for the cows. The creek had frozen, too, but he had been able to break through the ice with a pitchfork.

Yolanda, a thin woman in a huge Eskimo parka, came lumbering out of the barn in heavy winter boots. Since she and Mortimer were taking turns using a generator with some of their farmer neighbors, she was milking many of the cows by hand. It was hard work, and the cows were so accustomed to their milking machines that they found the idea of being milked by an actual *person* rather primitive.

"Well, good for you, Santa Paws!" she said in a remarkably booming voice. "I wondered where our poor Jessica had gone."

He was good! How fun! The dog wagged his tail.

Then Daffodil, the Jorgensens' elderly Border collie, appeared in the barn doorway. She quickly took charge of the situation, and ushered Jessica into the stall where she belonged.

"Thank you, Santa Paws," Yolanda said. "Maybe you should run along over to Mark and Bill's farm now. They're missing a couple of cows, too. I'm sure you can find them."

The dog barked and trotted back out to the icy road.

"Find" and "cows" was a concept he understood perfectly!

Mrs. Callahan convinced the hospital to release her late that afternoon, and by then, Aunt Emily was at the house, too. They had all relocated to the sitting room, to gather around the fireplace. Mrs. Callahan would be able to convalesce on the couch, and since Aunt Emily was pretty short, she would be comfortable on the loveseat. Uncle Steve had brought over a couple of old Army cots, and Mr. Callahan had dragged an old roll-away bed down from the attic. Originally, Gregory and Patricia's grandparents had been planning to drive down from Vermont for the holiday, but because of the storm, they were now going to come for New Year's, instead. It was probably for the best, since the room would have been incredibly crowded.

When Mrs. Callahan got home, moving awkwardly on her new crutches, Patricia and Gregory had to be careful when they hugged her. She had broken one rib and cracked two others in the accident, and they didn't want to hurt her. But they were *so glad* that she was back!

Miranda was completely fascinated by the big white cast on Mrs. Callahan's leg. She immediately found some Magic Markers and began drawing on it.

"I am drawing *very nice* pictures," she informed Mrs. Callahan. "To make you feel better."

"Thank you," Mrs. Callahan said with a grin. "They look lovely, so far."

Since it was dark outside now, the only light in the room came from the fireplace, the dim glow of Aunt Emily's lantern, and flashlights. Mr. Callahan had set up an old transistor radio on the coffee table, so that they could get some news from the outside world. The reports were saying that more than 90% of the people in Oceanport were without power, and three quarters of the town had no telephone service, either. The power company was working to re-establish power at places like the hospital, first. Their spokesperson could not really estimate when the electricity would return elsewhere, because the damage was so extensive.

Patricia and Gregory had been allowed to take a brief walk outside earlier, to call for Santa Paws. He had never come, but about half an hour after they got home, they heard the living room door squeaking open. It was Abigail, returning from her adventures. She had been asleep in front of the fireplace ever since. Evelyn had come downstairs, too, and selected a strategic position on the couch, next to Mrs. Callahan.

Mr. Callahan had buried some of their food from the refrigerator outside in a snowbank, to try and keep it from spoiling. They were eating as much of the rest as they could, so that it wouldn't go to waste. Cooking boneless chicken breasts over the fire was beyond Mr. Callahan's abilities, but so far, he had been very successful with hotdogs and rolls. Only a couple had burned too badly to eat. His attempt at making scrambled eggs over the fire was best forgotten. And, of course, after supper, it would be time for Miranda's birthday cake! Uncle Steve had hidden it in a pantry cupboard earlier that day, along with a pile of gifts.

Patricia wanted to read, but it was hard to see in the flickering light. She and Gregory were playing cards, instead. Later, they were all going to play Monopoly — while figuring out a way to allow Miranda to participate. The only game she really knew was Candyland, and mostly, she just liked to toss the pieces around. She had spent most of the afternoon occupied by drawing pictures and telling long, involved stories to everyone.

"I'm just really worried about him," Gregory said to his father, for about the twentieth time.

A hotdog roll slid off Mr. Callahan's skewer and disappeared into the flames. He frowned and selected another. "I know, Greg. We'll go out on the patio later, and call him again."

The radio continued to drone on with storm updates in the background. These included statistics about how many motor vehicle accidents there had been, how many people had been hospitalized, where all of the Red Cross shelters were located, and a long series of safety tips for coping without power or heat. They also announced the football scores, which Gregory listened to with rapt attention.

Patricia was already tired of cards, jittery about not being able to use her computer or watch television, and just generally feeling rather cranky. "I think I would have been a very bad pioneer," she said. "Remember *The Long Winter*?" That was a book by Laura Ingalls Wilder, about surviving on the prairie during the 1800s. "When they were burning straw and eating wheat kernels and all? No, thank you."

"Why don't you listen to your Walkman?" Mrs. Callahan suggested. "That way, you can still feel reasonably modern."

"Oh, yeah!" Patricia rushed upstairs with her flashlight, returning with her Walkman and a stack of CDs.

"You going to share?" Gregory asked. His Walkman was broken, although he was hoping that there might be a new one among his Christmas presents.

"Maybe," Patricia said, lying down on her

sleeping bag to listen to John Coltrane. "If Miranda asks nicely."

"I am drawing," Miranda said sternly. "Please let me draw now."

The radio announcer said something with "Santa Paws" in the sentence, and they all looked up.

"And now, on the local front," he was saying. "There have been *numerous* Santa Paws sightings around town, as the legendary canine continues his usual practice of protecting the innocent. We now have a live report from our woman in the field, Margaret Saunders, about one of his latest exploits."

Margaret Saunders was a woman Santa Paws had been kind to long ago, when he was a stray. Back then, she had been recently widowed and miserable. Now she was newly engaged, working as a full-time reporter, and very happy.

The Callahans listened as Margaret breathlessly told about Santa Paws racing to the fire station to bring a truck back to the Nguyens' house only moments earlier. Apparently, a small fire had started when a candle tipped over, but Santa Paws had intervened before it could spread beyond the corner of one room. Margaret interviewed the grateful family at length, and then reported on the earlier incident, during which Santa Paws had helped free a man who had been locked in his garage overnight. The garage doors only worked with an electric door opener, and so, when the power went out, Mr. Garcia had been trapped. Santa Paws had brought Father Reilly over from the rectory, and the priest used a car jack to force the garage door open. Mr. Garcia was currently being treated at Oceanport Memorial Hospital for mild hypothermia.

"Sounds as though Santa Paws is having a busy day," Mr. Callahan remarked.

"At least we know where he is now," Patricia said, and paused. "Well — sort of."

"Please stay tuned to this station on your AM dial for further Santa Paws reports," Margaret, the reporter, said over the radio. "And if you can get to a telephone, please phone in your sightings. We want to bring you the very latest information about these thrilling events."

The Callahans would *definitely* be staying tuned in.

191

16

As the night wore on, the dog got more and more tired. He had been running around for hours, and his stomach was growling terribly. After he found Mr. Garcia, the man caught in his garage, Father Reilly had fixed a bowl of water for him, which made him feel somewhat better. But, he needed a snack! So he cruised by the public safety complex, where a group of firefighters was in the back room, gulping down some beef stew between alarms. They were eager to share a large portion with Santa Paws, and the dog wagged his tail the entire time he was eating. Except for the celery, the stew was delicious!

After his late supper, the dog felt much happier. The firefighters were smiling, too. Some hot food and a little bit of time to take it easy made all the difference.

"Go home now, Santa Paws," one of the firefighters, Karen Berringer, advised, when he trotted over to the exit. "I think you've done your share."

The dog barked pleasantly, and went out into the night.

"Merry Christmas, Santa Paws!" someone else shouted after him.

He *wanted* to go home — he hadn't seen his family *all day*! — but he knew he needed to take one last survey of the town before he could relax. So many people had needed help today, and he didn't want to leave anyone out!

The dog started at the far end of town, and slowly worked his way towards the ocean. Almost every block was dark, but he could easily pick out the houses which were still occupied. Mostly, families and neighbors seemed to be gathered together, waiting for the power to return. He was happy because he sensed almost no anxiety or anger. At worst, people seemed to be tired, or bored. He could tell that many others were *happy*, and enjoying the novelty of spending uninterrupted time together. Laughter and conversation filled the air.

There was singing coming from one house — it sounded like a lot of people! Maybe twenty! The dog stood outside in the ice and snow, and listened to the voices wistfully. The Callahans never really sang, but he was sure that they were talking quietly and laughing right now. He couldn't wait to go and join them! Frankly, he couldn't help wishing that Oceanport was even *smaller*.

There was lots of salt and sand on the roads now, and the dog walked on drifts of snow whenever possible. The salt just made his paws hurt too much. He had covered enough miles by now to make his paws hurt, anyway. He missed Abigail, but it was good that she had gone home, because he would probably be carrying her by now!

He finally reached the seawall right before dawn. It was still dark, but the skies were much lighter than they had been. He rested his front paws on the cold cement of the seawall and inhaled deeply. The ocean had a very strong briny smell, but he liked it. The sound of the waves rolling in and out was soothing, too.

He yawned widely and dropped onto all four paws. Finally! He had checked the entire town! He could go home! Yay!

The dog was too worn out to keep trotting, so he just walked. What fun it would be to have a nice, long nap! He was thinking about Milk-Bones — big ones, small ones, and beef-flavored ones — when a chill ran unexpectedly down his spine.

There was more trouble!

His first instinct took him down Larchmont Street, but he changed his mind and ran the other way. When he was tired, it was more difficult to guess correctly the first time. He turned up Acorn Lane, and *now* he knew he was right. There was something terrible going on inside the white house with red shutters. It belonged to Mr. and Mrs. Malone, who had four children, and Mrs. Malone's mother also lived there.

The dog barked repeatedly outside the front door. The house was full of people — seven, as far as he could tell, and a cat, too — so why didn't any of them come to let him in? As far as he could tell, they were very, *very* sick in some way, and maybe none of them wanted to get out of bed. Or maybe they *couldn't* get out of bed!

He could go find his friends in uniform, but he sensed that there wasn't enough time. He had to act *now*. Since no one had answered the front door, he ran around to the back and barked there, too. There was still no response. How could they not hear him when it was so quiet? He returned to the front of the house, but still, no one inside had stirred. They scarcely seemed to be breathing!

The dog was sure that there was no time to waste — not even enough time to try to wake up one of the neighbors. He would have to go inside on his own. The dog took a running start, and then plunged through the front picture window with a crash of shattering glass.

He landed on a thick carpet, which broke his

fall. He shook once to knock away as much glass as possible, and then looked around to locate the family. There was a bad smell inside the house that made him cough, and whenever he took a breath, he felt dizzy. This was not a good place to be!

The dog ran into the living room, barking at the top of his lungs. The whole family was sleeping in there, wrapped up in blankets or sleeping bags. No matter how fiercely he barked, not one of them moved. What was *wrong* with them?

There was a small child curled into a sleeping bag by his feet, and he dragged the bag — with the child still inside — into the front room by the open window. He was able to pull out two more children the same way, and then he carried the family cat by the scruff of the neck. All of the other people were heavy, and it would be hard to transport them.

Not sure what to do, he yanked the father off the couch. The father landed heavily on the floor and mumbled something garbled. The dog pawed at the man's chest, trying to rouse him. He felt so dizzy and sick himself now that it was an effort to stay conscious.

Hearing a voice out by the broken window, the dog went to see what the children were doing. The older girl seemed to be waking up and coughing a lot. Standing by the open window as the cold air and wind rushed in made the dog feel a little better, and it seemed to be helping the girl recover, too. Her name was Jill, and she was twelve. The other two children he had dragged out were Vicky and Owen, and they were eight-year-old twins.

"Santa Paws?" Jill asked dully.

The dog barked.

"What's — I don't — I — " She looked around in complete confusion.

The dog ran to the front door and barked again.

Jill lurched to her feet and went over to open the door for him. The dog quickly dragged Vicky and Owen's sleeping bags out to the porch. He carefully set the cat down next to them, then went back into the house.

"Is it a fire?" Jill asked, still sounding vague.

The dog returned to the living room and fastened his teeth firmly around the end of the oldest boy's sleeping bag. His name was Larry, and he was fourteen. Using every ounce of his strength, the dog hauled him out of the living room.

By now, Jill had grasped that there was something seriously wrong, and she helped Santa Paws get Larry outside. Then they both went back to get Jill's grandmother and parents.

"Mom? Dad? Gram? Wake up!" Jill shouted. "We have to get out!"

Her father tried to sit up, but slumped down again.

"Come on, Dad," Jill said, struggling to get him to his feet.

That gave the dog a chance to concentrate on helping the mother and grandmother. The grandmother felt sort of frail, and he was afraid to knock her off the mattress where she was sleeping. He grabbed the mother's nightgown sleeve with his jaw and tugged as hard as he could.

"Go back to sleep," she muttered.

The dog dragged her as far as the hall before her sleeve tore. So, he switched to the other sleeve and got her halfway into the living room. This was very strenuous!

Jill was helping her father outside, and her brother Larry had revived enough to be able to get his mother. In the meantime, the dog was in the living room, trying to figure out a way to help the grandmother. He was joined by Larry and Jill, who worked together to carry her to the porch.

Everyone was finally out! But it was so cold that the dog raced to the living room one last time to drag some blankets out to the stricken family.

While they sat groggily on the porch, he took off for the public safety complex. His legs didn't want to work right, and he stumbled every so often. He felt sick the way he had when he was stolen by bad, mean thieves who made him smell a handkerchief soaked in nasty drugs. This was terrible!

It took him longer than he expected, because his legs were so rubbery. But the fire and rescue personnel leaped up the second they saw him, and with the help of his paramedic friends, Fran and Saul, he was able to guide everyone back to the Malones' house.

The family had been using a kerosine heater to keep their house warm, but they had not ventilated it properly. So the house filled with fumes and — more dangerously — odorless carbon monoxide gas. If Santa Paws had not forced his way inside, the entire family would have suffocated in their sleep from lack of oxygen.

It took several ambulances to transfer all of them to the hospital for oxygen therapy. The family was doing better since they had spent time in the fresh air, but they still needed medical attention.

The sun had come up, and it looked as though it was going to be a beautiful day. Already, some of the ice was beginning to melt. While the firefighters worked on ventilating and fumigating the house, Santa Paws climbed slowly to his feet. He *really* needed a nap.

"Not so fast, Santa Paws," Saul said, and grabbed his collar. "You need a little help yourself." Then he fitted a mask over the dog's face so that he could inhale some pure oxygen, while Fran checked his vital signs.

The dog was impatient to get home, but the air he was breathing was making him feel so much stronger! He rested on a blanket in the back of an ambulance, inhaling deeply.

"We're going to drive you home, too," Fran said. "*You*, Santa Paws, are going to enjoy the rest of this holiday — and that's an order!"

The dog wagged his tail a few times.

"Home" was one of the very best words of all!

The Callahans were in their sitting room, opening Christmas gifts. Oceanport's traditional non-religious, interdenominational holiday service had been postponed for a few days, so that everyone in town would be able to attend. It felt strange not to be going to church on Christmas — and even stranger to be celebrating without Santa Paws. The radio had yet to report a sighting this morning! But the station *was* playing Christmas carols, which helped brighten the atmosphere.

"Where is Santa Paws?" Miranda asked. "It is very sad when he isn't here."

"I'm sure he'll be along, Miranda. He was working a long shift last night, too," Uncle Steve said, and handed her a brightly-wrapped gift. "Why don't you open this? I think Santa Claus picked it especially for you." Uncle Steve had come over to the house at about four in the morning, when his commanding officer finally forced him to take some time off.

Miranda tore off the wrapping paper and stared with great glee at a new Barbie doll. "Hooray for Santa Claus!" she said.

Gregory and Patricia were drinking the last of the orange juice, and eating a bizarre morning meal of boxed macaroni and cheese their father had cooked in a saucepan over the fire, plus a banana each, and some carrots. Abigail stole a carrot stick when no one was looking and was now batting it lazily from one paw to another. Their parents and Aunt Emily were eating unevenly heated chicken tetrazzini from the freezer, while Uncle Steve settled for a couple of hotdogs.

"Well, at least we didn't have to carve each other presents out of sticks or something," Patricia said.

Gregory grinned at her. "Not so fast. You haven't opened mine yet."

Mrs. Callahan looked thoughtful. "You know, in spite of everything, this has actually been one of our nicest Christmases ever. Instead of running around all over the place, we've just been spending time together. It's what Christmas is supposed to be, really."

"Okay," Mr. Callahan said, "but next year, in Jerusalem."

Mrs. Callahan and Aunt Emily both laughed.

"*Next* year I will get to play with the baby sister Mommy is giving me," Miranda said solemnly.

"What if it's a baby brother?" Aunt Emily asked.

"It will *not* be," Miranda said.

"Yeah, really," Patricia agreed. "Baby brothers are a big pain."

"Yeah, well, hope you like the comb I whittled you," Gregory said.

"I'm sure I will." Patricia reached into the pile of presents and tossed one to him. "Here, hope you like the necklace I made you out of dried leaves and beans."

Then they all heard a small truck pulling up outside, and saw a flashing red light through the open curtains.

"What is *that*?" Uncle Steve asked. He got up and looked out the window. "Well, it looks like we have company."

Gregory went to open the front door and saw — Santa Paws! He was hopping out of an ambulance, and two paramedics were right behind him.

The dog barked triumphantly and ran to jump on Gregory.

"Hey, boy, welcome home!" Gregory hugged him. "Merry Christmas!"

The dog barked again and rushed into the house to greet everyone else.

"Is he all right?" Mr. Callahan asked Fran and Saul.

"He's fine," Saul promised. "He was saving the Malones from carbon monoxide poisoning and he inhaled some himself. But he's had oxygen, and we stopped off at Dr. Kasanofsky's house on the way over here just to be sure." Dr. Kasanofsky was Santa Paws' veterinarian. "He said just to keep him quiet for a few days."

"And only walk him on a leash," Fran added.

Then she and Saul looked at each other.

"And *no more rescues* this week," they said together.

"Well, I think we can manage all of that," Mr. Callahan said. "Thank you for helping him."

When he invited the paramedics inside, they told him that it was time to go home and see *their* families. So, after a quick exchange of Merry Christmases and Happy Holidays, Saul and Fran left.

In the sitting room, Santa Paws ran to each person — or cat — in turn to jump on them, kiss them, and otherwise say hello. Everyone was overjoyed to see him, except for Abigail who yawned, and stretched, and went back to sleep. But she *did* allow herself a tiny, little purr — which the dog heard.

"Well, okay," Gregory said. "*Now* it feels like Christmas!"

The dog sat down with very straight posture and lifted one paw expectantly.

"How about a Milk-Bone?" Patricia suggested.

The dog barked noisily. Yes! That would be perfect! Patricia was *so smart*! He loved her! He loved *everyone*.

It was so nice to be together that they all sat quietly, and looked at one another fondly, and listened to the holiday music playing on the radio. It didn't even seem important to open any more of their presents. Being safe, and together, was all that mattered. Then, a radio announcer cut in, right in the middle of "O Come, All Ye Faithful."

"Ladies and gentlemen, we have a very special report," he said, sounding very excited. "We have had one final Santa Paws sighting! Our beloved local hero has just been spotted by one of our eagle-eyed reporters entering his house to rejoin his family. Welcome home, Santa Paws, and Merry Christmas, everyone!"

Mr. Callahan lifted his cup of somewhat warm coffee. "I'll second that."

The rest of the family nodded. How could any of them argue with *those* sentiments?

"We now return you to our regular scheduled programming," the radio announcer said, and then, "We Wish You a Merry Christmas" began to play.

Santa Paws wagged his tail and curled up on the rug between Abigail and Evelyn. Each cat

reached out a paw and gave him a light pat before going back to sleep. That made the dog very
happy, and looking down at his Milk-Bone made
him even happier.

It was a great day!

SANTA
PAWS

Santa Paws

by
Nicholas Edwards

AN
APPLE
PAPERBACK

SCHOLASTIC INC.
New York Toronto London Auckland Sydney

ISBN 0-590-62400-8

22 21 20   123/0

Printed in the U.S.A.   40

First Scholastic printing, November 1995

Santa
Paws

1

When the dog woke up, it was very cold. On winter nights, his mother always brought him, along with his brother and sisters, to some safe place out of the wind. She would scratch up some dry leaves to make them a little nest, and they would all cuddle up together. Then, in the morning, his mother would go off and try to find food for them. Sometimes she would let them come along, although they were too small to be much help. Mostly, she would forage for food while he and his siblings would scuffle and play someplace nearby.

Once, his mother had lived in a big, nice house with a lot of college students. But then, when it got warm, they all left. She wasn't sure why they hadn't wanted her to come with them. Some of the students had even left without patting her, or saying goodbye. Her favorite, Jason, had filled up her water dish, given her some biscuits, and told her what a good dog she was. But then, he got in his car and drove away, too.

She had waited in front of the house for a long time, but none of them came back. Ever since then, she had lived on the streets. Sometimes, nice people would give her food, but more often, she was on her own. There were even times when people would be mean and throw things at her, or chase her away.

Then, when he and his siblings were born, she had to spend most of her time taking care of them. She had a special route of trash cans and other places she would check for discarded food. If she found anything, like stale bread or old doughnuts, she would drag the food back and they would all gobble it down. On special days, she might even find some meat in funny plastic packages. They would tear them open and gulp down the old hamburger or bacon or chicken. He and his siblings would always fight playfully over the last little bits, but when his mother growled at them, they would stop right away and be good. The days when she brought home meat were the best days of all. Too often though, when they went to sleep, they were all still very hungry.

He was the smallest of the four puppies, but he had the biggest appetite and slept the most, too. Lots of mornings, he would wake up and be the only one left under the abandoned porch, or in a deep gully, or wherever they had spent the night.

Lately, they had been sleeping in an old forgotten shed, behind a house where no people lived. It was safer that way. Lots of times, even if they wagged their tails, people would yell at them or act afraid. But when he saw big scary cars speed by, with happy dogs looking out the windows, he wished he knew *those* people. He also liked the people who would saunter down the street, with dogs on leashes walking proudly next to them. He really wanted to *be* one of those lucky dogs.

But, he wasn't, and he was happy, anyway. His mother always took care of them, and he loved his brother and sisters. They were a family, and as long as they were together, they were safe.

On this particular morning, he yawned a few times, and then rolled to his feet. None of the others were around, but he was sure they would be back soon with some breakfast. Maybe today they would even find some meat! Once he had stood up, he stretched a few times and yawned again. It was *really* cold, and he shivered a little. In fact, it would be nice to curl up again and get some more sleep. But he decided that he was more thirsty than he was sleepy and that it was time to go outside.

There was a hole in the back part of the old shed that they used for a door. He squirmed through it and immediately felt ice-cold snow under his paws. He shivered again, and shook the snow off each paw. It was *much* windier outside

than it had been in the shed and he stepped tentatively through the fresh drifts of snow.

In the woods nearby, there was a small stream,
where they would always drink. On some mornings lately, the water would be frozen, but his
mother had shown him how to stamp his paw on
the ice to break it. Today, there was so much snow
that he couldn't even *find* the water at first. Then,
when he did, he couldn't break the ice. He jumped
with all four feet, slipping and sliding, but nothing
happened. The ice was just too thick. Finally, he
gave up and sat down in the snow, whimpering a
little. Now he was going to be hungry *and* thirsty.

He swallowed a few mouthfuls of snow, but he
still felt thirsty. The snow also made his insides
feel cold. Where was his mother? Where were his
brother and sisters? They had never left him for
such a long time before. He ran back and forth in
front of the frozen stream, whining anxiously.
What if they were lost? What if they were hurt?
What if they *never* came back? What would happen to him?

Maybe they were back at the shed, waiting for
him. Maybe they had brought back food, and he
and his brother could roll and play and pretend to
fight over it. He should have waited for them,
instead of wandering away.

He ran through the woods to the shed. Some
of the snowdrifts were so tall that they were almost over his head and it took a lot of energy to

4

bound through them. No, they would never go away and forget him. Never, ever.

But the shed was still deserted. He barked a few times, then waited for answering barks. Lately, his bark had been getting bigger and deeper, so he filled his chest with air and tried again. His bark echoed loudly through the silent backyard and woods. When there was still no answer, he whimpered and lay down to wait for them.

He rested his head on his numb front paws. They would probably come back through the big field behind the shed, and he watched the empty acres miserably. If he moved, he might miss them, so he would just stay here and wait. No matter how long it took, he would stay.

The sun was out and shining on him, which made him feel better. He waited patiently, staring at the field with his ears pricked forward alertly. He could hear birds, and squirrels, and faraway cars — but, no dogs. He lifted his nose to try and catch their scent in the air, but he couldn't smell them, either.

So, he just waited. And waited, and waited, and waited. The sun went away after a while, and dark grey clouds rolled in to cover the sky. But still, he waited.

A light snow started falling, but he didn't abandon his post. He wanted to be able to *see* his family the second they came back. Every so often he would stand up to shake off the fresh flakes of snow that had landed on his fur. Then he would shiver, stamp out a new bed for himself, and lie back down. He had never felt so cold, and lonely, and miserable in his life.

Once it began to get dark, he couldn't help whimpering some more and yelping a few times. Something very bad must have happened to his family. Maybe, instead of waiting so long, he should have tried to follow their trail. Maybe they were hurt somewhere, or trapped. But if he went to look for them, they might come back while he was gone and think *he* was lost for good. Then they might go away and he would *never* find them.

There was a street running in front of the boarded-up house and a car was cruising slowly by. A bright beam of light flashed across the house and yard. The dog cringed and tried to duck out of the way. His mother had taught them that when people came around, it was usually safer to hide, just in case.

The car braked to a stop and two big men in uniforms got out. They were both local police officers, out on their nightly patrol.

"Come on, Steve," the man who had been driving said, as he stood by the squad car. "I didn't see anything."

Steve, who was about thirty years old with thick dark hair, aimed his flashlight around the yard. "We've had three break-ins in the last week," he answered. "If we have drifters in town, this is the kind of place where they might hide out."

"I know," the other cop, who was named Bill, said, sounding defensive. He was heavier than Steve was, with thinning blond hair and a neatly trimmed mustache. "I went to the academy, too, remember?"

Steve grinned at him. "Well, yeah, Bill," he agreed. "But *I* studied."

Bill laughed and snapped on his own flashlight. "Okay, fair enough," he said, and directed the beam at the boarded-up windows of the house. "But, come on. Oceanport isn't exactly a high crime area."

"Law and order," Steve said cheerfully. "That's our job, pal."

The men sounded friendly, but the dog uneasily hung back in the shadows. One of the lights passed over him, paused, and came whipping back.

"There!" Steve said, and pointed towards the shed. "I told you I saw something!"

"Whoa, a *dog*," Bill said, his voice a little sarcastic. "We'd better call for back-up."

Steve ignored that and walked further into the yard. "It must be one of those strays," he said. "I thought Charlie finally managed to round all of them up this morning." Charlie was the animal control officer in Oceanport.

Bill shrugged. "So, he missed one. We'll put a

7

report in, and he can come back out here tomorrow."

"It's *cold*," Steve said. "You really want to leave the poor thing out here all night? He looks like he's only a puppy."

Bill made a face. "I don't feel like chasing around after him in the snow, either. Let Charlie do it. He needs the exercise."

Steve crouched down, holding his gloved hand out. "Come here, boy! Come on, pup!"

The dog hung back. What did they want? Should he go over there, or run away and hide? His mother would know. He whined quietly and kept his distance.

"He's wild, Steve," Bill said. "This'll take all night."

Steve shook his head, still holding his hand out. "Charlie said they were just scared. He figured once the vet checked them over and they got a few decent meals, they'd be fine." He snapped his fingers. "Come here, boy. Come on."

The dog shifted his weight and stayed where he was. He had to be careful. It might be some kind of trap.

"He's pretty mangy-looking," Bill said critically.

Steve frowned at him. "Are you kidding? That dog's at least half German shepherd. Clean him up a little, and he'd be something to see. And he's young, too. He'd be easy to train."

8

Bill looked dubious. "Maybe. Give me a good retriever, any day."

Steve stood up abruptly. "Wait a minute. I've got an idea. I still have a sandwich in the car."

"I'm starved," Bill said, trailing after him. "Don't give it to the dog, give it to *me*."

Steve paid no attention to that. He dug into a brown paper bag below the front seat of the squad car and pulled out a thick, homemade sandwich wrapped in waxed paper. "If I catch him, can you take him home?" he asked.

"Are you serious? You know how tough my cat is," Bill said. "Besides, you're the one who likes him so much."

"Yeah," Steve agreed, "but I can't keep him. Not with Emily due any day now. I don't want to do anything to upset her. Besides, she's *already* bugged about me not getting the lights on the Christmas tree yet."

"You'd better get moving," Bill said, laughing. "There's only a week to go."

Steve nodded wryly. "I know, I know. I'm going to do it tomorrow, before my shift — I swear."

As he crossed the yard, carrying the sandwich, the dog shrank away from him. After all, it *could* be some kind of trick. His mother always helped him decide who they could trust, and who they couldn't. He didn't know *how* to take care of himself.

"Hey, what about your brother?" Bill sug-

9

gested. "Didn't he have to have that old collie of his put to sleep recently?"

"Yeah, a few weeks ago," Steve said, and held the sandwich out in the dog's direction. "My niece and nephew are still heartbroken."

Bill shrugged. "So, bring the dog to them."

Steve thought about that, then shook his head. "I don't know, you can't force a thing like that. They might not be ready yet."

Just then, the police radio in their squad car crackled. They both straightened up and listened, as the dispatcher called in a burglar alarm in their sector.

"Looks like the dog is going to have to wait," Bill said. He hurried over to the car and picked up the radio to report in.

Steve gazed across the dark yard at the shivering little dog. "I'm sorry, pal," he said. "We'll send Charlie out after you tomorrow. Try to stay warm tonight." Gently, he set the meatloaf sandwich down in the snow. "Enjoy your supper now." Then he hustled back to the car.

The dog waited right where he was, even after the police car was gone. Then, tentatively, he took a couple of steps out of the woods. He hesitated, sniffed the air, and hesitated some more. Finally, he got up his nerve and bolted across the yard. He was so hungry that he gobbled each sandwich half in two huge bites, and then licked the surrounding snow for any crumbs he might have missed.

It was the best meal he had had for a long time.

Once he was finished, he ran back to the shed and wiggled inside through the hole in the back. If he waited all night, maybe his family would come back. No matter what, he would stay on guard until they did. He was very tired, but he would *make* himself stay awake.

The night before, he and his family had slept in a tangle of leaves and an old musty tarpaulin. The shed had felt crowded, but very warm and safe.

Tonight, all the dog felt was afraid, and very, very alone.

2

It was a long cold night, and even though he tried as hard as he could to remain on guard, the dog finally fell asleep. When he woke up in the grey dawn light, he was still alone. His family really *had* left him!

He crept over to the jagged wooden hole in the back of the shed and peeked outside. Even more snow had fallen during the night, and the whole world looked white and scary. Just as he started to put his front paws through the hole, he heard a small truck parking on the street. Instantly, he retreated.

It was Charlie Norris, who was the animal control officer for the small town of Oceanport. He climbed out of his truck, with some dog biscuits in one hand, and a specially designed nooselike leash in the other.

Inside the shed, the dog could hear the man tramping around through the snow, whistling and calling out, "Here, boy!" But the dog didn't move, afraid of what the man might do to him. The biscuits smelled good, but the leash looked dangerous. He *wanted* to go outside, but if the man tried to take him away, he would miss his family when they came back to get him.

"Don't see any footprints," the man mumbled to himself as he wandered around the snowy yard. "Guess the poor little thing took off last night." He looked around some more, then finally gave up and went back to his truck.

After the truck had driven away, the dog ventured outside. Today, he was going to go *look* for his family. No more waiting. First, he lifted his leg to mark a couple of spots near the shed. That way, if they came back, they would know that he hadn't gone far.

He stuck his muzzle in the wind, and then down in the snow. With the new drifts, it was hard to pick up a scent. But he found a faint whiff and began following it.

The trail led him through the woods, in the opposite direction from the frozen stream. A couple of times, he lost the scent and had to snuffle around in circles to pick it up again.

Then, he came to a wide road and lost the trail completely. He ran back and forth, sniffing frantically. The smells of exhaust fumes and motor oil were so strong that they covered up everything else. He whined in frustration and widened his search, but the trail was gone.

He galloped across the street, and sharp crystals of road salt and gravel cut into his paws. He limped the rest of the way and plunged into the mammoth drifts on the other side. Again, he ran in wide circles, trying to pick up the trail.

It was no use. His family was *gone*.

He was on his own.

He ran back to where he had first lost the scent, his paws stinging again from the road salt. He searched some more, but the trail just plain disappeared. Finally, he gave up and lay down in the spot where his family had last been.

He stayed there, curled into an unhappy ball, for a very long time. Cars drove by, now and then, but no one noticed him huddled up behind the huge bank of snow.

Finally, he rose stiffly to his feet. His joints felt achy and frozen from the cold. He had tried to lick the salt from his paws to stop the burning, but the terrible taste only made him more thirsty. He needed food, and water, and a warm place to sleep.

If he couldn't find his family, he was going to have to find a way to survive by himself.

He limped slowly down the side of the icy road. Cars would zip by, and each time, he did his best to duck out of the way so he wouldn't get hit. None of the cars stopped, or even slowed down. A couple of them beeped their horns at him, and the sound was so loud that he would scramble to safety, his heart pounding wildly.

By the time he got to the center of town, it was almost dark. Even though there were lots of people around, no one seemed to notice him. One building seemed to be full of good smells, and he trotted around behind it.

There was a tall dumpster back there, and the delicious smells coming from inside it made him so hungry that his stomach hurt. He jumped as high as he could, his claws scrabbling against the rusty metal. He fell far short and landed in a deep pile of snow.

Determined to get some of that food, he picked himself up, shook off the snow, and tried again. He still couldn't reach the opening, so he took a running start. This time, he made it a little higher, but he didn't even get close to the top. He fell down into the same drift, panting and frustrated.

The back door of the building opened and a skinny young man about sixteen years old came out. He was wearing a stained white apron and carrying a bulging plastic sack of trash. Just as he was about to heave it into the dumpster, he paused.

"Hey!" he said.

The dog was going to run, but he was so hungry that he just stood there and wagged his tail, instead.

"What are you doing here?" the young man asked. Then, he reached out to pat him.

The dog almost bolted, but he made himself stay and let the boy pat him. It felt so good that he wagged his tail even harder.

"Where's your collar?" the boy asked.

The dog just wagged his tail, hoping that he would get patted some more.

"Do you have a name?" the boy asked. "I'm Dominic."

The dog leaned against the boy's leg, still wagging his tail.

Dominic looked him over and then stood up. "*Stay*," he said in a firm voice.

The dog wasn't quite sure what that meant, so he wagged his tail more tentatively. He was very disappointed when he saw the boy turn to go.

Dominic went back inside the building and the door closed after him. He had left the trash bag behind and the dog eagerly sniffed it. There was *food* in there. *Lots* of food. He nosed around, looking for an opening, but the bag seemed to be sealed. He nudged at the heavy plastic with an experimental paw, but nothing happened.

He was about to use his teeth when the back door opened again.

Dominic was holding a plate of meatballs and pasta, and glancing back over his shoulder. "Shhh," he said in a low voice as he set the plate down. "My boss'll flip if he sees me doing this."

16

The dog tore into the meal, gobbling it down so quickly that he practically ate the Styrofoam plate, too. After licking away every last morsel, he wagged his tail at the boy.

"Good dog," Dominic said, and patted him. "Go home now, okay? Your owners must be worried about you."

Patting was *nice*. Patting was *very* nice. Dogs who got to live with people and get patted all the time were *really* lucky. Maybe this boy would bring him home. The dog wagged his tail harder, hoping that the boy liked him enough to want to keep him.

"Hey, Dominic!" a voice bellowed. "Get in here! We've got tables to bus!"

"Be right there!" Dominic called back. He gave the dog one last pat and then stood up. With one quick heave, he tossed the trash bag into the dumpster. "I have to go. Go home now. Good dog," he said, and went back inside.

The dog watched him leave and slowly lowered his tail. He waited for a while, but the boy didn't come back. He gave the already clean plate a few more licks, waited another few minutes, and then went on his way again.

Oceanport was a small town. Most of the restaurants and stores were clustered together on a few main streets. The town was always quaint, but it looked its best at Christmastime. Brightly colored lights were strung along the old-fashioned

17

lampposts, and fresh wreaths with red ribbons hung everywhere.

The town square was a beautiful park, where the local orchestra played concerts on the bandstand in the summer. The park also held events like the annual art festival, occasional craft shows, and a yearly small carnival. During the holiday season, the various decorations in the park celebrated lots of different cultures and religions. The town council had always described the exhibit of lights and dioramas as "The Festival of Many Lands." Oceanport was the kind of town that wanted everyone to feel included.

Unfortunately, the dog felt anything *but* included. He wandered sadly through the back alley that ran behind the stores on Main Street. All of the dumpsters were too high for him to reach, and the only trash can he managed to tip over was empty. The spaghetti and meatballs had been good, but he was still hungry.

There was water dripping steadily out of a pipe behind a family-owned grocery store. The drip was too fast to freeze right away and the dog stopped to drink as much of the water as he could. The ice that had formed underneath the drip was very slippery and it was hard to keep his balance. But he managed, licking desperately at the water. Until he started drinking, he hadn't realized how thirsty he really *was*. He licked the water until his stomach was full and he was no longer panting.

Then, even though he was alone, he wagged his tail.

Now that he had eaten, and had something to drink, he felt much better. He trotted into the snowy park to look for a place to sleep. After food, naps were his favorite. The wind was blowing hard, and his short brown fur suddenly felt very thin. He lowered his head and ears as gusts of snow whipped into him.

The most likely shelter in the park was the bandstand and he forced himself through the uneven drifts towards it. The bandstand was an old wooden frame shaped in a circle, with a peaked roof built above it. The steps were buried in snow, and the floor up above them was too exposed to the wind. He could try sleeping on the side facing *away* from the wind, but that would mean curling up in deep snow. It would be much warmer and more comfortable if he could find a way in underneath it.

The bandstand was set above the ground, with latticelike boards running around the entire structure. The slats were set fairly far apart and he tried to squeeze between them. Even when he pushed with all of his might, he still couldn't fit. He circled the bandstand several times, looking for a spot where the slats might be broken, but they were in perfect repair.

He was too cold to face lying down in the snow yet, so he decided to keep moving. There was a small white church at the very edge of the park. Its walk and steps were neatly shovelled, and when he passed the building, he saw that the front door was ajar.

Heat seemed to be wafting out through the opening and the dog was drawn towards it. Shivering too much to think about being scared, he slipped through the open door.

It was *much* warmer than it had been outside. He gave himself a good, happy shake to get rid of any lingering snow. Then he looked around for a place to rest.

It was a big room, with high, arched ceilings. There were rows of hard wooden benches, separated by a long empty aisle. The church was absolutely silent, and felt very safe. Not sure where to lie down, the dog stood in the center aisle and looked around curiously. What kind of place was it? Did people *live* here? Would they chase him away, or yell at him? Should he run out now, or just take a chance and hope for the best?

He was so cold and tired that all he wanted to do was lie down. Just as he was about to go and sleep in a back corner, he sniffed the air and then stiffened. There *was* a person in here somewhere! He stood stock-still, his ears up in their full alert position. Instinctively, he lifted one paw, pointing without being sure why he was doing it.

All he knew for sure, was that he wasn't alone in here — and he might be in danger!

3

He sniffed cautiously and finally located where the scent was. A person was sitting alone in one of the front pews, staring up at the altar. Her shoulders were slouched, and she wasn't moving, or talking. She also didn't seem threatening in any way. In fact, the only thing she seemed to be was unhappy.

The dog hesitated, and then walked up the aisle to investigate. He paused nervously every few steps and sniffed again, but then he would make himself keep going.

It was a young woman in her late twenties, all bundled up in a winter hat, coat, and scarf. Her name was Margaret Saunders, and she had lived in Oceanport her whole life. She was sitting absolutely still in the pew, with her hands knotted in her lap. She wasn't making a sound, but there were tears on her cheeks.

The dog stopped at the end of her pew and waved his tail gently back and forth. She seemed very sad, and maybe he could make her feel better.

At first, Margaret didn't see him, and then she flinched.

"You scared me!" she said, with her voice shaking.

The dog wagged his tail harder. She was a nice person; he was *sure* of it.

"You shouldn't be in here," Margaret said sternly.

He cocked his head, still wagging his tail.

"Go on now, before Father Reilly comes out and sees you," she said, and waved him away. "Leave me alone. *Please.*" Then she let out a heavy sigh and stared up at the dark altar.

The dog hesitated, and then made his way clumsily into the pew. He wasn't sure how, but maybe he could help her. He rested his head on her knee, and looked up at her with worried brown eyes.

Margaret sighed again. "I thought I said to go away. Where did you come from, anyway? Your owner's probably out looking for you, worried sick."

The dog pushed his muzzle against her folded hands. Automatically, she patted him, and his tail thumped against the side of the pew.

"I hope you're not lost," she said quietly. "It's a bad time of year to feel lost."

The dog put his front paws on the pew. Then,

since she didn't seem to mind, he climbed all the way up. He curled into a ball next to her, putting his head on her lap.

"I really don't think you should be up here," she said, but she patted him anyway. She was feeling so lonely that even a scruffy little dog seemed like nice company. She had never had a pet before. In fact, she had never even *wanted* one. Dogs were noisy, and needed to be walked constantly, and shed fur all over the place. As far as she was concerned, they were just more trouble than they were worth. But this dog was so friendly and sweet that she couldn't help liking him.

So they sat there for a while. Sometimes she patted him, and when she didn't, the dog would paw her leg lightly. She would sigh, and then pat him some more. He was getting fur all over her wool coat, but maybe it didn't matter.

"I don't like dogs," she said to him. "Really, I don't. I never have."

The dog thumped his tail.

"*Really*," she insisted, but she put her arm around him. He was pretty cute. If it *was* a he. "Are you a boy dog, or a girl dog?"

The dog just wagged his tail again, looking up at her.

"You know, you have very compassionate eyes," she said, and then shook her head. "What am I, crazy? Talking to a *dog*? Like you're going to *answer* me?" She sighed again. "I don't know, though. I guess I have to talk to *someone*. It's been a long time."

The dog snuggled closer to her. He had never gotten to sit like this with a person before, but somehow, it felt very natural. Normal. Almost like cuddling with his brother and sisters.

"My husband died," the woman told him. Then she blinked a few times as her eyes filled with more tears. "We hadn't even been married for two years, and one night — " She stopped and swallowed hard. "He was in a terrible accident," she said finally. "And now — I don't know what to do. It's been almost a year, and — I just feel so alone. And *Christmas* makes it worse." She wiped one hand across her eyes. "We didn't even have time to start a family. And we wanted to have a *big* family."

The dog wanted to make her feel better, but he wasn't sure what to do. He tilted his head, listening intently to words he couldn't understand. Then, for lack of a better idea, he put his paw on her arm. She didn't seem to mind, so he left it there.

"People around here are trying to be really nice to me, especially my parents, but I just can't — I don't know," Margaret said. "I can't handle it. I feel like I can't handle *anything* anymore."

The dog cocked his head attentively.

"That's why I only come here at night," she

24

explained, "so I won't have to run into anyone. I used to go to church all the time, but now I don't know how to feel, or what to believe, or — everything's *so hard*. You know?"

The dog watched her with great concentration.

"I can't believe I'm talking to a dog. I must really be losing it." Tentatively, the woman touched his head, and then rubbed his ears. "Is that how I'm supposed to do it? I mean, I've never really patted a dog before."

He wagged his tail.

"What kind of dog are you, anyway?" she asked. "Sort of like one of those police dogs? Except, you're pretty little."

The dog thumped his tail cooperatively.

"Your owners shouldn't let you run around without a collar and license tag," she said. "They should be more careful."

He lifted his paw towards her, and she laughed. The laugh sounded hesitant, as though she hadn't used it for a very long time.

"Okay," she said, and shook his paw. "Why not. Like I told you, I'm not much for dogs, but — that's pretty cute. You seem *smart*."

When she dropped his paw, he lifted it again — and she laughed again.

"Hello?" a voice called from the front of the church. "Is anyone there?"

Now Margaret stiffened. She reached for her purse, getting ready to leave.

Not sure what was wrong, the dog sat up uneasily, too.

An older man wearing black pants and a black shirt with a white collar came out of a small room near the altar. He was also wearing a thick, hand-knit grey cardigan over his shirt. When he saw the woman, he looked surprised.

"I'm sorry, Margaret, I didn't realize you were here," he said. "I was going to lock up for the night."

Margaret nodded, already on her feet. "Excuse me. I was just leaving, Father."

"There's no need for that," he said, and then came partway down the aisle. He paused, leaning against the side of an empty pew. "I haven't seen you for a long time. How have you been?"

Margaret avoided his eyes as she buttoned her coat and retied her scarf. "Fine, Father Reilly. Everything's just fine. Just — super."

"I saw your parents at eleven o'clock Mass last Sunday," he said conversationally. "They looked well."

Margaret nodded, her head down.

Slowly, Father Reilly let out his breath. "This time of year can be difficult for *anyone*, Margaret. I hope you know that if you ever want to talk, my door is always open."

Margaret started to shake her head, but then she looked down at the dog and hesitated. Maybe it would be nice to talk to someone who could talk *back*. Maybe the dog had been good practice for the real thing.

"I was just going to make myself some tea," Father Reilly said, "if you'd like to come for a few minutes. Maybe we could talk about things, a little. How you're doing."

Margaret looked down at the dog, then back at Father Reilly. She had known Father Reilly since she was a child, and he had always been very sympathetic and understanding. The kind of priest who was so nice that even people who weren't Catholic would come and talk to him about their problems. "I think I'd like that," she said, her voice hesitant. "Or, anyway, I'd like to try."

"Okay, then," Father Reilly said with a kind smile. "It's a place to start, right?" Then his eyebrows went up as he noticed the dog standing in the pew. "Wait a minute. Is that a dog?"

Margaret nodded and patted him again. He wagged his tail in response, but kept his attention on Father Reilly. Was this stranger safe — or someone who was going to chase him away? Would the stranger be nice to his new friend?

"*Your* dog?" Father Reilly asked. "I don't think I've ever seen him around before."

Margaret shook her head. "Oh, no. I really don't even like dogs." Well, maybe she did *now*. A little. "He was just — here."

"Well, maybe we'd better call the police," Father Reilly suggested. "See if anyone has reported him missing. He shouldn't be running around alone in weather like this." He reached his hand out. "Come here, puppy."

Seeing the outstretched hand, the dog panicked. His mother had taught him that a raised hand usually meant something *bad*. He squirmed out of the pew and bolted down the aisle.

"No, it's okay," Margaret said, hurrying after him. "Come back, dog! You don't have to run away."

The dog stayed uncertainly by the door. Then, as Father Reilly headed down the aisle, too, he made up his mind and raced outside. The winter wind immediately bit into his skin, but he made himself keep running.

The strange man *might* be okay — but he couldn't take that chance.

He ran for what seemed like a long time. When he was exhausted, and quivering from the cold, he finally stopped. He was in an empty, plowed parking lot. There was a long, low red brick building beyond the lot and he followed a shovelled path over to the main entrance. There was some sand on the path, but it didn't hurt his paws the way the road salt had.

The wind was still whipping around and he ducked his head to avoid it. He couldn't remember *ever* being this cold. Cautiously, he circled the big building until he found a small, sheltered corner.

He climbed through a deep drift and then used his front paws to dig some of the snow away.

Once he had cleared away enough snow to make a small nest for himself, he turned around three times and then curled up in a tight ball. The icy temperature of his bed made him shiver, but gradually, his body heat began to fill the space and he felt warmer.

His snow nest wasn't the best bed he had ever had — but, for tonight, it would have to do.

It was going to be another long, lonely night.

4

He woke up when he heard children's voices. In fact, there were children *everywhere*. His joints felt frozen, and he had a hard time standing up. He had *never* been cold like this when he slept with his family. He stood there for a minute, in the snow, missing them. In fact, he missed them so much that he didn't even notice how hungry he was. Would he ever find them? Would they ever find *him*?

There were lots of children running around in the snow, yelling and throwing snowballs at each other. Some of them were playing a game with a round red rubber ball, and he *wanted* to bound over and join them.

He ventured out of the sheltered alcove a few steps, then paused. Could he play with them? Would they mind? The game looked like fun.

While he was still making up his mind, the big red ball came rolling in his direction and he barked happily. Then he galloped after it, leaping through the broken snow.

Two boys who were running after the ball stopped when they saw him.

"Where did he come from?" one of the boys, whose name was Gregory Callahan, asked.

The other boy, Oscar Wilson, laughed. "He *looks* like Rudolph!"

Gregory laughed, too. "Oh, so he came from the North Pole?"

"Yep," Oscar said solemnly. "He flew down early. Wanted to beat the holiday traffic."

Gregory laughed again. In a lot of ways, the dog *did* look like Rudolph. Since he was still a puppy, his nose and muzzle were too big for his face. His short fur had the same reddish tint a deer's coat might have, and his legs were very skinny compared to his body. If his nose was red, instead of black, it would be a perfect match.

"Hurry up, you guys!" a girl yelled from the kickball field. "Recess is almost over."

Gregory and Oscar looked at each other, and then chased after the ball.

It was too large to fit in the dog's mouth, so he was pushing it playfully with his paws. Each time the ball veered in a new direction, the dog would lope after it, barking. The whole time, he kept it under control, almost like he was playing soccer.

"Check it out," Oscar said, and pushed his

glasses up to see better. "We can put him in center field."

Gregory shook his head, watching the dog chase the ball in circles. "On Charlie Brown's team, maybe. Or, I don't know, the *Cubs*."

Gregory and Oscar were in the fifth grade, and they had been best friends since kindergarten. Although they both loved recess more than anything else, Gregory's favorite class was math, while Oscar liked reading.

Harriet, the girl who had been playing left field, ran over to join them. "While you guys were standing here, they scored all three runs," she said, with a very critical expression.

Oscar sighed, pretending to be extremely sad. "Downer," he said.

"Big-time," Gregory agreed.

"So go get the ball," Harriet said.

The boys both shrugged, and watched the dog play.

Harriet put her hands on her hips. "You guys aren't *afraid* of that dumb puppy, are you?"

"Yep," Oscar said, sadly.

Gregory nodded. "*Way* scared."

Harriet was much too caught up in the game to be amused. Instead, she ran after the dog and tried to get the ball away from him.

A game! The dog barked happily and nudged the ball just out of her reach. He would wait until she could almost touch it, and then bat it out of her range again.

Harriet stamped one of her boots in frustration. "Bad dog!" she scolded him. "You bring that ball to me right now!"

The dog barked and promptly knocked the ball further away.

"*That* worked," Gregory said.

"Good effort," Oscar agreed.

Harriet glared at them. "You could *help* me, you know."

Gregory and Oscar thought that over.

"We could," Oscar admitted.

Gregory nodded. "We most definitely could."

"Totally," Oscar said.

But then, of course, they just stayed right where they were and grinned at her. Since she lost her sense of humor pretty easily, Harriet was a lot of fun to tease.

She stamped her foot again. "You're just immature babies! *Both* of you!" Then she ran after the dog as fast as she could.

In the spirit of the game, the dog dodged out of her way. Harriet dove for the ball, missed, and dove again. Then she slipped, landing face-first in a deep mound of snow.

Oscar and Gregory clapped loudly.

"It's not funny," Harriet grumbled as she picked herself up.

Gregory reached behind his back and pretended to hold up a large card. "I don't know about you folks judging at home," he said, "but I have to give that one a nine."

Oscar shook his head and held up his own imaginary scoring card. "A seven-point-five is as high as I can go."

"But her compulsories were *beautiful*," Gregory pointed out.

"Well, that's true," Oscar conceded, "but — I'm sorry. The degree of difficulty *just wasn't there*."

"Babies," Harriet said under her breath as she brushed the snow off her down jacket and jeans. "Stupid, immature *babies*."

By now, the rest of the kickball players had given up on continuing the game and started a wild snowball fight instead. It was so rowdy that at least two teachers had already run over to try and break it up.

Gregory took his gloves off, and then put his pinkies in his mouth. It had taken his big sister, Patricia, a long time, but she had finally managed to teach him how to whistle that way. Patricia was convinced that, to have any hope of being cool in life, a person *had* to be able to let out a sharp, traffic-stopping whistle. And, hey, she was in the sixth grade — as far as Gregory was concerned, she *knew* these things.

His hands were a little cold, so his first whistle came out as a wimpy burst of air.

"That's good," Oscar said. "Patty taught you *great*."

Gregory ignored that, and tried again. This time, his whistle was strong and piercing, and half of the kids on the playground looked up from whatever they were doing.

Hearing the sound, the dog froze. His ears went up, and his tail stopped wagging.

"*Stay*," Gregory ordered, and walked over to him.

The dog tilted his head in confusion. Then he gave the ball a tiny, experimental nudge with his nose. Was this part of the game?

"*No*," Gregory said.

The dog stopped.

Gregory patted him on the head. "Good dog," he said. He picked up the ball and tossed it to Harriet.

She caught the ball, and then made a face. "Gross. There's drool all over it."

"Greg can't help it," Oscar said. "He *always* drools. They take him to doctors, but . . ."

"I almost have it licked," Gregory insisted. "All I have to do is Scotch-tape my mouth shut — and I'm fine."

"*So* immature," Harriet said in disgust, and trotted back to the kickball field.

A bell rang, signalling the end of recess. All over the playground, kids groaned and stopped whatever games they were playing. They headed for the school entrance, where they were supposed to line up by homeroom classes before going inside.

"We'd better go, Greg," Oscar said.

Gregory nodded, but he kept patting the dog. His family's collie, Marty, had died recently, and this was the first dog he had patted since then. Marty had been really old — his parents had had him since before he and Patricia were *born* — and life without him was lonely. All of them had cried about it, more than once. His parents had said that they would get another dog sometime soon, but none of them could really face the idea yet, since they still missed Marty so much.

"He doesn't have a collar," Gregory said aloud. "Do you think he's lost?"

Oscar shook his head. "I doubt it. He probably just got out of his yard or something."

Gregory nodded, but he *liked* this dog. If he thought his parents wouldn't get upset, he would bring him home.

Mr. Hastings, their teacher, strode over to them. "Come on, boys," he said sternly. "Leave the dog alone. Recess is over now."

Gregory would *much* rather have stayed and played with the dog. All afternoon, if possible. But he nodded, and gave the dog one last pat on the head.

"Good dog," he said. "Go home now, boy."

Then he and Oscar followed Mr. Hastings towards the school. The dog watched them go, very disappointed. The playground was completely empty now. Slowly, his tail drooped and he lowered his ears. He didn't know why, but for some reason, the game was over.

He was on his own again.

5

The dog waited in the playground for a while, but none of the children came back. He was *especially* waiting for the boy who had patted him for so long. He wished that he could *live* with that boy and play with him all the time.

When it was finally obvious that they had gone inside for good, he decided to move on. He walked slowly, with his head down, and his tail between his legs. He was so hungry that his stomach was growling. He ate some snow, but it only made his stomach hurt more.

There were some trash bins behind the school, overflowing with garbage bags. Smelling all sorts of wonderful food, he stopped short. He sniffed harder, then started wagging his tail in anticipation. Lunchtime!

The bins were taller than he was, but he climbed onto a pile of snow so he could reach. Then he leaned forward and grabbed onto one of the bags with his teeth. Using his legs for leverage, he was able to pull the bag free. It fell onto the ground and broke open, spilling half-eaten school lunches everywhere.

It was like a vision of dog heaven. Food, food, and *more* food!

In fact, there was so much food that he really wasn't sure where to start. Lots of sandwich crusts, carrot sticks, and apples with one bite out of them. He ate until he was full, switching from leftover peanut butter and jelly to cream cheese and olives to bologna. So far, the bologna was his favorite. He sniffed the crumpled brown paper bags, hoping to find more.

American cheese, part of a BLT, some tuna fish, pudding cups with some left inside, hard granola bars, a couple of drumsticks. He ate everything he could find, although he spit all of the lettuce out. He *definitely* didn't like lettuce. Or apples. The trash bin smelled more strongly of rotting apples than anything else, although he wasn't sure why.

Some of the milk cartons were still full, and he tore the cardboard containers open. Milk would spurt out onto the snow, and he would quickly lick it up before it drained away. Now his thirst was satisfied, too.

There was so much leftover food that even though he had been starving, he couldn't finish it all. Carefully, he used his front paws to cover the bag with snow. That way, he could come back later and eat some more. And there were other bags he hadn't even opened yet!

He trotted on his way in a much better mood, letting his tail sway jauntily. It didn't even seem as cold anymore. He didn't have anyplace special to go, so he decided to wander around town and look for his family. Could they have gone to live with some nice people? Maybe if he went down every street he could find, he would come across them.

The streets were busy with cars full of people doing last-minute holiday shopping. So, he was very cautious each time he had to cross one. Cars scared him. He would wait by the side of the road until they all seemed to be gone, take a deep breath, and dash across. When he got to the other side, his heart would be beating loudly and he could hear himself panting. No matter how many times he did it, it never got any easier.

He looked and looked, but found no signs that his family had ever existed. He even went back to the old abandoned house to check. The only thing he could find was faint whiffs of his own scent. If they hadn't come back for him by now, he knew they never would.

Tired and discouraged by his long search, it was an effort to keep walking. The sun was going down, and the temperature was dropping again. He wandered morosely through a quiet neighborhood, looking for a good place to take a nap. When in doubt, he always napped.

He could smell dogs inside some of the warmly lit houses he passed and felt very envious of them. They would bark when he went by, so they must smell him, too. A couple of dogs were outside in fenced yards, and they barked so fiercely at him that he would end up crossing to the other side of the street.

There were tantalizing smells of meat cooking and wood smoke from winter fires wafting out of many of the houses. He would stop on the sidewalk in front of the best-smelling houses and inhale over and over again. Beef, chicken, pork chops — all *kinds* of good things. He whimpered a little each time he caught a new scent, feeling very sorry for himself.

He was going by a small, unlit white house when he heard a tiny sound. A frail sound. He stopped, his ears flicking up. What was it? A bad sound. A *sad* sound.

He raised his nose into the wind to see if he smelled anything. A person, somewhere nearby. In the snow. He followed his nose — and the low moaning — around to the side of the little house.

There was a car parked in the driveway, and he could still smell gas and feel the warmth of the engine. Was it going to start up and run over him? He gave the car a wide berth, just in case, but kept tracking the sound.

Suddenly, he saw an old woman crumpled in the snow. She was so limp and still that he had almost stepped on her. There was a sheen of ice on the driveway, and she was lying at the bottom of a flight of steps leading to the back door. Two bags of groceries were strewn haphazardly around her.

She moaned weakly, and he went rigid. He backed away a few steps, and then circled around her a few times. Why didn't she move? When she didn't get up, he let out a small woof.

Her eyes fluttered open and she looked up at him dully. "Help," she whispered. "Please help me."

The dog put a tentative paw on her arm, and she moaned again. He jumped back, afraid. What was wrong? Why was she lying on the ground like that?

Unsure of himself, he ran up the back steps. They were covered with fresh ice and his paws skidded. He barked more loudly, standing up on his hind legs. He scratched at the door with his front paws, still barking.

"No one's there," the old woman gasped. "I live alone."

He barked some more, then ran back down the steps. Why didn't anyone come? Should he bark more?

"*Go,*" she said, lifting one arm enough to give him a weak push. "Go get your owner."

He nosed at her sleeve, and she pushed him harder.

"*Go home*," she ordered, her teeth chattering from the cold. "Get some help!"

The dog didn't know what to do, and he circled her again. There *was* something wrong; he just wasn't sure exactly what it was. Should he curl up with her to keep her warm, or just run away?

At the house across the street, a station wagon was pulling into the driveway. He could hear people getting out of the car. There were at least three children, two of whom were bickering.

"Help!" the elderly woman called, but her voice was barely above a whisper. "Help me!"

There was so much urgency in her voice that the dog barked. Then he barked again and again, running back and forth in the driveway. The people noticed him, but still seemed to be going into their house.

He barked more frantically, running partway across the street and then back to the driveway. He repeated the pattern, barking the entire time.

A teenage girl, who was holding a grocery bag and a knapsack full of schoolbooks, laughed. "Whose dog is that?" she asked, pointing over at him. "He's acting like he thinks he's Lassie."

The dog barked loudly, ran up the driveway, and ran out to the street.

"He sure doesn't *look* like Lassie," one of the

girl's little brothers, Brett, scoffed. "He looks like a *mutt*."

Their mother, who was carrying her own bags of groceries, frowned. "Maybe something's wrong," she said. "Mrs. Amory usually has her lights on by now."

The teenage girl, Lori, shrugged. "Her car's in the driveway. Maybe she's just taking a nap or something."

Her mother still looked worried. "Do me a favor and go over there, will you, Lori? It can't hurt to check."

Lori shrugged, and gave her grocery bag to Brett and her knapsack to her other brother, Harold.

The dog kept barking and running back and forth as she walked over.

"Take it easy already," she said to him. "You been watching the Discovery Channel or something? Getting *dog ambitions*?"

The dog galloped over to the injured old woman and stood next to her, barking loudly.

Lori's mouth dropped open. "Oh, *whoa*," she said, and then ran over to join him. "Mom!" she yelled over her shoulder. "Call 911! Quick! Mrs. Amory's hurt!"

After that, things moved fast. Lori's mother, who was Mrs. Goldstein, dashed over to help. Brett went inside to call an ambulance and Harold hurried to get a blanket.

Hearing all the commotion, other neighbors on the block came outside. By the time the police and the EMS workers had arrived, a small, concerned crowd had gathered.

Since it was the northwest sector of town, two of the police officers were Steve and Bill. They worked with the other cops to move the neighbors aside so that the two EMS attendants could get through with a stretcher.

The whole time, the dog hung back nervously in the shadow of Mrs. Amory's garage, not sure if he was in trouble. There were so many people around that he might have done something bad. They all seemed very upset, and it might be his fault.

"What happened, Officer Callahan?" one of the neighbors asked Steve. "Is Mrs. Amory going to be okay?"

Steve nodded. "Looks like a broken hip, but the Goldsteins found her in time. She might have a little hypothermia, but she should be just fine."

The EMS workers shifted Mrs. Amory very gently onto the stretcher, and covered her with two more blankets. She was weak from pain, and shivering from the cold.

"Thank you," she whispered. "Thank you so much."

"Don't worry about a thing," one of the EMS workers assured her. "We'll have you over at the emergency room in a jiffy."

"He saved me," she said weakly. "I don't know where he came from, but he saved me."

"Well, don't worry, you're going to be fine," the EMS worker said comfortingly.

As she was lifted into the back of the ambulance, Steve and Bill and the other officers moved the onlookers aside.

"Let's clear away now," Bill said authoritatively. "Give them room to pull out."

The ambulance backed slowly out of the driveway, with its lights flashing and its siren beginning to wail. Everyone watched as the emergency vehicle drove away with Mrs. Amory safely inside.

"Okay, folks, show's over," Steve announced. "Thanks a lot for all of your help. You can head in for supper now."

Although there was still an eager buzz of conversation, most of the neighbors started drifting towards their houses.

Bill pulled out his notebook and went over to the Goldsteins. "We just need a few things for our report," he said to Mrs. Goldstein. "You and your daughter found her?"

"It was Lassie!" Lori's little brother Harold chirped. "He was totally cool!"

Bill looked skeptical. "What do you mean by that, son?"

Brett pointed at the dog crouching by the garage. "It was that dog!" he said, sounding just as excited as Harold. "He was barking and barking, and Lori followed him. It was just like TV!"

Bill's expression got even more doubtful. "You're saying that a *dog* came over to get help?"

"Exactly," Mrs. Goldstein answered for her sons. "I know it must sound strange — but he was very insistent, and that's when I sent Lori over. I was afraid that something might be wrong."

Bill digested that, his pen still poised over the empty notebook page. "So, wait, let me get this straight. It was *your* dog who alerted you?" he asked.

"We don't have a dog," Brett told him.

Harold nodded, looking sheepish. "On account of, I'm allergic," he said, and sniffled a little to prove it.

Bill considered all of that, and then squinted over towards the garage. "You sure the dog didn't knock her down in the first place?"

"I don't think so," Lori said doubtfully. "He was trying to help."

It was completely dark now, except for the headlights on the two remaining squad cars. Bill unclipped his flashlight from his equipment belt. He turned it on and flashed the light around the yard.

Seeing that, the dog instinctively shied away from the beam. But it was too late — Bill had already seen him.

"Hey!" Bill said, and nudged his partner. "It's that same stray dog you were so hot about catching the other night."

"What about him?" Steve asked, in the middle of taking a statement from one of the other neighbors.

"He's over there," Bill said, and gestured with the flashlight. "The Goldsteins say he sounded the alarm."

Steve's eyebrows went up. "Really? Hey, all right! I *told* you he was a great dog." He shoved his notebook in his jacket pocket. "Let's see if we can get him this time. Find him a good home."

All of the neighbors wanted to help capture the hero dog. So everyone fanned out and moved forward. Some of them shouted, "Here, boy!" while others whistled or snapped their fingers.

Seeing so many people coming towards him, the dog slipped deeper into the bushes. He *was* in trouble! They had taken the poor old lady away, and now they were *blaming* him. He squirmed towards the woods crouched down on all fours, trying to stay out of sight. Then, he gathered all of his energy and started running as fast as he could.

Lately, escaping to safety had become one of his best tricks!

6

The dog hid in the woods until he was *sure* that no one was coming after him anymore. It had been a very long day, and all he wanted to do now was *sleep*. He could walk back to the school and sleep in that little alcove, but it seemed too far.

There were a bunch of boulders to his right and he crept over to explore them. Most of the rocks were jammed close together and buried in snow. But a few had openings that looked like little caves. He chose the one that seemed to be the most private and wiggled inside.

He fit easily, and there was even room to stand up and turn around, if he wanted. Almost no snow had blown in, and there were lots of dry leaves to lie on. He could smell the musty, ancient odor of other animals who had used this cave for a shelter — squirrels, mostly, and maybe a skunk or two. But, as far as he could tell, no other animal had been in here for a long time.

As always, he turned around three times before

49

lying down. The cave was so warm, compared to being outside, that he slept for a long time.

When he woke up and poked his head out through the rock opening, it was snowing hard. He retreated back inside. He wanted to go over to the school and find some more discarded lunches to eat, but the storm was just too bad. No matter how much his stomach started growling, he would be much better off in here, out of the blizzard. The wind was howling, and he was glad to be in a place where he could avoid it.

So, he went back to sleep. Every so often, he would be startled by a noise and leap to his feet. Then, when it turned out to be nothing out of the ordinary, he would curl up again.

It snowed all day, and most of the night. He only went outside to go to the bathroom, and then he would return to his little rock cave. The snow was so deep now that his legs were completely buried when he tried to walk, and mostly he had to leap. Leaping was hard work, and made him tired after a while. He liked it better when there wasn't any snow at all. Grass and dirt were *easy* to walk on.

Once, he saw a chipmunk chattering away on a low tree branch. He was hungry, and thought about trying to catch the little animal. But before he could even *try* to lunge in that direction, the chipmunk had sensed danger and scampered further up the tree. He ducked back into his cave, not terribly disappointed. The poor little chipmunk was trying to survive the harsh winter, the same way he was. He would just go hungry today, that's all.

By the next morning, the storm had finally stopped. The temperature was higher than it had been, and the top layer of snow was already softening into slush.

He hadn't eaten for such a long time that he headed straight for the school trash bins. When he got to the school, he stopped in the parking lot and shook out each front paw, since he had snow caked between his toes. Now, it was time to eat some breakfast.

He ran around behind the building, but the trash bins were empty! Now what? He had been so sure that he would find more bologna, BLTs, and other treats.

He sank back onto his haunches and whimpered a couple of times. Where had all the food gone? The trash bins were closed now and piled high with snow. All he could smell was the lingering stench of rotten apples and sour milk. They weren't very nice smells, but his stomach still rumbled.

He prowled around the back of the school for a while. Then he came to a door where he could smell food. He barked a couple of times, then sat down to see what would happen. The *last* time he had smelled food behind a door, that teenage boy had given him those great meatballs. Maybe he would get lucky again.

The door opened and a very stout woman in a big white apron looked out. She was Mrs. Gustave, the school cook.

"What?" she asked in a loud, raspy voice.

The dog barked again and held up one paw.

"Hmmm," Mrs. Gustave said, and folded her arms across her huge stomach. "Is that the best you can do?"

She seemed to be waiting for something, so he sat back and lifted both paws in the air.

"That's better," she decided, and disappeared into the kitchen.

Even though she was gone, the dog stayed in the same position. Maybe if she came back, she would like it more the second time. Then he lost his balance and fell over on his side.

"*My* dog can do much better than that," Mrs. Gustave said. She had come outside just in time to see him tumble into the snow.

He quickly scrambled up and held out one paw. One paw was *definitely* safer than two.

"You're going to have to work on that," she said. With a grunt of effort, she bent over and set a steaming plate on top of the snow.

It was crumbled hamburger with gravy, served over mashed potatoes. He wagged his tail enthusiastically and started eating.

"Now, remember," Mrs. Gustave said. "From

now on, you should eat at *home* and not go around begging like a fool." Then she closed the door so she could go back to cooking the students' hot lunch.

He enjoyed his meal very much, and licked the plate over and over when he was done. It had been a hefty serving, but he still could have eaten five or six more. Still, the one big portion made him feel much better.

Cheerfully, he wandered around to the playground. Maybe his friends from the other day would come out again! Then he might get patted some more.

He waited for a long time, and then he got bored. He scratched a little, dug a couple of holes in the snow, and then rolled over a few times.

But he was still bored. He yawned, and scratched again. Still bored. It was time for a nap.

He trudged over to the sheltered area where he had slept that one night. He dug himself a new nest, stamping down the snow with all four feet. Then he lay down and went right to sleep. He slept very soundly, and even snored a little. The day passed swiftly.

"Hey, look!" a voice said. "He *did* come back!"

The dog opened his eyes to see Gregory and his friend Oscar standing above him. He wagged his tail and sprang to his feet.

"Where've you been?" Gregory asked, patting him. "We looked all over for you yesterday."

The dog wagged his tail harder and let them take turns patting him.

"You know, he's kind of scraggly," Oscar said. "Maybe he really *is* a stray."

Gregory shrugged. "Of course he is. Why else would he sleep here?"

Oscar bent down and sniffed slightly. Then he made a face and straightened up. "I think he needs a *bath*, too."

Gregory thought about that. "My father's always home writing, so I can't sneak him into *my* house. What about your house?"

Oscar shook his head. "Not today. Delia and Todd have the flu, so Mom had to stay home with them."

The dog tried to sit up with both paws in the air again, but fell over this time, too.

Both boys laughed.

"What a goofball," Oscar said.

Gregory nodded. "He's funny, though. I really like him."

"Why don't you just say you want a dog for Christmas?" Oscar suggested. "Then you can show up with him like it's a big surprise and all."

Gregory was very tempted by that idea, but he was pretty sure it wouldn't work. "I don't know," he said doubtfully. "My parents said we could maybe go and pick one out together in a month or two."

Oscar packed together a hard snowball and

flipped it idly from one hand to the other. "What does Patricia say?" he asked.

Gregory's big sister. Her advice was advice Gregory always took seriously. Gregory sighed. "That they're still way too sad to even *look* at other dogs right now."

Oscar nodded, then threw the snowball a few feet away. The dog promptly chased after it, and brought it back.

Gregory looked pleased. "He fetches! He's really smart!"

Oscar laughed and threw the snowball even further. "How smart is a dog who fetches *snow*?" he asked as the dog returned with the snowball, his tail beating wildly from side to side.

"*Extra*-smart," Gregory said.

Oscar shrugged and tossed the snowball twenty feet away. "If you say so."

The dog galloped happily after it.

"Boys!" a sharp voice yelled. "What are you doing over there?" It was Ms. Hennessey, one of their teachers. She was always *very* strict.

Gregory and Oscar looked guilty, even though they weren't really doing anything wrong at all.

"Science," Oscar said. "We were just standing here, talking a whole lot about science."

Gregory nodded. "Like, gravity and stuff." He made his own snowball and flicked it straight up into the air.

They both watched it come down, shook their heads, and exchanged admiring glances.

"Gravity again," Oscar observed solemnly. *"Cool."*

The dog picked up that snowball instead and offered it to Gregory.

Ms. Hennessey marched over, her face tight with concern. She was tall and extremely skinny, with lots of bright red hair. She liked to wear wide, billowy skirts, big sunglasses, and ponchos. "Don't you boys know better than to go up to a stray animal! It's *dangerous*!"

This little dog might be many things, but "dangerous" didn't seem to be one of them. Gregory and Oscar looked at each other, and shrugged.

"Get away from him right now!" Ms. Hennessey said with her hands on her hips. "He might have rabies!"

Gregory looked at the dog, who wagged his tail in a very charming way. "I don't think so, ma'am. He seems — "

"Look at him!" Ms. Hennessey interrupted, and pulled both of the boys away. "There's *foam* in his mouth!"

"That's just drool, ma'am," Oscar explained. "Because he's sort of panting."

Gregory gave him a small shove. "Saliva, Oscar. Us science types like to call it saliva."

"Well, I'm going to call the dog officer," Ms. Hennessey said grimly. "We can't have a dangerous dog roaming around near children. I just won't have it!"

For years, Gregory's parents had always explained to him that it was important to be *careful* around strange animals — but that it was *also* important to help any animal who might be in trouble. "Please don't call the dog officer, Ms. Hennessey," he said desperately. If the dog went to the pound, he would never get to see him again. "It's okay, he's — " Gregory tried to come up with a good excuse — "he's *my* dog! He just — followed me to school, that's all."

Ms. Hennessey narrowed her eyes. "Where's his collar?"

Gregory thought fast. "He lost it, when we were walking on the beach last weekend."

"A seagull probably took it," Oscar put in helpfully. "They like shiny things."

"*Raccoons* like shiny objects," Gregory told him. "Not seagulls."

"Oh." Oscar shrugged. "That's right, it was a raccoon. I heard it was a big old *family* of raccoons."

Ms. Hennessey wasn't buying any of this. "What's his name?" she asked.

Gregory and Oscar looked at each other.

"Sparky," Gregory said, just as Oscar said, "Rover."

Mrs. Hennessey nodded, her suspicions confirmed. "I see."

"His, um, his *other* nickname is Spot," Gregory said, rather lamely.

"I don't appreciate having you two tell me fibs," Ms. Hennessey said without a hint of a smile on her face. "I think you'd just better come along down to the office with me, and you can talk to Dr. Garcia about all of this."

Dr. Garcia was the vice principal — and she made Ms. Hennessey seem *laid-back*. Being sent to the office at Oceanport Middle School was always a major disaster, dreaded by one and all.

"But — " Gregory started to protest.

"Come along now," Ms. Hennessey ordered, taking each of them by the sleeve. She turned towards Ms. Keise, one of the other teachers. "Cheryl, chase this dog away from here! He's a threat to the children!"

"He's not," Gregory insisted. "He's a really *good* — "

"That will be quite enough of that," Ms. Hennessey said sharply, and led the two of them away.

The dog let the snowball fall out of his mouth. Where were his friends going? Then he saw a tall woman in a leather coat hurrying towards him. She was frowning and shaking her finger at him. Before the woman could get any closer, the dog started running.

He would much rather run away — than be *chased*.

7

The dog ended up hiding behind the trash bins. When he no longer heard any voices, he slogged back to his little alcove to sleep some more. Who knew when his friends might come back? He wanted to be here waiting when they did.

This time, though, the voice that woke him up was female. He opened one eye and saw a thin girl, with her hair tied back in a neat brown ponytail. She had the same very blue eyes Gregory had, and she was wearing a red, white, and blue New England Patriots jacket. It was Patricia, Gregory's big sister.

"So, you must be the dog my brother won't shut up about," she said aloud.

The dog cocked his head.

Patricia frowned at him. "He got *detention* because of you. So even though it's Christmas, Mom and Dad are probably going to have to ground him."

He wagged his tail tentatively. She didn't exactly sound mad, but she didn't sound friendly, either.

"Well," she said, and tossed her ponytail back. "The way he was going on and on, I figured you could *talk* or something. Tap dance and sing, maybe. But you just look regular. Even a little silly, if you want to know the truth."

Maybe she would like it if he rolled in the snow. Like *him*. So, he rolled over a couple of times.

"*A lot* silly," she corrected herself.

The dog scrambled up and shook vigorously. Snow sprayed out in all directions.

"Thanks a lot, dog," Patricia said, and wiped the soggy flakes from her face and jacket. "I enjoyed that."

He wagged his tail.

"We could still maybe talk Mom and Dad into it. I mean, it *is* almost Christmas," she said. "Although we really like *collies*." She studied him carefully. "It would be easier, if you had a limp, or your ear was chewed up, or something. Then my parents would feel sorry for you."

The dog barked. Then he sat down and held up his right paw.

Patricia nodded. "Not bad. If you could *walk* with your paw up like that, they could *never* say no. Here, try it." She clapped her hands to be sure she had his full attention. "*Come.*"

60

Obediently, the dog walked over to her. "Come" was an easy one.

"No, *limp*," she said, and demonstrated. "I want you to limp. Like this, see?" She hopped around on one red cowboy-booted foot. Cowboy boots might not be warm in the winter, but they *were* cool. Always. "Can you do that?"

The dog barked, and rolled over in the snow. Then he bounded to his feet and looked at her hopefully.

"Well, that's not right at all," she said, and then sighed. "If I tell you to play dead, you'll probably *sit*, right?" She shook her head in dismay. "I really don't know about this. I thought he said you were *smart*."

The dog barked and wagged his tail heartily.

"Right," Patricia said, and shook her head again. "And if I tell you to 'Speak,' you're going to look for a hoop to jump through — I can see it now."

Perplexed by all of this, the dog just sat down and looked at her blankly.

"Well, this is just a waste," Patricia said, and then straightened the tilt of her beret. "Until we can get you home and I have some serious training time with you, you're clearly *beyond* my help." She unzipped her knapsack and took out some crackers and cheese and two chicken sandwiches. "Here, we saved most of our lunches for you. The crackers are from Oscar." She placed the food down in the snow. "Don't ever say I didn't do anything for you."

The dog wagged his tail, and then gobbled up the food in several gulping bites.

"We'll bring more tomorrow, even though it's Saturday," Patricia promised. "Greg can't come back this afternoon because Dad's going to have to pick him up after detention and yell at him for a while. You know, for appearances."

The dog licked the napkin for any remaining crumbs. Then he stuck his nose underneath it, just in case. But he had polished off every last scrap.

"See you later then," she said, and jabbed her finger at him. "Stay. Okay? *Stay*."

The dog lifted his paw.

"Ridiculous," Patricia said, and walked away, shaking her head the entire time. "Just ridiculous."

The dog hung around the school until all the lights were out, and even the janitors had gone home. Then he decided to roam around town for a while. He took what had become his regular route, heading first to the abandoned house. There was no sign of his family — which didn't surprise him, but *did* disappoint him.

Again.

After that, he wandered through the various neighborhoods, looking longingly at all of the families inside their houses. He explored the back alleys behind Main Street. The drainpipe near the pizza place was still leaking, and he had a nice, long drink.

Visiting the park was the next stop on his route. There were lots of townspeople strolling down the winding paths and admiring the holiday exhibits. He was careful to stay out of sight, but he enjoyed being around all of the activity. It was almost like being *part* of it.

There was a traditional Nativity scene, complete with a manger and plastic models of barnyard animals and the Three Wise Men. Further along, there were displays honoring Chanukah, Kwanzaa, and various other ways of celebrating the holiday season.

There was also, of course, a big, wooden sleigh. A fat model Santa Claus sat inside it, surrounded by presents, and the sleigh was being pulled by eight tiny plastic reindeer. Colored lights decorated all of the trees, and the little diorama of Main Street had been built perfectly to scale, right down to the miniature people cluttering its sidewalks.

Christmas carols and other traditional songs played from the loudspeaker above the bandstand, every night from six to ten. On Christmas Eve, live carollers would gather there and hold an early evening concert for everyone to enjoy. Oceanport took the holiday season *seriously*.

He found a nice vantage point underneath a mulberry bush, and settled down for a short nap. When he opened his eyes, the park had cleared out and all of the holiday lights had been turned off for the night. The place *seemed* to be deserted.

He wasn't sure what had woken him up, but somewhere, he heard a suspicious noise. Laughter. Low male voices. Banging and crunching sounds. He stood up, the fur slowly rising on his back. Something wasn't right. He should go and investigate the situation.

The voices were coming from over near the crèche. The dog loped silently through the snow, approaching the Nativity scene from behind. The laughter was louder and he could hear people hissing "Shhh!" to one another.

Whatever they were doing, it didn't feel right. There was a crash, and then more laughter. The dog walked around to the front of the crèche, growling low in his throat.

Inside the Nativity scene, a group of boys from the high school were moving the plastic figures around. They had always been bullies, and vandalism was one of their favorite destructive pranks. They were especially active around the holidays.

One of them was just bending down to steal the baby Jesus figure from the manger. Two other boys were walking over to the Chanukah exhibit, holding cans of spray paint. The fourth boy was knocking over the Three Wise Men, one at a time.

The dog growled the most threatening growl he knew how to make, and all of the boys froze.

"Whose dog?" one of them, Luke, asked uneasily.

The other three shrugged.

"Dunno," the biggest one, Guillermo, said. "Never seen him before."

The dog growled and took a stiff-legged step forward.

"Hey, *chill*, dog!" Michael, the leader of the group, said impatiently. "We're only fooling around." He turned to his friends. "Ignore him — it's just a dumb puppy. Let's hurry up before someone sees us."

"Hey, he looks kind of like those reindeer," another boy, Rich, said, snickering. "Let's tie him up front there."

Luke held up his can of red spray paint. "If you guys hold him, I'll spray his nose!"

They all laughed.

"Let's do it!" Michael decided.

As they crept towards him, the dog growled, his lips curling away from his teeth.

"Oh, yeah," Guillermo said. "He thinks he's *tough*."

"Let's leave *him* in the manger," Rich suggested. "That'd be pretty funny!"

As Luke and Michael lunged for him, the dog snarled and leaped forward. With his teeth bared, he slashed at Michael's jacket. The sleeve tore, and Michael stopped short. He looked down at the jagged rip and started swearing.

"That's *Gore-Tex*, man," he protested. "You stupid dog!" He aimed a kick at the dog's head, but missed. "It was really expensive! How'm I going to *explain* this?" He tried another kick, but the dog darted out of the way.

Guillermo packed together a ball of ice and snow. Then he threw it as hard as he could. The chunk hit the dog square in the ribs and he yelped.

"Yeah, all right!" Guillermo shouted, and bent down to find some more ice. "Let's get 'im!"

The dog growled at them, and then started barking as loudly as he could. He barked over and over, the sound echoing through the still night.

"If he doesn't shut up, everyone in town's going to hear him," Luke said uneasily.

"We mess up these dumb exhibits *every* year," Rich complained. "We can't let some stupid dog ruin this — it's a *tradition*."

During all of the commotion, none of them had noticed the police squad car patrolling past the park. The car stopped and Officers Kathy Bronkowski and Tommy Lee got out. They had been two of the other cops at Mrs. Amory's house the night before, when she had broken her hip on the ice.

Officer Lee turned on his flashlight, while Officer Bronkowski reached for her nightstick.

When the beam passed over them, the boys were exposed in the bright light and they all stood stock-still for a few seconds.

"Hey!" Officer Bronkowski yelled. "What do you think you're doing over there!"

The boys started running, stumbling over one another in their hurry to get away.

"Get back here, you punks!" Officer Lee shouted. "You think we don't recognize you?"

Still furious, the dog raced after them. He snapped at their heels, just to scare them a little. It *worked*. He kept chasing them all the way to the end of the park. Then he trotted back to the crèche, barely panting at all.

The two police officers were carefully reassembling the exhibit. They brushed snow off the tipped-over figures, and then set each one in its proper place.

Officer Bronkowski picked up the two discarded cans of spray paint. "Those little creeps," she said under her breath. "Who do they think they are?"

Officer Lee put the baby Jesus figure gently in the manger. "I saw Michael Smith and Guillermo Jereda. Did you get a good look at the other two?"

Officer Bronkowski shook her head. She had long blond hair, but when she was on duty, she kept it pinned up in a bun. "No, but it was probably the Crandall twins, Luke and Rich. Those four are always together."

"So let's cruise by their houses," Officer Lee

suggested. "See what their parents have to say about this."

Officer Bronkowski nodded. "Good idea. It's about time we caught them in the act."

"The dog gave them away," Officer Lee said, with a shrug. He yawned, opened a pack of gum, and offered a piece to his partner before taking one for himself. "They shouldn't have brought him along."

Officer Bronkowski started to answer, but then she noticed the dog lurking around behind the scale model of the Oceanport town hall. "You know what? I don't think they did," she said slowly.

Officer Lee glanced up from the plastic donkey he was setting upright. "What do you mean?"

She pointed at the dog. "Unless I'm crazy, that's the same dog who found Mrs. Amory yesterday."

Officer Lee looked dubious. "Oh, come on. You mean you think there's some dog *patrolling* Oceanport? You're starting to sound like Steve Callahan." Steve Callahan was, of course, the police officer who had been trying to catch the dog ever since he saw him at the abandoned house. Steve Callahan was also, as it happened, Gregory and Patricia's uncle.

Officer Bronkowski nodded. "That's exactly what I'm saying. Would we have pulled over just now if we hadn't heard him barking?"

"Well, no," Officer Lee admitted, "but — "

Officer Bronkowski cut him off. "And if Gail Amory had been out much longer last night, the doctors say she might have frozen to death. She owes her *life* to that dog."

Officer Lee grinned at her. "So let's put him on the payroll. Maybe even arrange a Christmas bonus." He gave the dog a big thumbs-up. "Good dog! Way to go!"

The dog barked once, and then trotted off.

"Wait!" Officer Bronkowski called after him. "Come back!"

The dog kept going. It was time to be on his way again.

8

Remembering how warm it had been inside, the dog went back to the church. Unfortunately, tonight, the door was already locked. He leaned his shoulder against it and pushed, but the heavy wood wouldn't even budge.

Okay. New plan. He would go back to the school, maybe. In the morning, his friends might come back. Gregory, especially, although he liked Oscar and Patricia, too. Maybe they would even have more food for him! Those chicken sandwiches were *good*.

He was cutting across a parking lot, when he heard — crying. A child, crying. It might even be a baby. He stopped to listen, lifting his paw. The sound was coming from a car parked at the farthest end of the lot.

He ran right over, stopping every few feet to sniff the air. There were several people in the car — he could smell them — but the crying was coming from a small child. A small, miserable child. A sick child.

All of the car windows were rolled up, except for the one on the driver's side, which was cracked slightly. The car was a beat-up old station wagon, and it was *crammed* with people and possessions. He could hear a soothing female voice trying to calm the crying child. The baby would cry, and then cough, and then cry some more. There were two other children in the backseat, and he could hear them coughing and sneezing, too.

He barked one little bark.

Instantly, everyone inside the car, except for the baby, was silent. They were maybe even holding their breaths.

He barked again.

One of the doors opened partway, and a tow-headed little boy peeked out.

"Mommy, it's a dog!" he said. "Can we let him in?"

"No," his mother answered, sounding very tired. "Close the door, Ned. It's cold out there."

"*Please?*" Ned asked. "He won't eat much — I promise! He can have my share."

His mother, Jane Yates, just sighed. They had been homeless since the first of the month, and she could barely afford to feed her *children*. She, personally, had been living on one tiny meal a day for almost two weeks now. For a while, after the divorce, she had been able to keep things going fine. But then, her ex-husband left the state and right after Thanksgiving, she got laid off. Since then, their lives had been a nightmare. And now, all three of the children were sick with colds. The baby, Sabrina, was running a fever, and her cough was so bad that she was probably coming down with bronchitis. They didn't have any money to pay a doctor, so the baby was just getting sicker and sicker.

"I'm sorry, Ned," Jane said. "We just can't. I'm really sorry."

Now Ned started crying, too. His sister, Brenda, joined in — and the baby, Sabrina, had yet to stop.

"Go away," Jane said to the dog, sounding pretty close to tears herself. "Please just leave us alone." She reached over the front seat and yanked the back door closed.

The door slammed in the dog's face and he jumped away, startled. Now *all* he could hear was crying and coughing. What was going on here? It was bad, whatever it was.

He pawed insistently at the door, and barked again. No matter what he did, the crying wouldn't stop.

"Bad dog! Go away!" Jane shouted from inside the car. "Stop bothering us!"

The dog backed off, his ears flattening down against his head. He circled the car a couple of times, but none of the doors opened. These people needed help! With one final bark, he trotted uncertainly back towards the church.

When he got there, Margaret Saunders, the young widow he had met earlier that week, was just coming out with her mother. If they didn't exactly look overjoyed, at least they seemed to be at peace.

"Well, hi there," Margaret said, her face lighting up when she saw him. She reached down one gloved hand to pat him. "Mom, it's the dog I was telling you about. He's pretty cute, isn't he?"

Her mother nodded.

"Maybe I should *get* a dog, sometime," Margaret mused. "To keep me company."

"Sounds like a great idea," her mother agreed. Since Saunders had been Margaret's husband's last name, her mother was Mrs. Talbot.

Margaret patted the dog again. "I think so, too. Whoever owns *this* dog is pretty lucky."

"No doubt. But I can't help wondering if maybe someone *sent* him to you that night," her mother said softly, and smiled at her daughter.

Margaret smiled back. Her mother had a point. The dog *had* appeared out of nowhere. "Stranger things have happened, I guess."

Margaret might be patting his head, but otherwise, they didn't seem to be paying much attention to him. He could still, faintly, hear the sound of crying, and he barked loudly. One thing the dog had learned, was that if he barked a lot, he could get people to follow him. He just *knew* that baby shouldn't be crying like that. He dashed off a few steps, barked, and ran back to them.

Margaret grinned. She had been feeling a little happier over the last couple of days. Hopeful, for the first time in many months. "What do you think, Mom? *I* think he's telling us that Timmy fell down the mine shaft, and we're supposed to bring rope. Manila, preferably."

Her mother laughed. "It certainly looks that way." Of course, neither of them was used to dogs. But *this* one seemed to have come straight out of a movie.

The dog barked again, and ran a few steps away. He barked more urgently, trying to make them understand.

Father Reilly came outside to see what all the commotion was. "What's going on?" he asked, buttoning his cardigan to block out some of the wind.

"Look, Father," Margaret said, and gestured towards the street. "That nice dog is back."

Father Reilly nodded, and then shivered a little. "So he is. But — what's wrong with him?"

The dog barked, and ran away three more steps.

"I don't know," Margaret's mother answered. "I don't know much about animals, but he really seems to want us to follow him."

Father Reilly shrugged. "Well, he strikes me

as a pretty smart dog. Let's do it."

So, with that, they all followed him. The dog led them straight to the parking lot. He checked over his shoulder every so often to make sure that they were still behind him. If he got too far ahead, he would stop and wait. Then, when they caught up, he would set forth again.

He stopped right next to the sagging station wagon and barked. The baby was still coughing and wailing.

The driver's door flew open and Jane Yates got out.

"I told you to go away!" she shouted, clearly at the end of her rope.

Father Reilly stared at her. "Jane, is that you? What are you doing here?"

Realizing that the dog was no longer alone, Jane blushed. "Oh," she said, and avoided their eyes. She hadn't expected company. "Hi." Sabrina coughed and she automatically picked her up, wrapping a tattered blanket more tightly around her so she would be warm.

"You have the children in there with you?" Margaret's mother asked, sounding horrified.

"I couldn't help it," Jane said defensively. "We didn't have any other place to go. Not that it's anyone else's business. Besides, they're *fine*. We're all fine."

Since it was obvious to everyone that the family *wasn't* fine, nobody responded to that. Sometimes it was easy to forget that even in nice, small towns like Oceanport, people could still be homeless.

"Why didn't you come to the church?" Father Reilly asked. "Or the shelter? We would have helped you."

Jane scuffed a well-worn rubber boot against the snow. "I was too embarrassed," she muttered.

Again, no one knew what to say. The baby sneezed noisily, and clung to her mother.

Father Reilly broke the silence. "Still, you must know that you could *always* come to the church," he said. "No matter what."

"I'm not even *Catholic*," Jane reminded him.

Ned, and his sister Brenda, had climbed out of the car and were patting the dog. They got him to sit in the snow, and took turns shaking hands with him. Each time, they would laugh and the dog would wag his tail. Then, they would start the game all over again.

"It's not about religion, it's about community," Father Reilly answered. "About *neighbors*."

Jane's shoulders were slumped, but she nodded.

"Look," Margaret's mother said, sounding very matter-of-fact. "The important thing here is to get these poor children in out of the cold. And the baby needs to see a doctor, right away."

"I don't have any — " Jane started.

"We'll take her to the emergency room," Mrs. Talbot said. "Before she gets penumonia."

Father Reilly checked his watch. "We won't be

able to get into the shelter tonight, but after that, why don't I take you over to the convent and see if the sisters can put you up for the night. Then, tomorrow, we can come up with a better plan."

Jane hesitated, even though her teeth were chattering. "I'm not sure. I mean, I'd rather — "

"You have to do *something*," Margaret's mother said. "Once you're all inside, and get a hot meal, you'll be able to think more clearly."

"Come on," Father Reilly said. "I'll drive everyone in my car."

Throughout all of this, Margaret stayed quiet. Although Jane had been two years ahead of her, they had actually gone to high school together. Since then, their lives had moved in very different — if equally difficult — directions. It wouldn't have seemed possible that things could turn out this way, all those years ago, playing together on the softball team. The team had even been undefeated that year. In those days, they *all* felt undefeated. She shook her head and stuffed her hands into her pockets. Little had they known back then how easily — and quickly — things could go wrong.

Now, Jane looked at her for the first time. "Margaret, I, uh, I was really sorry to hear about what happened. I know I should have written you a note, but — I'm sorry."

Margaret nodded. When a person's husband was killed suddenly, it was hard for other people to know how to react. What to say, or do. "I guess we've both had some bad luck," she answered.

Jane managed a weak smile, and hefted Sabrina in her arms. "Looks that way, yeah."

They both nodded.

"So it's settled," Father Reilly said. "We'll lock up here, and then I'll run you all over to the hospital, and we can go to the convent from there."

Margaret's mother nodded. "Yes. I think that's the best plan, under the circumstances."

Seeing the shame and discomfort on Jane's face, Margaret felt sad. Then she thought of something. "I-I have an idea," she ventured.

They all looked at her.

Margaret turned to direct her remarks to Jane. "Dennis and I bought a big house, because — " Because they had wanted to have a *big* family. "Well, we just did," she said, and had to blink hard. "Anyway, I — " She stopped, suddenly feeling shy. "I have *lots* of room, and maybe — for a while, we could — I don't know. I'd like it if you came to stay with me, until you can get back on your feet again. What do you think?"

Jane looked shy, too. "We couldn't impose like that. It wouldn't be — "

"It *would* be," Margaret said with great confidence. "I think it would be *just* the right thing — for both of us." She bent down to smile at Ned and Brenda. "What do you think? Do you all want to come home with me and help me — deck my

78

halls?" This would give her a reason to buy a Christmas tree. Even to celebrate a little.

"Can we, Mom?" Brenda pleaded.

Jane hesitated.

"I think it's a wonderful idea," Father Reilly said, and Margaret's mother nodded.

"Please," Margaret said quietly. "You may not believe this, but it would probably help *me* out, more than it's going to help you."

Jane grinned wryly and gestured towards the possessions-stuffed station wagon. "You're right," she agreed. "I don't believe it."

Margaret grinned, too. "But you'll come?"

"If you'll have us," Jane said, looking shy.

"Actually, I think it's going to be great," Margaret said.

Standing alone, off to the side, the dog wagged his tail. Everyone seemed happy now. Even the baby wasn't really crying anymore, although she was still coughing and sneezing. He could go somewhere and get some much-needed sleep. In fact, he was *long* overdue for a nap.

"Can we bring the dog with us, too, Mommy?" Ned asked. "Please?"

"Well — " Jane glanced at Margaret, who nodded. "Sure. I think we should."

They all looked around to see where the dog was.

Margaret frowned as she scanned the empty parking lot. The dog was nowhere in sight. "That's funny," she said. "I'm sure he was here just a minute ago."

They all called and whistled, but there was no response.

The dog was gone.

9

Walking along the dark streets, the dog was just plain tuckered out. The park was much closer than the school, so he went there to find a place to sleep. He was going to go back underneath his mulberry bush, but it was a little bit too windy. So he took a couple of minutes to scout out another place, instead.

There was lots of straw piled up in the Nativity scene, but it felt scratchy against his skin. None of the other dioramas were big enough for him to squeeze inside. He was about to give up and go under the bush, when he saw the sleigh. It was stuffed tight with the Santa model and the make-believe gifts, but maybe there would be room for him, too.

Wool blankets were piled around the gifts to make it look as though they were spilling out of large sacks. He took a running start, and leaped right into Santa's lap. Then he squirmed out of sight underneath the blankets. The blankets were almost as scratchy as the hay had been, but they were much warmer. This would do just fine.

He let out a wide, squeaky yawn. Then he twisted around until he found a comfortable position. This was an even better place to sleep than his rock cave had been. Snuggling against the thick blankets was — almost — like being with his family again.

He yawned again and rested his head on his front paws. Then, almost before he had time to close his eyes, he was sound asleep.

It had been a very eventful day.

The blankets were so comfortable that he slept well into the morning. When he opened his eyes, he felt too lazy to get up. He stretched out all four paws and gave himself a little "good morning" woof.

Food would be nice. He crawled out from underneath the heavy blankets. The sun was shining and the sky was bright and clear. The ocean was only a couple of blocks away, and he could smell the fresh, salty air. Oceanport was at its best on days like this.

Instead of jumping down, he kept sitting in the sleigh for a while. Being up so high was fun. He could see lots of cars driving by, and people walking around to do their errands. He kept his nose in the wind, smelling all sorts of intriguing smells.

A sanitation worker named Joseph Robinson,

who was emptying the corner litter basket, was the first person to notice him.

"Hey, check it out!" he said to his coworker. "It's Santa Paws!"

His coworker, Maria, followed his gaze and laughed. "I wish I had a camera," she said.

The town mailman, Rasheed, who was passing by on his morning delivery route, overheard them. "Santa Paws?" he repeated, not sure if he had heard right.

Joseph and Maria pointed at the dog sitting up in the sleigh, looking remarkably like the Grinch's dog, Max.

Rasheed shook his head in amusement. "That *is* pretty goofy." He shook his head again. "Santa Paws. I like that."

Then they all went back to work, still smiling.

Unaware of that whole conversation, the dog enjoyed his high perch for a while longer before jumping down. It was time to find something good to eat.

There was a doughnut shop at the corner of Tidewater Road and Main Street. The dog nosed through the garbage cans in the back. Finally, he unearthed a box of old-fashioneds that had been discarded because they were past the freshness deadline. To him, they tasted just fine. A little dry, maybe.

From there, he went to the ever-leaking drain-pipe behind the pizza place and drank his fill.

There was so much ice now that the flow was slowing down, but he was still able to satisfy his thirst. He cut his tongue slightly on the jagged edge of the pipe and had to whimper a few times. But then, he went right back to drinking.

With breakfast out of the way, he decided to make the rounds. The middle school would be his last stop. He visited all of his usual places, neither seeing — nor smelling — anything terribly interesting. It was three days before Christmas, and everything in Oceanport seemed to be just fine.

He was ambling down Meadowlark Way when he noticed something unusual in the road. To be precise, there were cows *everywhere*. Lots and lots of *cows*.

He stopped, his ears moving straight up. He had seen cows before, but never up close. They were *big*. Their hooves looked sharp, too. Dangerous.

The cows belonged to the Jorgensens, who owned a small family farm. They sold milk, and eggs, and tomatoes, in season. The weight of all of the snow had been too much for one section of their fence, and the cows had wandered through the opening. Now they were all standing in the middle of the street, mooing pensively and looking rather lost.

The dog's first instinct was to bark, so he did. Most of the cows looked up, and then shuffled a few feet down the road. Then they all stood around some more.

Okay. If he kept barking, they would probably keep moving, but he wasn't sure if that's what he wanted them to do. Except they were in the middle of the road. They were *in his way*. And what if scary cars came? That would be bad.

He barked again, experimentally, and the cows clustered closer together. They looked at him; he looked at them.

Now what? The dog barked a very fierce bark and the cows started shuffling down the lane. The more he barked, the faster they went. In fact, it was sort of fun.

The cows seemed to know where they were going, and the dog followed along behind. If they slowed down, he would bark. Once, they sped up too much, and he had to race up ahead. Then he skidded to a stop and barked loudly at them.

The cows stopped, and turned to go back the other way. That didn't seem right at all, so the dog ran back behind them. He barked a rough, tough bark, and even threw in a couple of growls for good measure.

With a certain amount of confusion, the cows faced forward again. Relieved, the dog barked more pleasantly, and they all resumed their journey down the road. He didn't know where they were going, but at least they were making progress.

When they came to a long, plowed driveway, the cows all turned into it. The dog was a little perplexed by this, but the cows seemed pretty sure of themselves. He barked until they got to the end of the driveway where there was a sprawling old farmhouse and a big wooden barn.

The cows all clustered up by the side of the barn, and mooed plaintively. The dog ran back and forth in a semicircle around them, trying to keep all of them in place. If he barked some more, who knew *where* they might go next.

A skinny woman wearing overalls and a hooded parka came out of the barn. She stared at the scene, and then leaned inside the barn. "Mortimer," she bellowed in a voice that sounded too big for someone so slim. "Come here! Something very strange has happened."

Her husband, who had a big blond beard, appeared in the doorway, holding a pitchfork. "What is it, Yolanda?" he asked vaguely. "Did I leave the iron on again?"

"Look, Morty," she said, and pointed. *"The cows came home."*

He thought about that, and then frowned. "Weird," he said, and went back into the barn.

Yolanda rolled her eyes in annoyance. There was a fenced-in paddock outside the barn and she went over to unlatch the gate. "Come on, you silly cows," she said, swinging the gate open. "You've caused more than enough trouble for one day. Let's go."

The cows didn't budge.

"Great," she said. She turned and whistled in the direction of the barn.

After a minute, a very plump Border collie loped obediently outside.

"Good girl," Yolanda praised her. "Herd, girl!"

The Border collie snapped into action. She darted over to the cows, her body low to the ground. She barked sharply, and herded them into a compact group.

Wanting to help, the dog barked, too. The Border collie didn't seem to want any interference and even snapped at him once, but when she drove the cows towards the open gate, he ran along behind her. It was almost like being with his mother again. *She* liked him to stay out of the way when she was busy, too.

One cow veered away from the others, and the Border collie moved more swiftly than seemed to be physically possible for such a fat dog. She nipped lightly at the cow's hooves and nudged it back into the group.

Imitating her, the dog kept the cows on the other side in line. Whatever the Border collie did, he would promptly mimic. In no time, the cows were safely in the paddock.

"Good girl, Daffodil," Yolanda said, and handed

the Border collie a biscuit from her coat pocket. "That's my little buttercup."

The Border collie wagged her tail and waddled off to eat her treat.

The biscuit smelled wonderful. The dog sat down and politely lifted his paw. Maybe he would get one, too.

"Yeah, I think you've earned one," Yolanda said, and tossed him a Milk-Bone. "Whoever you are."

He had never had a Milk-Bone before, but he liked it a lot. Nice and crunchy. When he was finished, he barked.

"No, just one," Yolanda told him. "Run along now. I have work to do."

The dog barked, trotted partway down the driveway, and trotted back.

"Oh." Yolanda suddenly understood what he was trying to tell her. "The cows had to come from *somewhere*, didn't they? I bet there's a big hole in the fence." She turned towards the barn. "Mortimer! The fence is down again! We have to go fix it!"

"Okay. You do that, honey," he called back.

"It doesn't sound like he's going to *help* me, now does it," she said to the dog.

The dog cocked his head.

"Men," Yolanda pronounced with great disgust, and went to get her tools.

The dog led her down the road to the broken spot.

"Well, how about that," she said. She bent down and lifted the fallen fence post. Then she pounded it back in place. "I don't suppose you want to stay," she said conversationally. "Our Daffodil would probably like some help herding."

Stay. He had heard "Stay" before. It meant *something*, but he wasn't sure what. He rolled over a couple of times, to be cooperative, but she didn't even notice. So he just sat down to wait for her to finish. Maybe she would give him another one of those good biscuits.

Yolanda hefted the two wooden bars that had collapsed and slid them into place. "There we go!" she said, and brushed her hands off triumphantly. She reached into her pocket for another Milk-Bone and held it out. "Here's your reward."

The dog barked happily and took the biscuit. Then he headed down the road, carrying it in his mouth. He had places to go, things to do — and a school to visit!

"Well, wait a minute," Yolanda protested. "You don't have to go, you can — "

The dog had already disappeared around the curve and out of sight.

10

It was fun to walk along carrying his biscuit, like he was a *real* dog, with a *real* owner, who loved him. But soon, he couldn't resist stopping and eating it.

When he got to the middle school, the building was deserted. No cars, no buses, no teachers, no students, no Mrs. Gustave.

No Patricia, no Oscar, no *Gregory*.

Where was everyone? They should be here!

He slumped down right where he was and lay in a miserable heap. Maybe they had gone away forever, the way his family had. Why did everyone keep leaving him?

He stayed there on the icy front walk until his body was stiff from the cold. Then he got up and slunk around to the back of the building. Maybe he would be able to find some garbage to eat.

When he passed his little sleeping alcove by the playground, he caught a fresh scent. Gregory and Oscar had been here! Not too long ago! He ran into the alcove and found a big red dish full of some dark meaty food. What was it? There were lots of chunks and different flavors. It tasted soft and delicious, like a *special* food, made just for dogs. It was *great*.

Next to the red dish, there was a yellow dish full of water. The top had frozen, but he slapped his paw against it, and the ice shattered. He broke a hole big enough for his muzzle to fit through. Then he drank at least half of the water in the bowl in one fell swoop.

What a nice surprise! Food *and* water! They hadn't forgotten him, after all.

If he waited long enough, maybe they would come again. He lay down next to the dishes and watched the empty playground with his alert brown eyes.

Several hours passed, but no one came. He still lay where he was, on full-alert, without moving. A couple of birds flew by. A squirrel climbed from one tree to another, and then disappeared inside a hole. A big chunk of ice fell off the school roof, landing nearby.

That was it.

Maybe they had just come back *once*, and never would again. Maybe he was doomed to be alone forever.

Discouraged, the dog dragged himself to his feet. His back itched, but he was too sad to bother scratching. It would take too much energy.

He wandered off in a new direction, exploring a different part of town. Soon, he came upon the largest parking lot he had ever seen. There were only a few cars in it, but the smell of exhaust fumes was so strong that there must have been many other cars here, not too long ago. He marked several places, just to cover up the ugly stench of gasoline and oil.

The parking lot went on and on and on. It seemed endless. In the middle, there were a lot of low buildings. They were different sizes, but they seemed to be attached.

He walked closer, sniffing the air curiously. *Many* people had been walking around here. Recently. There were food smells, too. His feet touched a rubber mat, and to his amazement, two glass doors swung open in front of him.

Alarmed, he backed away. Why did the doors open like that? For no good reason?

Gingerly, he stepped on the mat again — and the doors opened again! Since it seemed to be all right, he walked cautiously through the doors and inside.

It was a very strange place. There was a wide open space in the center, with lots of benches scattered around. Water bubbled inside a big fountain, and the lights were very dim. He could smell the sharp odor of industrial cleaner, and hear people talking about a hundred feet away. A radio was playing somewhere, too.

He wasn't sure if he liked this place, but then he saw a sleigh. It was just like the one in the park! He wagged his tail, and happily leaped inside. Mounds of soft cloth were tucked around the cardboard presents in the back. He wiggled around until he had made enough room to sleep among the boxes. This was even *better* than the sleigh in the park!

He yawned and rolled onto his back. Sometimes he liked to sleep with his feet up in the air. It was restful.

Off to the side of the Santa Claus display, two mall custodians walked by with mops and pails. Hearing them, the dog crouched down in the sleigh. This was *such* a nice place to sleep that he didn't want them to see him. In the dark, they probably wouldn't, but he wanted to be sure.

"You two about finished?" a woman called to the two men.

"Yeah!" one of the custodians answered. "The food court was a real mess, though."

The woman, who was their supervisor, walked down the mall with a clipboard in her hand. "Well, let's lock up those last two electric doors, and get out of here. We open at nine tomorrow, and this place is going to be *packed* with all the last-minute shoppers."

The other custodian groaned. "I'm glad Christmas only comes once a year."

"Wait until the after-Christmas sales," his partner said glumly. "That's even crazier."

Their supervisor shrugged, making check marks on her clipboard. "Hey, with this economy, we should just be *glad* to have the business." She tucked the clipboard under her arm. "Come on. We'll go check in with the security people, and then you two can take off."

As they walked away, the dog relaxed. It looked like he was safe. He yawned again, shut his eyes, and went to sleep with no trouble whatsoever.

During the night, he would hear someone walk by every so often, along with the sound of keys clanking. But he just stayed low, and the guards would pass right by without noticing him. He got up a couple of times to lift his leg against a big, weird plant, but then, went back to bed each time. It was morning now, but he was happy to sleep late.

Then, a lot of people came, and he could hear metal gates sliding up all over the place. Different kinds of food started cooking somewhere nearby, and Christmas music began to play loudly.

He started to venture out, but he was afraid. What would happen if the people saw him? Maybe he *shouldn't* have come in here, after all. It might have been bad.

Suddenly, the weight of the sleigh shifted as a hefty man sat down on the wide vinyl bench in the front. He was wearing a big red suit with a broad black belt, and he smelled strongly of coffee and bacon.

The dog scrunched further back into the presents. He wanted to panic and run away, but for now, he decided to stay hidden. There were just too many people around.

"Ready for another long day of dandling tots on your lap, Chet?" a man standing next to the sleigh said.

All decked out in his Santa Claus costume, Chet looked tired already. "Oh, yeah," he said. "I *love* being one of his helpers."

"Better you than me," the man said, and moved on to open up his sporting goods store.

Soon, there were people *everywhere*. So many people that the dog quivered with fear as he hid under the soft layers of red and green felt. All of the voices, and music, and twinkling lights were too much for him to take. Too many sounds. Too many *smells*. He closed his eyes, and tried to sleep some more. For once in his life, it was *difficult*.

Tiny children kept getting in and out of the sleigh. They would talk and talk, and Chet would bounce them on his big red knee. Sometimes, they cried, and every so often, a bright light would flash.

It was *horrible*. And — he had to go to the bathroom again. Could he go on the presents, or would that be bad? He would try to wait, maybe.

Unknown to the dog, Gregory and Patricia Callahan had come to the mall with their mother. They still had some presents to buy, and the next day was Christmas Eve. Mrs. Callahan had told them that they could each bring along a friend. So Gregory invited Oscar, and Patricia called up *her* best friend, Rachel. Mrs. Callahan was going to buy all of them lunch and then, if they behaved, they would get to go to a movie later.

"I'm going to have a burrito," Gregory decided as they walked along.

His mother looked up from her lengthy Christmas list. Mrs. Callahan taught physics at the high school, so she had had to do most of her shopping on the weekends. She had been doing her best, but she was still very far behind. She was a woman of *science*, but not necessarily one of precision.

"We just had breakfast, Greg," she said. "Besides, I thought you wanted sweet and sour chicken."

"Dad said we could order in Chinese tonight," Gregory reminded her. "So he could finish his chapter, instead of cooking."

"Pizza," Patricia said flatly. "Pizza's *way* better."

Hearing that, their mother stopped walking. "If you two start fighting . . ."

They gave her angelic smiles.

"Never, *ever*, Mommy," Gregory promised, trying to sound sweet.

96

"We *love* each other," Patricia agreed.

Then, when their mother turned her back, Gregory gave his sister a shove. Patricia retaliated with a quick kick to his right shin. Gregory bit back a groan, and hopped for a few feet until it stopped hurting.

"You think the dog ever came back?" Oscar asked him, as they paused to admire the window of the computer store.

Gregory shrugged. "I sure hope so. If we keep leaving food, he'll know he can trust us. Then we'll be able to catch him."

"What did your parents say?" Rachel asked, tapping the floor just ahead of her with her cane. She had been blind since she was four, but she got around so well that they all usually forgot about it. Her eyes hadn't been physically scarred, but she still *always* wore sunglasses. If people asked, she would explain that it was "a coolness thing." No one who knew the two of them was surprised that she and Patricia had been best friends since kindergarten. "Do you think they'll let you bring him home?" she asked.

"Well — we're working on them," Patricia assured her. "They still really miss Marty, so I think they want to wait a while before we get another dog." Then she touched her friend's arm lightly. "Trash can, at nine o'clock."

Rachel nodded and moved to avoid the obstacle.

"Next year, you're old enough to get a dog,

97

right?" Gregory said, meaning a guide dog.

Rachel nodded. "I can't wait. Except I have to *stay* at that school for a while, to learn how. Live away from home."

Patricia shrugged. "It's not so far. We can come and visit you and all."

Rachel pretended to be disgusted by that idea. "And that would be a *good* thing?"

"For *you*," Patricia said, and they both laughed.

"Those guide dogs are really smart," Gregory said, and paused. "Although not as smart as *my* new dog is going to be. He's the best dog *ever*."

Oscar snorted. "Oh, yeah. He's a whiz, all right." He turned towards Patricia and Rachel. "Fetches *snowballs*, that dog."

The girls laughed again.

"Well, that makes him about Gregory's speed," Rachel said.

"Absolutely," Patricia agreed. "He doesn't even know how to *sit* right." She glanced a few feet ahead. "Baby carriage, two o'clock," she said, and then went on without pausing. "Rachel, you're going to have to help me train him, so he won't *embarrass* us."

Rachel grinned, tapping her cane and deftly avoiding the baby carriage. "You mean, Gregory, or the dog?"

"*Gregory*, of course," Patricia said.

"What if he never comes back?" Oscar said. "I mean, he might belong to someone, or — I don't know. He could be really far away by now."

Gregory looked worried. He was so excited about the dog that he had forgotten that he might not even see him again. Someone else might find him, or he might get hurt, or — all sorts of terrible things could happen! The worst part would be that he would never even *know* why the dog hadn't come back. He would just be — gone.

"Cheer up, Greg," Patricia said. "He's probably still hanging around the school. I mean, he didn't exactly seem like, you know, a dog with a lot of *resources.*"

Gregory just looked worried.

"Are you kids coming or not?" Mrs. Callahan asked, about ten feet ahead of them. "We have a lot of stops to make."

They all nodded, and hurried to catch up.

Down in front of the Thom McAn shoe store, a young father was trying to balance a bunch of bulging shopping bags and a stroller, which held his two-year-old son, Kyle. At the same time, he was trying to keep track of his other three children, who were four, six, and seven. His wife was down in the Walden bookstore, and they were all supposed to meet in the food court in half an hour.

"Lucy, watch it," he said to his six-year-old as she bounced up and down in place, croaking. She was pretending to be a frog. His four-year-old, Marc, was singing to himself, while the seven-year-old, Wanda, was trying to peek inside the

Toys "R" Us bags. "Wanda, put that down! Marc, will you — " He stopped, realizing that the stroller was empty. "Kyle? Where's Kyle?"

The other three children stopped what they were doing.

"I haven't seen him, Daddy," Wanda said. "Honest."

The other two just looked scared.

Their father spun around, searching the crowd frantically. "Kyle?" he shouted. "Where are you? Kyle, come back here!"

His two-year-old was missing!

11

Immediately, a crowd gathered around the little family. Everyone was very concerned, and spread out to look for the lost little boy. The mall security guards showed up, and quickly ran to block off all of the exits. Children got lost at the mall all the time, and the guards just wanted to make sure that when it happened, they didn't *leave* the mall.

"What's going on?" Mrs. Callahan asked, as they came out of the Sharper Image store. One of her contact lenses had fogged up a little, and she blinked to clear it.

"Oh, no!" Patricia said, with great drama. "Maybe it's a run on the bank!"

"You mean, a run on the ATMs," Rachel corrected her.

"Maybe there's a movie star here or something," Oscar guessed. "Someone *famous*."

That idea appealed to Gregory, and he looked around in every direction. "What if it was someone like Michael Jordan," he said. "That'd be great!"

"*Shaquille,*" Oscar said, and they bumped chests in the same dumb-jock way NBA players did.

Mrs. Callahan reached out to stop a woman in a pink hat who was rushing by. "Excuse me," she said. "What's going on?"

"A little boy is lost," the woman told her. "Curly hair, two years old, wearing a Red Sox jacket. They can't find him anywhere!"

"Can we look, Mom?" Gregory asked.

"We'll look *together,*" Mrs. Callahan said firmly. "I don't want us to get separated in this crowd."

Up in the sleigh, the dog had heard all of the sudden chaos, too. The noise had woken him up. What was going on? Why was everyone so upset? He couldn't resist poking his head up and looking around. People were running around all over the place, and shouting, "Kyle! Kyle! Where are you, Kyle?"

The dog didn't know what to think. But, once again, he was sure that something was very wrong. Then, amidst all of the uproar, he heard a distinct little sound. A strange sound. He stood up in the sleigh and pricked his ears forward, listening intently.

It had been a *splash.* Now, he could hear a tiny *gurgle.* Where was it coming from? The fountain. Something — some*one*? — must have fallen into the huge, bubbling fountain in the middle of the mall. The dog stood there indecisively. What should he do? Run away? Run to the *fountain*? Stay here?

A man searching for Kyle right near the sleigh stared at him. It was Rasheed, the mailman, who had seen the dog in the park the day before — sitting up in Santa's sleigh. The dog that Joseph, the sanitation worker, had called Santa Paws.

Rasheed had come to the mall on his day off to buy some presents for his coworkers. This was certainly the *last* place he would have expected to see that dog.

"Look at that!" he gasped to his wife, who was standing next to him. "It's Santa Paws!"

She looked confused. "What?"

"Santa Paws!" he said, pointing up at the sleigh.

The dog had his full concentration on the distant fountain. There was something *in* there. Under the water. Movement. It was — a child! A drowning child!

He sailed off the sleigh in one great leap. Then he galloped through the crowded mall as fast as he could. The top of the fountain was very high, but he gathered his legs beneath him and sprang off the ground.

He landed in the fountain with a huge splash and water splattered everywhere. He dug frantically through the water with his paws, searching for the child.

By now, Kyle had sunk lifelessly to the bottom

of the fountain. The dog dove underneath the churning water and grabbed the boy's jacket between his teeth. Then he swam furiously to the surface, using all of his strength to pull the boy along behind him.

All at once, both of their heads popped up. Kyle started choking weakly, and the dog dragged him to the edge of the fountain. He tried to pull him over the side, but the little boy was too heavy, and the dog was too small. He tightened his jaws on the boy's jacket, and tried again. But it was no use. The edge of the fountain was just too high.

The dog used his body to keep the little boy pressed safely against the side of the fountain. Then he started barking, as he dog-paddled to try and keep them both afloat.

"I hear a dog barking," one of the security guards yelled. "Where's it coming from? Someone find that dog!"

In the meantime, Rasheed was running down the mall towards the fountain.

"In there!" he panted, gesturing towards the fountain. "The little boy's in there! Don't worry, Santa Paws has him!"

Even in the midst of all the excitement, people stared at him when they heard the name, "Santa Paws."

"Santa *Paws*?" the security guard repeated. "Well. Hmmm. I think you mean — "

Rasheed ignored him, climbing over the side of

the fountain. He plucked Kyle out of the water and lifted him to safety. Everyone nearby began to clap.

"Is he all right?" Kyle's father asked, frantic with worry. "Oh, please, tell me he's all right!"

Kyle was coughing and choking, but fully conscious. He would be just fine. Very carefully, Rasheed climbed back over the side of the fountain, holding the little boy in his arms.

Kyle's sisters and brother promptly burst into tears.

"Oh, *thank you*, sir," Kyle's father said, picking up his wet son in a big hug. Kyle started crying, too, and hung on to him tightly. "I don't know how I can ever thank you," his father went on.

"It wasn't me," Rasheed said. "It was Santa Paws."

All of the people who had gathered by the fountain to watch stared at him.

"Are you new to this country?" one of them asked tentatively. "Here, in America, we call him Santa *Claus*."

Rasheed looked irritated. "Oh, give me a break," he said, sounding impatient. "I'm *third-generation*."

Now, the dog struggled over the edge of the fountain. He jumped down to the wet pavement and shook thoroughly. Water sprayed all over the place.

"*There's* your hero," Rasheed proclaimed proudly. "It's Santa Paws!"

Everyone clapped again.

Several stores away, still trying to get through the crowd, Gregory saw the dog. Instantly, he grabbed his mother's arm.

"Mom, that's him!" he said eagerly. "My dog! Isn't he great? Can we keep him? Please?"

His mother shook her head, not sure if she could believe the coincidence. "What? Are you sure?" she asked. "Here, in the *mall*?"

"That's the dog!" Gregory insisted. "The one we want to come live with us!"

"That's no dog," a woman next to them said solemnly. "That's *Santa Paws*!"

"He just saved that little boy," one of the workers from the taco stand agreed. "He's a hero!"

Patricia looked disgusted. "*Santa Paws?*" she said. "What a *completely* dumb name."

Rachel nodded. "It's embarrassing. It's . . ." — she paused for effect — "not cool."

Patricia nodded, too. It wasn't cool *at all*.

"I have to get him!" Gregory said, and started trying to push his way through the crowd.

Down by the fountain, the dog was shrinking away from all of the people and attention. Everyone was trying to touch him and pat him at once. There were too many people. Too much noise. Too much *everything*.

So unexpectedly that everyone was startled, the dog raced away from them.

"Someone catch him!" Kyle's father shouted. "He saved my little boy!"

People started chasing the dog, but he was much too fast. He ran until he found one of the rubber mats and then jumped on it. The doors opened and he tore out of the mall. He raced through the parking lot, dodging cars and customers.

It was a scary place, and he was never going back!

Inside the mall, Gregory got to the fountain only seconds after the dog had left.

"Where's my dog?" he asked urgently. "I mean — where's Santa Paws!"

Everyone turned and pointed to the exit.

"Thanks!" Gregory said, and ran in that direction. But when he got outside, the dog was already long gone.

Disappointed, he walked slowly back inside. He had *almost* gotten him, this time. What if he never got another chance?

Oscar caught up to him. "Where'd he go? Is he still here?"

Gregory shook his head unhappily. "Lost him again. What if he disappears for good, this time?"

"I'm sorry," Oscar said. Then he threw a comforting arm around his friend's shoulders. "Don't worry. We'll find him again. Count on it."

"I sure *hope* so," Gregory said glumly.

Just then, Kyle's mother came walking up to the fountain. She was carrying lots of bags and whistling a little. She gave her husband and children a big smile.

"Well, *there* you are," she said. "I've been waiting in the food court *forever* — I was starting to worry."

Then, seeing the large crowd around her family, she frowned.

"Did I miss something?" she asked.

Everyone just groaned.

12

The name "Santa Paws" caught on, and news of the hero dog spread quickly all over Oceanport. People began coming forward with tales about *their* experiences with Santa Paws. Some of these stories were more plausible than others. There were people who thought that a stray dog on his own might be wild — and possibly dangerous. They thought that he should be caught, and taken to the pound as soon as possible. One man even claimed that Santa Paws had growled viciously at him on Hawthorne Street, but since he was a Yankees fan living in the middle of New England, nobody took him very seriously.

Most of the town was behind Santa Paws one hundred percent. Officers Bronkowski and Lee told how the dog had scared the vandals away from the Nativity scene. Mrs. Amory spoke from her hospital bed about how he had saved her life when she fell on the ice and broke her hip. Yolanda's husband Mortimer said, vaguely, "Oh, yeah, that was the weird dog who brought the cows home." One woman said that Santa Paws had magically cleared the snow from her front walk and driveway earlier that week. Another family claimed that he had been up on the roof and suddenly their television reception was much better. A little girl in the first grade was *sure* that he had come into her room while she was asleep and chased the monsters from her closet.

By now, the dog's brother and sisters and mother had all been adopted. Seeing the strong resemblance, their new owners were boasting that they owned dogs who might be *related* to the great Santa Paws. Although they had originally just gone to the pound to adopt nice stray dogs, these owners now felt very lucky, indeed.

In short, Santa Paws was the talk of the town. There was even a group who hung out at Sally's Diner & Sundries Shop taking bets on when, and where, Santa Paws might show up next. What heroic acts he would perform. Everyone who came into the diner had an enthusiastic prediction.

The newscasters on television had set up a Santa Paws hotline so people could phone in sightings. He was described as being small, and brown, and very, very wise.

In the meantime, the poor dog had barely stopped running since he had left the mall. He ran and ran and ran. He had gotten so wet from diving into the fountain that his fur froze. No matter

110

what he did, he couldn't get warm. He ended up huddling against a tree in a vacant lot, as his body shook uncontrollably from the cold. He was glad that the little boy hadn't drowned, but it had still been a bad, scary day.

He was so tired and cold that he felt like giving up. He didn't *like* being on his own. It was too hard. He wanted a home. He wanted a family. He wanted to feel *safe*.

Instead, he sat in the vacant lot all by himself and shivered. Every few minutes, he whimpered a little, too.

He was just plain *miserable*.

The same afternoon, Mrs. Callahan let Gregory and Oscar skip going to the movies and leave the mall early. As long as they got home before dark, they had permission to go over to the school and leave some more food and water for the dog. If they could catch him, she said, Gregory could bring him home.

Gregory was overjoyed. Getting to keep the dog would be the best Christmas present he ever had! He just prayed that the dog would be there waiting for him. If not — well, he didn't want to think about the possibility of never finding him again. His parents would probably take him to the pound in a couple of weeks to get a different dog — but the *only* dog he wanted was Santa Paws. He had to be over at the school, he just *had* to be.

So, he and Oscar gathered up a bunch of supplies. Then Gregory's father left his word processor long enough to drive them over to the school. Gregory and Oscar were in such good moods that they didn't even complain when Mr. Callahan made them listen to Frank Sinatra on the radio. They also didn't laugh when Mr. Callahan sang along. Much.

Just as the chorus from "New York, New York" was over, Mr. Callahan pulled up in front of the school. When he was in the middle of a new book, he was sometimes very absentminded. Today, he still had on his bunny slippers. Gregory and Oscar were afraid that they would laugh more, so they pretended not to notice.

"Okay, guys," Mr. Callahan said, as he put the car in park. "You want me to wait, or would you rather walk home?"

Gregory and Oscar looked at each other.

"Would we have to listen to more Sinatra, Mr. Callahan?" Oscar asked politely.

Gregory's father nodded. He was tall and a little bit pudgy, with greying hair and thick horn-rimmed glasses. "I'm afraid so," he said.

"Well, then," Oscar answered, very politely, "maybe it would be very good exercise for us to walk."

"Thanks for driving us, though," Gregory added.

Mr. Callahan grinned, raised the volume on the radio, and drove away. He beeped the horn twice, waved, and then turned onto the main road to head home.

"For Christmas, you should give him a CD of *good* music," Oscar said. "So he'll know what it sounds like."

Gregory laughed. His father's idea of modern music was the Eagles. Mr. Callahan liked the Doobie Brothers, too.

He and Oscar had brought more dog food, some biscuits, a couple of thick beach towels, and a new collar and leash. Gregory was also carrying a big cardboard box the dog could use for shelter, in case they missed him again. He hoped that as long as they kept leaving things, the dog would keep coming back.

When they got to the little alcove, they saw that all of the food was gone. Most of the water was, too.

"Good!" Gregory said happily. "He found it!" He would have been very sad if the bowls hadn't been touched.

Oscar nodded, bending down to refill the water dish. "I hope so. I mean, I wouldn't want *other* dogs to be eating his food."

Now, Gregory frowned. "Whoa. I didn't even think of that."

Oscar shrugged. "Don't sweat it. It was probably him, anyway." Then he took out a big can of Alpo. To open it, he used a special little can opener his father had had in Vietnam. Oscar was very proud that his father had given it to him, and he always carried it on his key chain.

Gregory set up the cardboard box in the most protected corner. It had come from some catalog when his mother ordered new comforters, so it was pretty big. Then he packed some snow against the side, so it wouldn't blow away. Right now, the wind wasn't blowing very hard, but it might pick up later.

"On the top, too," Oscar advised. "Just in case."

Gregory considered that, and then frowned. The box was *only* made of cardboard. "Maybe a little. I don't want it to collapse."

"It might be good insulation, though," Oscar said.

That made sense, so Gregory did it. Then he folded the beach towels and put them neatly inside. One was yellow, and the other had a faded Bugs Bunny on it. He arranged them until they formed a nice, warm bed. He had also brought three dog biscuits, and he laid them out in a row on the top towel. That way, the dog could have a bedtime snack.

"Think he'll like this?" he asked.

Oscar nodded. "Totally." He put his key chain back in his pocket and dumped the Alpo into the big red dish. "I think he'll be really happy."

"Me, too," Gregory agreed. What he wanted more than anything was for the dog to feel *special*. Loved.

Once they had set everything up, they sat down in the snow to wait for a while. If they were lucky, maybe the dog would show up. If not, tomorrow was Christmas Eve, and they had a whole week of holiday vacation ahead. They could come here and wait around all day, every day, if they wanted. He would have to come back at some point — wouldn't he?

It was pretty cold, sitting there in the snow, but they stayed for over an hour. The dog was probably busy saving people somewhere. Oscar searched his jacket pockets and found a deck of cards. To pass the time, they played Hearts, and Go Fish, and Old Maid.

The sun was starting to go down, and shadows were creeping across the playground.

Gregory sighed. "We'd better go. We promised we'd get home before dark."

Oscar nodded and stood up. He put his cards in the pocket of his Bruins jacket, and brushed the snow off his jeans. "Don't worry, Greg. We'll just keep coming back until we find him."

"What if someone *else* finds him?" Gregory asked. Now that Santa Paws was famous, *everyone* was going to want him.

"*Nobody* is going to think to look here," Oscar pointed out. "Nobody."

Gregory sure hoped not.

The dog quivered against the tree in the vacant lot for a long time. The ice particles in his fur felt sharp. He couldn't remember ever feeling so uncomfortable. He was very hungry, too. He was *always* hungry.

He was also still scared from having been in the big place with all those people. He didn't like the noise, or all the unfamiliar faces staring at him. He *never* wanted to go to a place like that again.

He was very hungry. If he started walking around again, he might find some more food. Maybe it would also seem warmer, if he kept moving.

He was afraid of running into strangers, so he waited until it was dark. Then he waited until he didn't hear any cars going by. Finally, he got up enough nerve to leave the vacant lot.

He decided to travel along side roads and back alleys. It might be safer. He took a route that went along the ocean, so that he could avoid the center of town.

The dog walked very slowly along Overlook Drive. His paws hurt. He was hungry and thirsty. There was still lots of ice on his coat. Instead of carrying his tail up jauntily, the way he usually did, he let it drag behind him. He just wasn't feeling very happy right now.

He wandered unhappily off the road and down to the beach in the dark. The cold sand felt strange under his paws, but he kind of liked it. He kept slipping and sliding.

The water was very noisy. It was almost high tide, and big waves were rolling in and out. The dog trotted down to the edge of the water to drink some.

Just as he put his head down, foamy water came rushing towards him. He yelped in surprise and jumped out of the way. Why did the water *move* like that?

He waited for a minute, and then tried again. The water rushed in his direction, almost knocking him off his feet. And it was cold!

He ran back onto the dry sand and shook himself vigorously. It was like the water was *playing* with him. He decided that it would be fun to join the game. A lot more fun than feeling sad. So he chased the waves back and forth until he got tired.

A bunch of seagulls flew past him in the night sky and he barked happily at them. This was a nice place, even though the water smelled sort of funny. He tasted some and then made gagging noises. It was awful!

The taste in his mouth was so sour and salty that he lost interest in chasing the waves. It was too cold, anyway.

He trotted along the sand until he came to a big stone seawall. It took him three tries, but he finally managed to scramble over it. He landed hard on the icy sidewalk on the other side with his legs all splayed out. It hurt. But he picked himself up and only limped for about ten feet. Then he forgot that he had hurt himself at all, and went back to trotting.

Fifteen minutes later, the dog found himself at the middle school. He paused at the trash bins and lifted his nose in the air for a hopeful sniff. Even if he could have reached the garbage, what little there was smelled rotten.

Even so, his stomach churned with hunger. When had he eaten last? That nice meaty food yesterday? It had been so good that he could *still* almost taste it.

He ran behind the school to the playground. He stopped before he got to the alcove, and whined a little. If there wasn't any food there, he was going to be very disappointed. What if they had forgotten him?

He took his time walking over, pausing every few steps and whining softly. Then he caught a little whiff of that special meaty smell. There *was* food waiting for him!

He raced into the alcove so swiftly that he almost knocked the dishes over. Food and water! All for him! He *loved* Gregory and Oscar. There was another familiar smell, too. He sniffed a few more times and then barked with delight.

Milk-Bones!

The dog was very happy when he went to sleep that night.

13

The next day was Christmas Eve. The sky was overcast and the temperature was just above freezing. But the dog had been warm and comfortable inside his cardboard box. The thick towels felt very soft and clean next to his body.

He had eaten one of the biscuits right before he went to sleep. His plan was to save the other two for the morning. But they smelled so good that he woke up in the middle of the night and crunched down one more.

When he woke up just before dawn, he yawned and stretched out all four paws. He liked his box-home a whole lot! There was still one biscuit left and he held it between his front paws. It was so nice to have his own bone that he just looked at it, wagging his tail.

Then he couldn't stand it anymore, and he started crunching. It tasted just as good as the other two! He was so happy!

It was time to go outside. Feeling full of energy,

he rolled to his feet. He hit his head against the top of the box, but that was okay. He *liked* that it was cozy. He yawned again and ambled outside.

His water bowl had frozen again. He jumped on the ice with his front paws, and it broke easily. He lapped up a few mouthfuls and then licked his chops. He could still taste the Milk-Bone, a little. It still tasted delicious!

He galloped around the playground twice to stretch his legs. Because he was happy, he barked a lot, too.

Would his friends come back soon? He sat down to wait. Then he got bored. So he rolled on his back for a while. But that got boring, too.

Next, he took a little nap until the sun rose. When he woke up, Gregory and Oscar still hadn't come. He was very restless, so he decided to go for a walk. Maybe he would go back to the beach and play with the moving water some more.

After about an hour of wandering, he walked up Prospect Street, near a little strip mall. A girl was standing on the sidewalk without moving. She was holding a funny-looking stick, and she seemed worried.

It was Patricia's best friend Rachel. She was on her way to the 7-Eleven to pick up some milk and rye bread for her mother. Unfortunately, her wallet had fallen out of her pocket on the way, and now she couldn't find it.

She hated to ask people for help. So she was

retracing her steps and using her red and white cane to feel for the missing object. She could go home and tell her mother what happened, but she would rather not. It wasn't that she was afraid someone would *steal* the wallet if she left. She just liked to do things by herself.

The dog cocked his head. Why was she moving *so slowly*? Why was she swinging the little stick around? He didn't want the stick to hit him, so he kept his distance.

"Now, where is it?" Rachel muttered. She bent down and felt the snow with her gloved hands. This was so frustrating! "Why can't I find the stupid thing?" she asked aloud.

The dog woofed softly.

Rachel stiffened. "Who's there?" she said, and got ready to use her cane as a weapon. She knew that it was a dog, but how could she be sure that it was friendly? Sometimes, dogs weren't.

The dog walked closer, wagging his tail.

Rachel felt something brush against her arm. The dog? She reached out and felt a wagging tail, and then a furry back.

"Are you a dog I know?" she asked.

Naturally, the dog didn't answer.

She took off her left glove and felt for the dog's collar. Her fingertips were so sensitive from reading Braille that she could usually read the inscriptions on license tags. But this dog wasn't wearing a collar at all.

Could he be — Santa Paws? She ran her hand along his side and felt sharp ribs. He was *very* skinny. His fur felt rough and unbrushed, too. This dog had been outside for a very long time.

The dog liked the way she was patting him, so he licked her face.

"You're that dog Gregory's trying to catch, aren't you," Rachel said. "You must be."

The dog licked her face again.

It felt pretty slobbery, but Rachel didn't really mind. "Can you fetch?" she asked. "Or find? Do you know 'find'?"

The dog lifted his paw.

"I lost my wallet," she said. "I have to find it."

The dog barked and pawed at her arm.

"Okay, okay." Rachel shook her head. Patricia was right — this dog needed some *serious* training. "Stay. I have to keep looking for it."

Stay. "Stay" meant something, but right now, the dog couldn't remember what. He barked uncertainly.

"*Stay*," she said over her shoulder.

He followed her as she kept retracing her steps. She would take a step, bend down and feel the snow, and then take another step.

Was she looking for something? The dog sniffed around. The girl was walking so slowly that he leaped over a big drift to pass her. He could cover more ground that way.

He could smell that she had already walked on

123

this part of the sidewalk. There were little boot-steps in the snow. He followed them until he smelled something else. He wasn't sure what it was, but the object had her scent on it. It was square and made of some kind of sturdy material.

So he picked the object up in his mouth and romped back up to the street to where she was.

"I really can't play with you now," Rachel said, pushing him away. "I have to keep searching."

He pressed his muzzle against her arm, and then dropped the object in front of her.

Rachel heard it hit the ground and reached out to feel — her wallet!

"Good dog!" she said, and picked it up. "No wonder they call you Santa Paws. Good boy!"

The dog wagged his tail and woofed again.

Rachel couldn't help wondering what he looked like. She had vague memories of things like colors and shapes. Mostly, though, she had to use her hands to picture things.

"Is it okay if I see what you look like?" she asked, surprised to find herself feeling shy. He was only a *dog*, even if he was a particularly good one.

The dog wagged his tail.

She put her hand out and felt the sharp ribs again. His fur was short and fairly dense. His winter undercoat, probably. The fur wasn't silky at all. Her family had a cocker spaniel named

Trudy and *she* was very silky. This dog's fur was much more coarse.

The dog's hips were narrow, but his chest was pretty broad. Gregory had said that he wasn't full grown yet, but he was already at least forty or fifty pounds. He felt bony and athletic, not solid and stocky. That was the way her friend Gary's Labrador retriever felt. This dog was built differently.

She ran her hand down the dog's legs. They were very thin. His paws were surprisingly *big*. That meant Gregory was right, and the dog was going to grow a lot more.

She left his head for last. His ears seemed to be pointy, although they were a little crooked right at the very tip. His head and muzzle were long and slim. His mouth was open, but he was so gentle that she knew he wouldn't bite her.

"Thank you," she said, and removed her hands. She always felt better when she could *picture* something in her mind. She had a very clear picture, now, of this dog. A nice picture.

She was almost sure that the 7-Eleven was only about half a block away. There was a pay phone there. She should call Patricia's house right away and tell them to come pick up the dog.

"Come here, Santa Paws," she said. "Just follow me down to this telephone, okay?"

There was no answering bark.

"Santa Paws?" she called. "Are you still here?"

She listened carefully, trying to hear him panting or the sound of his tail beating against the air. She could almost always sense it when any living being was near her.

The only thing she could sense right now was that the dog had gone away.

Rachel sighed. Oh, well. She could still call Patricia and tell her that the dog *had* been here. Briefly.

She wasn't sure if that would make Gregory feel better — or worse.

The dog's next stop was behind the doughnut shop. He checked the garbage cans, but all he found were coffee grounds and crumpled napkins. He was more lucky at the pizza place, because he found a box full of discarded crusts. They were a little hard, but they tasted fine.

Now it was time to go to the beach. A couple of people shouted and pointed when they saw him, but he just picked up his pace. They sounded very excited to see him, but he had no idea why. So he kept running along until he outdistanced them.

Trotting down Harbor Cove Road, he heard several dogs barking and growling. They sounded like they were just around the next corner. He could also hear an elderly man shouting, "No, no! Bad dogs!" There was definitely trouble up ahead!

More alarmed than curious, he broke into a full

run. He stretched his legs out as far as they would go, feeling the wind blow his ears back.

Just up ahead, at the base of an old oak tree, a big Irish setter, a Dalmatian, and a husky-mix were all barking viciously. They had chased a kitten up the tree and were still yapping wildly at her from the bottom.

The elderly man, Mr. Corcoran, was brandishing a stick and trying to make the dogs run away. The kitten belonged to him, and he loved her very much.

"Bad dogs!" he shouted. "Go home!"

The little kitten trembled up on the icy tree branch. Even though she was tiny, the branch was swaying under her weight and might break at any second.

The dog growled a warning, and then ran straight into the fray. He butted the Dalmatian in the side, and then shoved past the husky-mix, still growling.

At first, since he was obviously a puppy, the other dogs ignored him. They were having too much fun tormenting the kitten. The Irish setter seemed to be the leader of the pack, so the puppy confronted him with a fierce bark.

This got the Irish setter's attention, but the puppy refused to back down. He showed his teeth and the Irish setter returned the favor. The Dalmatian and the husky-mix decided to join in, and the odds were three against one.

The dog was ready to fight *all* of them! He would probably lose, but he wasn't afraid. He stood his ground, trying to keep all three dogs in sight at once and not let any of them sneak up on him from behind. It was much harder than herding cows! And this time, Daffodil wasn't here to help him!

"Bad dogs!" Mr. Corcoran yelled. "Leave him alone!"

Just as the husky-mix lunged towards the puppy, with her teeth bared, the kitten fell out of the tree with a shrieking meow. She landed in a clumsy heap in the snow, mewing pitifully.

Before the other dogs could hurt her, the puppy jumped past them, ready to protect her with his body. The other three dogs circled him slowly, planning their next moves. The puppy kept his teeth bared and growled steadily.

Swiftly and silently, the husky-mix leaped forward and bit his shoulder. The puppy yelped in pain, but snapped at one of the husky's back legs and heard the husky yelp, too.

Now the Irish setter moved in. At the last second, the puppy ducked and the setter sailed right over him. While the setter was trying to recover his balance, the puppy whirled around to face the Dalmatian.

The Dalmatian didn't like to fight, and he took one nervous step forward. Then he backed up, whining uneasily. The puppy made a short, fierce move towards him and the Dalmatian hesitated for a second. Then he tucked his tail between his legs and started running home.

Before the puppy had time to enjoy that victory, the Irish setter and the husky had already jumped on him. The puppy fought back, trying not to let them get between him and the mewing kitten.

He was ready to fight for his life — and the kitten's life!

14

The fight was fast, confusing, and brutal.

"Stop it!" Mr. Corcoran kept yelling helplessly. "Stop it right now!" He tried to break the fight up, using a stick he had found on the ground. It took a while, but he finally managed to knock the snarling husky away.

The husky growled at him, but then just limped off towards his owner's house. He had had enough fighting for one day.

Mrs. Quigley, who lived across the street, came tearing outside in her bathrobe. "Pumpkin!" she shouted. "Bad dog, Pumpkin! You come here *right now*!"

Hearing the voice of authority, the Irish setter instantly cringed. Mrs. Quigley grabbed him by the collar and hauled him away a few feet. "Bad, bad dog! You, *sit*!"

The Irish setter sat down, looking guilty.

"I'm so sorry, Carl," she said to Mr. Corcoran,

out of breath. "I don't know what could have gotten into him."

"*Eggnog*, probably," Mr. Corcoran grumbled.

Mrs. Quigley sniffed her dog's breath and then glared down at him. "Pumpkin! How could you? You bad, bad dog!" She looked up at Mr. Corcoran. "I am so sorry. Are Matilda and your puppy all right?"

Mr. Corcoran reached down and gently lifted his terrified kitten out of the snow. She was a calico cat, and her name was Matilda. He checked her all over, but except for being very frightened, she wasn't hurt.

"Oh, thank God," he said gratefully. "She's okay. I don't know what I would have done if they'd hurt her."

"I'm sorry," Mrs. Quigley said, wringing her hands. "I promise I won't let Pumpkin get out like that again."

Hearing his name — and his owner's disappointment — the Irish setter cringed lower. He was very ashamed.

In the meantime, feeling dazed, the puppy dragged himself to his feet. He hurt in a lot of places. He could feel blood on his left shoulder and his right ear was dripping blood, too. He had lots of other small cuts and slashes, but his ear and shoulder hurt the most. He shook his head from side to side, trying to clear away the dizziness.

Suddenly, Mrs. Quigley looked horrified. "That

131

isn't Santa Paws, is it?" she asked.

Mr. Corcoran's eyes widened. "I don't know. I guess it could be. Who else would come save Matilda?" He studied the dog more carefully. "The TV *did* say that he was small, and brown, and wise."

At that moment, the dog mainly looked *small*.

"Well, we're going to have to take him straight to the vet," Mrs. Quigley said decisively. She aimed a stern finger at her Irish setter. "You are *very bad*, Pumpkin! You're going to have to go back to obedience school!"

The Irish setter wagged his tail tentatively at the puppy. Now that the heat of the battle was over, he couldn't remember how, or why, the fight had started.

The puppy ignored him and tried to put weight on his injured shoulder. It hurt so much that he whimpered.

"Oh, you poor thing," Mrs. Quigley cooed. "You just come here, snook'ums, and I'll take you to the vet."

The puppy veered away from her. He was in so much pain that he just wanted to be alone. Mrs. Quigley and Mr. Corcoran both tried to stop him, but he staggered off down the street. Then he forced himself into a limping run.

He wanted to get as far away from Harbor Cove Road as possible!

* * *

The dog only managed to run a couple of blocks before he had to stop. He lurched over to the side of the road and into the woods. His injured leg didn't want to work at all.

He collapsed next to an old tree stump. He rested on his bad side, and the snow numbed the pain a little. But it still hurt. A lot.

The dog whimpered and tried to lick the blood away from his wounds. He had never been in a fight with other dogs before. Dog fights were terrible! Especially when it was three against one!

His ear was stinging badly. He rubbed it against the snow to try and get rid of the pain. Instead, it started bleeding even more.

The dog whimpered pitifully and then closed his eyes. Right now, he was too weak to do anything else. Then, before he had a chance to fall asleep, he passed out.

It would be a long time before he woke up again.

Gregory and Oscar met on the school playground at ten-thirty. Patricia had insisted on coming along, too. Since the food was gone and the towels in the cardboard box were rumpled, they knew that the dog had been there. But he was gone now — and they had no way of knowing if he would ever come back.

"Where does he *go* every day?" Gregory asked, frustrated. "Doesn't he want us to find him?"

Oscar shrugged as he opened a brand-new can

of Alpo stew. "He's off doing hero stuff, probably."

Patricia didn't like to see the towels looking so messy. She bent down to refold them. "You know, that was really something at the mall," she remarked. "I've never seen a dog do anything like that before."

"He's not just any dog," Gregory said proudly.

Patricia nodded. For once, her brother was right. "I have to say, it was pretty cool." She reached into the open Milk-Bone box. "How many should I leave him?"

"Three," Gregory told her. "In a nice, neat row."

"Since it's Christmas Eve, let's give him four," Oscar suggested.

"Sounds good," Patricia said, and took out four biscuits.

When they were done, they sat down on a wool blanket Oscar had brought. It was much more pleasant than sitting in the cold snow. Mrs. Callahan had packed them a picnic lunch, too.

So they spent the next couple of hours eating sandwiches, drinking out of juice boxes, and playing cards. Patricia hated Hearts, so mostly they played inept poker.

"Is this going to get any more interesting?" Patricia asked at one point.

Gregory and Oscar shook their heads.

"Great," Patricia said grumpily. Then she slouched down to deal another hand of cards.

"Aces wild, boys. Place your bets."

They waited and waited, but the dog never showed up. They had stayed so long that the batteries in Gregory's portable tape deck were running down.

"Is it okay if we go now?" Patricia asked. "I'm *really* tired of playing cards."

"Me, too," Oscar confessed.

"We might as well," Gregory said with a sigh. He was pretty sick of cards, too. "I don't think he's coming." He reached for a small plastic bag and started collecting all of their trash. "Do you think Mom and Dad would let us come here at night? Maybe we'd find him here, asleep."

"They wouldn't let us come *alone*," Patricia said. "But if we asked really nicely, they might come with us. I mean, they're the ones who are always telling us to be kind to animals, right?"

Gregory nodded. His parents had always *stressed* the importance of being kind to animals.

"You should write down what you're going to say first," Oscar advised them. He never really liked to leave things to chance. In the Cub Scouts, he had learned a lot about being prepared. "That way, you can practice how you're going to do it. Work out all the bugs."

"Let me write it," Patricia told her brother. "I have a bigger vocabulary."

Gregory just shrugged. All he wanted to do was find the dog — one way or another.

He was beginning to be afraid that the dog didn't *want* to be found.

Hours passed before the dog regained consciousness. It was well past midnight, and the woods were pitch-black. His shoulder had stiffened so much that at first, he couldn't get up. But finally, he staggered to his feet. He wanted to lie right back down, but he made himself stay up.

He stood there, swaying. He felt dizzy and sick. What he wanted right now, more than anything, was to be inside that warm cardboard box, sleeping on those soft towels that smelled so clean and fresh.

He limped out to the road, whimpering every time his bad leg hit the ground. The bleeding had stopped, but now that he was moving around, it started up again.

The only way he was going to make it back to the school was if he put one foot after the other. He limped painfully up the road, staring down at his front paws the whole way. One step. Two. Three. Four. It was hard work.

Whenever possible, he took shortcuts. He cut through alleys, and parking lots, and backyards. The lights were off all over town. People were sound asleep, dreaming about Christmas morning. The dog just staggered along, putting one foot in front of the other. Over and over.

He was plodding through someone's front yard

when he felt the hair on his back rise. Oh, now what? He was *too tired*. But — he smelled smoke! Even though he was dizzy, he lifted his head to sniff the air. Where was it coming from?

He followed the trail across several yards and up to a yellow two-story house. Smoke was billowing out through a crack in the living room window. Someone had left the Christmas tree lights on, and the tree had ignited! The lights were snapping and popping, and the ornaments were bursting into flames. He could hear the crackle of electricity, and smell the smoke getting stronger.

The house was on fire!

He lurched up the front steps and onto the porch. He was too weak to paw on the door, but he *could* still bark. He threw his head back and howled into the silent night. He barked and barked until the other dogs in the neighborhood woke up and started joining in. Soon, there were dogs howling and yapping everywhere.

After a few minutes of that, lights started going on in houses up and down the block. The dog was losing strength, but he kept barking. Why didn't the people come outside? Didn't they know that their house was burning?

The living room windows were getting black from the smoke, as the fire spread. Why wouldn't the people wake up? Maybe he was going to have to go in and *get* them. But, how?

He started throwing his body feebly against the

front door, but it wouldn't budge. Why couldn't the people hear him barking? Where were they? If they didn't wake up soon, they might die from the smoke!

The dog limped to the farthest end of the porch, trying to gather up all of his strength. Then he raced towards the living room window and threw himself into the glass at full speed. The window shattered and he landed in the middle of the burning room. He was covered with little shards of glass, but he didn't have time to shake them off. He had to go find the family! The floor was very hot, and he burned the bottom of his paws as he ran across the room. It was scary in here!

The doorway was blocked by fire, but he launched himself up into the air and soared through the flames. He could smell burned fur where his coat had been singed, but he ignored that and limped up the stairs as fast as he could. He kept barking and howling the entire way, trying to sound the alarm. A burning ember had fallen onto his back and he yelped when he felt the pain, but then he just went back to barking.

A man came stumbling out of the master bedroom in a pair of flannel pajamas. It was Mr. Brown, who lived in the house with his wife and two daughters, and he was weak from smoke inhalation.

"Wh-what's going on?" Mr. Brown mumbled. "It's the middle of the — "

The dog barked, and tugged at his pajama leg with his teeth, trying to pull him down the stairs.

Mr. Brown saw the flames downstairs and gasped. "Fire!" he yelled, and ran into his children's bedroom. "Wake up, everyone! The house is on fire!"

The dog ran into the master bedroom, barking as loudly as he could until Mrs. Brown groggily climbed out of bed. She was coughing from the smoke, and seemed very confused. The dog barked, and nudged her towards the door.

Mr. Brown rushed down the stairs with his two sleepy children and a squirming Siamese cat, and then went back for his wife. By now, she was only steps behind him, carrying a cage full of gerbils.

The dog was exhausted, but he kept barking until they were all safely outside. Once he was sure the house was empty, he staggered out to the yard, his lungs and eyes hurting from the thick smoke. He sank down in the snow, coughing and gagging and quivering from fear.

One of the neighbors had called 911, and the first fire engine was just arriving. The firefighters leaped out, carrying various pieces of equipment and grabbing lengths of hose. By now, the fire had spread from the living room to the dining room.

"Is anyone still in there?" the engine company lieutenant yelled.

"No," Mrs. Brown answered, coughing from the

smoke she had inhaled. "It's okay! We all got out."

Because they had been called only a minute or two after the fire started, the fire department was able to put the fire out quickly. Although the living room and dining room were destroyed, the rest of the house had been saved. Instead of losing everything, including their lives, the Browns would still have a place to live.

During all of this, the dog had limped over to the nearest bush. He crawled underneath it as far as he could go. Then he collapsed in exhaustion. His injured shoulder was throbbing, he was still gagging, and all he could smell was smoke. His paws hurt, and he licked at the pads, trying to get rid of the burning sensation. They hurt so much that he couldn't stop whimpering. His back was stinging from where the ember had hit it, and he had lots of new cuts from leaping through the glass. He huddled into a small ball, whimpering to himself. He had never been in so much pain in his life.

While the other firefighters checked to make sure that the fire was completely out, the chief went over to interview Mr. and Mrs. Brown. The Oceanport Fire Department was staffed by volunteers, and Fire Chief Jefferson had run the department for many years.

"How did you get out?" Chief Jefferson asked, holding an incident report form and a ballpoint pen. "Did your smoke detector wake you up?"

140

Mr. and Mrs. Brown exchanged embarrassed glances.

"We, um, kind of took the battery out a few days ago," Mr. Brown mumbled. "See, the remote control went dead, and . . ." His voice trailed off.

"We were going to get another battery for the smoke detector," Mrs. Brown said, coming to his defense. "But, with the holidays and all, we just — "

"Hadn't gotten around to it yet," Chief Jefferson finished the sentence for her.

The Browns nodded, and looked embarrassed.

Chief Jefferson sighed. "Well, then, all I can say is that you were very lucky. On a windy night like tonight, a fire can get out of control in no time."

Mr. and Mrs. Brown and their daughters nodded solemnly. They knew that they had had a very close call.

"So, what happened?" Chief Jefferson asked. "Did you smell the smoke?"

The Browns shook their heads.

"We were all asleep," Mrs. Brown said.

Chief Jefferson frowned. "Then I don't understand what happened. Who woke you up?"

The Browns looked at one another.

"It was Santa Paws!" they all said in unison. "Who else?"

15

It was Christmas morning, and the Callahans were getting ready to go to church. On Christmas Eve, they had gone over to the Oceanport Hospital maternity ward to visit their brand-new niece. Mr. Callahan's brother Steve and his wife Emily had had a beautiful baby girl named Miranda. Gregory and Patricia thought she was kind of red and wrinkly, but on the whole, pretty cute.

On the way home, they talked their parents into stopping at the middle school. But when they went to the little alcove, the food and water dishes hadn't been touched. The towels were still neatly folded, too. For some reason, the dog had never returned. Maybe he was gone for good.

Gregory knew that something terrible must have happened to him, but right now, there wasn't anything he could do about it. As far as he knew, no one had seen the dog since he had found Rachel's wallet that morning. And that was *hours* ago. Now, for all Gregory knew, the dog could be lying somewhere, alone, and scared, and *hurt*.

His father put his hand on his shoulder. "Come on, Greg," he said gently. "It'll be okay. We'll come back again tomorrow."

Gregory nodded, and followed his family back to the car.

They went home and ate cookies and listened to Christmas carols. Mrs. Callahan made popcorn. Mr. Callahan read *The Night Before Christmas* aloud. Patricia told complicated jokes, and Gregory pretended that he thought they were funny. Then they all went to bed.

Gregory didn't get much sleep. He was too upset. Deep inside, he knew that the dog was gone for good. He was sure that he would never see him again — and the thought of that made him feel like crying.

When he got up, even though it was Christmas Day, he was more sad than excited. He and his father both put on suits and ties to wear to church. His mother and Patricia wore long skirts and festive blouses. Patricia also braided red and green ribbons into her hair.

Every year, on Christmas morning, there was a special, nonreligious, interdenominational service in Oceanport. No matter what holiday they celebrated, everyone in town was invited. This year, the Mass was being held at the Catholic church, but Rabbi Gladstone was going to be the main speaker. Next year, the service would be at the Baptist church, and the Methodist minister would lead the ceremony. As Father Reilly always said, it wasn't about religion, it was about *community*. It was about *neighbors*.

"Come on, Gregory," Mrs. Callahan said as they got into the station wagon. "Cheer up. It's Christmas."

Gregory nodded, and did his best to smile. Inside, though, he was miserable.

"When we get home, we have all those presents to open," Patricia reminded him. "And I spent *a lot* of money on yours."

Gregory smiled again, feebly.

The church was very crowded. Almost the entire town had shown up. People were smiling, and waving, and shaking hands with each other. There was a definite feeling of goodwill in the air. Oceanport was *always* a friendly and tolerant town, but the holiday season was special.

Gregory sat in his family's pew with his eyes closed and his hands tightly folded. He was wishing with all of his heart that the dog was okay. No matter how hard he tried, he couldn't seem to feel *any* Christmas spirit. How could he believe in the magic of Christmas, if he couldn't even save one little stray dog?

Rabbi Gladstone stepped up to the podium in the front of the church. "Welcome, everyone," he said. "Seasons greetings to all of you!"

Then, the service began.

After the fire had been put out and the Browns had gone across the street to stay with neighbors, the dog was alone underneath his bush. He dragged himself deeper into the woods, whimpering softly. He knew he was badly hurt, and that he needed help.

He crawled through the woods until he couldn't make it any further. Then he lay down on his side in the snow. He stayed in that same position all night long. By now, he was too exhausted even to *whimper*.

In the morning, he made himself get up. If he stayed here by himself, he might die. Somehow, he had to make it back to the school. If he could do that, maybe his friends Gregory and Oscar would come and help him. He *needed* help, desperately.

Each limping step was harder than the one before, and the dog had to force himself to keep going. The town seemed to be deserted. He limped down Main Street, undisturbed.

The park was empty, too. The dog staggered across the wide expanse, falling down more than once. He was cold, he was in pain, and he was *exhausted*.

Naturally, he was also hungry.

When he tottered past the church, he paused

at the bottom of the stairs. The doors were open and welcoming, warm air rushed out at him. For days, he had been trying to *give* help. Maybe now it was time to *get* some.

He dragged himself up the steps. His shoulder throbbed and burned with pain the entire way. When he got to the top, he was panting heavily. Could he make it any further, or should he just fall down right here?

He could smell lots of people. Too many people. Too many different scents. Some of the scents were familiar, but he was too confused to sort them all out. *Walking* took up all of his energy.

He hobbled into the church, weaving from side to side. He started down the center aisle, and then his bad leg gave out under his weight. He fell on the floor and then couldn't get up again. He let his head slump forward against his front paws and then closed his eyes.

A hush fell over the church.

"I don't believe it," someone said, sounding stunned. "It's Santa Paws!"

Now that the silence had been broken, everyone started talking at once.

Hearing the name "Santa Paws," Gregory sat up straight in his pew. Then he stood up so he could see better.

"That's my dog," he whispered, so excited that he was barely able to breathe. "Look at my poor dog!" Then he put his pinkies in his mouth, and let out — noisy *air*.

Sitting next to him, Patricia sighed deeply. "*Really*, Greg," she said, and shook her head with grave disappointment. "Is that the best you can do?" She sighed again. Then she stuck her fingers in her mouth, and sent out a sharp, clear, and *earsplitting* whistle.

Instantly, the dog lifted his head. His ears shot up, and his tail began to rise.

"That's my dog!" Gregory shouted. He climbed past his parents and stumbled out into the aisle.

The dog was still too weak to get up, but he waved his tail as Gregory ran over to him.

"Are you all right?" Gregory asked, fighting back tears. "Don't worry, I'll take care of you. You're safe now."

Everyone in the church started yelling at once, and trying to crowd around the injured dog.

Patricia lifted her party skirt up a few inches so that she wouldn't trip on it. Then she stepped delicately into the aisle on her bright red holiday high heels.

"Quiet, please," she said in her most commanding voice. Then she raised her hands for silence. "Is there a veterinarian in the house?"

A man and a woman sitting in different sections of the church each stood up.

"Good." Patricia motioned for them both to

come forward. "Step aside, please, everyone, and let them through."

A few people did as she said, but there was still a large, concerned group hovering around Gregory and the dog. The veterinarians were trying to get through, but the aisle was jammed.

Patricia's whistle was even more piercing this time. "I *said*," she repeated herself in a no-nonsense voice, "please step aside, in an orderly fashion."

The people standing in the aisle meekly did as they were told.

Watching all of this from their pew, Mr. Callahan leaned over to his wife.

"Do you get the sudden, sinking feeling that someday, we're going to have another cop in the family?" he asked.

Mrs. Callahan laughed. "I've had that feeling since she was *two*," she answered.

Gregory waited nervously as the two veterinarians examined the dog.

"Don't worry," the female vet announced after a couple of minutes. "He's going to be just fine."

Her colleague nodded. "Once we get him cleaned up and bandaged, and put in a few stitches, he'll be as good as new!"

Everyone in the church started clapping.

"Hooray for Santa Paws!" someone yelled.

"Merry Christmas, and God bless us everyone!" a little boy in the front row contributed.

Mr. Callahan leaned over to his wife again. "If that kid is holding a crutch, I'm *out* of here."

Mrs. Callahan grinned. "That's just Nathanial Haversham. His parents are *actors*."

"Oh." Mr. Callahan looked relieved. "Good."

Up in the front of the church, Rabbi Gladstone tapped on the microphone to get everyone's attention. Gradually, the church quieted down.

"Thank you," he said. "I think that this week, we've all seen proof that there *can* be holiday miracles. Even when it's hard to believe in magic, wonderful, unexplained things can still happen. That dog — an ordinary dog — has been saving lives and helping people throughout this season." He smiled in the dog's direction. "Thank you, and welcome to Oceanport, Santa Paws!"

Gregory didn't want to be rude, but he had to speak up. "Um, I'm sorry, Rabbi, but that's not his name," he said shyly.

"Whew," Patricia said, and pretended to wipe her arm across her forehead. "Promise me you're not going to call him Brownie, or Muffin, or anything else *cute*."

Gregory nodded. If he came up with a cute name, his sister would never let him live it down. Somehow, the name would have to be *cool*.

"What *is* his name, son?" Rabbi Gladstone asked kindly from the podium.

Gregory blinked a few times. His mind was a complete blank. "Well, uh, it's uh — "

"Sparky!" Oscar shouted, sitting with his family several rows away.

Everyone laughed.

"It's *not* Sparky," Gregory assured them. "It's, uh — "

"Solomon's a very nice name," Rabbi Gladstone suggested. "Isaiah has a nice ring to it, too."

Now, everyone in the church started shouting out different ideas. Names like Hero, and Rex, and Buttons.

"Oh, yeah, *Buttons*," Patricia said under her breath. "Like we wouldn't be totally humiliated to have a dog named *Buttons*."

Other names were suggested. Champ, and Sport, and Dasher, and Dancer. Frank, and Foxy, and Bud.

Bud?

Gregory looked at his dog for a long time. The dog wagged his tail and then lifted his paw into his new owner's lap. Gregory thought some more, and then, out of nowhere, it came to him. After all, what was another name for Santa Claus?

"His name's Nicholas," he told everyone. Then he smiled proudly and shook his dog's paw. "We call him *Nick*."

The dog barked and wagged his tail.

Then, Gregory stood up. "Come on, Nicky," he said. "It's time to go home."

The dog got up, too, balancing on three legs.

He wagged his tail as hard as he could, and pressed his muzzle into Gregory's hand. He had a new owner, he had a new home, and he was going to have a whole new life.

He could hardly wait to get started!

APPLE®PAPERBACKS

Pick an Apple and Polish Off Some Great Reading!

BEST-SELLING APPLE TITLES

❏ MT43944-8	**Afternoon of the Elves** Janet Taylor Lisle	**$3.99**
❏ MT41624-3	**The Captive** Joyce Hansen	**$3.50**
❏ MT43266-4	**Circle of Gold** Candy Dawson Boyd	**$3.99**
❏ MT44064-0	**Class President** Johanna Hurwitz	**$3.50**
❏ MT45436-6	**Cousins** Virginia Hamilton	**$3.99**
❏ MT43130-7	**The Forgotten Door** Alexander Key	**$3.99**
❏ MT44569-3	**Freedom Crossing** Margaret Goff Clark	**$3.99**
❏ MT42858-6	**The Hot and Cold Summer** Johanna Hurwitz	**$3.99**
❏ MT22514-2	**The House on Cherry Street 2: The Horror** Rodman Philbrick and Lynn Harnett	**$3.50**
❏ MT41708-8	**The Secret of NIMH** Robert C. O'Brien	**$4.50**
❏ MT42882-9	**Sixth Grade Sleepover** Eve Bunting	**$3.50**
❏ MT42537-4	**Snow Treasure** Marie McSwigan	**$3.99**

Available wherever you buy books, or use this order form

Scholastic Inc., P.O. Box 7502, 2931 East McCarty Street, Jefferson City, MO 65102

Please send me the books I have checked above. I am enclosing $_____ (please add $2.00 to cover shipping and handling). Send check or money order—no cash or C.O.D.s please.

Name_____**Birthdate**_____

Address_____

City_____**State/Zip**_____

Please allow four to six weeks for delivery. Offer good in U.S. only. Sorry, mail orders are not available to residents of Canada. Prices subject to change.   APP997